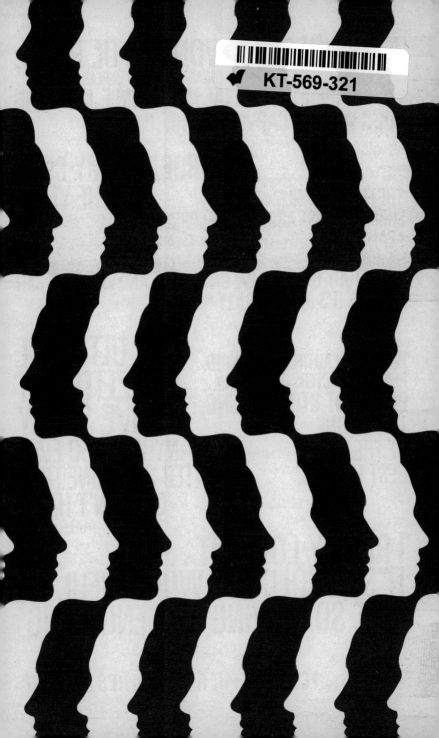

DAVID NICHOLLS trained as an actor before making the switch to writing. His TV credits include the third series of *Cold Feet*, *Rescue Me*, and *I Saw You*, as well as a much-praised modern version of *Much Ado About Nothing* and an adaptation of *Tess of the D'Urbervilles*, both for BBC TV. David has continued to write for film and TV as well as writing novels, and he has twice been nominated for BAFTA awards.

David's bestselling first novel, STARTER FOR TEN, was selected for the Richard and Judy Book Club in 2004, and David wrote the screenplay for the film version, which was released in 2006 and starred James McAvoy.

Also by David Nicholls

Starter For Ten
The Understudy

www.oneday-twopeople.com

DAVID NICHOLLS

ONE DAY

HODDER

First published in Great Britain in 2009 by Hodder & Stoughton
An Hachette UK company
First published in paperback in 2010
This paperback edition published in 2011

8

A CIP catalogue record for this title is available from the British Library.

B format ISBN 978 1 444 72458 5
A format ISBN 978 1 444 72459 2

Typeset in Sabon MT by Palimpsest Book Production Limited,
Grangemouth, Stirlingshire

Printed and bound by
Clays Ltd, St Ives plc

Hodder & Stoughton policy is to use papers that are natural, renewable and
recyclable products and made from wood grown in sustainable forests.
The logging and manufacturing processes are expected to conform to the
environmental regulations of the country of origin.

Hodder & Stoughton Ltd
338 Euston Road
London NW1 3BH

www.hodder.co.uk

To Max and Romy, for when you're older.
And Hannah, as always.

'What are days for?
Days are where we live.
They come, they wake us
Time and time over.
They are to be happy in:
Where can we live but days?

Ah, solving that question
Brings the priest and the doctor
In their long coats
Running over the fields.'

Philip Larkin, 'Days'

Part One

1988–1992

Early Twenties

'That was a memorable day to me, for it made great changes in me. But, it is the same with any life. Imagine one selected day struck out of it and think how different its course would have been. Pause, you who read this, and think for a long moment of the long chain of iron or gold, of thorns or flowers, that would never have bound you, but for the formation of the first link on that memorable day.'

Charles Dickens, *Great Expectations*

CHAPTER ONE
The Future

FRIDAY 15 JULY 1988

Rankeillor Street, Edinburgh

'I suppose the important thing is to make some sort of difference,' she said. 'You know, actually change something.'

'What, like "change the world", you mean?'

'Not the whole entire world. Just the little bit around you.'

They lay in silence for a moment, bodies curled around each other in the single bed, then both began to laugh in low, predawn voices. 'Can't believe I just said that,' she groaned. 'Sounds a bit corny, doesn't it?'

'A bit corny.'

'I'm trying to be inspiring! I'm trying to lift your grubby soul for the great adventure that lies ahead of you.' She turned to face him. 'Not that you need it. I expect you've got your future nicely mapped out, ta very much. Probably got a little flow-chart somewhere or something.'

'Hardly.'

'So what're you going to do then? What's the great plan?'

'Well, my parents are going to pick up my stuff, dump it at theirs, then I'll spend a couple of days in their flat in London, see some friends. Then France—'

'Very nice—'

'Then China maybe, see what that's all about, then maybe onto India, travel around there for a bit—'

'*Travelling,*' she sighed. 'So predictable.'

'What's wrong with travelling?'

'Avoiding reality more like.'

'I think reality is over-rated,' he said in the hope that this might come across as dark and charismatic.

She sniffed. 'S'alright, I suppose, for those who can afford it. Why not just say "I'm going on holiday for two years"? It's the same thing.'

'Because travel broadens the mind,' he said, rising onto one elbow and kissing her.

'Oh I think you're probably a bit too broad-minded as it is,' she said, turning her face away, for the moment at least. They settled again on the pillow. 'Anyway, I didn't mean what are you doing next month, I meant the future-future, when you're, I don't know . . .' She paused, as if conjuring up some fantastical idea, like a fifth dimension. '. . . *Forty* or something. What do you want to be when you're forty?'

'*Forty?*' He too seemed to be struggling with the concept. 'Don't know. Am I allowed to say "rich"?'

'Just so, so shallow.'

'Alright then, "famous".' He began to nuzzle at her neck. 'Bit morbid, this, isn't it?'

'It's not morbid, it's . . . exciting.'

'"Exciting!"' He was imitating her voice now, her soft Yorkshire accent, trying to make her sound daft. She got this a lot, posh boys doing funny voices, as if there was something unusual and quaint about an accent, and not for the first time she felt a re-assuring shiver of dislike for him. She shrugged herself away until her back was pressed against the cool of the wall.

'Yes, exciting. We're meant to be excited, aren't we? All those possibilities. It's like the Vice-Chancellor said, "the doors of opportunity flung wide . . ."'

'"Yours are the names in tomorrow's newspapers . . ."'

'*Not* very likely.'

'So, what, are you excited then?'

'Me? God no, I'm crapping myself.'

'Me too. Christ . . .' He turned suddenly and reached for the cigarettes on the floor by the side of the bed, as if to steady his nerves. 'Forty years old. Forty. Fucking hell.'

Smiling at his anxiety, she decided to make it worse. 'So what'll you be doing when you're forty?'

He lit his cigarette thoughtfully. 'Well the thing is, Em—'

'"Em"? Who's "Em"?'

'People call you Em. I've heard them.'

'Yeah, *friends* call me Em.'

'So can I call you Em?'

'Go on then, *Dex*.'

'So I've given this whole "growing old" thing some thought and I've come to the decision that I'd like to stay exactly as I am right now.'

Dexter Mayhew. She peered up at him through her fringe as he leant against the cheap buttoned vinyl headboard and even without her spectacles on it was clear why he might want to stay exactly this way. Eyes closed, the cigarette glued languidly to his lower lip, the dawn light warming the side of his face through the red filter of the curtains, he had the knack of looking perpetually posed for a photograph. Emma Morley thought 'handsome' a silly, nineteenth-century word, but there really was no other word for it, except perhaps 'beautiful'. He had one of those faces where you were aware of the bones beneath the skin, as if even his bare skull would be attractive. A fine nose, slightly shiny with grease, and dark skin beneath the eyes that looked almost bruised, a badge of honour from all the smoking and late nights spent deliberately losing at strip poker with girls from Bedales. There was something feline about him: eyebrows fine, mouth pouty in a self-conscious way, lips a shade too dark and full, but dry and chapped now, and rouged with Bulgarian red wine. Gratifyingly his hair was terrible, short at the back and sides, but with an awful little quiff at the front. Whatever gel he used had worn off, and now the quiff looked pert and fluffy, like a silly little hat.

Still with his eyes closed, he exhaled smoke through his nose.

5

Clearly he knew he was being looked at because he tucked one hand beneath his armpit, bunching up his pectorals and biceps. Where did the muscles come from? Certainly not sporting activity, unless you counted skinny-dipping and playing pool. Probably it was just the kind of good health that was passed down in the family, along with the stocks and shares and the good furniture. Handsome then, or beautiful even, with his paisley boxer shorts pulled down to his hip bones and somehow here in her single bed in her tiny rented room at the end of four years of college. 'Handsome'! Who do you think you are, Jane Eyre? Grow up. Be sensible. Don't get carried away.

She plucked the cigarette from his mouth. 'I can imagine you at forty,' she said, a hint of malice in her voice. 'I can picture it right now.'

He smiled without opening his eyes. 'Go on then.'

'Alright—' She shuffled up the bed, the duvet tucked beneath her armpits. 'You're in this sports car with the roof down in Kensington or Chelsea or one of those places and the amazing thing about this car is it's silent, 'cause all the cars'll be silent in, I don't know, what – 2006?'

He scrunched his eyes to do the sum. '2004—'

'And this car is hovering six inches off the ground down the King's Road and you've got this little paunch tucked under the leather steering wheel like a little pillow and those backless gloves on, thinning hair and no chin. You're a big man in a small car with a tan like a basted turkey—'

'So shall we change the subject then?'

'And there's this woman next to you in sunglasses, your third, no, fourth wife, very beautiful, a model, no, an *ex*-model, twenty-three, you met her while she was draped on the bonnet of a car at a motor-show in Nice or something, and she's stunning and thick as shit—'

'Well that's nice. Any kids?'

'No kids, just three divorces, and it's a Friday in July and you're heading off to some house in the country and in the tiny boot of your hover car are tennis racquets and croquet mallets and a hamper full of fine wines and South African grapes and poor little quails and asparagus and the wind's in your widow's peak and you're feeling very, very pleased with yourself and wife number three, four, whatever, smiles at you with about two hundred shiny white teeth and you smile back and try not to think about the fact that you have nothing, absolutely nothing, to say to each other.'

She came to an abrupt halt. You sound insane, she told herself. Do try not to sound insane. 'Course if it's any consolation we'll all be dead in a nuclear war long before then!' she said brightly, but still he was frowning at her.

'Maybe I should go then. If I'm so shallow and corrupt—'

'No, don't go,' she said, a little too quickly. 'It's four in the morning.'

He shuffled up the bed until his face was a few inches from hers. 'I don't know where you get this idea of me, you barely know me.'

'I know the type.'

'The type?'

'I've seen you, hanging round Modern Languages, braying at each other, throwing black-tie dinner parties—'

'I don't even own black-tie. And I certainly don't bray—'

'Yachting your way round the Med in the long hols, ra ra ra—'

'So if I'm so awful—' His hand was on her hip now.

'—which you are.'

'—then why are you sleeping with me?' His hand was on the warm soft flesh of her thigh.

'Actually I don't think I have slept with you, have I?'

'Well that depends.' He leant in and kissed her. 'Define your terms.' His hand was on the base of her spine, his leg slipping between hers.

'By the way,' she mumbled, her mouth pressed against his.

'What?' He felt her leg snake around his, pulling him closer.

'You need to brush your teeth.'

'I don't mind if you don't.'

'S'really horrible,' she laughed. 'You taste of wine and fags.'

'Well that's alright then. So do you.'

Her head snapped away, breaking off the kiss. 'Do I?'

'I don't mind. I like wine and fags.'

'Won't be a sec.' She flung the duvet back, clambering over him.

'Where are you going now?' He placed his hand on her bare back.

'Just the bog,' she said, retrieving her spectacles from the pile of books by the bed: large, black NHS frames, standard issue.

'The "bog", the "bog" . . . sorry I'm not familiar . . .'

She stood, one arm across her chest, careful to keep her back to him. 'Don't go away,' she said, padding out of the room, hooking two fingers into the elastic of her underpants to pull the material down at the top of her thighs. 'And no playing with yourself while I'm gone.'

He exhaled through his nose and shuffled up the bed, taking in the shabby rented room, knowing with absolute confidence that somewhere in amongst the art postcards and photocopied posters for angry plays there would be a photograph of Nelson Mandela, like some dreamy ideal boyfriend. In his last four years he had seen any number of bedrooms like this, dotted round the city like crime scenes, rooms where you were never more than six feet from a Nina Simone album, and though he'd rarely seen the same bedroom twice, it was all too familiar. The burnt out nightlights and desolate pot plants, the smell of washing powder on cheap, ill-fitting sheets. She had that arty girl's passion for photomontage too; flash-lit snaps of college friends and family jumbled in amongst the Chagalls and Vermeers and Kandinskys, the Che Guevaras and Woody Allens and Samuel Becketts. Nothing here was neutral, everything displayed an allegiance or a point of view. The room was a manifesto, and with a sigh Dexter recognised her as one of

8

those girls who used 'bourgeois' as a term of abuse. He could understand why 'fascist' might have negative connotations, but he liked the word 'bourgeois' and all that it implied. Security, travel, nice food, good manners, ambition; what was he meant to be apologising for?

He watched the smoke curl from his mouth. Feeling for an ashtray, he found a book at the side of the bed. *The Unbearable Lightness of Being*, spine creased at the 'erotic' bits. The problem with these fiercely individualistic girls was that they were all exactly the same. Another book: *The Man Who Mistook His Wife for a Hat*. Silly bloody fool, he thought, confident that it was not a mistake he would ever make.

At twenty-three, Dexter Mayhew's vision of his future was no clearer than Emma Morley's. He hoped to be successful, to make his parents proud and to sleep with more than one woman at the same time, but how to make these all compatible? He wanted to feature in magazine articles, and hoped one day for a retrospective of his work, without having any clear notion of what that work might be. He wanted to live life to the extreme, but without any mess or complications. He wanted to live life in such a way that if a photograph were taken at random, it would be a cool photograph. Things should look right. Fun; there should be a lot of fun and no more sadness than absolutely necessary.

It wasn't much of a plan, and already there had been mistakes. Tonight, for instance, was bound to have repercussions: tears and awkward phone-calls and accusations. He should probably get out of here as soon as possible, and he glanced at his discarded clothes in preparation for his escape. From the bathroom came the warning rattle and bang of an ancient toilet cistern, and he hurriedly replaced the book, finding beneath the bed a small yellow Colman's mustard tin that he flipped open to confirm that, yes, it did contain condoms, along with the small grey remains of a joint, like a mouse dropping. With the possibility of sex *and* drugs in a small yellow tin he felt hopeful again, and decided that he might stay a little longer at least.

In the bathroom, Emma Morley wiped the crescents of toothpaste from the corner of her mouth and wondered if this was all a terrible mistake. Here she was, after four romantically barren years, finally, finally in bed with someone she really liked, had liked since she'd first seen him at a party in 1984, and in just a few hours he'd be gone. Forever probably. He was hardly likely to ask her to go to China with him, and besides she was boycotting China. And he was alright, wasn't he? Dexter Mayhew. In truth she suspected he wasn't all that bright, and a little too pleased with himself, but he was popular and funny and – no point fighting it – very handsome. So why was she being so stroppy and sarcastic? Why couldn't she just be self-confident and fun, like those scrubbed, bouncy girls he usually hung around with? She saw the dawn light at the tiny bathroom window. Sobriety. Scratching at her awful hair with her finger-tips, she pulled a face, then yanked the chain of the ancient toilet cistern and headed back into the room.

From the bed, Dexter watched her appear in the doorway, wearing the gown and mortar board that they'd been obliged to hire for the graduation ceremony, her leg hooked mock-seductively around the doorframe, her rolled degree certificate in one hand. She peered over her spectacles and pulled the mortar board down low over one eye. 'What d'you think?'

'Suits you. I like the jaunty angle. Now take it off and come back to bed.'

'No way. Thirty quid this cost me. I'm going to get my money's worth.' She swirled the gown like a vampire's cape. Dexter grabbed at a corner but she swiped at him with the rolled-up certificate before sitting on the edge of the bed, folding her spectacles and shrugging off her gown. He had one last glimpse of her naked back and the curve of her breast before they disappeared beneath a black t-shirt that demanded unilateral nuclear disarmament now. That's that, he thought. Nothing was less conducive to sexual desire than a long black political t-shirt, except perhaps that Tracy Chapman album.

Resigned, he picked her degree certificate off the floor, rolled the elastic band along the length of the scroll, and announced 'English and History, Joint Honours, 1st Class.'

'Read it and weep, two-two boy.' She grabbed for the scroll. 'Eh, careful with that.'

'Getting it framed, are you?'

'My mum and dad are having it turned into wallpaper.' She rolled it tightly, tapping the ends. 'Laminated place mats. My mum's having it tattooed across her back.'

'Where are your parents anyway?'

'Oh, they're just next door.'

He flinched. 'God, really?'

She laughed. 'Not really. They drove back to Leeds. Dad thinks hotels are for toffs.' The scroll was stashed beneath the bed. 'Now budge up,' she said, nudging him to the cool side of the mattress. He allowed her in, sliding one arm somewhat awkwardly beneath her shoulders, kissing her neck speculatively. She turned to look at him, her chin tucked in.

'Dex?'

'Hm.'

'Let's just cuddle, shall we?'

'Of course. If you want,' he said gallantly, though in truth he had never really seen the point of cuddling. Cuddling was for great aunts and teddy bears. Cuddling gave him cramp. Best now to admit defeat and get home as soon as possible, but she was settling her head on his shoulder territorially, and they lay like this, rigid and self-conscious for some time before she said:

'Can't believe I used the word "cuddle". Bloody 'ell – *cuddle*. Sorry about that.'

He smiled. 'S'alright. Least it wasn't *snuggle*.'

'*Snuggle*'s pretty bad.'

'Or *smooch*.'

'*Smooch* is awful. Let's promise never, ever to *smooch*,' she said, regretting the remark at once. What, together? There seemed little chance of that. They lapsed into silence again. They had been talking, and kissing, for the last eight hours, and both had that deep, whole body fatigue that arrives at dawn. Blackbirds were singing in the overgrown back garden.

'I love that sound,' he mumbled into her hair. 'Blackbirds at dawn.'

'I hate it. Makes me think I've done something I'll regret.'

'That's why I love it,' he said, aiming once again for a dark, charismatic effect. A moment, then he added, 'Why, have you?'

'What?'

'Done something you regret?'

'What, this you mean?' She squeezed his hand. 'Oh, I expect so. Don't know yet, do I? Ask me in the morning. Why, have you?'

He pressed his mouth against the top of her head. 'Course not,' he said, and thought *this must never, ever happen again*.

Pleased with his answer, she curled closer into him. 'We should get some sleep.'

'What for? Nothing tomorrow. No deadlines, no work . . .'

'Just the whole of our lives, stretching ahead of us,' she said sleepily, taking in the wonderful warm, stale smell of him and at the same time feeling a ripple of anxiety pass across her shoulders at the thought of it: independent adult life. She didn't feel like an adult. She was in no way prepared. It was as if a fire alarm had gone off in the middle of the night and she was standing on the street with her clothes bundled up in her arms. If she wasn't learning, what was she doing? How would she fill the days? She had no idea.

The trick of it, she told herself, is to be courageous and bold and make a difference. Not change the world exactly, just the bit around you. Go out there with your double-first, your passion and your new Smith Corona electric typewriter and work hard at . . . something. Change lives through art maybe. Write beautifully. Cherish your friends, stay true to your principles, live passionately and fully and well. Experience new things. Love and be loved if at all possible. Eat sensibly. Stuff like that.

It wasn't much in the way of a guiding philosophy, and not one you could share, least of all with this man, but it was what she believed. And so far the first few hours of independent adult life had been alright. Perhaps in the morning, after tea and aspirin, she might even find the courage to ask him back to bed. They'd both be sober by then, which wouldn't make things any easier, but she might even enjoy it. The few times that she'd gone to bed with boys she had always ended up giggling or weeping and it might be nice to try for something in between. She wondered if there were condoms in the mustard tin. No reason why there shouldn't be, they were there last time she looked: February 1987, Vince, a hairy-backed Chemical Engineer who had blown his nose on her pillowcase. Happy days, happy days . . .

It was starting to get bright outside. Dexter could see the pink of the new day seeping though the heavy winter curtains that came with the rented room. Careful not to wake her, he stretched his arm across, dropped the end of his cigarette into the mug of wine and stared up at the ceiling. Not much chance of sleep now. Instead he would pick out patterns in the grey Artex until she was completely asleep, then slip out and away without waking her.

Of course leaving now would mean that he would never see her again. He wondered if she would mind, and presumed she would: they usually did. But would he mind? He had managed perfectly well without her for four years. Until last night he had been under the impression that she was called Anna, and yet at the party he hadn't been able to look away. Why had he not noticed her until now? He examined her face as she slept.

She was pretty, but seemed annoyed by the fact. Her bottled-red hair was almost wilfully badly cut, alone in front of the mirror probably, or by Tilly whatsername, that loud, large girl she shared this flat with. Her skin had a pallid puffiness that spoke of too much time in libraries or drinking pints in pubs, and her spectacles made her seem owlish and prim. Her chin was soft and a little plump, though perhaps that was just puppy-fat (or were 'plump' and 'puppy-fat' things you weren't meant to say now? in the same way that you couldn't tell her she had tremendous breasts, even if it was true, without her getting all offended).

Never mind that, back to her face. There was a slight greasy sheen on the tip of her small, neat nose and a spattering of tiny red spots on her forehead, but these aside there was no denying that her face – well, her face was a wonder. With her eyes closed he found that he couldn't recall their exact colour, only that they were large and bright and humorous, like the two creases in the corners of her wide mouth, deep parentheses that deepened when she smiled, which seemed to be often. Smooth, pink mottled cheeks, pillows of flesh that looked as if they would be warm to the touch. No lipstick but soft, raspberry-coloured lips that she kept tightly closed when she smiled as if she didn't want to show her teeth, which were a little large for her mouth, the front tooth slightly chipped, all of this giving the impression that she was holding something back, laughter or a clever remark or a fantastic secret joke.

If he left now he would probably never see this face again, except perhaps at some terrible reunion in ten years' time. She'd be overweight and disappointed and would complain about him sneaking off without saying goodbye. Best to leave quietly, and no reunions. Move on, look to the future. Plenty more faces out there.

But as he made his decision, her mouth stretched open into a wide smile and without opening her eyes she said:

'So, what do you reckon, Dex?'

'About what, Em?'

'Me and you. Is it love, d'you think?' and she gave a low laugh, her lips tightly closed.

'Just go to sleep, will you?'

'Stop staring up my nose then.' She opened her eyes, blue and green, bright and shrewd. 'What's tomorrow?' she mumbled.

'Today you mean?'

'Today. This bright new day that awaits us.'

'It's a Friday. Friday all day. St Swithin's Day as a matter of fact.'

'What's that then?'

'Tradition. If it rains today it'll rain for the next forty days, or all summer, or something like that.'

She frowned. 'That doesn't make any sense.'

'Not meant to. It's a superstition.'

'Raining where? It's always raining somewhere.'

'On St Swithin's grave. He's buried outside Winchester Cathedral.'

'How come you know all this?'

'I went to school there.'

'Well la-di-da,' she mumbled into the pillow.

'"If on St Swithin it doth rain/Something dum-di-dum again."'

'That's a beautiful poem.'

'Well, I'm paraphrasing.'

She laughed once again, then raised her head sleepily. 'But Dex?'

'Em?'

'If it doesn't rain today?'

'Uh-huh.'

'What are you doing later?'

Tell her that you're busy.

'Nothing much,' he said.

'So shall we do something then? Me and you, I mean?'

Wait 'til she's asleep then sneak away.

'Yeah. Alright,' he said. 'Let's do something.'

She allowed her head to drop onto the pillow once more. 'Brand new day,' she murmured.

'Brand new day.'

CHAPTER TWO
Back to Life

Wolverhampton and Rome

> *Girls' Changing Rooms*
> *Stoke Park Comprehensive School*
> *Wolverhampton*
> *15 July 1989*

Ciao, Bella!

How are you? And how is Rome? The Eternal City is all very well, but I've been here in Wolverhampton for two days now and that's felt pretty eternal (though I can reveal that the Pizza Hut here is excellent, just excellent).

Since I last saw you I have decided to take that job I was telling you about, with Sledgehammer Theatre Co-operative and for the last four months we have been devising, rehearsing and touring with 'Cruel Cargo', an Arts Council-funded spectacular about the slave-trade told through the medium of story, folk song and some pretty shocking mime. I have enclosed a crudely photocopied leaflet so that you can see what a classy number it really is.

Cruel Cargo is a TIE piece (that's Theatre-in-Education to you) aimed at 11–13-year-olds that takes the provocative view that slavery was a Bad Thing. I play Lydia, the, um, well, yes, the LEAD ROLE as a matter of fact, the spoilt and vain daughter of the wicked Sir Obadiah Grimm (can you tell from his name that he's not very nice?) and in the show's most powerful moment

16

it's beneath him to be seen with an object that isn't really there, and every other sentence begins 'when I was on telly' which is his way of saying 'when I was happy'. Sid pees in washbasins and has these scary polyester trousers which you WIPE DOWN instead of washing and subsists on service station minced beef pasties, and me and Kwame think he's secretly really racist, but apart from that he's a lovely man, a lovely, lovely man.

And then there's Candy, ah Candy. You'd like Candy, she's exactly what she sounds like. She plays Cheeky Maid, a Plantation Owner and Sir William Wilberforce, and is very beautiful and spiritual and even though I don't approve of the word, a complete bitch. She keeps asking me how old I am really and telling me I look tired or that if I got contact lenses I could actually be quite pretty, which I ADORE of course. She's very keen to make it clear that she's only doing this to get her Equity card and bide her time until she's spotted by some Hollywood producer who presumably just happens to be passing through Dudley on a wet Tuesday afternoon on the lookout for hot TIE talent. Acting is rubbish, isn't it? When we started STC (Sledgehammer Theatre Co-operative) we were really keen to set up a progressive theatrical collective with none of that ego-fame-getting-on-the-telly-ego-showing-off bullshit, and just do really good, exciting original political devised work. That may all sound dopey to you, but that's what we wanted to do. But the problem with democratic egalitarian collectives is that you have to listen to twots like Sid and Candy. I wouldn't mind if she could act but her Geordie accent is unbelievable, like she's had a stroke or something and she's also got this thing about doing yoga warm-ups in her lingerie. There, that's got your attention, hasn't it? It's the first time I've seen someone do the Sun Worship in hold-up stockings and a basque. That can't be right, can it? Poor old Sid can barely chew his curried beef slice, keeps missing his mouth. When the time finally comes for her to put some clothes on and go on stage one of the kids usually wolf-whistles or something and in the mini-bus afterwards she

always pretends to be really affronted and feminist about
hate being judged on my looks all my life I've been judge
my exquisite face and firm young body,' she says as she ad
her suspender belt, like it's a big POLITICAL issue, like we
should be doing agit-prop street theatre about the plight of
women cursed with great tits. Am I ranting? Are you in love
with her yet? Maybe I'll introduce you when you get back. I
can see you now, giving her that look where you clench your
jaw and play with your lips and ask about her careeeeeer. Maybe
I won't introduce you after all . . .

Emma Morley turned the page face down as Gary Nutkin entered, skinny and anxious, and it was time for the pre-show pep-talk from the director and co-founder of Sledgehammer Theatre Co-operative. The unisex dressing room was not a dressing room at all, just the girls' changing room at an inner-city comprehensive which, even at the weekend, still had that school smell she remembered: hormones, pink liquid soap, mildewed towels.

In the doorway, Gary Nutkin cleared his throat; pale and razor-burned, the top-button of his black shirt fastened tight, a man whose personal style icon was George Orwell. 'Great crowd tonight, people! Nearly half full which isn't bad considering!' though considering what exactly he didn't say, perhaps because he was distracted by Candy, performing pelvic rolls in a polka-dot all-in-one. 'Let's give 'em one hell of a show, folks. Let's knock 'em dead!'

'I'd like to knock 'em dead,' growled Sid, watching Candy while picking at pastry crumbs. 'Cricket bat with nails in, little bastards.'

'Stay positive, Sid, will you please?' implored Candy on a long, controlled out-breath.

Gary continued. 'Remember, keep it fresh, stay connected, keep it lively, say the lines like it's the first time and most importantly of all, *don't* let the audience intimidate or goad you in any way. Interaction is great. *Retaliation* is not. Don't let them rile you. Don't give them that satisfaction. Fifteen minutes, please!' and with that Gary closed the dressing room door on them, like a jailor.

Sid began his nightly warm-up now, a murmured incantation of i-hate-this-job-i-hate-this-job. Beyond him sat Kwame, topless and forlorn in tattered trousers, hands jammed in his armpits, head lolling back, meditating or trying not to cry perhaps. On Emma's left, Candy sang songs from *Les Miserables* in a light, flat soprano, picking at the hammer toes she'd got from eighteen years of ballet. Emma turned back to her reflection in the cracked mirror, plumped up the puffed sleeves of her Empire line dress, removed her spectacles and gave a Jane Austen sigh.

The last year had been a series of wrong turns, bad choices, abandoned projects. There was the all-girl band in which she had played bass, variously called Throat, Slaughterhouse Six and Bad Biscuit, which had been unable to decide on a name, let alone a musical direction. There was the alternative club night that no-one had gone to, the abandoned first novel, the abandoned second novel, several miserable summer jobs selling cashmere and tartan to tourists. At her very, very lowest ebb she had taken a course in Circus Skills until it transpired that she had none. Trapeze was not the solution.

The much-advertised Second Summer of Love had been one of melancholy and lost momentum. Even her beloved Edinburgh had started to bore and depress her. Living in her University town felt like staying on at a party that everyone else had left, and so in October she had given up the flat in Rankeillor Street and moved back to her parents for a long, fraught, wet winter of recriminations and slammed doors and afternoon TV in a house that now seemed impossibly small. 'But you've got a double-first! What happened to your double-first?' her mother asked daily, as if Emma's degree was a super-power that she stubbornly refused to use. Her younger sister, Marianne, a happily married nurse with a new baby, would come round at nights just to gloat at mum and dad's golden girl brought low.

But every now and then, there was Dexter Mayhew. In the last few warm days of the summer after graduation she had gone to stay at his family's beautiful house in Oxfordshire; not a house, but a mansion to her eyes. Large, 1920s, with faded rugs and large abstract canvases and ice in the drinks. In the large, herb-scented garden they had spent a long, languid day between the swimming pool and tennis court, the first she'd ever seen that had not been built by the local council. Drinking gin and tonics in wicker chairs, looking at the view, she had thought of *The Great Gatsby*. Of course she had spoiled it; getting nervous and drinking too much at dinner, shouting at Dexter's father – a mild, modest, perfectly reasonable man – about Nicaragua, while all the time Dexter regarded her with a look of affectionate disappointment, as if she were a puppy who had soiled a rug. Had she really sat at their table, eating their food and calling his father a fascist? That night she lay in the guest bedroom, dazed and remorseful, waiting for a knock on the door that clearly would never come; romantic hopes sacrificed for the Sandinistas, who were unlikely to be grateful.

They had met again in London in April, at their mutual friend Callum's twenty-third birthday party, spending the whole of the next day in Kensington Gardens together, drinking wine from the bottle and talking. Clearly she had been forgiven, but they had also settled into the maddening familiarity of friendship; maddening for her at least, lying on the fresh spring grass, their hands almost touching as he told her about Lola, this incredible Spanish girl he'd met while ski-ing in the Pyrenees.

And then he was off travelling again, broadening his mind yet further. China had turned out to be too alien and ideological for Dexter's taste, and he had instead embarked on a leisurely year-long tour of what the guide books called 'Party Towns'. So they were pen pals now, Emma composing long, intense letters crammed with jokes and underlining, forced banter and barely concealed longing; two-thousand-word acts of love on air-mail paper. Letters, like compilation tapes, were really vehicles for unexpressed emotions and she was clearly putting far too much time and energy into them. In return, Dexter sent her postcards with insufficient postage: 'Amsterdam is MAD', 'Barcelona INSANE', 'Dublin ROCKS. Sick as DOG this morning.' As a travel writer, he was no Bruce Chatwin, but still she would slip the postcards in the pocket of a heavy coat on long soulful walks on Ilkley Moor, searching for some hidden meaning in 'VENICE COMPLETELY FLOODED!!!!'.

'Who's this *Dexter* then?' her mother asked, peering at the back of the postcards. 'Your boyfriend, is he?' Then, with a concerned look: 'Have you ever thought about working for the Gas Board?' Emma got a job pulling pints in the local pub, and time passed, and she felt her brain begin to soften like something forgotten at the back of the fridge.

Then Gary Nutkin had phoned, the skinny Trotskyist who had directed her in a stark, uncompromising production of Brecht's *Fears and Miseries of the Third Reich* back in '86, then kissed her for three stark, uncompromising hours at the last-night party. Shortly afterwards he had taken her to a Peter Greenaway double-bill, waiting until four hours in before reaching across and absent-mindedly placing his hand on her left breast as if adjusting a dimmer switch. They made Brechtian love that evening in a stale single bed beneath a poster for *The Battle of Algiers*, Gary taking care throughout to ensure that he was in no way objectifying her. Then nothing, not a word, until that late-night phone-call in May, and the hesitant words, softly spoken: 'How would you like to join my theatre co-operative?'

Emma had no ambitions as an actress or any great love of theatre, except as a medium to convey words and ideas. And Sledgehammer was to be a new kind of progressive theatre co-op, with shared intentions, a shared zeal, a written manifesto and a commitment to changing young lives through art. Maybe there'd be some romance too, Emma thought, or at the very least some sex. She packed her rucksack, said goodbye to her sceptical mum and dad, and set out in the mini-bus as if heading out on some great cause, a sort of theatrical Spanish Civil War, funded by the Arts Council.

But three months later, what had happened to the warmth, the camaraderie, the sense of social value, of high ideals coupled with fun? They were meant to be a co-operative. That's what was written on the side of the van, she had stencilled it there herself. *I-hate-this-job-I-hate this-job*, said Sid. Emma pressed her hands against her ears, and asked herself some fundamental questions.

Why am I here?

Am I really making a difference?

Why can't she put some clothes on?

What is that smell?

Where do I want to be right now?

She wanted to be in Rome, with Dexter Mayhew. In bed.

'Shaf-tes-bury Avenue.'

'No, Shafts-bury. Three syllables.'

'Lychester Square.'

'Leicester Square, two syllables.'

'Why not Ly-chester?'

'No idea.'

'But you are meant to be my teacher, you are meant to know.'

'Sorry,' Dexter shrugged.

'Well I think it is stupid language,' said Tove Angstrom, and punched him in the shoulder.

'*A* stupid language. I couldn't agree with you more. No need to hit me though.'

'I apologise,' said Tove, kissing his shoulder, then his neck and mouth, and Dexter was once again struck by how rewarding teaching could be.

They lay in a tangle of cushions on the terracotta floor of his tiny room, having given up on the single bed as inadequate for their needs. In the brochure for the Percy Shelley International School of English, the teachers' accommodation had been described as 'some comfortable with many mitigating features' and this summed it up perfectly. His room in the Centro Storico was dull and institutional, but there was at least a balcony, a foot-wide sill overlooking a picturesque square that, in a very Roman way, also functioned as a car park. Each morning he was woken by the sound of office-workers breezily reversing their cars into each other.

But in the middle of this humid July afternoon, the only sound came from the wheels of tourist suitcases rumbling on the cobbles below, and they lay with the windows wide open, kissing lazily, her hair clinging to his face, thick and dark and smelling of some Danish shampoo: artificial pine and cigarette smoke. She reached across his chest for the packet on the floor, lit two cigarettes and passed him one, and he shuffled up onto the pillows, letting the cigarette dangle from his lip like Belmondo or someone in a Fellini film. He had never seen a Belmondo or Fellini film, but was familiar with the postcards: stylish, black and white. Dexter didn't like to think of himself as vain, but there were definitely times when he wished there was someone on hand to take his photograph.

They kissed again, and he wondered vaguely if there was some moral or ethical dimension to this situation. Of course the time to worry about the pros and cons of sleeping with a student would have been after the College party, while Tove was perching unsteadily on the edge of his bed and unzipping her knee-length boots. Even then, in the muddle of red wine and desire he had found himself wondering what Emma Morley would say. Even as Tove twirled her tongue in his ear, he had conducted his defence: she's nineteen, an adult, and anyway I'm not a real teacher. Besides, Emma was a long way away at this moment, changing the world from a mini-bus on the ring road of a provincial town, and what was all this to do with Emma anyway? Tove's knee-length boots sagged in the corner of the room now, in the hostel where overnight visitors were strictly forbidden.

He shifted his body to a cooler patch of terracotta, peering out of the window to try to gauge the time from the small square of vivid blue sky. The rhythm of Tove's breathing was changing as she slipped into sleep, but he had an important appointment to keep. He dropped the last two inches of cigarette into a wine glass, and stretched for his wristwatch, which lay on an unread copy of Primo Levi's *If This is a Man*.

'Tove, I've got to go.'

She groaned in protest.

'I'm meeting my parents, I've got to leave now.'

'Can I come too?'

He laughed. 'Don't think so, Tove. Besides you've got a grammar test on Monday. Go and revise.'

'You test me. Test me now.'

'Okay, verbs. Present continuous.'

She coiled one leg around him, using the leverage to pull herself on top of him. 'I am kissing, you are kissing, he is kissing, she is kissing . . .'

He pulled himself up on his elbows. 'Seriously, Tove . . .'

'Ten more minutes,' she whispered in his ear, and he sank back to the floor. Why not, he thought? After all, I'm in Rome, it's a beautiful day. I am twenty-four years old, financially secure, healthy. I ache and I am doing something that I shouldn't be doing, and I am very, very lucky.

The attraction of a life devoted to sensation, pleasure and self would probably wear thin one day, but there was still plenty of time for that yet.

*And how is Rome? How is La Dolce Vita? (look it up). I imagine you right now at a café table, drinking one of those 'cappuccinos' we hear so much about, and wolf-whistling at **every-***

thing. You're probably wearing sunglasses to read this. Well take them off, you look ridiculous. Did you get the books I sent you? Primo Levi is a fine Italian writer. It's to remind you that life isn't all gelati and espadrilles. Life can't always be like the opening of Betty Blue. And how is teaching? Please promise me you're not sleeping with your students. That would just be so . . . disappointing.

Must go now. Bottom of page looms, and in the other room I can hear the thrilling murmur of our audience as they throw chairs at each other. I finish this job in two weeks THANK GOD, then Gary Nutkin, our director, wants me to devise a show for infant schools about Apartheid. With PUPPETS for fuck's sake. Six months in a Transit on the M6 with a Desmond Tutu marionette on my lap. I might give that one a miss. Besides, I've written this two-woman play about Virginia Woolf and Emily Dickinson called 'Two Lives' (either that or 'Two Depressed Lesbians'). Maybe I'll put that on in a pub-theatre somewhere. Once I'd explained to Candy who Virginia Woolf was, she said that she really, really wanted to play her, but only if she can take her top off, so that's the casting sorted. I'll be Emily Dickinson, and keep my top on. I'll reserve you tickets.

In the meantime, I have to choose whether to sign-on in Leeds or sign-on in London. Choices, choices. I've been trying to fight moving to London – it's so PREDICTABLE, moving to London – but my old flatmate Tilly Killick (remember her? Big red glasses, strident views, sideburns?) has a spare room in Clapton. She calls it her 'box room', which doesn't bode well. What's Clapton like? Are you coming back to London soon? Hey! Maybe we could be flatmates?

'Flatmates?' Emma hesitated, shook her head and groaned, then wrote 'Just kidding!!!!' She groaned again. 'Just kidding' was exactly what people wrote when they meant every word. Too late to scribble it out now, but how to sign off? 'All the best' was too formal, 'tout mon amour' too affected, 'all my love' too corny, and now Gary Nutkin was in the doorway once again.

'Okay, places everyone!' Sorrowfully he held the door open as if leading them to the firing squad, and quickly, before she could change her mind, she wrote—

God I miss you, Dex

—then her signature and a single kiss scratched deep into the pale blue air-mail paper.

In the Piazza della Rotunda, Dexter's mother sat at a café table, a novel held loosely in one hand, her eyes closed and her head tilted back and to the side like a bird to catch the last of the afternoon sun. Rather than arrive straightaway, Dexter took a moment to sit amongst the tourists on the steps of the Pantheon and watch as the waiter approached and picked up her ashtray, startling her. They both laughed, and from the theatrical movement of her mouth and arms he could tell that she was speaking her terrible Italian, her hand on the waiter's arm, patting it flirtatiously. With no apparent idea what had been said, the waiter nevertheless grinned and flirted back, then walked away, glancing over his shoulder at the beautiful English woman who had touched his arm and talked incomprehensibly.

Dexter saw all this and smiled. That old Freudian notion, first whispered at boarding school, that boys were meant to be in love with their mothers and hate their fathers, seemed perfectly plausible to him. Everyone he had ever met had been in love with Alison Mayhew, and the best of it was that he really liked his father too; as in so many things, he had all the luck.

Often, at dinner or in the large, lush garden of the Oxfordshire house, or on holidays in France as she slept in the sun, he would notice his father staring at her with his bloodhound eyes in dumb adoration. Fifteen years her elder, tall, long-faced and introverted, Stephen Mayhew seemed unable to believe this one remarkable piece of good fortune. At her frequent parties, if Dexter sat very quietly so as not to be sent to bed, he would watch as the men formed an obedient, devoted circle around her; intelligent, accomplished men, doctors and lawyers and people who spoke on the radio, reduced to moony teenage boys. He would watch as she danced to early Roxy Music albums, a cocktail glass in her hand, woozy and self-contained as the other wives looked on, dumpy and slow-witted in comparison. School-friends too, even the cool complicated ones, would turn into cartoons around Alison Mayhew, flirting with her while she flirted back, engaging her in water fights, complimenting her on her terrible cooking – the violently scrambled eggs, the black pepper that was ash from a cigarette.

She had once studied fashion in London but these days ran a village antiques shop, selling expensive rugs and chandeliers to genteel Oxford with great success. She still carried with her that aura of having been something-in-the-Sixties – Dexter had seen the photographs, the clippings from faded colour supplements – but with no apparent sadness or regret she had given this up for a resolutely respectable, secure, comfortable family life. Typically, it was as if she had sensed exactly the right moment to leave the party. Dexter suspected that she had occasional flings with the doctors, the lawyers, the people who spoke on the radio, but he found it hard to be angry with her. And always people said the same thing – that he had got it from her. No-one was specific about what 'it' was, but everyone seem to know; looks of course, energy and good health, but also a certain nonchalant self-confidence, the right to be at the centre of things, on the winning team.

Even now, as she sat in her washed-out blue summer dress, fishing in her immense handbag for matches, it seemed as if the life of the Piazza revolved around her. Shrewd brown eyes in a heart-shaped face under expensively dishevelled black hair, her dress undone one button too far, an immaculate mess. She saw him approach and her face cracked with a wide smile.

'Forty-five minutes late, young man. Where have you been?'

'Over there watching you chat up the waiters.'

'Don't tell your father.' She knocked the table with her hip as she stood and hugged him. 'Where have you been though?'

'Just preparing lessons.' His hair was wet from the shower he had shared with Tove Angstrom, and as she brushed it from his forehead, her hand cupping the side of his face fondly, he realised that she was already a little drunk.

'Very tousled. Who's been tousling you? What mischief have you been up to?'

'I told you, planning lessons.'

She pouted sceptically. 'And where did you get to last night? We waited at the restaurant.'

'I'm sorry, I got delayed. College disco.'

'A *disco*. Very 1977. What was that like?'

'Two hundred drunk Scandinavian girls vogue-ing.'

'"Vogue-ing". I'm pleased to say that I have absolutely no idea what that is. Was it fun?'

'It was hell.'

She patted his knee. 'You poor, poor thing.'

'Where's Dad?'

'He's had to go for one of his little lie-downs at the hotel. The heat, and his sandals were chafing. You know what your father's like, he's so *Welsh*.'

'So what have you been doing?'

'Just wandering around the Forum. I thought it was beautiful, but Stephen was bored out of his skull. All that mess, columns just left lying around all over the place. I think he thinks they should bulldoze it all, put up a nice conservatory or something.'

'You should visit the Palatine. It's at the top of that hill . . .'

'I know where the Palatine is, Dexter, I was visiting Rome before you were born.'

'Yes, who was emperor back then?'

'Ha. Here, help me with this wine, don't let me drink the whole bottle.' She already had, pretty much, but he poured the last inch into a water glass and reached for her cigarettes. Alison tutted. 'You know sometimes I think we took the whole liberal-parent thing a bit too far.'

'I quite agree. You ruined me. Pass the matches.'

'It's not clever, you know. I know you think it makes you look like a film star, but it doesn't, it looks awful.'

'So why do you do it then?'

'Because it makes me look sensational.' She placed a cigarette between her lips and he lit it with his match. 'I'm giving up anyway. This is my last one. Now quickly, while your father's not here—' She shuffled closer, conspiratorially. 'Tell me about your love-life.'

'No!'

'Come on, Dex! You know I'm forced to live vicariously through my children, and your sister's such a *virgin* . . .'

'Are you drunk, old lady?'

'How she got two children, I'll never know . . .'

'You are drunk.'

'I don't drink, remember?' When Dexter was twelve she had solemnly taken him into the kitchen one night and in a low voice instructed him how to make a dry martini, as if it were a solemn rite. 'Come on then. Spill the beans, all the juicy details.'

'I have nothing to say.'

'No-one in Rome? No nice Catholic girl?'

'Nope.'

'Not a student, I hope.'

'Of course not.'

'What about back home? Who's been writing you those long tear-stained letters we keep forwarding?'

'None of your business.'

'Don't make me steam them open again, just tell me!'

'There's nothing to tell.'

She sat back in her chair. 'Well I'm disappointed in you. What about that nice girl who came to stay that time?'

'What girl?'

'Pretty, earnest, Northern. Got drunk and shouted at your father about the Sandinistas.'

'That was Emma Morley.'

'Emma Morley. I liked her. Your father liked her too, even if she did call him a bourgeois fascist.' Dexter winced at the memory. 'I don't mind, at least she had a bit of fire, a bit of passion. Not like those silly sex-pots we usually find at the breakfast table. *Yes Mrs Mayhew, no Mrs Mayhew.* I can hear you, you know, tip-toeing to the guest room in the night . . .'

'You really are drunk, aren't you?'

'So what about this Emma?'

'Emma's just a friend.'

'Is she now? Well I'm not so sure. In fact I think she likes you.'

'Everyone likes me. It's my curse.'

In his head it had sounded fine: raffish and self-mocking, but now they sat in silence and he felt foolish once again, like at those parties where his mother would allow him to sit with the grown-ups and he would show-off and let her down. She smiled at him indulgently, and squeezed his hand as it rested on the table.

'Be nice, won't you?'

'I am nice, I'm always nice.'

'But not too nice. I mean don't make a religion out of it, niceness.'

'I won't.' Uncomfortable now, he began to glance around the Piazza.

She nudged his arm. 'So do you want another bottle of wine, or shall we go back to the hotel and see about your father's bunions?'

They began to walk north through the back streets that run parallel to the Via del Corso towards the Piazza del Popolo, Dexter adjusting the route as he went to make it as scenic as possible, and he began to feel better, enjoying the satisfaction of knowing a city well. She hung woozily on his arm.

'So how long are you planning to stay here then?'

'I don't know. 'Til October maybe.'

'But then you will come home and settle down to something, won't you?'

'Of course.'

'I don't mean live with us. I wouldn't do that to you. But you know we'd help you out with a deposit on a flat.'

'There isn't any rush, is there?'

'Well it's been a whole year, Dexter. How much holiday do you need? It's not as if you worked yourself ragged at University—'

'I'm not on holiday, I'm working!'

'What about journalism? Didn't you talk about journalism?'

He had mentioned it in passing, but only as a distraction and alibi. It seemed that as he ambled through his late teens his possibilities had slowly begun to narrow. Certain cool-sounding jobs – heart surgeon, architect – were permanently closed to him now and journalism seemed about to go the same way. He wasn't much of a writer, knew little about politics, spoke bad restaurant-French, lacked all training and qualifications, possessed only a passport and a vivid image of himself smoking beneath a ceiling fan in tropical countries, a battered Nikon and a bottle of whisky by his bedside.

Of course what he really wanted was to be a photographer. At sixteen he had completed a photo-project called 'Texture', full of black and white close-ups of tree bark and sea-shells which had apparently 'blown' his art teacher's mind. Nothing that he had done since had given him as much satisfaction as 'Texture' and those high-contrast prints of frost on windows and the gravel in the driveway. Journalism would mean grappling with difficult stuff like words and ideas, but he thought he might have the makings of a decent photographer, if only because he felt he had a strong sense of when things looked right. At this stage in his life, his main criterion for choosing a career was that it should sound good in a bar, shouted into a girl's ear, and there was no denying that 'I'm a professional photographer' was a fine sentence, almost up there with 'I report from war zones' or 'actually, I make documentaries.'

'Journalism's a possibility.'

'Or business. Weren't you and Callum going to start up some business?'

'We're giving it some thought.'

'All sounds a bit vague, just "business".'

'Like I said, we're giving it some thought.' In truth Callum, his old flatmate, had already started the business without him, something about computer refurbishment that Dexter didn't have the energy to understand. They'd be millionaires by the time they were twenty-five, Callum insisted, but what would it sound like in a bar? 'Actually, I refurbish computers.' No, professional photography was his best bet. He decided to try saying it out loud.

'Actually, I'm thinking about photography.'

'Photography?' His mother gave a maddening laugh.

'Hey, I'm a good photographer!'

'—when you remember to take your thumb off the lens.'

'Aren't you meant to be encouraging me?'

'What kind of photographer? *Glamour?*' She gave a throaty laugh. 'Or are you going to continue your work on *Texture!*' and they had to stop while she stood in the street laughing for some time, doubled over, holding onto his arm for support – 'All those pictures of *gravel!*' – until finally it was over, and she stood and straightened her face. 'Dexter, I am so, so sorry . . .'

'I'm actually much better now.'

'I know you are, I'm sorry. I apologise.' They began to walk again. 'You must do it, Dexter, if that's what you want.' She squeezed his arm with her elbow, but Dexter felt sulky. 'We've always told you that you can be anything you want to be, if you work hard enough.'

'It was just a thought,' he said, petulantly. 'I'm weighing up my options, that's all.'

'Well I hope so, because teaching's a fine profession, but this isn't really your vocation, is it? Teaching Beatles songs to moony Nordic girls.'

'It's hard work, Mum. Besides it gives me something to fall back on.'

'Yes, well, sometimes I wonder if you have a little too much to fall back on.' She was looking down as she spoke and the remark seemed to rebound off the flagstones. They walked a little further before he spoke.

'And what does *that* mean?'

'Oh, I just mean—' She sighed, and rested her head against his shoulder. 'I just mean that at some point you'll have to get serious about life, that's all. You're young and healthy and you look nice enough, I suppose, in a low light. People seem to like you, you're smart, or smart enough, not academically maybe, but you know what's what. And you've had luck, so much luck, Dexter, and you've been protected from things, responsibility, money. But you're an adult now, and one day things might not be this . . .' She looked around her, indicating the scenic little back street down which he had brought her. '. . . this serene. It would be good if you were prepared for that. It would do you good to be better equipped.'

Dexter frowned. 'What, a career you mean?'

'Partly.'

'You sound like Dad.'

'Good God, in what way?'

'A proper job, something to fall back on, something to get up for.'

'Not just that, not just a job. A direction. A purpose. Some drive, some ambition. When I was your age I wanted to change the world.'

He sniffed 'Hence the antiques shop,' and she jabbed him in the ribs with her elbow.

'That's now, this was then. And don't get smart with me.' She took hold of his arm and they began walking slowly again. 'I just want you to make me proud, that's all. I mean I'm already proud of you, and your sister, but, well, you know what I mean. I'm a little drunk. Let's change the subject. I wanted to talk to you about something else.'

'What else?'

'Oh – too late.' They were in sight of the hotel now, three stars, smart but not ostentatious. Through the smoked plate glass window he could glimpse his father hunched in a lobby armchair, one long thin leg bent up to his knee, sock bunched up in his hand as he scrutinised the sole of his foot.

'Good God, he's picking his corns in the hotel lobby. A little bit of Swansea on the Via del Corso. Charming, just charming.' Alison unlooped her arm and took her son's hand in hers. 'Take me for lunch tomorrow, will you? While your father sits in a darkened room and picks his corns. Let's go out, just you and me, somewhere outside on a nice square. White tablecloths. Somewhere expensive, my treat. You can bring me some of your photographs of interesting pebbles.'

'Okay,' he said, sulkily. His mother was smiling but frowning too, squeezing his hand a little too hard, and he felt a sudden pang of anxiety. 'Why?'

'Because I want to talk to my handsome son and I'm a little too drunk right now, I think.'

'What is it? Tell me now!'

'It's nothing, nothing.'

'You're not getting divorced, are you?'

She gave a low laugh. 'Don't be ridiculous, of course not.' In the hotel lobby his father had seen them, and was standing and tugging on the 'push to open' door. 'How could I ever leave a man who tucks his shirts into his underpants?'

'So tell me, what is it?'

'Nothing bad, sweetheart, nothing bad.' Standing on the street she gave him a consoling smile and put her hand in the short hair at the back of his neck, pulling him down to her height so that their foreheads were touching. 'Don't you worry about a thing. Tomorrow. We'll talk properly tomorrow.'

35

CHAPTER THREE
The Taj Mahal

SUNDAY 15 JULY 1990

Bombay and Camden Town

'ATTENTION PLEASE! Can I have your attention? Some attention if you don't mind? If you could listen? Don't throw things, listen please? Please? ATTENTION, PLEASE? Thank you.'

Scott McKenzie settled on his bar stool and looked out at his team of eight staff: all under twenty-five, all dressed in white denim jeans and corporate baseball caps, all of them desperate to be anywhere but here, the Sunday lunch-time shift at Loco Caliente, a Tex-Mex restaurant on the Kentish Town Road where both food and atmosphere were hot hot hot.

'Now before we open the doors for brunch I'd just like to run through today's so-called "specials", if I may. Our soup is that repeat offender, the sweetcorn chowder, and the main course is a very delicious and succulent fish burrito!'

Scott blew air out through his mouth and waited for the groaning and fake retching to subside. A small, pale pink-eyed man with a degree in Business Management from Loughborough, he had once hoped to be a captain of industry. He had pictured himself playing golf at conference centres or striding up the steps of a private jet, and yet just this morning he had scooped a plug of yellow pork fat the size of a human head from the kitchen drains. With his bare hands. He could still feel the grease between his fingers. He was thirty-nine years old, and it wasn't meant to be this way.

'Basically, it's your standard beef-stroke-chicken-stroke-pork burrito but with, and I quote, "delicious moist chunks of cod and salmon". Who knows, they may even get a prawn or two.'

'That's just . . . *awful*,' laughed Paddy from behind the bar, where he sat cutting limes into wedges for the necks of beer bottles.

'Bringing a little touch of the North Atlantic to the cuisine of Latin America,' said Emma Morley, tying on her waitress's apron and noticing a new arrival appearing behind Scott, a large, sturdy man, fair curly hair on a large cylindrical head. The new boy. The staff watched him warily, weighing him up as if he were a new arrival on G-wing.

'On a brighter note,' said Scott, 'I'd like to introduce you to Ian Whitehead, who will be joining our happy team of highly trained staff.' Ian slapped his regulation baseball cap far back on his head and, raising an arm in salute, high-fived the air. 'Yo, my people!' he said, in what might have been an American accent.

'*Yo my people?* Where does Scott *find* them?' sniggered Paddy from behind the bar, his voice calibrated just loud enough for the new arrival to hear.

Scott slapped a palm on Ian's shoulder, startling him: 'So I'm going to hand you over to Emma, our longest serving member of staff!—'

Emma winced at the accolade, then smiled apologetically at the new boy, and he smiled back with his mouth closed tight; a Stan Laurel smile.

'—She'll show you the basics, and that's it, everyone. Remember! Fish burritos! Now, music please!'

Paddy pressed play on the greasy tape deck behind the bar and the music began, a maddening forty-five minutes loop of synthetic mariachi music, beginning aptly enough with 'La Cucaracha', the cockroach, to be heard twelve times in an eight-hour shift. Twelve times a shift, twenty-four shifts a month, for seven months now. Emma looked down at the baseball cap in her hand. The restaurant logo, a cartoon donkey, peered up at her goggle-eyed from beneath his sombrero, drunk it would

37

seem, or insane perhaps. She settled the cap on her head and slid off the bar stool as if lowering herself into icy water. The new guy was waiting for her, beaming, his fingertips jammed awkwardly into the pockets of his gleaming white jeans, and Emma wondered once again what exactly she was doing with her life.

Emma, Emma, Emma. How are you, Emma? And what are you doing right this second? We're six hours ahead here in Bombay, so hopefully you're still in bed with a Sunday morning hang-over in which case WAKE UP! IT'S DEXTER!

This letter comes to you from a downtown Bombay hostel with scary mattresses and hot and cold running Australians. My guide book tells me that it has character i.e. rodents but my room also has a little plastic picnic table by the window and it's raining like crazy outside, harder even than in Edinburgh. It's CHUCKING IT DOWN, Em, so loud that I can barely hear the compilation tape you made me which I like a lot incident-ally except for that jangly indie stuff because after all I'm not some GIRL. I've been trying to read the books you gave me at Easter too, though I have to admit I'm finding Howards End quite heavy-going. It's like they've been drinking the same cup of tea for two hundred pages, and I keep waiting for someone to pull a knife or an alien invasion or something, but that's not going to happen is it? When will you stop trying to educate me, I wonder? Never I hope.

By the way, in case you hadn't guessed from the Exquisite Prose and all the SHOUTING I'm writing this drunk, beers at lunch time! As you can tell I'm not a great letter writer not like you (your last letter was so funny) but all I will say is that India is incredible. It turns out that being banned from Teaching English as a Foreign Language was the best thing that ever happened to me (though I still think they over-reacted. Morally Unfit? Me? Tove was twenty-one). I won't bore you with all that sunrise over the Hindu-kesh prose except to say that all the clichés are true (poverty, tummy upsets blah blah blah). Not only is it a rich and ancient civilization but you wouldn't BELIEVE what you can get in the chemists without a prescription.

So I've seen some amazing things and while it's not always fun it is an Experience and I've taken thousands of photographs which I will show you very very slooooooowly when I get back. Pretend to be interested, won't you? After all I pretended to be interested when you banged on about the Poll Tax Riots. Anyway, I showed some of my photos to this TV producer who I met on a train the other day, a woman (not what you think, old, mid-thirties) and she said I could be a professional. She was here producing a sort of young people's TV travel show thing and she gave me her card and told me to call her in August when they're back again, so who knows maybe I'll do some researching or filming even.

What's happening with you work-wise? Are you doing another play? I really, really enjoyed your Virginia-Woolf-Emily-whatsername play when I was in London, and like I said I think it showed loads of promise which sounds like bullshit but isn't. I think you're right to give up acting though, not because you're not good but because you so obviously hate it. Candy was nice too, much nicer than you made out. Send her my love. Are you doing another play? Are you still in that box room? Does the flat still smell of fried onions? Is Tilly Killick still soaking her big grey bras in the washing-up bowl? Are you still at Mucho Loco or whatever it's called? Your last letter made me laugh so much, Em, but you should still get out of there because while it's good for gags it's definitely bad for your soul. You can't throw years of your life away because it makes a funny anecdote.

Which brings me to my reason for writing to you. Are you ready? You might want to sit down . . .

* * *

'So, Ian – welcome to the graveyard of ambition!'

Emma pushed open the staffroom door, immediately knocking over a pint glass on the floor, last night's fags suspended in lager. The official tour had brought them to the small, dank staffroom which overlooked the Kentish Town Road, packed already with students and tourists on their way to Camden Market to buy large furry top hats and smiley face t-shirts.

'Loco Caliente means Crazy Hot; "Hot" because the air-conditioning doesn't work, "crazy" because that's what you'd have to be to eat here. Or work here, come to that. Mucho mucho loco. I'll show you where to put your stuff.' Together they kicked through the mulch of last week's newspapers to the battered old office cabinet. 'This is your locker. It doesn't lock. Don't be tempted to leave your uniform here overnight either because someone'll nick it, God knows why. Management flip if you lose your baseball cap. They drown you face down in a vat of tangy barbecue relish—'

Ian laughed, a hearty, slightly forced chortle, and Emma sighed and turned to the staff dining table, still covered with last night's dirty plates. 'Lunch hours are twenty minutes and you can have anything from the menu except the jumbo prawns, which I believe is what's known as a blessing in disguise. If you value life, don't touch the jumbo prawns. It's like Russian Roulette, one in six'll kill you.' She began to clear the table.

'Here, let me—' said Ian, gingerly picking up a meatily smeared plate with the tips of his fingers. New boy – still squeamish, thought Emma, watching him. He had a pleasant, large open face beneath the loose straw-coloured curls, smooth ruddy cheeks and a mouth that hung open in repose. Not exactly handsome, but, well – sturdy. For some reason, not entirely kind, it was a face that made her think of tractors.

Suddenly he met her gaze and she blurted out: 'So tell me, Ian, what brings you down Mexico Way.'

'Oh, you know. Got to pay the rent.'

'And there's nothing else you can do? You can't temp, or live with your parents or something?'

'I need to be in London, I need flexible hours . . .'

'Why, what's your stroke?'

'My what?'

'Your stroke. Everyone who works here has a stroke. Waiter-stroke-artist, waiter-stroke-actor. Paddy the bartender claims to be a model, but frankly I'm doubtful.'

'Weeeeeell,' said Ian, in what she took to be a Northern accent, 'I suppose I'd have to say that I'm a comedian!' Grinning, he splayed his hands either side of his face and gave them an end-of-pier waggle.

'Right. Well, we all like to laugh. What, like a stand-up or something?'

'Stand-up mainly. What about you?'

'Me?'

'Your stroke? What else do you do?'

She thought about saying 'playwright' but even after three months the humiliation of being Emily Dickinson to an empty room still burned bright. She might as well say 'astronaut' as 'playwright', there was as much truth in it. 'Oh, I do this—' She peeled an old burrito from its carapace of hardened cheese. 'This is what I do.'

'And do you like it?'

'*Like* it? I love it! I mean I'm not made of wood.' She wiped the day-old ketchup onto a used napkin and headed for the door. 'Now, let me show you the toilets. Brace yourself . . .'

Since I started this letter I've drank (drunken? dronk?) two more beers and so am ready to say this now. Here goes. Em, we've known each other five or six years now, but two years properly, as, you know, 'friends', which isn't that long but I think I know a bit about you and I think I know what your problem is. And be aware that I have a lowish 2.2 in Anthropology, so

I know what I'm talking about. If you don't want to know my theory, stop reading now.

Good. Here it is. I think you're scared of being happy, Emma. I think you think that the natural way of things is for your life to be grim and grey and dour and to hate your job, hate where you live, not to have success or money or God forbid a boyfriend (and a quick discersion here – that whole self-deprecating thing about being unattractive is getting pretty boring I can tell you). In fact I'll go further and say that I think you actually get a kick out of being disappointed and under-achieving, because it's easier, isn't it? Failure and unhappiness is easier because you can make a joke out of it. Is this annoying you? I bet it is. Well I've only just started.

Em, I hate thinking of you sitting in that awful flat with the weird smells and noises and the overhead lightbulbs or sat in that launderette, and by the way there's no reason in this day and age why you should be using a launderette, there's nothing cool or political about launderettes it's just depressing. I don't know, Em, you're young, you're practically a genius, and yet your idea of a good time is to treat yourself to a service wash. Well I think you deserve more. You are smart and funny and kind (too kind if you ask me) and by far the cleverest person I know. And (am drinking more beer here – deep breath) you are also a Very Attractive Woman. And (more beer) yes I do mean 'sexy' as well, though I feel a bit sick writing it down. Well I'm not going to scribble it out because it's politically incorrect to call someone 'sexy' because it is also TRUE. You're gorgeous, you old hag, and if I could give you just one gift ever for the rest of your life it would be this. Confidence. It would be the gift of Confidence. Either that or a scented candle.

I know from your letters and from seeing you after your play that you feel a little bit lost right now about what to do with your life, a bit rudderless and oarless and aimless but that's okay that's alright because we're all meant to be like that at twenty-four. In fact our whole generation is like that. I read an article about it, it's because we never fought in a war or watched too much television or something. Anyway, the only people with oars and rudders and aims are dreary bores and squares and careerists like Tilly-bloody-Killick or Callum O'Neill and his refurbished computers. I certainly don't have a master plan I know you think I've got it all sorted out but I haven't I worry too I just don't worry about the dole and housing benefit and the future of the Labour Party and where I'm going to be in twenty years' time and how Mr Mandela is adjusting to freedom.

So time for another breather before the next paragraph because I've barely got started. This letter builds to a life-changing climax. I wonder if you're ready for it yet.

Somewhere between the staff toilets and the kitchen, Ian Whitehead slipped into his stand-up act.

'Have you ever been in, like, a supermarket, and you're in the six items or less queue, and there's an old lady in front of you, and she's got, like *seven* items? And you stand there counting them, and you're like, soooo angry . . .'

'Ay caramba,' mumbled Emma under her breath before kicking open the swing doors to the kitchen where they were met by a wall of hot air that stung their eyes, acrid and infused with jalapeno peppers and warm bleach. Loud acid house played on the battered radio cassette as a Somalian, an Algerian and a Brazilian prised the lids off white plastic catering tubs.

'Morning, Benoit, Kemal. Hiya, Jesus,' said Emma cheerfully and they smiled and nodded cheerfully back. Emma and Ian crossed to a noticeboard where she pointed out a laminated sign that showed what to do if someone choked on their food, 'as well they might'. Next to this was pinned a large document, ragged at the edges, a parchment map of the Texas–Mexico border. Emma tapped it with her finger.

'This thing that looks like a treasure map? Well don't get your hopes up, because it's just the menu. No gold here, compadre, just forty-eight items, all the different permutations of your five key Tex-Mex food groups – minced beef and beans, cheese, chicken and guacamole.' She traced her finger across the map. 'So, moving east–west, we've got chicken on beans under cheese, cheese on top of chicken under guacamole, guacamole on top of mince on top of chicken under cheese . . .'

'Right, I see . . .'

'. . . occasionally for the thrill of it we'll throw some rice or a raw onion in, but where it gets really exciting is what you put it in. It's all to do with wheat or corn.'

'Wheat or corn, right . . .'

'Tacos are corn, burritos are wheat. Basically if it shatters and burns your hand it's a taco, if it flops around and leaks red lard down your arm it's a burrito. Here's one—' She pulled a soft pancake from a catering pack of fifty and dangled it like a wet flannel. 'That's a burrito. Fill it, deep fry it, melt cheese on it, it's an enchilada. A tortilla that's been filled is a taco and a burrito that you fill yourself is a fajita.'

'So what's a tostada?'

'We'll get to that. Don't run before you can walk. Fajitas come on these red-hot iron platters.' She hefted a greasy ridged-iron pan, like something from a blacksmith's. 'Careful with these, you wouldn't believe how many times we've had to peel a customer off these things. Then they don't tip.' Ian was staring at her now, grinning goofily. She drew attention to the bucket at her feet. 'This white stuff here is sour cream, except it's not sour, it's not cream, just some sort of hydrogenated fat, I think. It's what's left over when they make petrol. Handy if the heel comes off your shoe, but apart from that . . .'

'I have a question for you.'

'Go on then.'

'What are you doing after work?'

Benoit, Jesus and Kemal all stopped what they were doing as Emma readjusted her face and laughed. 'You don't hang about, do you, Ian?'

He had taken his cap off now, and was turning it in his hand, a stage suitor. 'Not a date or anything, you've probably got a boyfriend anyway!' A moment, while he waited for a response, but Emma's face didn't move. 'I just thought you might be interested in my—' in a nasal voice '—unique comedy stylings, that's all. I'm doing a—' finger apostrophes '—"gig" tonight, at Chortles at the Frog and Parrot in Cockfosters.'

'Chortles?'

'In Cockfosters. It's Zone 3 which seems like Mars I know on a Sunday night, but even if I'm shit there are still some other really top notch comics there. Ronny Butcher, Steve Sheldon, the Kamikaze Twins—' As he spoke Emma became aware of his real accent, a slight, pleasant West Country burr, not yet wiped away by the city, and she thought once again of tractors. 'I'm doing this whole new bit tonight, about the difference between men and women—'

No doubt about it, he was asking her out on a date. She really ought to go. After all, it wasn't like it happened very often, and what was the worst thing that could happen?

'And the food's not bad there either. Just the usual, burgers, spring rolls, curly fries—'

'It sounds enchanting, Ian, the curly fries and all, but I can't tonight, sorry.'

'Really?'

'Evensong at seven.'

'No, but really.'

'It's a nice offer, but after my shift here I'm wiped out. I like to just go home, comfort-eat, cry. So I'll have to give it a miss, I'm afraid.'

'Another time then? I'm playing the Bent Banana at the Cheshire Cat in Balham on Friday—'

Over his shoulder Emma could see the cooks watching, Benoit

laughing with his hand to his mouth. 'Maybe another time,' she said, kindly but decisively, then sought to change the subject.

'Now, this—' She tapped another bucket with her toe. 'This stuff here is salsa. Try not to get it on your skin. It burns.'

The thing is, Em, running back to the hostel in the rain just now – the rain is warm here, hot even sometimes, not like London rain – I was, like I said, pretty drunk and I found myself thinking about you and thinking what a shame Em isn't here to see this, to experience this, and I had this revelation and it's this.

You should be here with me. In India.

And this is my big idea, and it might be insane, but I'm going to post this before I change my mind. Follow these simple instructions.

1 – Leave that crappy job right now. Let them find someone else to melt cheese on tortilla chips for 2.20 an hour. Put a bottle of tequila in your bag and walk out the door. Think what that will feel like, Em. Walk out now. Just do it.

2 – I also think you should leave that flat. Tilly's ripping you off, charging all that money for a room without a window. It isn't a box room, it's a box, and you should get out of there and let someone else wring out her great big grey bras for her. When I get back to the so-called real world I'm going to buy a flat because that's the kind of over-privileged capitalist monster I am and you're always welcome to come and stay for a bit, or permanently if you like, because I think we'd get on, don't you? As, you know, FLATMATES. That's providing you can over-come your sexual attraction to me ha ha. If the worst comes to the worst, I'll lock you in your room at nights. Anyway, now the big one—

3 – As soon as you've read this, go to the student travel agency on Tottenham Court Road and book an OPEN RETURN flight to Delhi to arrive as near as possible to August 1st, two weeks' time, which in case you've forgotten is my birthday. The night before get a train to Agra and stay in a cheap motel. Next morning get up early and go to the Taj Mahal. Perhaps you've heard of it, big white building named after that Indian restaurant on the Lothian Road. Have a look around and at precisely 12 midday you stand directly under the centre of the dome with a red rose in one hand and a copy of Nicholas Nickleby *in the other and I will come and find you, Em. I will be carrying a white rose and my copy of* Howards End *and when I see you I will throw it at your head.*

Isn't that the greatest plan you've ever heard of in your life?

Ah, typical Dexter you say, isn't he forgetting something? Money! Plane tickets don't grow on trees and what about social security and the work ethic etc. etc. Well don't worry, I'm paying. Yes, I'm paying. I'm going to wire the money to you for your plane ticket (I've always wanted to wire money) and I'm going to pay for everything when you're here which sounds swanky but isn't because it is so DAMN CHEAP here. We can live for months, Em, me and you, heading down to Kerala or across to Thailand. We could go to a full moon party – imagine staying awake all night not because you're worried about the future but because it's FUN. (Remember when we stayed up all night after graduation, Em? Anyway. Moving on.)

For three hundred pounds of someone else's money, you could change your life, and you mustn't worry about it because frankly I have money that I haven't earned, and you work really hard and yet you don't have money, so it's socialism in action isn't it? And if you really want you can pay me back when you're a famous playwright, or when the poetry-money kicks in or whatever. Besides it's only for three months. I've got to come back in the autumn anyway. As you know Mum's not been well. She tells me the operation went fine and maybe it did or maybe she just doesn't want me to worry. Either way I've got to come home eventually. (By the way, my mother has a theory about you and me, and if you meet me at the Taj Mahal I will tell you all about it, but only if you meet me.)

On the wall in front of me is this massive sort of praying mantis thing and he's looking at me as if to say shut up now so I will. It's stopped raining, and I'm about to go to a bar and meet up with some new friends for a drink, three female medical students from Amsterdam which tells you all you need to know. But on the way I'm going to find a post box and send this before I change my mind. Not because I think you coming here is a bad idea – it isn't, it's a great idea and you must come – but because I think I might have said too much. Sorry if this has annoyed you. The main thing is that I think about you a lot, that's all. Dex and Em, Em and Dex. Call me sentimental, but there's no-one in the world that I'd like to see get dysentery more than you.

Taj Mahal, 1st August, 12 noon.

I will find you!

Love

D

. . . and then he stretched and scratched at his scalp, drained the last of his beer and picked the letter up, tapped the edges together and laid the stack solemnly in front of him. He shook the cramp from his hand; eleven pages written at great speed, the most he had written since his finals. Stretching his arms above his head in satisfaction he thought: this isn't a letter, it's a gift.

He slid his feet back into his sandals, stood a little unsteadily and steeled himself for the communal showers. He was deeply tanned now, his great project of the last two years, the colour penetrating deep into his skin like a creosoted fence. With his head shaved very close to the skull by a street barber, he had also lost some weight but secretly liked the new look: hero-ically gaunt, as if he'd just been rescued from the jungle. To complete the image he had acquired a cautious tattoo on his ankle, a non-committal yin-and-yang that he would probably regret back in London. But that was fine. In London he would wear socks.

Sobered by the cold shower, he returned to the tiny room and dug deep in his rucksack to find something to wear for the Dutch medical students, smelling each item of clothing until they lay in a damp, ripe pile on the worn raffia rug. He settled on the least offensive item, a vintage American short-sleeved shirt, and pulled on some jeans, cut off at the calves and worn with no underwear, so that he felt bold and daredevil. An adventurer, a pioneer.

And then he saw the letter. Six blue sheets densely written on both sides. He stared at it as if an intruder had left it behind, and with his new sobriety came the first twinge of doubt. Picking it up gingerly, he glanced at a page at random and immediately looked away, his mouth puckered tight. All those capitals and exclamation marks and awful jokes. He had called her 'sexy', he had used the word 'discersion' which wasn't even a proper word. He sounded like some poetry-reading sixth-former, not a pioneer, an adventurer with a shaved head and a tattoo and no underpants beneath his jeans. *I will find you, I've been thinking about you, Dex and Em, Em and Dex* – what was he thinking? What had seemed urgent and touching an hour ago now seemed mawkish and gauche and sometimes frankly deceitful; there had been no praying mantis on the wall, he hadn't been listening to her compilation tape as he wrote, had lost his cassette player in Goa. Clearly the letter would change everything, and weren't things fine just as they were? Did he really want Emma with him in India, laughing at his tattoo, making smart remarks? Would he have to kiss her at the airport? Would they have to share a bed? Did he really want to see her that much?

Yes, he decided, he did. Because for all its obvious idiocy, there was a sincere affection, more than affection, in what he had written and he would definitely post it that night. If she over-reacted, he could always say he was drunk. That much at least was true.

49

Without further hesitation he packed the letter into an air-mail envelope and slipped it into his copy of *Howards End*, next to Emma's handwritten dedication. Then he headed off to the bar to meet his new Dutch friends.

Shortly after nine that night, Dexter left the bar with Renee van Houten, a trainee pharmacist from Rotterdam with fading henna on her hands, a jar of temazepam in her pocket and a poorly executed tattoo of Woody Woodpecker at the base of her spine. He could see the bird leering at him lewdly as he stumbled through the door.

In their eagerness to leave, Dexter and his new friend accidentally jostled Heidi Schindler, twenty-three years old, a chemical engineering student from Cologne. Heidi swore at Dexter, but in German, and quietly enough for them not to hear. Pushing through the crowded bar, she shrugged off her immense backpack and searched the room for somewhere to collapse. Heidi's features were red and round, like a series of overlapping circles, an effect exaggerated by her round spectacles, now steamy in the hot humid bar. Bad-tempered, bloated on Diocalm, angry with the friends who kept running off without her, she collapsed backwards on a decrepit rattan sofa and absorbed the full scale of her misery. She removed her steamy spectacles, wiped them on the corner of her t-shirt, settled on the sofa and felt something hard jab into her hip. Quietly, she swore again.

Tucked between the ragged foam cushions was a copy of *Howards End*, a letter tucked into the opening pages. Even though it was intended for someone else, she felt an automatic thrill of anticipation at the red and white trim of the air-mail envelope. She tugged the letter out, read it to the end, then read it again.

Heidi's English wasn't particularly strong, and some words were unfamiliar – 'discersion' for example, but she understood enough to recognise this as a letter of some importance, the kind of letter that she would like to receive herself one day. Not quite a love-letter, but near enough. She pictured this 'Em' person reading it, then re-reading it, exasperated but a little pleased too, and she imagined her acting upon it, walking out of her terrible flat and the rotten job and changing her life. Heidi imagined Emma Morley, who looked not unlike herself, waiting at the Taj Mahal as a handsome blond man approached. She imagined a kiss and Heidi began to feel a little happier. She decided that, whatever happened, Emma Morley must receive this letter.

But there was no address on the envelope and no return address for 'Dexter' either. She scanned the pages for clues, the name of the restaurant where Emma worked perhaps, but there was nothing of use. She resolved to ask at the reception of the hostel over the road. This was, after all, the best that she could do.

Heidi Schindler is Heidi Klauss now. Forty-one years old, she lives in a suburb of Frankfurt with a husband and four children, and is reasonably happy, certainly happier than she expected to be at twenty-three. The paperback copy of *Howards End* is still on the shelf in the spare bedroom, forgotten and unread, with the letter tucked neatly just inside the cover, next to an inscription in small, careful handwriting that reads:

To dear Dexter. A great novel for your great journey. Travel well and return safely with no tattoos. *Be good, or as good as you are able. Bloody hell, I'll miss you.*

All my love, your good friend Emma Morley, Clapton, London, April 1990

CHAPTER FOUR
Opportunities

MONDAY 15 JULY 1991

Camden Town and Primrose Hill

'ATTENTION PLEASE! Can I have your attention? Attention everyone? Stop talking, stop talking, stop talking. Please? Please? Thank you. Right I just want to go through today's menu if I may. First of all the so-called "specials". We've got a sweetcorn chowder and a turkey chimi-changa.'

'Turkey? In July?' said Ian Whitehead from the bar, where he was cutting lime wedges to jam into the necks of bottles of beer.

'Now it's Monday today,' continued Scott. 'Should be nice and quiet, so I want this place spotless. I've checked the rota, and Ian, you're on toilets.'

The other staff scoffed. 'Why is it always me?' moaned Ian.

'Because you do it so *beautifully*,' said his best friend Emma Morley, and Ian took the opportunity to throw an arm around her hunched shoulders, jokily wielding a knife in a light-hearted downwards stabbing motion.

'And when you two have finished, Emma, can you come and see me in my office please?' said Scott.

The other staff sniggered insinuatingly, Emma disentangled herself from Ian, and Rashid the bartender pressed play on the greasy tape deck behind the bar, 'La Cucaracha', the cockroach, a joke that wasn't funny anymore, repeated until the end of time.

'So I'll come straight out with it. Take a seat.'

Scott lit a cigarette and Emma hoisted herself onto the bar

stool opposite his large, untidy desk. A wall of boxes filled with vodka, tequila and cigarettes – the stock deemed most 'nickable' – blocked out the July sunlight in a small dark room that smelt of ashtrays and disappointment.

Scott kicked his feet up onto the desk. 'The fact is, I'm leaving.'

'You are?'

'Head office have asked me to head up the new branch of Hail Caesar's in Ealing.'

'What's Hail Caesar's?'

'Big new chain of contemporary Italians.'

'Called Hail Caesar's?'

'That is correct.'

'Why not Mussolini's?'

'They're going to do to Italian what they've done to Mexican.'

'What, fuck it up?'

Scott looked hurt. 'Give me a break, will you, Emma?'

'I'm sorry, Scott, really. Congratulations, well done, really—' She stopped short, because she realised what was coming next.

'The point is—' He interlocked his fingers and leant forward on the desk, as this was something that he'd seen businessmen do on television, and felt a little aphrodisiac rush of power. 'They've asked me to appoint my own replacement as manager, and that's what I wanted to talk to you about. I want someone who isn't going anywhere. Someone reliable who isn't going to run off to India without giving proper notice or drop it all for some exciting job. Someone I can rely onto stick around here for a couple of years and really devote themselves to . . . Emma, are you . . . are you *crying?*'

Emma shielded her eyes with both hands. 'Sorry, Scott, it's just you've caught me at a bad time, that's all.'

Scott frowned, stalled between compassion and irritation. 'Here—' He yanked a roll of coarse blue kitchen paper from a catering pack. 'Sort yourself out—' and he tossed the roll across the desk so that it bounced off Emma's chest. 'Is it something I said?'

'No, no, no, it's just a personal, private thing, just boils up every now and then. So embarrassing.' She pressed two wads of rough blue paper against her eyes. 'Sorry, sorry, sorry, you were saying.'

'I've lost my place now, you bursting into tears like that.'

'I think you were telling me that my life was going nowhere,' and she began to laugh and cry at the same time. She grabbed a third piece of kitchen paper and wadded it against her mouth.

Scott waited until her shoulders had stopped heaving. 'So are you interested in the job or not?'

'You mean to say—' She placed her hand on a twenty-litre tub of Thousand Island Dressing '—all this could one day be mine?'

'Emma, if you don't want the job, just say, but I have been doing it for four years now—'

'And you've done it really well, Scott—'

'The money's adequate, you'd never have to clean the toilets again—'

'And I appreciate the offer.'

'So why the waterworks then?'

'Just I've been a little . . . depressed that's all.'

'De-pressed.' Scott frowned as if hearing the word for the first time.

'You know. Bit blue.'

'Right. I see.' He contemplated putting a paternal arm around her, but it would mean climbing over a ten-gallon drum of mayonnaise, so instead he leant further across the desk. 'Is it . . . boy trouble?'

Emma laughed once. 'Hardly. Scott, it's nothing, you just caught me at a low ebb, that's all.' She shook her head vigorously. 'See, all gone, right as rain. Let's forget it.'

'So what do you think? About being manager?'

'Can I think about it? Tell you tomorrow?'

Scott smiled benignly and nodded. 'Go on then! Take a break—' He stretched an arm towards the door, adding with infinite compassion: 'Go get yourself some nachos.'

In the empty staff room, Emma glared at the plate of steaming cheese and corn chips as if it was an enemy that must be defeated.

Standing suddenly, she crossed to Ian's locker and plunged her hand into the densely packed denim until she found some cigarettes. She took one, lit it, then lifted her spectacles and inspected her eyes in the cracked mirror, licking her finger to remove the tell-tale smears. Her hair was long these days, style-less in a colour that she thought of as 'Lank Mouse'. She pulled a strand from the scrunchie that held it in place and ran finger and thumb along its length, knowing that when she washed it she would turn the shampoo grey. City hair. She was pale from too many late shifts, and plump too; for some months now she had been putting skirts on over her head. She blamed all those refried beans; fried then fried again. 'Fat girl,' she thought, 'stupid fat girl' this being one of the slogans currently playing in her head, along with 'A Third of Your Life Gone' and 'What's the Point of Anything?'

Emma's mid-twenties had brought a second adolescence even more self-absorbed and doom-laden than the first one. 'Why don't you come home, sweetheart?' her mum had said on the phone last night, using her quavering, concerned voice, as if her daughter had been abducted. 'Your room's still here. There's jobs at Debenhams' and for the first time she had been tempted.

Once, she had thought she could conquer London. She had imagined a whirl of literary salons, political engagement, larky parties, bittersweet romances conducted on Thames embankments. She had intended to form a band, make short films, write novels, but two years on the slim volume of verse was no fatter, and nothing really good had happened to her since she'd been baton-charged at the Poll Tax Riots.

The city had defeated her, just like they said it would. Like some overcrowded party, no-one had noticed her arrival, and no-one would notice if she left.

It wasn't that she hadn't tried. The idea of a career in publishing had floated itself. Her friend Stephanie Shaw had got a job on graduation, and it had transformed her. No more pints of lager and black for Stephanie Shaw. These days she drank white wine, wore neat little suits from Jigsaw and handed out Kettle Chips at dinner parties. On Stephanie's advice Emma had written letters to publishers, to agents, then to bookshops, but nothing. There was a recession on and people were clinging to their jobs with grim determination. She thought about taking refuge in education, but the government had ended student grants, and there was no way she could afford the fees. There was voluntary work, for Amnesty International perhaps, but rent and travel ate up all her money, Loco Caliente ate up all her time and energy. She had a fanciful notion that she might read novels aloud to blind people, but was this an actual job, or just something that she'd seen in a film? When she had the energy, she would find out. For now she would sit at the table and glare at her lunch.

The industrial cheese had set solid like plastic, and in sudden disgust Emma pushed it away and reached into her bag, pulling out an expensive new black leather notebook with a stubby fountain pen clipped to the cover. Turning to a fresh new page of creamy white paper, she quickly began to write.

Nachos

It was the nachos that did it.
The steaming variegated mess like the mess of her life
Summing up all that was wrong
With
Her
Life.

'Time for change' comes the voice from the street.
Outside on the Kentish Town Road
There is laughter
But here, in the smoky attic room
There are only
The Nachos.
Cheese, like life, has become
Hard and
Cold
Like Plastic
And there is no laughter in the high room.

Emma stopped writing, then looked away and stared at the ceiling, as if giving someone a chance to hide. She looked back at the page in the hope of being surprised by the brilliance of what was there.

She shuddered and gave a long groan, then laughed, shaking her head as she methodically scratched out each line, cross-hatching on top of this until each word was obliterated. Soon there was so much ink that it had soaked through the paper. She turned back a page to where the blots had seeped through and glanced at what was written there.

<u>Edinburgh morning, 4 a.m.</u>

We lie in the single bed and talk about the
Future, make our guesses
and as he speaks I look at him, think
'Handsome', stupid word, and think
'might this be it? The elusive thing?'

Blackbirds sing outside and the
Sunlight warms the curtains . . .

Once more she shuddered, as if peeking beneath a bandage, and snapped the notebook shut. Good God, 'the elusive thing'. She had reached a turning point. She no longer believed that a situation could be made better by writing a poem about it.

Putting the notebook away, she reached for yesterday's *Sunday Mirror* instead and began to eat the nachos, the elusive nachos, surprised all over again at how very comforting very bad food can be.

Ian was in the doorway. 'That guy's here again.'

'What guy?'

'Your friend, the handsome one. He's got some girl with him.' And immediately Emma knew which guy Ian was talking about.

She watched them from the kitchen, nose pressed against the greasy glass of the circular window as they slumped insolently in a central booth, sipping gaudy drinks and laughing at the menu. The girl was long and slim with pale skin, black eye make-up and black, black hair, cut short and expensively asymmetrical, her long legs in sheer black leggings and high-ankled boots. Both a little drunk, they were behaving in that self-consciously wild and reckless way that people slip into when they know they're being watched: pop-video behaviour, and Emma thought how satisfying it would be to stride out onto the restaurant floor and cosh them both with tightly packed burritos-of-the-day.

Two big hands draped on her shoulders. 'Schhhhhwing,' said Ian, resting his chin on her head. 'Who is she?'

'No idea.' Emma rubbed at the mark her nose had made on the window. 'I lose track.'

'She's a new one then.'

'Dexter has a very short attention span. Like a baby. Or a monkey. You need to dangle something shiny in front of him.' That's what this girl is, she thought: something shiny.

'So do you think it's true what they say? About girls liking bastards.'

'He's not a bastard. He's an idiot.'

'Do girls like idiots then?'

Dexter had stuck his cocktail umbrella behind his ear now, the girl collapsing into enchanted laughter at the genius of it.

'Certainly seems that way,' said Emma. What was it, she wondered, this need to brandish his shiny new metropolitan life at her? As soon as she'd met him at the arrivals gate on his return from Thailand, lithe and brown and shaven-headed, she knew that there was no chance of a relationship between them. Too much had happened to him, too little had happened to her. Even so this would be the third girlfriend, lover, whatever, that she had met in the last nine months, Dexter presenting them up to her like a dog with a fat pigeon in his mouth. Was it some kind of sick revenge for something? Because she got a better degree than him? Didn't he know what this was doing to her, sat at table nine with their groins jammed in each other's faces?

'Can't you go, Ian? It's your section.'

'He asked for you.'

She sighed, wiped her hands on her apron, removed the baseball cap from her head to minimise the shame and pushed the swing door open.

'So – do you want to hear the specials or what?'

Dexter stood up quickly, untangling himself from the girl's long limbs, and threw his arms around his old, old friend. 'Hey there, how are you, Em? Big hug!' Since starting to work in the TV industry he had developed a mania for hugging, or for Big Hugging. The company of TV presenters had rubbed off on him, and he spoke to her now less like an old friend, more like our next very special guest.

'Emma, this—' He placed one hand on the girl's bare, bony shoulder, forming a chain between them. 'This is Naomi, pronounced Gnome-y.'

'Hello, Gnome-y,' smiled Emma. Naomi smiled back, the drinking straw nipped tight between white teeth.

'Hey, come and join us for a margarita!' Boozy and sentimental, he tugged on Emma's hand.

'Can't, Dex, I'm working.'

'Come on, five minutes. I want to buy you a drunk. A *drink*! I mean a drink.'

Ian joined them now, his notebook poised. 'So shall I get you guys something to eat?' he asked convivially.

The girl wrinkled her nose. 'I don't *think* so!'

'Dexter, you've met Ian, haven't you?' said Emma quickly.

'No, no, I haven't,' said Dexter. 'Yes, several times,' said Ian, and there was a moment of silence as they stood there, the staff and the customers.

'So, Ian, can we get two, no, three of the "Remember the Alamo" margaritas. Two or three? Em, are you joining us?'

'Dexter, I told you. I'm working.'

'Okay, in that case, do you know what? We'll leave it then. Just the bill, please, um . . .' Ian left and Dexter beckoned to Emma and in a low voice said, 'Hey, look, is there any way I can, you know . . .'

'What?'

'Give you the money for the drinks.'

Emma stared blankly. 'I don't understand.'

'What I mean is, is there any way I can, you know, *tip* you?'

'Tip me?'

'Exactly. Tip you.'

'Why?'

'No reason, Em,' said Dex. 'I just really, really want to tip you,' and Emma felt another small portion of her soul fall away.

On Primrose Hill, Dexter slept in the evening sun, shirt unbuttoned, hands beneath his head, a half-empty bottle of grocer's white wine warming by his side as he slipped from the hangover of the afternoon into drunkenness again. The parched yellow grass of the hill was crowded with young professional people, many straight from their offices, talking and laughing as three different stereos competed with each other, and Dexter lay in the centre of it all and dreamt about television.

The idea of being a professional photographer had been abandoned without much of a fight. He knew that he was a decent amateur, probably always would be, but to become exceptional, a Cartier-Bresson, a Capa or a Brandt, would require toil, rejection and struggle, and he wasn't sure if struggle suited him. Television, on the other hand, television wanted him right now. Why hadn't he thought of it before? Growing up there had always been a television in the home, but there was something a little unwholesome about watching the thing. Now, in the last nine months it had suddenly come to dominate his life. He was a convert, and with the passion of the new recruit he found himself getting quite emotional about the medium, as if he had finally found a spiritual home.

And no, it didn't have the arty gleam of photography or the credibility of reporting from a war zone, but TV mattered, TV was the future. Democracy in action, it touched people's lives in the most immediate way, shaped opinions, provoked and entertained and engaged far more effectively than all those books that no-one read or plays that no-one went to see. Emma could say what she liked about the Tories (Dexter was no fan either, though more for reasons of style than principle) but they had certainly shaken up the media. Until recently, broadcasting had seemed stuffy, worthy and dull; heavily unionised, grey and bureaucratic, full of bearded lifers and do-gooders and old dears pushing tea-trolleys; a sort of showbiz branch of the Civil Service. Redlight Productions, on the other hand, was part of the boom of new, youthful, privately owned independent companies wresting the means of production away from those fusty old Reithian dinosaurs. There was money in the media; the fact sang out from the primary-coloured open-plan offices with their state-of-the-art computer systems and generous communal fridges.

His rise through this world had been meteoric. The woman he had met on a train in India with the glossy black bob and tiny spectacles had given him his first job as a runner, then a researcher, and now he was Assistant Producer, Asst Prod, on *UP4IT*, a weekend magazine programme that mixed live music and outrageous stand-up with reports on issues that 'really affect young people today': STDs, drugs, dance music, drugs, police brutality, drugs. Dexter produced hyperactive little films of grim housing estates shot from crazy angles through fish-eye lenses, the clouds speeded up to a soundtrack of acid house. There was even talk of putting him in front of the cameras in the next series. He was excelling, he was flying and there seemed to be every possibility that he might make his parents proud.

'I work in TV'; just saying it gave him satisfaction. He liked striding down Berwick Street to an edit-suite with a jiffy bag of videotapes, nodding at people just like him. He liked the sushi platters and the launch parties, he liked drinking from water coolers and ordering couriers and saying things like 'we've got to lose six seconds'. Secretly, he liked the fact that it was one of the better-looking industries, and one that valued youth. No chance, in this brave new world of TV, of walking into a conference room to find a group of sixty-two-year-olds brainstorming. What happened to TV people when they reached a certain age? Where did they go? Never mind, it suited him, as did the preponderance of young women like Naomi: hard, ambitious, metropolitan. In rare moments of self-doubt, Dexter had once worried that a lack of intellect might hold him back in life, but here was a job where confidence, energy, perhaps even a certain arrogance were what mattered, all qualities that lay within his grasp. Yes, you had to be smart, but not Emma-smart. Just politic, shrewd, ambitious.

He loved his new flat in nearby Belsize Park, all dark wood and gunmetal, and he loved London, spread out vast and hazy before him on this St Swithin's Day, and he wanted to share all this excitement with Emma, introduce her to new possibilities, new experiences, new social circles; to make her life more like his own. Who knows, perhaps Naomi and Emma might even become friends.

Soothed by these thoughts, and on the verge of sleep, he

was woken by a shadow across his face. He opened one eye, squinting up.

'Hello, beautiful.'

Emma kicked him sharply in the hip.

'Ow!'

'Don't you ever, *ever* do that again!'

'Do what?'

'You know what! Like I'm in a zoo, you poking me with a stick, laughing—'

'I wasn't laughing at you!'

'I watched you, sat straddling your girlfriend, chuckling away—'

'She isn't my girlfriend, and we were laughing at the menu—'

'You were laughing at where I work.'

'So? You do!'

'Yes, because I *work* there. I'm laughing in the face of adversity, you're just laughing in my face!'

'Em, I would never, ever—'

'That's what it feels like.'

'Well I apologise.'

'Good.' She folded her legs beneath her and sat next to him. 'Now do your shirt up and pass me the bottle.'

'And she really isn't my girlfriend.' He fastened three low shirt buttons, waiting for her to take the bait. When she didn't, he prodded again. 'We're just sleeping together every now and then, that's all.'

As the possibility of a relationship had faded, Emma had endeavoured to harden herself to Dexter's indifference and these days a remark like this caused no more pain than, say, a tennis ball thrown sharply at the back of her head. These days she barely even flinched. 'That's nice for you both, I'm sure.' She poured wine into a plastic cup. 'So if she's not your girlfriend, what do I call her?'

'I don't know. "Lover"?'

'Doesn't that imply affection?'

63

'How about "conquest"?' he grinned. 'Can I say "conquest" these days?'

'Or "victim". I like "victim".' Emma lay back suddenly and squeezed her fingers awkwardly into the pockets of her jeans. 'You can have that back 'n' all.' She tossed a tightly wadded ten-pound note onto his chest.

'No way.'

'Yes way.'

'That's yours!'

'Dexter, listen to me. You don't tip friends.'

'It's not a tip, it's a gift.'

'And cash is not a gift. If you want to buy me something, that's very nice, but not cash. It's embarrassing.'

He sighed, and stuffed the money back into his pocket. 'I apologise. Again.'

'Fine,' she said, and lay down beside him. 'Go on then. Tell me all about it.'

Grinning, he raised himself up on his elbows. 'So we were having this wrap party at the weekend—'

Wrap party, she thought. *He has become someone who goes to wrap parties.*

'—and I'd seen her around at the office so I went over to say hi, hello, welcome to the team, very formal, hand outstretched, and she smiled up at me, winked, put her hand on the back of my head and pulled me towards her and she—' He lowered his voice to a thrilled whisper. '—kissed me, right?'

'Kissed you, right?' said Emma, as another tennis ball struck home.

'—and slipped something into my mouth with her tongue. "What was that?" I said and she just winked and said, "You'll find out".'

A silence followed before Emma said 'Was it a peanut?'

'No—'

'Little dry-roasted peanut—'

'No, it was a pill—'

'What, like a tic-tac or something? For your bad breath?'

'I don't have bad—'

'Haven't you told me this story before anyway?'

'No, that was another girl.'

The tennis balls were coming thick and fast now, the odd cricket ball mixed in there too. Emma stretched and concentrated on the sky. 'You've got to stop letting women slip drugs into your mouth, Dex, it's unhygienic. And dangerous. One day it'll be a cyanide capsule.'

Dexter laughed. 'So do you want to hear what happened next?'

She placed a finger on her chin. 'Do I? Nope, I don't think so. No, I don't.'

But he told her anyway, the usual narrative about dark backrooms at clubs and late-night phone-calls and taxis across the city at dawn; the endless, eat-as-much-as-you-can buffet that was Dexter's sex-life, and Emma made a conscious effort not to listen and just watch his mouth instead. It was a nice mouth as she remembered, and if she were fearless, bold and asymmetrical like this Naomi girl she would lean over now and kiss him, and it occurred to her that she had never kissed anyone, that is never *initiated* the kiss. She had been kissed of course, suddenly and far too hard by drunken boys at parties, kisses that came swinging out of nowhere like punches. Ian had tried three weeks ago while she was mopping out the meat locker, looming in so violently that she had thought he was going to head-butt her. Even Dexter had kissed her once, many, many years ago. Would it really be so strange to kiss him back? What might happen if she were to do it now? Take the initiative, remove your spectacles, hold onto his head while he's still talking and kiss him, kiss him—

'—so Naomi calls at three in the morning, says, "Get in a cab. Right. Now."'

She had a perfectly clear mental picture of him wiping his mouth with the back of his hand: the kiss as custard-pie. She let her head loll to the other side to watch the others on the hill. The evening light was starting to fade now, and two hundred prosperous, attractive young people were throwing frisbees, lighting disposable barbecues, making plans for the evening. Yet she felt as far removed from these people, with their interesting careers and CD players and mountain bikes, as if it had been a TV commercial, for vodka perhaps or small sporty cars. 'Why don't you come home, sweetheart,' her mother had said on the phone last night, 'Your room's still here . . .'

She looked back to Dexter, still narrating his own love-life, then over his shoulder at a young couple, kissing aggressively, the woman kneeling astride the man, his arms flung back in surrender, their fingers interlocked.

'. . . basically we didn't leave the hotel room for, like, three days.'

'Sorry, I stopped listening a while ago.'

'I was just saying . . .'

'What do you think she sees in you?'

Dexter shrugged, as if he didn't understand the question. 'She says I'm complicated.'

'Complicated. You're like a two-piece jigsaw—' She sat and brushed the grass from her shin. '—in thick ply,' then tugged the leg of her jeans a little higher. 'Look at these legs.' She held a tiny twist of hair between her finger and thumb. 'I've got the legs of some fifty-eight-year-old fell-walker. I look like the President of the Ramblers Association.'

'So wax 'em then. Hairy Mary.'

'Dexter!'

'And anyway, you've got great legs.' He leant across and pinched her calves. 'You're gorgeous.'

She knocked his elbow away so that he fell back onto the grass. 'Can't believe you called me Hairy Mary.' Beyond him the couple were still kissing. 'Look at these two here – don't stare.' Dexter peered over his shoulder. 'I can actually hear them. Over this distance, I can hear the suction. Like someone unblocking a sink. I said don't stare!'

'Why not? It's a public place.'

'Why would you go to a public place to behave like that? It's like a nature documentary.'

'Maybe they're in love.'

'And is that what love looks like – all wet mouths and your skirt rucked up?'

'Sometimes it is.'

'Looks like she's trying to fit his entire head into her mouth. She'll dislocate her jaw if she's not careful.'

'She's alright though.'

'Dexter!'

'Well she is, I'm just saying.'

'You know some people might think it's a bit weird, this obsession you've got with being in a constant state of intercourse, some people might think it's a bit desperate and sad . . .'

'Funny, I don't feel sad. Or desperate.'

Emma, who did feel these things, said nothing. Dexter nudged her with his elbow. 'You know what we should do? Me and you?'

'What?'

He grinned. 'Take E together.'

'E? What's E?' she deadpanned. 'Oh, yes, I believe I read an article about that. Don't think I'm cut out for mind-bending chemicals. I left the lid off the Tipp-Ex once and I thought my shoes were trying to eat me.' He laughed gratifyingly and she hid her own smile in her plastic cup. 'Anyway I prefer the pure, natural high of booze.'

'It's very disinhibiting, E.'

'Is that why you're hugging everybody all the time?'

'I just think you might have fun, that's all.'

'I *am* having fun. You have no idea how much fun.' Lying on her back and staring at the sky, she could feel him looking at her.

'So. What about you?' he said, in what she thought of as his psychiatrist voice. 'Any news? Any action? Love-life-wise.'

'Oh you know me. I have no emotions. I'm a robot. Or a nun. A robot nun.'

'No you're not. You pretend to be, but you're not.'

'Oh, I don't mind. I quite like it, getting old alone—'

'You're twenty-five, Em—'

'—turning into this bluestocking.'

Dexter wasn't sure what a bluestocking was, but nevertheless still felt a Pavlovian twinge of arousal at the word 'stocking'. As she talked, he pictured her wearing blue stockings before deciding blue stockings wouldn't suit her, or anyone in fact, and that stockings should really only ever be black or possibly red like those ones Naomi had worn once, before deciding that maybe he was missing the point about the phrase 'bluestocking'. This kind of erotic reverie occupied great swathes of Dexter's mental energy, and he wondered if perhaps Emma was right, perhaps he was a little too distracted by the sexual side of things. Hourly he was rendered idiotic by billboards, magazine covers, an inch of crimson bra-strap on a passing stranger, and it was even worse in summer. Surely it wasn't natural to feel as if he'd just got out of prison *all the time*? Concentrate. Someone he cared for dearly was engaged in some kind of nervous collapse, and he should concentrate on that, rather than the three girls behind her who had just started a water-fight . . .

Concentrate! Concentrate. He steered his thoughts away from the subject of sex, his brain as nimble as an aircraft carrier.

'How about that guy?' he said.

'What guy?'

'At work, the waiter. Looks like captain of the computer club.'

'Ian? What about him?'

'Why don't you go out with Ian?'

'Shut up, Dexter. Ian's just a friend. Now pass the bottle, will you?'

He watched as she sat and drank the wine, which had become warm and syrupy now. While not sentimental, there were times when Dexter could sit quietly and watch Emma Morley laughing or telling a story and feel absolutely sure that she was the finest person he knew. Sometimes he almost wanted to say this out loud, interrupt her and just tell her. But this was not one of those times and instead he thought how tired she looked, sad and pale, and when she looked at the floor her chin had started to pouch. Why didn't she get contact lenses, instead of those big ugly spectacles? She wasn't a student anymore. And the velour scrunchies, she wasn't doing herself any favour with the scrunchies. What she really needed, he thought, ablaze with compassion, was someone to take her in hand and unlock her potential. He imagined a sort of montage, looking on patrician and kindly as Emma tried on a series of incredible new outfits. Yes, he really should pay Emma more attention, and he would do it too if he didn't have so much happening at present.

But in the short term, wasn't there something he could do to make her feel better about herself, lift her spirits, give her self-confidence a boost? He had an idea, and reached for her hand before announcing solemnly:

'You know, Em, if you're still single when you're forty I'll marry you.'

She looked at him with frank disgust. 'Was that a *proposal*, Dex?'

'Not *now*, just at some point if we both get desperate.'

She laughed bitterly. 'And what makes you think I'd want to marry you?'

'Well, I'm sort of taking that as a given.'

She shook her head slowly. 'Well you'll have to join the queue, I'm afraid. My friend Ian said exactly the same thing to me while we were disinfecting the meat fridge. Except he only gave me until I was thirty-five.'

'Well no offence to Ian, but I think you should definitely hold out for the extra five years.'

'I'm not holding out for either of you! I'm never getting married anyway.'

'How do you know that?'

She shrugged. 'Wise old gypsy told me.'

'I suppose you disagree on *political* grounds or something.'

'Just . . . not for me, that's all.'

'I can see you now. Big white dress, bridesmaids, little page boys, blue garter . . .' *Garter*. His mind snagged on the word like a fish on a hook.

'As a matter of fact, I think there are more important things in life than "relationships".'

'What, like your career, you mean?' She shot him a look. 'Sorry.'

They turned back to the sky, shading into night now and after a moment she said, 'Actually my career took a bit an upturn today if you must know.'

'You got fired?'

'Promotion.' She started to laugh. 'I've been offered the job of manager.'

Dexter sat up quickly. 'In that place? You've got to turn it down.'

'Why do I have to turn it down? Nothing wrong with restaurant work.'

'Em, you could be mining uranium with your teeth and that would be fine as long as you were happy. But you hate that job, you hate every single moment.'

'So? Most people hate their jobs. That's why they're called jobs.'

'I love my job.'

'Yeah, well, we can't all work in the *media*, can we?' She hated the tone of her voice now, sneering and sour. Worse still, she could feel hot, irrational tears starting to form in the back of her eyes.

'Hey, maybe I could get you a job!'

She laughed. 'What job?'

'With me, at Redlight Productions!' He was warming to the idea now. 'As a researcher. You'd have to start as a runner, which is unpaid, but you'd be brilliant—'

'Dexter, thank you, but I don't want to work in the media. I know we're all meant to be desperate to work in the *media* these days, like the *media*'s the best job in the world—' *You sound hysterical*, she thought, jealous and hysterical. 'In fact I don't even know what the *media* is—' *Stop talking, stay calm.* 'I mean what do you people do all day except stand around drinking bottled water and taking drugs and photocopying your *bits*—'

'Hey, it's hard work, Em—'

'I mean if people treated, I don't know, nursing or social work or teaching with the same respect as they do the bloody *media*—'

'So be a teacher then! You'd be a fantastic teacher—'

'I want you to write on the board, "I will not give my friend careers advice!"' She was talking too loud now, shouting almost, and a long silence followed. Why was she being like this? He was only trying to help. In what way did he benefit from this friendship? He should get up and walk away, that's what he should do. They turned to look at each other at the same time.

'Sorry,' he said.

'No, I'm sorry.'

'What are you sorry for?'

'Rattling on like a . . . mad old cow. I'm sorry, I'm tired, bad day, and I'm sorry for being so . . . boring.'

'You're not that boring.'

'I am, Dex. God, I swear, I bore myself.'

'Well you don't bore me.' He took her hand in his. 'You could never bore me. You're one in a million, Em.'

'I'm not even one in three.'

He kicked her foot with his. 'Em?'

'What?'

'Just take it, will you? Just shut up and take it.'

They regarded each other for a moment. He lay down once more, and after a moment she followed and jumped a little when she found out that he had slid his arm beneath her shoulders. There was a self-conscious moment of mutual discomfort before she turned onto her side and curled towards him. Tightening his arm around her, he spoke into the top of her head.

'You know what I can't understand? You have all these people telling you all the time how great you are, smart and funny and talented and all that, I mean endlessly, I've been telling you for years. So why don't you believe it? Why do you think people say that stuff, Em? Do you think it's a conspiracy, people secretly ganging up to be nice about you?'

She pressed her head against his shoulder to make him stop or else she felt she might cry. 'You're nice. But I should go.'

'No, stay a bit longer. We'll get another bottle.'

'Isn't Naomi waiting for you somewhere? Her little mouth crammed full of drugs like a little druggy hamster.' She puffed out her cheeks and Dexter laughed, and she began to feel a little better.

They stayed there for a while, then walked down to the off-licence and back up the hill to see the sun set over the city, drinking wine and eating nothing but a large bag of expensive crisps. Strange animal cries could be heard from Regents Park Zoo, and finally they were the last people on the hill.

'I should get home,' she said, standing woozily.

'You could stay at mine if you wanted.'

She thought of the journey home, the Northern Line, the top deck of the N38 bus, then the long perilous walk to the flat that smelt unaccountably of fried onions. When she finally got home the central heating would probably be on and Tilly Killick would be there with her dressing-gown hanging open, clinging to the radiators like a gecko and eating pesto out of the jar. There would be teeth marks in the Irish Cheddar and *thirtysomething* on TV, and she didn't want to go.

'Borrow a toothbrush?' said Dexter, as if reading her thoughts. 'Sleep on the sofa?'

She imagined a night spent on the creaking black leather of Dexter's modular sofa, her head spinning with booze and confusion, before deciding that life was already complicated enough. She made a firm resolution, one of the resolutions she was making almost daily these days. No more sleepovers, no more writing poetry, no more wasting time. Time to tidy up your life. Time to start again.

CHAPTER FIVE
The Rules of Engagement

The Dodecanese Islands, Greece

And then some days you wake up and everything is perfect.

This fine bright St Swithin's Day found them under an immense blue sky with not the smallest chance of rain, on the sun deck of the ferry that steamed slowly across the Aegean. In new sunglasses and holiday clothes they lay side by side in the morning sun, sleeping off last night's taverna hangover. Day two of a ten-day island-hopping holiday, and The Rules of Engagement were still holding firm.

A sort of platonic Geneva Convention, The Rules were a set of basic prohibitions compiled before departure to ensure that the holiday didn't get 'complicated'. Emma was single again; a brief, undistinguished relationship with Spike, a bicycle repairman whose fingers smelt perpetually of WD40, had ended with barely a shrug on either side, but had at least served to give her confidence a boost. And her bicycle had never been in better shape.

For his part Dexter had stopped seeing Naomi because, he said, it was 'getting too intense', whatever the hell *that* meant. Since then he had passed through Avril, Mary, a Sara, a Sarah, a Sandra and a Yolande before alighting on Ingrid, a ferocious model turned fashion-stylist who had been forced to give up modelling – she had told Emma this with a straight face – because 'her breasts were too large for the catwalk', and as she said this it seemed as if Dexter might explode with pride.

Ingrid was the kind of sexually confident girl who wore her bra on top of her shirt, and although she was by no means threatened by Emma or indeed by anyone on this earth, it had been decided by all parties that it might be better to get a few things straight before the swimwear was unveiled, the cocktails were drunk. Not that anything was likely to happen; that brief window had closed some years ago and they were immune to each other now, secure in the confines of firm friendship. Nevertheless, on a Friday night in June, Dexter and Emma had sat outside the pub on Hampstead Heath and compiled The Rules.

Number One: separate bedrooms. Whatever happened, there were to be no shared beds, neither double nor single, no drunken cuddles or hugs; they were not students anymore. 'And I don't see the point of cuddling anyway,' Dexter had said. 'Cuddling just gives you cramp,' and Emma had agreed and added:

'No flirting either. Rule Two.'

'Well I don't flirt, so . . .' said Dexter, rubbing his foot against the inside of her shin.

'Seriously though, no having a few drinks and getting frisky.'

'"Frisky"?'

'You know what I mean. No funny business.'

'What, with you?'

'With me or anyone. In fact that's Rule Three. I don't want to have to sit there like a lemon while you're rubbing oil into Lotte from Stuttgart.'

'Em, that is not going to happen.'

'No, it isn't. Because it's a Rule.'

Rule Number Four, at Emma's insistence, was the no nudity clause. No skinny-dipping: physical modesty and discretion at all times. She did not want to see Dexter in his underpants or in the shower or, God forbid, going to the toilet. In retaliation, Dexter proposed Rule Number Five. No Scrabble. More and more of his friends were playing it now, in a knowing ironic way, triple-word-score-craving freaks, but it seemed to him like a game designed expressly to make him feel stupid and bored. No Scrabble and no Boggle either; he wasn't dead yet.

Now on Day Two, with The Rules still in place, they lay on the deck of the ancient rust-spotted ferry as it chugged slowly from Rhodes towards the smaller Dodecanese islands. Their first night had been spent in the Old Town, drinking sugary cocktails from hollowed-out pineapples, unable to stop grinning at each other with the novelty of it all. The ferry had left Rhodes while it was still dark and now at nine a.m. they lay quietly nursing their hangovers, feeling the throb of the engines in their churning liquid stomachs, eating oranges, quietly reading, quietly burning, entirely happy in each other's silence.

Dexter cracked first, sighing and placing his book on his chest: Nabokov's *Lolita*, a gift from Emma who was responsible for selecting all the holiday reading, a great breeze-block of books, a mobile library that took up most of her suitcase.

A moment passed. He sighed again, for effect.

'What's up with you?' said Emma, without looking up from Dostoyevsky's *The Idiot*.

'I can't get into it.'

'It's a masterpiece.'

'Makes my head hurt.'

'I should have got something with pictures or flaps.'

'Oh, I am enjoying it—'

'*Very Hungry Caterpillar* or something—'

'I'm just finding it a bit dense. It's just this bloke banging on about how horny he is all the time.'

'I thought it would strike a chord.' She raised her sunglasses. 'It's a very erotic book, Dex.'

'Only if you're into little girls.'

'Tell me one more time, why were you sacked from that Language School in Rome?'

'I've told you, she was twenty-three years old, Em!'

'Go to sleep then.' She picked up her Russian novel. 'Philistine.'

He settled his head once more against his rucksack, but two

people were by his side now, casting a shadow over his face. The girl was pretty and nervous, the boy large and pale, almost magnesium white in the morning sun.

'Scuse me,' said the girl in a Midlands accent.

Dexter shielded his eyes and smiled broadly up at them. 'Hi there.'

'Aren't you that bloke off the telly?'

'Might be,' said Dexter, sitting and removing his sunglasses with a raffish little flick of his head. Emma quietly groaned.

'What's it called? *largin' it*!' The title of the TV show was always spelt in lower case, lower being the more fashionable of the two cases at this time.

Dexter held his hand up. 'Guilty as charged!'

Emma laughed briefly through her nose, and Dexter shot her a look. 'Funny bit,' she explained, nodding towards her Dostoyevsky.

'I knew I'd seen you on the telly!' The girl nudged her boyfriend. 'I said so, didn't I?'

The pale man shuffled and mumbled, then silence. Dexter became aware of the chug of the engines and *Lolita* lying open on his chest. He slipped it quietly into his bag. 'On holiday, are ya?' he asked. The question was clearly redundant, but allowed him to slip into his television persona, that of a really great, down to earth guy who they'd just met at the bar.

'Yeah, holiday,' mumbled the man.

More dead air. 'This is my friend Emma.'

Emma peered over her sunglasses. 'Hi there.'

The girl squinted at her. 'Are you on television too?'

'Me? God, no.' She widened her eyes. 'Though it is my dream.'

'Emma works for Amnesty International,' said Dexter proudly, one hand on her shoulder.

'Part-time. Mainly I work in a restaurant.'

'As a manager. But she's just about to pack it in. She's trainin' to be a teacher in September, aren't you, Em?'

Emma looked at him levelly. 'Why are you talking like that?'

76

'Like wha'?' Dexter laughed defiantly, but the young couple were shifting uneasily, the man looking over the ship's side as if contemplating the jump. Dexter decided to round up the interview. 'So we'll see you on the beach, yeah? Maybe get a beer or summink?' and the couple smiled and headed back to their bench.

Dexter had never consciously set out to be famous, though he had always wanted to be successful, and what was the point of being successful in private? People should know. Now that fame had happened to him it did make a certain sense, as if fame were a natural extension of being popular at school. He hadn't set out to be a TV presenter either – did anyone? – but was delighted to be told that he was a natural. Appearing on camera had been like sitting at a piano for the first time and discovering he was a virtuoso. The show itself was less issue-based than other shows he had worked on, really just a series of live bands, video exclusives, celebrity interviews, and yes, okay, it wasn't exactly demanding, all he really did was look at the camera and shout 'make some noise!' But he did it so well, so attractively, with such swagger and charm.

But public recognition remained a new experience. He was self-aware enough to know that he possessed a certain facility for what Emma would call 'prattishness' and with this in mind he had been investing some private effort into working out what to do with his face. Anxious not to appear affected or cocky or a fake, he had been devising an expression that said *hey, it's no big deal, it's only TV* and he assumed this expression now, replacing his sunglasses and returning to his book.

Emma watched this performance, amused; the straining for nonchalance, the slight flare of the nostrils, the smile that flickered at the corners of his mouth. She pushed her sunglasses up onto her forehead.

'It's not going to change you, is it?'

'What?'

'Being very, very, very, very slightly famous.'

'I hate that word. "Famous".'

'Oh and what would you prefer? "Well known".'

'How about "notorious"?' he grinned.

'Or "annoying"? How about "annoying"?'

'Leave it out, will ya?'

'And you can drop that now, please?'

'What?'

'The cockney accent. You went to Winchester College for Christ's sake.'

'I don't do a cockney accent.'

'When you're being Mr TV you do. You sound like you've left your whelk stall to go and do this 'ere fancy telly programme.'

'You've got a Yorkshire accent!'

'Because I'm *from* Yorkshire!

Dexter shrugged. 'I've got to talk like that, otherwise it alienates the audience.'

'And what if it alienates me?'

'I'm sure it does, but you're not one of the two million people who watch my show.'

'Oh, *your* show is it now?'

'The TV show on which I feature.'

She laughed and went back to her book. After a while Dexter spoke again.

'Well, do you?'

'What?'

'Watch me? On *largin' it*?'

'I might have had it on. In the background once or twice, while I'm balancing my cheque-book.'

'And what do you think?'

She sighed and fixed her eyes on the book. 'It's not my thing, Dex.'

'Tell me anyway.'

'I don't know about TV . . .'

'Just say what you think.'

'Okay, well I think the programme is like being screamed at for an hour by a drunk with a strobe-light, but like I said—'

'Alright, point taken.' He glanced at his book, then back at Emma. 'And what about me?'

'What about you?'

'Well – am I any good? As a presenter?'

She removed her sunglasses. 'Dexter, you are possibly the greatest presenter of Youth TV that this country has ever known, and I don't say that kind of thing lightly.'

Proudly, he raised himself onto one elbow. 'Actually, I prefer to think of myself as a journalist.'

Emma smiled and turned a page. 'I'm sure you do.'

'Because that's what it is, journalism. I have to research, shape the interview, ask the right questions—'

She held her chin between finger and thumb. 'Yes, yes, I believe I saw your in-depth piece on MC Hammer. Very sharp, very provoking—'

'Shut up, Em—'

'No, seriously, the way you got under MC's skin, his musical inspirations, the trousers. It was, well – untouchable.'

He swatted at her with his book. 'Shut up and read, will you?' He lay back down and closed his eyes. Emma glanced over to check that he was smiling, and smiled too.

Mid-morning approached and while Dexter slept, Emma caught her first sight of their destination: a blue-grey granite mass rising from the clearest sea that she had ever seen. She had always assumed that water like this was a lie told by brochures, a trick with lenses and filters, but there it was, sparkling and emerald green. At first glance the island seemed unpopulated except for the huddle of houses spreading up from the harbour, buildings the colour of coconut ice. She found herself laughing quietly at the sight of it. Until now travel had always been a fraught affair. Each year until she was sixteen, it had been two weeks fighting with her sister in a caravan in Filey while her parents drank steadily and looked out at the rain, a sort of harsh experiment in the limits of human proximity. At University she had gone camping in the Cairngorms with Tilly Killick, six days in a tent that smelt of cup-a-soup; a larky, so-awful-it's-funny holiday that had ended up just awful.

Now, standing at the railing as the town came into clearer view, she began to understand the point of travel; she had never felt so far away from the launderette, the top deck of the night bus home, Tilly's box room. It was as if the air was somehow different here; not just how it tasted and smelt, but the element itself. In London the air was something you peered through, like a neglected fish tank. Here everything was bright and sharp, clean and clear.

She heard the snap of a camera shutter and turned in time to see Dexter take her photo again. 'I look terrible,' she said as a reflex, though perhaps she didn't. He joined her, his arms holding the rail on either side of her waist.

'Beautiful, isn't it?'

'S'alright,' she said, unable to recall a time when she had felt happier.

They disembarked – the first time she felt that she had ever *disembarked* – and immediately found a flurry of activity on the quayside as the casual travellers and backpackers began the scramble for the best accommodation.

'So what happens now?'

'I'll find us somewhere. You wait in that café, I'll come and get you.'

'Somewhere with a balcony—'

'Yes, ma'am.'

'And a sea view please. And a desk.'

'I'll see what I can do,' and, sandals slapping, he strolled towards the crowd on the quay.

She shouted after him: 'And don't forget!'

He turned and looked at her, standing on the harbour wall, holding her wide-brimmed hat to her head in the warm breeze that pressed her light blue dress against her body. She no longer wore spectacles, and there was a scattering of freckles across her chest that he had never seen before, the bare skin turning from pink to brown as it disappeared below the neckline.

'The Rules,' she said.

'What about them?'

'We need *two* rooms. Yes?'

'Absolutely. Two rooms.'

He smiled and headed off into the crowd. Emma watched him go, then dragged the two backpacks along the quay to a small, wind-blown café. There she reached into her bag and pulled out a pen and notebook, an expensive, cloth-bound affair, her journal for the trip.

She opened it on the first blank page and tried to think of something she could write, some insight or observation other than that everything was fine. Everything was fine, and she had the rare, new sensation of being exactly where she wanted to be.

Dexter and the landlady stood in the middle of the bare room: whitewashed walls and cool stone floor, bare save for an immense iron-framed double bed, a small writing desk and chair and some dried flowers in a jar. He walked through louvred double-doors onto a large balcony painted to match the colour of the sky, overlooking the bay below. It was like walking out onto some fantastic stage.

'You are how many?' asked the landlady, mid-thirties, quite attractive.

'Two of us.'

'And for how long?'

'Not sure, five nights, maybe more?'

'Well here is perfect I think?'

Dexter sat on the double bed, bouncing on it speculatively. 'But my friend and I we are just, well, just good friends. We need two rooms?'

'Oh. Okay. I have second room.'

Emma has these freckles that I've never seen before scattered across her chest just above the neckline.

'So you do have two rooms?'

'Yes, of course, I have two rooms.'

'There's good news and there's bad news.'

'Go on,' said Emma, closing her notebook.

'Well I've found this fantastic place, sea view, balcony, a bit higher up in the village, quiet if you want to write, there's even a little desk, and it's free for the next five days, longer if we want it.'

'And the bad news?'

'There's only one bed.'

'Ah.'

'Ah.'

'I see.'

'Sorry.'

'Really?' she said, suspiciously. 'One bedroom on the whole island?'

'It's peak season, Em! I've tried everywhere!' *Stay calm, don't get shrill. Maybe play the guilt card instead.* 'But if you want me to carry on looking . . .' Wearily he made to get up from the chair.

She put her hand on his forearm. 'Single or double bed?'

The lie seemed to be holding. He sat again. 'Double. A big double.'

'Well it would have to be a pretty massive bed though, wouldn't it? To conform to The Rules.'

'Well,' Dexter shrugged, 'I suppose I prefer to think of them as guidelines.'

Emma frowned.

'What I mean, Em, is I don't mind if you don't.'

'No, I know *you* don't mind—'

'But if you really don't think you can keep your hands off me—'

'Oh, I can manage, it's you I worry about—'

'Because I'm telling you now, if you lay one finger on me—'

82

Emma loved the room. She stood on the balcony and listened to the cicadas, a noise that she had only heard in films before and had half suspected to be an exotic fiction. She was delighted, too, to see lemons growing in the garden; actual lemons, in trees; they seemed glued on. Keen not to appear provincial, she said none of this out loud, simply saying 'Fine. We'll take it.' Then, while Dexter made arrangements with the landlady, she slipped into the bathroom to continue fighting with her contact lenses.

At University Emma had held firm private convictions about the vanity of contact lenses, nurturing as they did conventional notions of idealised feminine beauty. A sturdy, honest, utilitarian pair of National Health spectacles showed that you didn't care about silly trivia like looking nice, because your mind was on higher things. But in the years since leaving college this line of argument had come to seem so abstract and specious that she had finally succumbed to Dexter's nagging and got the damn things, realising only too late that what she had really been avoiding for all those years was that moment in the movies: the librarian removes her spectacles and shakes out her hair. 'But Miss Morley, you're beautiful.'

Her face in the mirror seemed strange to her now, bare and exposed, as if she had just removed her spectacles for the last nine months. The lenses had a tendency to make her prone to random and alarming facial spasms, ratty blinks. They stuck to her finger and face like fish scales or, as now, slid beneath her eyelid, burying themselves deep in the back of her skull. After a rigorous bout of facial contortion and what felt like surgery, she managed to retrieve the shard, stepping out of the bathroom, red-eyed and blinking tearfully.

Dexter was sitting on the bed, his shirt unbuttoned. 'Em? Are you crying?'

'No. But it's still early.'

They headed out in the oppressive lunch-time heat, finding their way towards the long crescent of white sand that stretched for a mile or so from the village, and it was time to unveil the swimming costumes. Emma had put a lot of thought, perhaps too much, into her swimsuit, settling finally for a plain black all-in-one from John Lewis that might have been branded The Edwardian. As she pulled her dress over her head, she wondered if Dexter thought she was in some way chickening-out by not wearing a bikini, as if a one-piece swimming costume belonged with spectacles, desert boots and bike helmets as somehow prudish, cautious, not quite feminine. Not that she cared, though she did wonder, as her dress passed over her head, if she had caught his eyes flickering in her direction. Either way, she was pleased to note that he had gone for the baggy shorts look. A week of lying next to Dexter in Speedos would be more uncomfortable than she could bear.

'Excuse me,' he said, 'but aren't you the Girl from Ipanema?'

'No, I'm her auntie.' She sat and attempted to apply suntan lotion to her legs in a way that wouldn't make her thighs wobble.

'What is that stuff?' he said.

'Factor thirty.'

'You might as well lie under a blanket.'

'I don't want to overdo it on the second day.'

'It's like house paint.'

'I'm not used to the sun. Not like you, you globetrotter. You want some?'

'I don't agree with suntan lotion.'

'Dexter, you are so *hard*.'

He smiled, and continued to watch her from behind his dark glasses, noting the way her raised arm lifted her breast beneath the black material of the swimming costume, the bulge of soft pale flesh about the elasticated neckline. There was something about the gesture too, the tilt of the head and the pulling back of her hair as she applied the lotion to her neck, and he felt the pleasant nausea that accompanied desire. Oh God, he thought, eight more days of *this*. Her swimming costume was scooped low at the back and she could do no more than dab ineffectually at the lowest point. 'Want me to do your back?' he said.

Offering to apply sun cream was a corny old routine, beneath him really, and he thought it best to pass it off as medical concern. 'You don't want to burn.'

'Go on then.' Emma shuffled over and sat between his legs, her head resting forward on her knees. He began to apply the lotion, his face so close that she could feel his breath on her neck, while he could feel the heat reflecting off her skin, both of them working hard on the impression that this was everyday behaviour and in no way a clear contravention of Rules Two and Four, those prohibiting Flirtation and Physical Modesty.

'Scooped quite low, isn't it?' he said, aware of his fingers at the base of her spine.

'Good job I didn't put it on backwards!' she said and a silence followed while both of them thought *oh God, oh God, oh God, oh God*.

As a distraction she placed her hand on his ankle and yanked it towards her. 'What's this?'

'My tattoo. From India.' She rubbed it with her thumb as if trying to wipe it off. 'It's faded a bit. It's a yin-and-yang,' he explained.

'Looks like a road sign.'

'It means the perfect union of opposites.'

'It means "end of national speed limit". It means put some socks on.'

He laughed and placed his hands on her back, his thumbs aligned with the hollows of her shoulder blades. A moment passed. 'There!' he said, brightly. 'That's your undercoat. So. Let's swim!'

And so the long, hot day crawled on. They swam and slept and read, and as the fiercest heat faded and the beach become more populated a problem became apparent. Dexter noticed it first.

'Is it just me or—'

'What?'

'Is everyone on this beach completely naked?'

Emma looked up. 'Oh yeah.' She returned to her book. 'Don't *ogle*, Dexter.'

'I'm not ogling, I'm observing. I'm a qualified anthropologist, remember?'

'Low third, wasn't it?'

'High two-two. Look, there's our friends.'

'What friends?'

'From the ferry. Over there. Having a barbecue.' Twenty metres away the man crouched pale and naked over a smoky aluminium tray as if for warmth, while the woman stood on tip-toes and waved, two triangles of white, one of black. Dexter waved back cheerily: 'You've got no cloooothes oooon!'

Emma averted her eyes. 'You see, I couldn't do that.'

'What?'

'Barbecue naked.'

'Em, you're so conventional.'

'That's not conventional, it's basic health and safety. It's food hygiene.'

'I'd barbecue naked.'

'And that's the difference between us, Dex, you're so dark, so complicated.'

'Maybe we should go and say hi.'

'No!'

'Just have a chat.'

'With a chicken drumstick in one hand and his knob in the other? No thanks. Besides, isn't it a breach of nudist etiquette or something?'

'What?'

'Talking to someone naked and us not being naked.'

'I don't know, is it?'

'Just concentrate on your book, will you?' She turned to face the tree-line, but over the years she had reached a level of famil-iarity with Dexter where it had become possible to hear an idea enter his mind, like a stone thrown into mud, and sure enough:

'So what do you think?'

'What?'

'Should we?'

'What?'

'Take all our clothes off?'

'No, we should *not* take all our clothes off!'

'Everyone else has!'

'That's no reason! And what about Rule Four?'

'Not a rule, a guideline.'

'No, a rule.'

'So? We can bend it.'

'If you bend it, it's not a rule.'

Sulkily he flopped back down on the sand. 'Just seems a bit rude, that's all.'

'Fine, you go ahead, I'll try to tear my eyes away.'

'No point if it's just me,' he mumbled petulantly.

She lay her back down once again. 'Dexter, why on earth are you so desperate for me to take my clothes off?'

'I just thought we might be more relaxed, with our clothes off.'

'Un-believable, just unbelievable—'

'You don't think you'd be more relaxed?'

'NO!'

'Why not?'

'It doesn't matter why not! Besides, I don't think your girl-friend would be very pleased.'

'Ingrid wouldn't care. She's very open-minded, Ingrid. She'd have had her top off at WH Smiths in the airport—'

'Well, I'm sorry to disappoint you, Dex—'

'You don't disappoint me—'

'But there's a difference—'

'What difference?'

'Well Ingrid used to be a model for one thing—'

'So? You could be a model.'

Emma laughed sharply. 'Oh, Dexter, do you really think so?'

'For catalogues or something. You've got a lovely figure.'

'"A lovely figure", God help me—'

'All I'm saying is completely objectively, you're a very attractive woman—'

'—who is keeping her clothes on! If you're so desperate to tan your bits, fine, go ahead. Now can we change the subject?'

He turned and lay down on his front alongside her, head resting on his arms, their elbows touching, and once again she could hear the sound of his thoughts. He nudged her with his elbow.

'Course it's nothing we've not seen before.'

Slowly she lay her book down, lifted her sunglasses onto her forehead, her face resting sideways on her forearms, the mirror of him.

'Beg pardon?'

'I'm just saying that neither of has got anything that the other hasn't seen before. Nudity-wise.' She stared. 'That night, remember? After the graduation party? Our one night of love?'

'Dexter?'

'I'm just saying it's not as if we've got any surprises, genitally-speaking.'

'I think I'm going to be sick—'

'You know what I mean—'

'It was a long time ago—'

'Not that long. If I close my eyes, I can picture it—'

'Don't do that—'

'Yep, there you are—'

'It was dark—'

'Not that dark—'

'I was drunk—'

'That's what they always say—'

'*They?* Who's *they?*'

'And you weren't that drunk—'

'Drunk enough to lower my standards. Besides, as I recall nothing happened.'

88

'Well I wouldn't call it *nothing*, not from where I was laying. "Lying"? "Laying" or "lying"?'

'Lying. I was young, I didn't know any better. In fact I've blanked it out, like a car crash.'

'Well I haven't. If I close my eyes I can picture you right now, silhouetted against the morning light, your discarded dungarees splayed provocatively on the Habitat dhurri—'

She tapped him sharply on the nose with her book.

'Ow!'

'Look I'm not taking my clothes off, alright? And I wasn't wearing dungarees, I've never worn dungarees in my life.' She retrieved her book, then started to laugh quietly to herself.

'What's funny?' he asked.

'"Habitat dhurri".' She laughed and looked at him fondly. 'You make me laugh sometimes.'

'Do I?'

'Every now and then. You should be on television.'

Gratified, he smiled and closed his eyes. He had in fact retained a vivid mental picture of Emma from that night, lying on the single bed, naked except for the skirt around her waist, her arms thrown up above her head as they kissed. He thought about this, and eventually fell asleep.

In the late afternoon they returned to the room, tired and sticky and tingling from the sun, and there it was again: the bed. They stepped around it and walked out onto the balcony that overlooked the sea, hazy now as the sky shaded from blue into the pink of the evening.

'So. Who wants first shower?'

'You go ahead. I'm going to sit out here and read.'

She lay on the faded sun-lounger in the evening shade, listening to the sound of the running water and trying to concentrate on the tiny typeface of her Russian novel, which seemed to be getting smaller with each page. She stood suddenly and crossed to the small fridge that they'd filled with water and beer, took a can and noticed that the bathroom door had swung open.

There was no shower curtain, and she could see Dexter standing side on beneath the cold water, eyes closed against the spray, head back, arms raised. She noticed his shoulder blades, the long brown back, the two hollows at the base of his spine above the small white bottom. But oh God, he was turning now, and the can of beer slipped through her hand and exploded, fizzing and foaming, propelling itself noisily around the floor. She threw a towel over it as if capturing some wild rodent, then looked up to see Dexter, her platonic friend, naked except for his clothes held loosely in front of him. 'Slipped out of my hand!' she said, stamping the beer foam into the towel and thinking *eight more days and nights of this and I will self-combust.*

Then it was her turn to shower. She closed the door, washed the beer from her hands then contorted herself as she struggled to undress in the tiny, humid bathroom that still smelt of his aftershave.

Rule Four required that Dexter go and stand on the balcony while she dried herself and got dressed but after some experimentation he found that if he kept his sunglasses on and turned his head just so, he could see her reflection in the glass door as she struggled to rub lotion onto the low parabola of her newly tanned back. He watched the wriggle of her hips as she pulled on her underwear, the concave curve of her back and arch of shoulder blades as she fastened her bra, the raised arms and the blue summer dress coming down like a curtain.

She joined him on the balcony.

'Maybe we should just stay here,' he said. 'Instead of island-hopping, hang out here for a week, then back to Rhodes then home.'

She smiled. 'Okay. Maybe.'

'Don't think you'd get bored?'

'I don't think so.'

'Happy then?'

'Well my face feels like a grilled tomato, but apart from that—'

'Let me see.'

Closing her eyes she turned towards him and lifted her chin, her hair still wet and combed back off her face, which was shiny and scrubbed clean. It was Emma, but all new. She glowed, and he thought of the words sun-kissed, then thought *kiss her, take hold of her face and kiss her.*

She opened her eyes suddenly. 'What now?' she said.

'Whatever you want.'

'Game of Scrabble?'

'I have my limits.'

'Okay, how about dinner. Apparently they have this thing called Greek Salad.'

The restaurants in the small town were remarkable for being all identical. The air hung smoky with burning lamb, and they sat in a quiet place at the end of the harbour where the crescent of the beach began and drank wine that tasted of pine.

'Christmas trees,' said Dexter.

'Disinfectant,' said Emma.

Music played from speakers concealed in the plastic vines, Madonna's 'Get into the Groove' performed on the zither. They ate stale bread rolls, burnt lamb, salad soused in acetic acid, all of which tasted just fine. After a while even the wine became delicious, like some interesting mouthwash, and soon Emma felt ready to break Rule Two. No flirting.

She had never been a proficient flirt. Her spasms of kittenish behaviour were graceless and inept, like normal conversation on roller skates. But the combination of the retsina and sun made Emma feel sentimental and light-headed. She reached for her roller skates.

'I've got an idea.'

'Go on.'

'Well if we're going to stay here for eight days we're going to run out of things to talk about, right?'

91

'Not necessarily.'

'But to be on the safe side.' She leant forward, put her hand on his wrist. 'I think we should tell each other something that the other person doesn't know.'

'What, like a secret?'

'Exactly, a secret, something surprising, one a night every night for the rest of the holiday.'

'Sort of like spin-the-bottle?' His eyes widened. Dexter considered himself a world-class spin-the-bottle player. 'Okay. You first.'

'No, you first.'

'Why me first?'

'You've got more to choose from.'

And it was true, he had an almost bottomless supply of secrets. He could tell her that he'd watched her getting dressed that night, or that he'd left the bathroom door open on purpose when he showered. He could tell her that he'd smoked heroin with Naomi, or that just before Christmas he'd had fast, unhappy sex with Emma's flatmate Tilly Killick; a foot massage that had spun horribly out of control while Emma was at Woolworths buying fairy lights for the tree. But perhaps it would be better to go for something that didn't reveal him as shallow or seedy, duplicitous or conceited.

He thought for some time.

'Okay, here goes.' He cleared his throat. 'A couple of weeks ago at this club, I got off with this guy.'

Her mouth fell open. 'A guy?' and she started to laugh. 'Well I take my hat off to you, Dex, you're really full of surprises—'

'No big deal, just a snog, and I was off my face—'

'That's what they all say. So tell me – what happened?'

'Well it was this hardcore gay night, Sexface, at this club called Strap in Vauxhall—'

'"Sexface at Strap"! Whatever happed to discos called "Roxys" or "Manhattans"?'

'It's not a "disco", it's a gay club.'

'And what were you doing in a gay club?'

'We always go. The music's better. More hardcore, less of that happy house shit—'

'You *mentalist*—'

'Anyway, I was there with Ingrid and her mates and I was dancing and this guy just came up to me and started kissing me and I suppose I just sort of, you know, kissed him back.'

'And did you . . . ?'

'What?'

'Like it?'

'It was alright. Just a kiss. A mouth is just a mouth, isn't it?'

Emma laughed once, loudly. 'Dexter, you've the soul of a poet. "A mouth is just a mouth". Oh, that's nice, that's lovely. Isn't that from "As Time Goes By"?'

'You know what I mean.'

'A mouth is just a mouth. They should put that on your tombstone. What did Ingrid say?'

'She just laughed. She doesn't mind, she quite liked it.' He gave a blasé shrug. 'Ingrid's bisexual anyway, so—'

Emma rolled her eyes. 'Of *course* she's bisexual,' and Dexter smiled as if Ingrid's bisexuality had been his idea.

'Hey, it's not a big deal, is it? We're meant to be experimenting with sexuality at our age.'

'We are? No-one tells me anything.'

'You must get up to stuff.'

'I left the lights on once, but I wouldn't do it again.'

'Well you better get on with it, Em. Shed those inhibitions.'

'Oh Dex, you're such a *sexpert*. What was he wearing then, your friend at The Strap?'

'Not *The* Strap, just Strap. A harness and leather chaps. A British Telecom engineer called Stewart.'

'And do you think you'll be seeing Stewart again?'

'Only if my phone breaks down. He wasn't my type.'

'Seems to me like everyone's your type.'

'It was just a colourful episode, that's all. What's funny?'

'Just you look soooo pleased with yourself.'

'No, I don't! Homophobe.' He started to peer over her shoulder.

'Hey are you making a pass at the waiter?'

'I'm trying to get us another drink. Your turn now. Your secret.'

'Oh I give in. I can't compete with that kind of thing.'

'No girl/girl?'

She shook her head, resigned. 'You know one day you're going to say something like that to a real-life lesbian and they're going to break your jaw.'

'So you've never been attracted to a—?'

'Don't be pathetic, Dexter. Now do you want to hear my secret or what?'

The waiter arrived with complimentary Greek brandies, the kind of drink that can only be given away. Emma took a sip and winced then carefully rested her cheek on her hand in a way that she knew suggested a tipsy intimacy. 'A secret. Let me see.' She tapped her chin with her finger. She could tell him that she had watched him in the shower, or that she knew all about Tilly Killick at Christmas, the foot massage that had spun horribly out of control. She could even tell him that in 1983 she had kissed Polly Dawson in her bedroom, but knew that she would never hear the end of it. Besides, she had known all evening what she intended to say. As the zither played 'Like a Prayer', she licked her lips and made her eyes sultry along with other tiny readjustments, until she had constructed what she believed to be her best, most attractive face, the one she used in photographs.

'When we first met, at University, before we became, you know, *pals*, well, I had a bit of a crush on you. Not a bit of a crush, a massive crush actually. For ages. Wrote dopey poems and everything.'

'Poems? Really?'

'I'm not proud of myself.'

'I see. I see.' He folded his arms, put them on the edge of the

94

table and looked down. 'Well I'm sorry, Em, but that doesn't count.'

'Why not?'

'Because you said it had to be something that I didn't know.' He was grinning, and she was reminded once more of his almost limitless capacity to disappoint.

'God, you're annoying!' She slapped the reddest part of his sunburn with the back of her hand.

'Ow!'

'How did you know?'

'Tilly told me.'

'Nice one, Tilly.'

'So what happened?'

She looked into the bottom of her glass. 'I suppose it was something you get over in time. Like shingles.'

'No, really, what happened.'

'I got to know you. You cured me of you.'

'Well I want to read these poems. What rhymes with "Dexter"?'

'"Bastard". It's a half-rhyme.'

'Seriously, what happened to them?'

'They've been destroyed. I built a bonfire, years ago.' Feeling foolish and let down, she drank once more from the empty glass. 'Too much brandy. We should go.' She began to look distractedly for the waiter, and Dexter began to feel foolish too. So many things he might have said, so why be smug, glib, ungenerous? Keen to find a way to make amends, he nudged her hand. 'So shall we go for a walk?'

She hesitated. 'Okay. Let's go for a walk.'

They headed out along the bay past the half-built houses of the town as it spread itself along the coast, a new tourist development that they deplored in a conventional way, and while they talked Emma silently resolved to be more sensible in future. Recklessness, spontaneity didn't really suit her, she couldn't carry it off, the results were never what she hoped for. Her confession to Dexter had felt like swinging wildly at a ball, watching it sail high into the air then moments later hearing the sound of breaking glass. For the remainder of their time together she resolved to stay level-headed, sober and remember The Rules. Remember Ingrid, beautiful uninhibited bisexual Ingrid, waiting for him back in London. No more inappropriate revelations. In the meantime she would just have to drag the stupid conversation round with her, like toilet paper on the heel of her shoe.

They had left the town behind now, and Dexter took her hand to support her as they stumbled woozily over the dry dunes, still warm from the day's sun. They walked towards the sea to where the sand was wet and firm and Emma noticed that he was still holding her hand.

'Where are we going anyway?' she asked, noting the slur in her voice.

'I'm going for a swim. You coming?'

'You're insane.'

'Come on!'

'I'll drown.'

'You won't. Look, it's beautiful.' The sea was very calm and clear like some wonderful aquarium, jade with a phosphorescent gleam; if you scooped it up it would glow in your hands. Dexter was already pulling his shirt off over his head. 'Come on. It'll sober us up.'

'But I haven't got my swimming cost—' A realisation dawned. 'Oh, I get it,' she laughed. 'I see what's going on here—'

'What?'

'I've walked right into it haven't I?'

'What?'

'The old skinny-dip routine. Get a girl drunk and look for the nearest large body of water—'

'Emma, you are such a prude. Why are you such a prude?'

'You go on, I'll wait here.'

'Fine, but you'll regret it.' His back was to her now, taking down his trousers then his underwear.

'Leave your underpants on!' she shouted after him, watching

his long brown back and white buttocks as he strode down to the sea. 'You're not at Sexface now you know!' He fell forward into the surf and she stood, swaying woozily, feeling solitary and absurd. Wasn't this exactly one of the experiences she craved? Why couldn't she be more spontaneous and reckless? If she was too scared to swim without a costume how could she ever be expected to tell a man that she wanted to kiss him? Before the thought was finished she had reached down, grabbed the hem of her dress and in a single movement peeled it over her head. She removed her underwear, kicking it off her foot high into the air, letting it lie where it fell, and ran, laughing and swearing to herself, towards the water's edge.

Standing on tip-toe as far out as he dared to go, Dexter wiped the water from his eyes, looked out to sea and wondered what would happen next. Qualms; he felt the onset of qualms. A Situation loomed, and hadn't he resolved to try and avoid Situations for a while, to be less reckless and spontaneous? This was Emma Morley after all, and Em was precious, his best friend probably. And what about Ingrid, privately known as Scary Ingrid? He heard a garbled shout of exhilaration from the beach and turned just too late to see Emma stumble naked into the water as if pushed from behind. Honesty and frankness, those would be his watchwords. She splashed towards him with a messy crawl, and he decided to be frank and honest for a change and see where that got him.

Emma arrived, gasping. Suddenly aware of the sea's translucency, she was struggling to find a way to tread water with one arm folded across her chest. 'So this is it then!'

'What?'

'Skinny-dipping!'

'It is. What d'you think?'

'S'alright I suppose. Very larky. What am I meant to do now, just goof around or splash you or what?' She cupped her hand, threw water lightly at his face. 'Am I doing it right?' Before he could splash her back the current caught her and pulled her towards Dexter, who stood with his feet braced against the sea-bed. He caught her, their legs interlacing like clasped fingers, bodies touching then held apart again, like dancers.

'That's a very soulful face,' she said, to break the silence. 'Hey, you're not having a wee in the water, are you?'

'No—'

'So?'

'So anyway what I meant to say was sorry. For what I said—'

'When?'

'Back in the restaurant, for being a bit glib or whatever.'

'S'alright. I'm used to it.'

'And also to say I thought the same thing too. At the time. What I mean is I liked you too, "romantically", I mean. I mean I didn't write poems or anything, but I thought about you, think about you, you and me. I mean I fancy you.'

'Really? Oh. Really? Right. Oh. Right.' *It's going to happen after all*, she thought, *right here and now, standing naked in the Aegean Sea.*

'My problem is—' and he sighed and smiled with one side of his mouth. 'Well I suppose I fancy pretty much *everybody*!'

'I see,' was all she could say.

'—anyone really, just walking down the street, it's like you said, everyone's my type. It's a nightmare!'

'Poor you,' she said flatly.

'What I mean is that I don't think I was – am – ready for, you know, Boyfriend Girlfriend. I think we'd want different things. From a relationship.'

'Because . . . you're a gay man?'

'I'm being serious here, Em?'

'Are you? I can never tell.'

'Are you angry with me?'

'No! I don't care! I told you, it was a long, long time ago—'

'However!' Under the water, his hands found her waist and held on. 'However, if you wanted a bit of fun—'

'Fun?'

'Break the Rules—'

'Play Scrabble?'

'You know what I mean. A fling. Just while we're away, no strings, no obligations, not a word to Ingrid. Our little secret. Because I'd be up for it. That's all.'

She made a noise in her throat somewhere between laughter and a growl. *Up for it*. He was grinning expectantly like a salesman offering great deals on finance. *Our little secret*, to add to all the others presumably. A phrase entered her mind: a mouth is just a mouth. There was only one thing she could do, and oblivious to her own nakedness she bounced up out of the water and with all her weight pushed his head under the water and held it there. She began a slow count. One, two, three—

You arrogant, self-satisfied little—

Four, five, six—

And you stupid, stupid woman, stupid for caring, stupid for thinking that he cared—

Seven, eight, nine—

He's flailing now, better let him up I suppose, and make a joke, make a joke of it—

Ten, and she took her hands from the top of his head and let him bounce up. He was laughing, shaking the water from his hair and eyes and she laughed too, a rigid ha ha ha.

'I take it that's a no then,' he said eventually, pinching the sea-water from his nose.

'I think so. I think our moment passed some time ago.'

'Oh. Really. Are you sure? Because I think we'd feel much better if we got it out of the way.'

'Got it out of the way?'

'I just think we'd feel closer. As friends.'

'You're worried that *not* sleeping together could spoil our friendship?'

'I'm not expressing myself very well—'

'Dexter, I understand you perfectly, that's the problem—'

99

'If you're scared of Ingrid—'

'I'm not scared of her, I'm just not going to *do it* so that we can say that we've *done it*. And I'm not going to *do it* if the first thing you say afterwards is "please don't tell anyone" or "let's forget it ever happened". If you have to keep something secret it's because you shouldn't be doing it in the first place!'

But he was peering past her, eyes narrowed, towards the beach, and she turned towards the shore just in time to see a small, slim figure hurtling at great speed along the sand, carrying something over his head in triumph like a captured flag: a shirt, a pair of trousers.

'OIIIIIIIIII!' shouted Dexter, barrelling towards the shore now, yelling through mouthfuls of water, then taking startling high-kneed strides up the beach, pounding after the thief who had stolen all his clothes.

By the time he made it back to Emma, breathless and fuming, she was sitting on the beach fully dressed and sober once again.

'Any sign of them?'

'Nope! Gone!' he said tragically. 'Just completely fucked off and gone' and it took a light breeze to remind him that he was naked, and he angrily cupped one hand between his legs.

'Did he take your wallet?' she asked, her face fixed in an earnest rictus.

'No, just some cash, I don't know, ten, fifteen quids' worth, little bastard.'

'Well I suppose that's just one of the perils of skinny-dipping,' she mumbled, the corners of her mouth twitching.

'It's the trousers that wind me up. They were Helmut Lang! The underpants were Prada. Thirty bloody quid a go, those underpants. What's up with you?' But Emma couldn't speak for laughter, 'It's not funny Em! I've been robbed!'

'I know, I'm sorry—'

'They were Helmut Lang, Em!'

'I know! It's just you . . . so angry, and . . . no clothes . . .' She crouched over, her fists and forehead pressed into the sand before keeling over sideways.

'Pack it in, Em. It's not funny. Emma? Emma! That's enough!'

When she could stand again they spent a while walking up the beach in silence, Dexter suddenly very cold and coy, Emma walking discreetly ahead, looking at the sand and trying to contain herself. 'What kind of little bastard steals someone's underpants?' muttered Dexter. 'Know how I'm going to find the little sod? I'm going to look for the only well-dressed bastard on the whole bloody island!' and Emma collapsed onto the sand once more, head between her knees.

When the search proved fruitless, they beachcombed for emergency clothing. Emma found a heavy-duty sack in blue plastic. Dexter held it daintily round his waist like a mini-skirt while Emma suggested that they cut slits and make it into a pinafore dress, then collapsed once more.

The route home took them along the harbour front. 'It's a lot busier than I expected,' said Emma. Dexter adjusted his face into an expression of larky self-deprecation and marched on past the pavement taverna, eyes fixed forward, ignoring the wolf-whistles. They headed into the town, and coming up a narrow alley they suddenly found themselves facing the couple from the beach, red-faced with booze and sun, clinging to each other drunkenly as they tottered down the steps towards the harbour. They stared, bemused, at Dexter's blue sacking mini-skirt.

'Someone stole my clothes,' he explained curtly.

The couple nodded sympathetically and squeezed past them, the girl pausing to turn and shout after them—

'Nice sack.'

'It's Helmut Lang,' said Emma and Dexter narrowed his eyes at her treachery.

The sulk lasted all the long way home and by the time they were back in the room, the fact of the shared bed had somehow lost its significance. Emma went into the bathroom to change into an old grey t-shirt. When she came out, the blue plastic coal-sack lay on the floor at the foot of the bed. 'You should hang this up,' she said, nudging the sack with her toe. 'It'll get creased.'

'Ha,' he said, lying on the bed, in new underwear.

'So is that them?'

'What?'

'The famous thirty-quid underpants. What are they, lined with ermine?'

'Let's just go to sleep, shall we? So – which side?'

'This one.'

They lay on their backs in parallel, Emma relishing the sensation of the cold white sheets against tender skin.

'Nice day,' she said.

'Til that last bit,' he mumbled.

She turned to look at him, his face in profile, staring petulantly at the ceiling. She nudged his foot with hers. 'S'only trousers and a pair of pants. I'll buy you some nice new ones. Three-pack of cotton briefs.' Dexter sniffed and she took his hand beneath the sheet, squeezed it hard until he turned his head to look at her. 'Seriously, Dex,' she smiled. 'I'm really pleased to be here. I'm having a really nice time.'

'Yeah. Me too,' he mumbled.

'Eight more days,' she said.

'Eight more days.'

'Think you can hack it?'

'Who knows?' He smiled affectionately and, for good or ill, everything was just as it had been before. 'So how many Rules did we break tonight?'

She thought for a moment. 'One, Two and Four.'

'Well at least we didn't play Scrabble.'

'There's always tomorrow.' She reached above her head, turned the light off, then lay on her side with her back to him. Everything was just how it had been before, and she was unsure how she felt about this. For a moment she worried that she might not be able to sleep for dwelling on the day, but to her relief she soon found herself overcome with weariness, sleep creeping through her veins like anaesthetic.

Dexter lay for a while looking at the ceiling in the blue light, feeling that he had not been at his best tonight. Being with Emma demanded a certain level of behaviour, and he was not always up to the mark. Glancing over at Emma, her hair falling away from the nape of her neck, the newly tanned skin dark against the white sheets, he contemplated touching her shoulder to apologise.

'Night, Dex,' she murmured while she could still speak.

'Night, Em,' he replied, but she was already gone.

Eight days to go, he thought, eight whole days. Almost anything could happen in eight days.

Part Two

1993–1995

Late Twenties

'We spent as much money as we could and got as little for it as people could make up their minds to give us. We were always more or less miserable, and most of our acquaintance were in the same condition. There was a gay fiction among us that we were constantly enjoying ourselves, and a skeleton truth that we never did. To the best of my belief, our case was in the last aspect a rather common one.'

Charles Dickens, *Great Expectations*

CHAPTER SIX
Chemical

THURSDAY 15 JULY 1993,
Part One – Dexter's Story

Brixton, Earls Court and Oxfordshire

These days the nights and mornings have a tendency to bleed into one another. Old-fashioned notions of a.m. and p.m. have become obsolete and Dexter is seeing a lot more dawns than he once used to.

On the 15th of July 1993 the sun rises at 05.01 a.m. Dexter watches it from the back of a decrepit mini-cab as he returns home from a stranger's flat in Brixton. Not a stranger exactly, but a brand new friend, one of many he is making these days, this time a graphic designer called Gibbs or Gibbsy, or was it maybe Biggsy, and his friend, this mad girl called Tara, a tiny birdlike thing with woozy, heavy eyelids and a wide scarlet mouth who doesn't talk much, preferring to communicate through the medium of massage.

It's Tara he meets first, just after two a.m. in the night-club underneath the railway arches. All night he has noticed her on the dance floor, a broad grin on her pretty pixie face as she appears suddenly behind strangers and starts to rub their shoulders or the small of their backs. Finally it's Dexter's turn, and he nods and smiles and waits for the slow dawn of recognition. Sure enough the girl frowns, brings her fingers close to the tip of his nose and says what they all say now, which is:

'You're famous!'

'Who are you then?' he shouts over the music, taking both

her small bony hands in his, holding them out to the side as if this were some great reunion.

'I'm Tara!'

'Tara! Tara! Hello, Tara!'

'You're famous? Why are you famous? Tell me!'

'I'm on TV. I'm on a TV programme called *largin' it*. I interview pop stars.'

'I knew it! You *are* famous!' she shouts, delighted, and she cranes up on tip-toe and kisses his cheek, and she does this so nicely that he's moved to shout over the music, 'You're lovely, Tara!'

'I am lovely!' she shouts back. 'I am lovely, but I'm not famous.'

'But you should be famous!' shouts Dexter, his hands on her waist. 'I think everybody should be famous!'

The remark is without thought or meaning, but the sentiment seems to move Tara because she says 'Aaaaaaaah', stands on tip-toe and rests her little elfin head on his shoulder. 'I think you're so lovely,' she shouts in his ear, and he doesn't disagree. 'You're lovely too,' he says, and they find themselves caught in a 'you're lovely' loop that could potentially go on forever. They're dancing together now, sucking in their cheeks and grinning at each other and once again Dexter is struck by how easy conversation can be when no-one is in their right mind. In the olden days, when people only had alcohol to fall back on, talking to a girl would involve all kinds of eye-contact, the buying of drinks, hours of formal questioning about books and films, parents and siblings. But these days it's possible to segue almost immediately from 'what's your name?' to 'show me your tattoo', say, or 'what underwear are you wearing?' and surely this has got to be progress.

'You're lovely,' he shouts, as she grinds her buttocks against his thighs. 'You're really tiny. Like a bird!'

'But I'm strong as an ox,' she shouts back over her shoulder and flexes a neat bicep the size of a tangerine. It's such a great little bicep that he is moved to kiss it. 'You're nice. You're sooooo nice.'

'You're nice too,' he fires back and thinks, God, this is really going just incredibly well, this back and forth, just so well. She's so small and neat that she reminds him of a little wren, but he can't summon up the word 'wren' so he takes hold of her hands, pulls her towards him, shouts in her ear, 'What's the name of that tiny bird that fits in a matchbox?'

'What?'

'A BIRD THAT YOU PUT IN A MATCHBOX YOU CAN FIT IT IN A MATCHBOX A TINY BIRD YOU'RE LIKE A LITTLE BIRD CAN'T THINK OF ITS NAME.' He holds his finger and thumb an inch apart. 'SMALL BIRD TINY YOU'RE LIKE THAT.'

And she nods, either in agreement or to the music, her heavy eyelids fluttering now, pupils dilated, her eyeballs rolling back in her head like one of those dolls his sister used to have and Dexter has forgotten what he's talking about, is unable for a moment to make sense of anything, so that when Tara takes his hands and squeezes them and tells him once again that he really is lovely and that he must come and meet her friends because they're lovely too, he doesn't disagree.

He looks around for Callum O'Neill, his old flatmate from University and sees him pulling on his coat. Once the laziest man in Edinburgh, Callum is a successful businessman now, a large man in expensive suits, made wealthy by refurbished computers. But with the success has come sobriety; no drugs, not too much booze on a weeknight. He looks uncomfortable here, square. Dexter crosses to him and grabs both hands.

'Where are you going, mate?'

'Home! It's two in the morning. I've got work to do.'

'Come with me. I want you to meet Tara!'

'Dex, I don't want to meet Tara. I've got to go.'

'You know what you are? You're a lightweight!'

'And you are off your face. Go on, do what you've got to do. I'll call tomorrow.'

Dexter hugs Callum, and tells him how great he is, but Tara

is tugging on his hand once again, and so he turns and allows himself to be led through the crowds towards one of the chill-out rooms.

The club is expensive and supposedly upmarket, though Dexter rarely pays for anything these days. It's also a little quiet for a Thursday night, but at least there's none of that scary techno marching music here, or those scary kids, the bony shaven-headed ones who take their shirts off and leer in your face with their teeth bared, their jaws clenched. Instead there are mainly lots of pleasant, attractive, middle-class people in their twenties, people he belongs with, like Tara's friends here, lolling around on big cushions, smoking and talking and chewing. He meets Gibbsy, or was it Biggsy, The Lovely Tash and her boyfriend Stu Stewpot, and Spex who wears spectacles and his boyfriend Mark who, disappointingly, seems to be just called Mark, and they all offer him their gum and water and Marlboro Lights. People make a big deal about friendship but it really does seem incredibly easy here, and soon he is imagining everyone hanging out together, going on holiday in a camper van, having barbecues on the beach as the sun goes down, and they seem to like him too, asking him what it's like, being on TV, asking him what other famous people he's met, and he tells them some salacious gossip and all the while Tara perches behind him, working on his neck and shoulders with her tiny bony fingers, giving him little shudders of elation until suddenly for some reason there's a pause in conversation, perhaps five seconds of silence, but just long enough for a flash of sobriety to take him by surprise and he remembers what he has to do tomorrow, no, not tomorrow, today, oh God, later today, and he feels the night's first shiver of panic and dread.

But it's okay, it's fine, because Tara is saying let's go and dance before it wears off, so they all go and stand in the railway arches in a loose group facing the DJ and the lights, and they dance for a while in the dry ice, grinning and nodding and exchanging that strange puckered frown, eyebrows knitted, but the nodding and grinning are less from elation now, more from a need for reassurance that they're still having fun, that it isn't all about to end. Dexter wonders if he should take his shirt off, that sometimes helps, but the moment has passed. Someone nearby shouts 'tune' half-heartedly, but no-one's convinced, there are no tunes. The enemy, self-consciousness, is creeping up on them and Gibbsy or Biggsy is the first to crack, declaring that the music is shit and everyone stops dancing immediately as if a spell has been broken.

As he heads for the exit Dexter imagines the journey home, the menacing crowd of illicit cabbies who will be outside the club, the irrational fear of being murdered, the empty flat in Belsize Park and hours of sleeplessness as he does the washing-up and rearranges his vinyl until the thumping in his head stops and he is able to sleep and face the day, and once again he feels a wave of panic. He needs company. He looks around for a payphone. He could see if Callum's still awake, but male company is no good to him now. He could call Naomi, but she'll be with her boyfriend, or Yolande but she's filming in Barcelona, or Scary Ingrid but she has said that if she sees him again she'll rip his heart out, or Emma, yes Emma, no not Emma, not in this state, she doesn't get it, won't approve. And yet it's Emma that he wants to see the most. Why isn't she with him tonight? He has all these things he wants to ask her like why have they never got together, they'd be great together, a team, a pair, Dex and Em, Em and Dex, everybody says so. He is taken aback by this sudden rush of love he feels for Emma, and he decides to get in a cab to Earls Court and tell her how great she is, how he really, really loves her and how sexy she is if only she knew it and why not just do it, just to see what happens, and if none of that works, even if they just sit up and talk, at least it will be better than being alone tonight. Whatever happens, he mustn't be alone . . .

The phone is in his hand when, thank God, Biggsy or is it Gibbsy, suggests they all go back to his place, it isn't far, and so they head out of the club, safe in a crowd as they walk back to Coldharbour Lane.

The flat is a large space on top of an old pub. Kitchen and living room, bedroom and bathroom are all laid out without walls, the one concession to privacy being the semi-transparent shower curtain that encircles the free-standing toilet. While Biggsy sorts out his decks everyone else goes and lolls in a great tangled pile on the huge four-poster bed, which is covered in ironic acrylic tiger skins and black synthetic sheets. Above the bed is a semi-ironic mirror, and they stare up at it through heavy eyelids, admiring themselves as they sprawl beneath, heads resting in laps, hands searching around for other hands, listening to the music, young and smart, attractive and successful, in the know and not in their right minds, all of them thinking how great they look and what good friends they're going to be from now on. There will be picnics on the Heath, and long lazy Sundays in the pub, and Dexter is enjoying himself once more. 'I think you're amazing,' someone says to someone else, but it doesn't matter who, because they're all amazing really. People are amazing.

Hours slip by with no-one noticing. Someone is talking about sex now, and they compete to make personal revelations that they'll regret in the morning. People are kissing, and Tara is still fiddling with his neck, probing the top of his spine with her hard little fingers, but all the drugs have gone now and what was once a relaxing massage is now a series of jabs and pokes, and when he peers up at Tara's pixie face it suddenly seems pinched and menacing, the mouth too wide, the eyes too round, like some sort of small hairless mammal. He also notices that she's older than he thought – my God she must be like *thirty-eight* – and that there's some sort of white paste between her little teeth, like grouting, and Dexter can no longer control his terror of the day ahead from crawling up his spinal column, dread, fear and shame manifesting itself as a sticky chemical sweat. He sits suddenly, shivers and drags both hands slowly down his face as if physically wiping something away.

It is starting to get light. Blackbirds are singing on Coldharbour Lane and he has the sensation, so vivid that it is almost an hallucination, that he is entirely hollow; empty, like an easter egg. Tara the masseuse has created a great twisted knot of tension between his shoulders, the music has stopped, and someone on the bed is asking for tea, and everyone wants tea, tea, tea, so Dexter disentangles himself and crosses to the immense fridge, the same model as his own, sinister and industrial like something you'd find in a genetics lab. He opens the door and stares blankly inside. A salad is rotting in its bag, the plastic swollen and about to burst. His eyes flicker in their sockets, making his vision judder one last time, and coming back into focus he sees a bottle of vodka. Hiding behind the fridge door he drinks a good two inches, washing it down with a sour gulp of apple juice that fizzes repulsively on his tongue. He winces, swallows the liquid down, taking his chewing gum with it. Someone calls for tea again. He finds the milk carton, weighs it in his hand, has an idea.

'There's no milk!' he shouts.

'Should be,' shouts Gibbsy or Biggsy.

'Nope. Empty. I'll go and get some.' He puts the full, unopened carton back in the fridge. 'Back in five minutes. Anyone want anything? Ciggies? Gum?' There's no reply from his new friends, so he quietly lets himself out, then tumbles down the stairs and out onto the street, barrelling through the door as if coming up for air then breaking into a run, never to see any of these amazing people ever again.

On Electric Avenue he finds a mini-cab office. On the 15th of July 1993 the sun rises at 05.01 a.m. and already Dexter Mayhew is in hell.

Emma Morley eats well and drinks in moderation. These days she gets eight good hours sleep then wakes promptly of her own accord at just before six-thirty and drinks a large glass of water, the first 250ml of a daily 1.5 litres, which she pours from the brand new carafe and matching glass that stand in a shaft of fresh morning sunlight next to her warm, clean double bed. A carafe. She owns a carafe. She can hardly believe it's true.

She owns furniture too. At twenty-seven she is too old to live like a student anymore, and she now owns a bed, a large wrought-iron and wickerwork affair bought in the summer sales from a colonial-themed store on the Tottenham Court Road. Branded the 'Tahiti' it occupies the whole bedroom of her flat off the Earls Court Road. The duvet is goosedown, the sheets are Egyptian cotton which is, the saleswoman informed her, the very best cotton known to man, and all of this signifies a new era of order, independence and maturity. On Sunday mornings she lounges alone on the Tahiti as if it were a raft, and listens to *Porgy and Bess* and Mazzy Star, old Tom Waits and a quaintly crackling vinyl album of Bach's Cello Suites. She drinks pints of coffee and writes little observations and ideas for stories with her best fountain pen on the linen-white pages of expensive note-books. Sometimes, when it's going badly, she wonders if what she believes to be a love of the written word is really just a fetish for stationery. The true writer, the born writer, will scribble words on scraps of litter, the back of a bus tickets, on the wall of a cell. Emma is lost on anything less than 120gsm.

But at other times she finds herself writing happily for hours, as if the words had been there all along, content and alone in her one-bedroom flat. Not that she's lonely, or at least not very often. She goes out four nights a week, and could go out more often if she wanted to. Old friendships are holding up, and there are new ones too, with her fellow students from the Teacher Training College. At the weekend she makes full use of the listing magazines, everything except the clubbing section, which might as well be written in runic script for all its talk of shirts-off-up-for-it crowds. She suspects that she will never, ever dance in her bra in a room full of foam, and that's fine. Instead she visits independent cinemas and galleries with friends, or sometimes they hire cottages, go for hearty walks in the country and pretend they live there. People tell her she looks better, more confident. She has thrown away the velour scrunchies, the cigarettes, the take-away menus. She owns a cafetiere and for the first time in her life she is considering investing in some pot-pourri.

The clock radio clicks on but she allows herself to lie in bed and listen to the news headlines. John Smith is in conflict with the unions, and she feels torn because she likes John Smith, who seems the right sort, headmasterly and wise. Even his name suggests solid man-of-the-people principles, and she reminds herself once again to look into the possibility of joining the Labour Party; perhaps it will ease her conscience now that her CND membership has lapsed. Not that she doesn't sympathise with their aims, but demanding multilateral disarmament has started to seem a bit naïve, a bit like demanding universal kindness.

At twenty-seven, Emma wonders if she's getting old. She used to pride herself on her refusal to see two sides of an argument, but increasingly she accepts that issues are more ambiguous and complicated than she once thought. Certainly she doesn't understand the next two news items, which concern the Maastricht Treaty and the war in Yugoslavia. Shouldn't she have an opinion, take a side, boycott something? At least with apartheid you knew where you stood. Now there's a war in Europe and she has personally done absolutely nothing to stop it. Too busy shopping for furniture. Unsettled, she throws off her new duvet and slides into the tiny corridor of space between the side of the bed and the walls, shuffling sideways to the hall and into the tiny bathroom, which she never has to wait for because she lives alone. She drops her t-shirt into the wicker laundry basket – a great deal of wicker in her life since that fateful summer sale on Tottenham Court Road – puts on her old spectacles and stands naked in front of the mirror, her shoulders pushed back. Could be worse, she thinks and steps into the shower.

She eats breakfast looking out of the window. The flat is six floors up in a red brick mansion block and the view is of an identical red brick mansion block. She doesn't care for Earls Court particularly; shabby and temporary, it's like living in London's spare room. The rent on a single flat is insane too, and she may have to get somewhere cheaper when she gets her first teaching job, but for the moment she loves it here, a long way from Loco Caliente and the gritty social realism of the box room in Clapton. Free of Tilly Killick after six years together, she loves knowing that there'll be no underwear lurking greyly in the kitchen sink, no teeth marks in the Cheddar.

Because she is no longer ashamed of how she lives, she has even allowed her parents to visit her, Jim and Sue occupying the Tahiti while Emma slept on the sofa. For three fraught days they commented endlessly on London's ethnic mix and the cost of a cup of tea, and although they didn't actually express their approval of her new lifestyle at least her mother no longer suggests that she come back to Leeds to work for the Gas Board. 'Well done, Emmy,' her father had whispered as she saw them onto the train at King's Cross, but well done for what? For finally living like a grown-up perhaps.

Of course there's still no boyfriend, but she doesn't mind. Occasionally, very occasionally, say at four o'clock in the afternoon on a wet Sunday, she feels panic-stricken and almost breathless with loneliness. Once or twice she has been known to pick up the phone to check that it isn't broken. Sometimes she thinks how nice it would be to be woken by a call in the night: 'get in a taxi now' or 'I need to see you, we need to talk'. But at the best of times she feels like a character in a Muriel Spark novel – independent, bookish, sharp-minded, secretly romantic. At twenty-seven years old Emma Morley has a double-first in English and History, a new bed, a two-roomed flat in Earls Court, a great many friends, and a post-graduate certificate in education. If the interview goes well today she will have a job teaching English and Drama, subjects that she knows and loves. She is on the brink of a new career as an inspiring teacher and finally, finally, there is some order in her life.

There is also a date.

Emma has a proper, formal date. She is going to sit in a restaurant with a man and watch him eat and talk. Someone wants to climb aboard the Tahiti, and tonight she will decide if she is going to let him. She stands at the toaster, slicing a banana, the first of seven portions of fruit and veg today, and stares at the calendar. The 15th of July 1993, a question mark, and exclamation mark. The date looms.

Dexter's bed is imported, Italian, a low, bare black platform that stands in the centre of the large bare room like a stage or a wrestling ring, both of which functions it sometimes serves. He lies there awake at 9.30, dread and self-loathing combined with sexual frustration. His nerve-endings have been turned up high and there is an unpleasant taste in his mouth, as if his tongue has been coated with hairspray. Suddenly he leaps up and pads across high-gloss black floorboards to the Swedish kitchen. There in the freezer compartment of his large, industrial fridge, he finds a bottle of vodka and he pours an inch into his glass then adds the same amount of orange juice. He reassures himself with the thought that, as he hasn't been to sleep yet, this is not the first drink of the day, but the last drink of last night. Besides, the whole taboo about drinking during daytime is exaggerated; they do it in Europe. The trick is to use the uplift of the booze to counteract the downward tumble of the drugs; he is getting drunk to stay sober which when you think about it is actually pretty sensible. Encouraged by this logic, he pours another inch and a half of vodka, puts on the *Reservoir Dogs* soundtrack and swaggers to the shower.

Half an hour later he is still in the bathroom, wondering what he can do to stop the sweating. He has changed his shirt twice, showered in cold water, but still the perspiration comes bubbling up on his back and forehead, oily and viscous like vodka which perhaps is what it is. He looks at his watch. Late already. He decides that he'll try driving with the windows down.

There's a brick-sized parcel by the door so that he won't forget it, elaborately wrapped in layers of different coloured tissue paper, and he picks this up, locks the flat and steps out into the leafy avenue where his car waits for him, a Mazda MRII convertible in racing green. No room for passengers, no possibility of a roof rack, barely room for a spare tyre let alone a pram, it's a car that screams of youth, success, bachelorhood. Concealed in the boot is a CD changer, a futuristic miracle of tiny springs and matt black plastic and he chooses five CDs (freebies from the record companies, another perk of the job) and slides the shiny disks into the box as if loading a revolver with bullets.

He listens to The Cranberries as he negotiates the wide residential streets of St John's Wood. It's not really his thing, but it's important to stay on top of stuff when you're forging people's tastes in music. The Westway has cleared of rush-hour traffic and before the album ends he is on the M40, heading westward through the light-industrial estates and housing developments of the city in which he lives so successfully, so fashionably. Before long the suburbs have given way to the conifer plantations that pass as countryside. Jamiroquai is playing on the stereo and he's feeling much, much better, raffish and boysy in his sporty little car, and only a little queasy now. He turns up the volume. He has met the band's lead singer, has interviewed him several times, and though he wouldn't go so far as to call him a friend, he knows the guy who plays the congas pretty well and feels a little personal connection as they sing about the emergency on planet earth. It's the extended mix, massively extended, and time and space take on an elastic quality as Dexter scats along for what seems like many, many hours until his vision blurs and judders one last time, the remnants of last night's drugs in his veins, and there's a blare of horn as he realises that he is driving at 112 miles an hour in the exact centre of two lanes.

He stops scatting and tries to steer the car back into the

middle lane, but finds that he has forgotten how to steer, his arms locked at the elbows as he tries to physically wrench the wheel from some invisible grasp. Suddenly Dexter's speed has dropped to fifty-eight miles an hour, his feet on the brake and the accelerator simultaneously, and there's another blast of horn from a lorry the size of a house that has appeared behind him. He can see the contorted face of the driver in the rearview mirror, a big bearded man in black mirror shades screaming at him, his face three black holes, like a skull. Dexter wrenches the wheel once more without even checking what is in the slow lane and he is suddenly sure that he is going to die, right here and now, in a ball of searing flame while listening to an extended Jamiroquai remix. But the slow lane is empty, thank God, and he breathes sharply through his mouth, once, twice, three times, like a boxer. He jabs the music off and drives in silence at a steady sixty-eight until he reaches his exit.

Exhausted, he finds a lay-by on the Oxford Road, reclines his seat and closes his eyes in the hope of sleep, but can only see the three black holes of the lorry driver screaming at him. Outside the sun is too bright, the traffic too noisy, and besides there's something shabby and unwholesome about this anxious young man wriggling in a stationary car at eleven forty-five on a summer's morning, so he sits up straight, swears and drives on until he finds a roadside pub that he knows from his teenage years. The White Swan is a chain affair offering all-day breakfasts and impossibly cheap steak and chips. He pulls in, picks up the gift-wrapped parcel from the passenger seat and enters the large, familiar room that smells of furniture polish and last night's cigarettes.

Dexter leans matily on the bar and orders a half of lager and a double vodka tonic. He remembers the barman from the early Eighties when he used to drink here with mates. 'I used to come here years ago,' says Dexter, chattily. 'Is that right?' replies the gaunt, unhappy man. If the barman recognises him he doesn't say, and Dexter takes a glass in each hand, walks to a table and drinks in silence with the gift-wrapped package in front of him, a little parcel of gaiety in the grim room. He looks around and thinks about how far he's come in the last ten years, and all that he's achieved – a well-known TV presenter, and not yet twenty-nine years old.

Sometimes he thinks the medicinal powers of alcohol border on the miraculous because within ten minutes he is trotting nimbly out to the car and listening to music again, The Beloved chirruping away, making good time so that within ten minutes he is turning into the gravel drive of his parents' house, a large secluded 1920s construction, its front criss-crossed with fake timber framing to make it look less modern, boxy and sturdy than it really is. A comfortable, happy family home in the Chilterns, Dexter regards it with dread.

His father is already standing in the doorway, as if he's been there for years. He is wearing too many clothes for July; a shirt-tail is hanging down beneath his sweater, a mug of tea is in his hand. Once a giant to Dexter, he now looks stooped and tired, his long face pale, drawn and lined from the six months in which his wife's condition has deteriorated. He raises his mug in greeting and for a moment Dexter sees himself through his father's eyes, and winces with shame at his shiny shirt, the jaunty way he drives this sporty little car, the raffish noise it makes as it swoops to a halt on the gravel, the chill-out music on the stereo.

Chilled-out.

Idiot.

Loved up.

Buffoon.

Sorted, you tawdry little clown.

He jabs off the CD player, unclips the removable facia from the dashboard, then stares at it in his hand. *Calm down, this is the Chilterns, not Stockwell. Your father is not going to steal your stereo. Just calm down.* In the doorway, his father raises his mug once again, and Dexter sighs, picks up the present from the passenger seat, summons up all his powers of concentration, and steps out of the car.

'What a ridiculous machine,' tuts his father.

'Well you don't have to drive it, do you?' Dexter takes comfort from the ease of the old routine, his father stern and square, the son irresponsible and cocky.

'Don't think I'd fit in it anyway. Toys for boys. We were expecting you some time ago.'

'How are you, old man?' says Dexter, feeling a sudden swell of affection for his dear old dad, and instinctively he loops his arms around his father's back, rubs it and then, excruciatingly, kisses his father's cheek.

They freeze.

Somehow Dexter has developed a kiss reflex. He has made the 'mmmmoi' noise in his father's tufted ear. Some unconscious part of him thinks that he is back under the railway arches with Gibbsy and Tara and Spex. He can feel the saliva, wet on his lip and he can see the consternation on his father's face as he looks down at his son, an Old Testament look. Sons kissing fathers – a law of nature has been broken. Not yet through the front door and already the illusion of sobriety has shattered. His father sniffs – either with distaste or because he is sniffing his son's breath, and Dexter is not sure which is worse.

'Your mother is in the garden. She's been waiting for you all morning.'

'How is she?' he asks. Perhaps he'll say 'much better'.

'Go and see. I'll put the kettle on.'

The hallway is dark and cool after the sun's glare. His older sister Cassie is entering from the back garden, a tray in her hands, her face aglow with competence, commonsense and piety. At thirty-four she has settled into the role of stern hospital matron, and the part suits her. Half smile, half scowl, she touches her cheek against his. 'The prodigal returns!'

Dexter's mind is not so addled that he can't recognise a dig, but he ignores the remark and glances at the tray. A bowl of grey brown cereal dissolved in milk, the spoon by its side, unused. 'How is she?' he asks. Perhaps she'll say 'much improved'.

'Go and find out,' says Cassie, and he squeezes past and wonders: Why will no-one tell me how she is?

From the doorway he watches her. She is sitting in an old-fashioned wing-backed chair that has been carried out to face the view across the fields and woods, Oxford a grey hazy smudge in the distance. From this angle, her face is obscured by a large sunhat and sunglasses – the light hurts her eyes these days – but he can tell by the slender arms and the way her hand lolls on the padded arm of the chair that she has changed a great deal in the three weeks since he last came to see her. He has a sudden urge to cry. He wants to curl up like a child and feel her put her arms around him, and he also wants to run from here as fast as he can, but neither are possible, so instead he trots down the steps, an artificially buoyant jog, a chat-show host.

'Hellooo there!'

She smiles as if smiling itself has become an effort. He stoops beneath the brim of her hat to kiss her, the skin of her cheek disconcertingly cool, taut and shiny. A headscarf is tied beneath her hat to disguise her hair loss, but he tries not to scrutinise her face too closely as he quickly reaches for a rusting metal garden chair. Noisily, he pulls it close and arranges it outwards so that they are both facing the view, but he can feel her eyes on him.

'You're sweating,' she says.

'Well it's a hot day.' She looks unconvinced. Not good enough. Concentrate. Remember who you're talking to.

'You're soaked through'

'It's this shirt. Artificial fibre.'

She reaches across and touches his shirt with the back of her hand. Her nose wrinkles with distaste. 'Where from?'

'Prada.'

'Expensive.'

'Only the best,' then keen to change the subject he retrieves the parcel from the rockery wall. 'Present for you.'

'How lovely.'

'Not from me, from Emma.'

'I can tell, from the wrapping.' Carefully she undoes the ribbon. 'Yours come in taped-up bin bags . . .'

'That's not true . . .' he smiles, keeping things light-hearted.

'. . . when they come at all.'

He's finding it harder to maintain this smile, but thankfully her eyes are on the parcel as she carefully folds the paper back, revealing a pile of paperback books: Edith Wharton, some Raymond Chandler, F. Scott Fitzgerald. 'How kind of her. Will you thank her for me? Lovely Emma Morley.' She looks at the cover of the Fitzgerald. '*The Beautiful and Damned*. It's me and you.'

'But which is which?' he says without thinking, but thankfully she doesn't seem to have heard. Instead she's reading the back of the postcard, a black and white agit-prop collage from '82; 'Thatcher Out!' She laughs. 'Such a kind girl. So funny.' She takes the novel and measures its thickness between finger and thumb. 'A little optimistic maybe. You might want to push her towards short stories in future.'

Dexter smiles and sniffs obediently but he hates this type of thing, gallows humour. It's meant to show pluck, to lift the spirits, but he finds it boring and stupid. He would prefer the unsayable to be left unsaid. 'How is Emma anyway?'

'Very good, I think. She's a fully qualified teacher now. Job interview today.'

'Now there's a profession.' She turns her head to look at him. 'Weren't you going to be a teacher once? What happened there?'

He recognises the dig. 'Didn't suit me.'

'No' is all she says. There is a silence and he feels the day slip from his control once more. Dexter had been led to believe, by TV, by films, that the only up-side of sickness was that it brought people closer, that there would be an opening-up, an effortless understanding between them. But they have always been close, always been open, and their habitual understanding has instead been replaced by bitterness, resentment, a rage on both their parts at what is happening. Meetings that should be fond and comforting descend into bickering and recrimination. Eight hours ago he was telling complete strangers his most intimate secrets, and now he can't talk to his mother. Something isn't right.

'So. I saw *largin' it* last week,' she says.

'Did you?'

She is silent, so he's forced to add, 'What did you think?'

'I think you're very good. Very natural. You look very nice on the screen. As I've said before, I don't care for the programme very much.'

'Well it's not really meant for people like you, is it?'

She bridles at the phrase, and turns her head imperiously. 'What do you mean, people like me?'

Flustered, he continues, 'I mean, it's just a silly, late-night programme, that's all. It's post-pub—'

'You mean I wasn't *drunk* enough to enjoy it?'

'No—'

'I'm not a prude either, I don't mind vulgarity, I just don't understand why it's suddenly necessary to humiliate people all the time—'

'No-one's humiliated, not really, it's fun—'

'You have competitions to find Britain's ugliest girlfriend. You don't think that's humiliating?'

'Not really, no—'

'Asking men to send in photos of their ugly girlfriends . . .'

'It's fun, the whole point is the guys love them even though they're . . . not conventionally attractive, that's the whole point, it's fun!'

'You keep saying it's fun, are you trying to convince me, or yourself?'

'Let's just not talk about it, shall we?'

'And do you think they find it fun, the girlfriends, the "mingers"—'

'Mum, I just introduce the bands, that's all. I just ask pop stars about their exciting new video, that's my job. It's a means to an end.'

'But to *what* end, Dexter? We always raised you to believe that you can do anything you wanted. I just didn't think you'd want to do *this*.'

'What do you want me to do?'

'I don't know; something *good*.' Abruptly she places her left hand on her chest, and sits back in her chair.

After a moment, he speaks. 'It is good. In its own terms.' She sniffs. 'It's a silly programme, just entertainment, and of course I don't like all of it, but it's an experience, it'll lead to other things. And actually I think I'm good at it, for what it's worth. Plus I'm enjoying myself.'

She waits a moment, then says, 'Well you must do it then, I suppose. You must do what you enjoy. And I know you'll do other things in time, it's just . . .' and she takes his hand, without finishing the thought. Then she laughs, breathlessly, 'I still don't see why it's necessary for you to pretend to be a cockney.'

'It's my man of the people voice,' he says, and she smiles, a very slight smile, but one which he latches onto.

'We shouldn't argue,' she says.

'We're not arguing, we're discussing,' he says, though he knows that they are arguing.

Her hand goes to her head. 'I'm taking this morphine. Sometimes I don't know what I'm saying.'

'You haven't said anything. I'm a little tired myself.' The sun is bouncing off the paving slabs and he can actually feel the skin on his face and forearms burning, sizzling, like a vampire. He feels another wave of perspiration and nausea coming on. Stay calm, he tells himself. It's just chemical.

'Late night?'

'Quite late.'

'Larging it, were you?'

'A little.' He rubs his temples to indicate soreness, says, without thinking, 'Don't suppose you've got any of that morphine going spare, have you?'

She doesn't even bother to look at him. Time passes. Recently he has noticed idiocy creeping up on him. His resolve to keep his head on straight, his feet on the ground, is failing and he has observed, quite objectively, that he is becoming more thought-less, selfish, making more and more stupid remarks. He has tried to do something about this but it almost feels out of his control now, like pattern baldness. Why not just give in and be an idiot? Stop caring. Time passes and he notices that grass and weeds have started to push their way through the surface of the tennis court. The place is falling apart already.

Eventually she speaks.

'I'm telling you now, your father's cooking lunch. Tinned stew. Be warned. At least Cassie should be back in time for dinner. You are staying the night, I suppose?'

He could stay the night, he thinks. Here is an opportunity to make amends. 'Actually, no,' he says.

She half turns her head.

'I've got tickets for *Jurassic Park* tonight. The premiere actu-ally. Lady Di is going! Not with me, I hasten to add,' and as he speaks the voice he hears is of someone he despises. 'I can't skip it, it's a work thing, it was arranged ages ago.' His mother's eyes narrow, almost imperceptibly, and in mitigation he quickly tells a lie. 'I'm taking Emma, you see. I'd skip it, but she really wants to go.'

'Oh. Well.' And there's a silence.

'The life you lead,' she says levelly.

Silence once more.

'Dexter, you'll have to excuse me, but I'm afraid the morning has taken it out of me. I'm going to need to go to sleep upstairs for a while.'

'Okay.'

'I'm going to need some help.'

Anxiously, he looks around for his sister, or father, as if they had some kind of qualification that he doesn't possess, but they're nowhere to be seen. His mother's hands are on the arms of the chair now, straining uselessly, and he realises that he must do this. Lightly, without conviction, he loops his arm under hers and helps her up. 'Do you want me to . . . ?'

'No, I'm fine getting indoors, I just need help with the stairs.'

They walk across the patio, his hand just touching the fabric of the blue summer dress that hangs loosely off her like a hospital gown. Her slowness is maddening, an affront to him. 'How is Cassie?' he asks, to fill the time.

'Oh fine. I think she enjoys bossing me around a little too much, but she's very attentive. Eat this, take these, sleep now. Strict but fair, that's your sister. It's revenge for not buying her that pony.'

So if Cassie's so good at this, he wonders, where is she when she's needed? They are inside, at the bottom of the staircase. He had never realised there were so many stairs.

'How do I? . . .'

'It's best if you just lift me. I'm not heavy, not these days.'

I am not up to this. I am not capable. I thought I would be, but I'm not. Some part of me is missing, and I cannot do this.

'Does it hurt anywhere? I mean is there anywhere I should? . . .'

'Don't worry about that.' She removes her sunhat and settles her headscarf. He takes a firmer hold of her below her shoulder blade, the fingers of his hand aligning with the grooves of her ribs, then bends at the knee, feels the back of her legs beneath her dress against his forearm, smooth and cool, and when he thinks she is ready he lifts, scooping her up and feeling her body loosen in his arms. She exhales deeply, and her breath is sweet and hot on his face. Either she is heavier than he expected or he is weaker than he thought, and he bumps her shoulder against the stair post, then readjusts, turning sideways as he starts to climb the stairs. Her head rests against his shoulder, the headscarf slippery against his face. It feels like a parody of a stock situation, the husband carrying the bride over the threshold perhaps, and several light-hearted remarks run through his head, none of which will make this any easier. As they reach the landing, she obliges instead – 'My hero,' she says, looking up at him, and they both smile.

He kicks open the door to the dark room, and lays her on the bed.

'Can I get you anything?'

'I'm fine.'

'Are you due anything? Medicine or . . .'

'No, I'm fine.'

'Dry martini with a twist?'

'Oh yes please.'

'Do you want to get under the covers?'

'Just that blanket, please.'

'Curtains closed?'

'Please. But leave the window open.'

'See you later then.'

'Goodbye, darling.'

'See you.'

He smiles tightly at her, but she is already lying on her side with her back to him, and he steps out of the room, pulling the door loosely closed. One day quite soon, probably within the year, he will walk out of a room and never see her again, and this thought is so hard to conceive of that he shoves it away violently, concentrating instead on himself: his hangover, how tired he feels, how the pain throbs in his temples as he trots down the stairs.

The large, untidy kitchen is empty so he crosses to the fridge, which is almost empty too. A wilted celery heart, a chicken carcass, opened cans and economy ham all indicate that his father has taken over the domestic duties. In the fridge door is an opened bottle of white wine. He takes the bottle out and swigs from it, taking four, five gulps of the sweet liquid before he hears father's footsteps in the hall. He replaces the bottle, wipes his mouth with the back of the hand just as his father enters, carrying two plastic bags from the village supermarket.

'Where's your mother?'

'Tired. I carried her upstairs for a lie-down.' Dexter wants him to know that he is brave and mature, but his father seems unimpressed.

'I see. Did you chat?'

'A little. Just about this and that.' His voice sounds strange in his own head, booming and slurred and self-conscious. Drunk. Can his father tell, he wonders? 'We'll talk more when she wakes up.' He opens the fridge door again, and pretends to see the wine for the first time. 'Mind if I?' He takes it, empties the dregs into a glass then heads out past his father. 'I'm just going to be in my room for a bit.'

'What for?' scowls his father.

'I'm looking for something. Old books.'

'Don't you want lunch? Little food with your wine perhaps?'

Dexter glances at the shopping bag at his father's feet, splitting from the weight of all the tins. 'Maybe later,' he says, already out of the room.

On the landing, he notices the door of his parents' room has swung open, and silently he steps inside once again. The curtains move in the afternoon breeze, and the sunlight comes and goes on her sleeping form beneath an old blanket, the dirty soles of her feet visible, toes curled up tight. The smell that he remembers from his childhood, of expensive lotions and mysterious powders, has been replaced with a vegetable odour that he would rather not think about. A hospital smell has invaded his childhood home. He closes her door, and pads to the bathroom.

As he pees, he checks in the medicine cabinet: his father's copious sleeping pills tell of night fears, and there's an old bottle of his mother's valium dated March 1989, long superseded by more potent medication. He shakes out two of each and slips them into his wallet, then a third valium, which he swallows with water from the hand basin's tap, just to take the edge off.

His old bedroom is used for storage now, and he has to squeeze past an old chesterfield, tea chest and cardboard boxes. On the walls, a few dog-eared family snapshots, and his own black and white prints of shells and leaves that he took as a teenager, imperfectly fixed and fading now. Like a child sent to his room he lies on the old double bed, hands behind his head. He had always imagined that some sort of emotional mental equipment was meant to arrive, when he was forty-five, say, or fifty, a kind of kit that would enable him to deal with the impending loss of a parent. If he were only in possession of this equipment, he would be just fine. He would be noble and selfless, wise and philosophical. Perhaps he might even have kids of his own, and would presumably possess the maturity that comes with father-hood, the understanding of life as a process.

But he isn't forty-five, he is twenty-eight years old. His mother is forty-nine. There has been some terrible mistake, the timing is out, and how can he possibly be expected to deal with this, the sight of his extraordinary mother diminishing like this? It isn't fair on him, not with so many other distractions. He is a busy young man on the edge of a successful career. Expressed in its frankest terms, he has better things to do. He feels another sudden urge to cry, but he hasn't cried for fifteen years, so he puts this down to the chemicals and decides to sleep a little. He balances the glass of wine on a packing case by the side of the bed, and rolls onto his side. Being a decent human being will require effort and energy. A little rest, then he will apologise and show how much he loves her.

He wakes with a start and looks at his watch, then looks again. 6.26 p.m. He has slept for six hours, clearly impossible, but when he pulls open the curtains the sun is starting to dip in the sky. His head still hurts, his eyes are somehow gummed shut, there's a metallic taste in his mouth, and he is parched and hungrier than he has ever been before. The glass of wine, when he reaches for it, is warm in his hand. He drinks half of it, then recoils – a fat bluebottle has found its way into the glass and buzzes against his lip. Dexter drops the glass, spilling the wine down his shirt and onto the bed. He stumbles to his feet.

In the bathroom, he splashes his face. The perspiration on the shirt has gone sour, taking on an unmistakeable alcoholic stench. A little queasily he paints himself with his father's old roll-on deodorant. Downstairs he can hear pots and pans, the babble of the radio, family sounds. Bright; be bright and happy and polite, then go.

But as he passes his mother's room he sees her sitting on the edge of the bed in profile, looking out across the fields as if she too has been waiting for him. Slowly she turns her head, but he hovers on the threshold like a child.

'You've missed the whole day,' she says quietly.

'I overslept.'

'So I see. Feeling better?'

'No.'

'Oh well. Your father is a little angry with you, I'm afraid.'

'No change there then.' She smiles indulgently and, encouraged, he adds, 'Everyone seems pissed-off with me at the moment.'

'Poor little Dexter,' she says and he wonders if she is being sarcastic. 'Come and sit here.' She smiles, places one hand on the bed next to her. 'Next to me.' Obediently he enters the room, and sits, so that their hips are touching. She knocks her head against his shoulder. 'We're not ourselves, are we? I'm certainly not myself, not anymore. And you're not either. You don't seem yourself. Not as I remember you.'

'In what way?'

'I mean . . . can I speak frankly?'

'Do you have to?'

'I think I do. It is my prerogative.'

'Go on then.'

'I think . . .' She lifts her head from his shoulder. 'I think that you have it in you to be a fine young man. Exceptional even. I have always thought that. Mothers are supposed to, aren't they? But I don't think you're there yet. Not yet. I think you've got some way to go. That's all.'

'I see.'

'You mustn't take this badly, but sometimes . . .' She takes his hand in hers, rubbing the palm of it with her thumb. 'Sometimes I worry that you're not very nice anymore.'

They sit there for a while until eventually he says, 'There's nothing I can say to that.'

'There's nothing that you have to say.'

'Are you angry with me?'

'A little. But then I'm angry with pretty much everyone these days. Everyone who isn't sick.'

'I'm sorry, Mum. I am so, so sorry.'

She presses her thumb into the palm of his hand. 'I know you are.'

'I'll stay. Tonight.'

'No, not tonight. You're busy. Come back and start again.'

He stands, holds her shoulders lightly, and presses his cheek against hers – he can hear her breathing in his ear, the warm, sweet breath – then he walks to the door.

'Thank Emma for me,' she says. 'For the books.'

'I will.'

'Send her my love. When you see her tonight.'

'Tonight?'

'Yes. You're seeing her tonight.'

He remembers his lie. 'Yes, yes I will. And I'm sorry if I haven't been very . . . very good today.'

'Well. I suppose there's always the next time,' she says, and smiles.

Dexter takes the stairs at a run, counting on the momentum to hold him together, but his father is in the hallway reading the local newspaper, or pretending to. Once again, it's as if he has been waiting for him, a sentry on duty, the arresting officer.

'I overslept,' says Dexter, to his father's back.

He turns a page of the newspaper. 'Yes, I know.'

'Why didn't you wake me, Dad?'

'There didn't seem much point. Also I tend to think that I shouldn't have to.' He turns another page. 'You're not fourteen years old, Dexter.'

'But it means I've got to go now!'

'Well, if you've got to go . . .' The sentence peters out. He can see Cassie in the living room, also pretending to read, her face flush with condemnation and self-righteousness. *Get out of here now, just go, because this is all about to break.* He places one hand on the hall table for his keys, but it comes up empty.

'My car keys.'

'I've hidden them,' says his father, reading the paper.

Dexter can't help but laugh. 'You can't *hide my keys*!'

'Well clearly I can because I have. Do you want to play looking for them?'

'May I ask why?' he says, indignant.

His father lifts his head from the paper, as if sniffing the air. 'Because you are drunk.'

In the living room, Cassie gets up from the sofa, crosses to the door and pushes it closed.

Dexter laughs, but without conviction. 'No, I'm not!'

His father glances over his shoulder. 'Dexter, I know when someone is drunk. You in particular. I've been seeing you drunk for twelve years now, remember?'

'But I'm not drunk, I'm hungover, that's all.'

'Well either way, you are not driving home.'

Again, Dexter gives a scoffing laugh, and rolls his eyes in protest, but no words will come out, except for a feeble, high-pitched 'Dad, I am twenty-eight years old!'

On cue his father says, 'Could have fooled me,' then reaches into his pocket for his own car keys, tossing them in the air and catching them in feigned joviality. 'Come on. I'll give you a lift to the station.'

Dexter does not say goodbye to his sister.

Sometimes I worry that you're not very nice. His father drives in silence, Dexter steeping in shame in the big old Jaguar. When the silence can no longer be borne, his father speaks, quietly and soberly, eyes fixed on the road. 'You can come and get your car on Saturday. When you're sober.'

'I'm sober now,' says Dexter, hearing his own voice, still whining and petulant, the voice of his sixteen-year-old self. 'For Christ's sake!' he adds, redundantly.

'I'm not going to argue with you, Dexter.'

He huffs and slides down in his seat, his forehead and nose pressed against the window as the country lanes and smart houses flash by. His father, who has always abhorred all confrontation and is clearly in agony here, punches on the radio to cover the silence and they listen to classical music: a march, banal and bombastic. They approach the train station. The car pulls into the car park, emptied now of commuters. Dexter opens the car door, places one foot on the gravel, but his father makes no gesture of goodbye, just sits and waits with the engine running, as neutral as a chauffeur, his eyes fixed on the dashboard, fingers tapping to that lunatic march.

Dexter knows he should accept his chastisement and go, but pride won't let him. 'Okay, I'm going now, but can I just say, I think you're completely over-reacting to this . . .'

And suddenly there is real rage in his father's face, his teeth bared and clenched tight, his voice cracking: 'Do not *dare* to insult my intelligence or your mother's, you are a grown man now, you are not a child.' Just as quickly the rage is gone, and instead he thinks his father might be about to cry. His bottom lip is trembling, one hand is gripping the wheel, the long fingers of the other hand wrapped around his eyes like a blindfold. Dexter hurriedly backs out of the car and is about to stand and close the door, when his father turns off the radio and speaks again. 'Dexter—'

Dexter stoops, and looks in at his father. His eyes are wet, but his voice is steady as he says—

'Dexter, your mother loves you very, very much. And I do too. We always have and we always will. I think you know that. But in whatever time your mother has left to her—' He falters, glances down as if looking for the words, then up. 'Dexter, if you ever come and see your mother in this state again, I swear, I will not let you into the house. I will not let you through our door. I will close the door in your face. I mean this.'

Dexter's mouth is open, though there are no words.

'Now. Please go home.'

Dexter closes the car door, but it doesn't lock. He closes it again just as his father, flustered too, jolts forwards, then into reverse, leaving the car park at speed. Dexter stands and watches him go.

The rural train station is empty. He looks along the length of the platform for the payphone, the old familiar payphone that he used as a teenager to make his plans of escape. It's 6.59 p.m. The London connection will be here in six minutes, but he has to make this call.

At 7 p.m., Emma takes one last look in the mirror to ensure that it doesn't seem as if she has made any kind of effort. The mirror leans precariously against the wall and she knows that it has a foreshortening, hall-of-mirrors effect, but even so she clicks her tongue at her hips, the short legs below her denim skirt. It's too warm for tights but she can't bear the sight of her scuffed red knees so is wearing them anyway. Her hair, newly washed and smelling of something called forest fruits, has fallen into a 'do', flicked and fragrant, and she scrubs at it with her fingertips to muss it up, then uses her little finger to wipe smears of lipstick from the corner of her mouth. Her lips are very red, and she wonders if she's overdoing it. After all, nothing's likely to happen, she'll be home by 10.30. She drains the last of a large vodka and tonic, winces as it reacts metallically with the toothpaste, picks up her keys, drops them in her best handbag, and closes the door.

The phone rings.

She is halfway down the institutional hallway when she hears it. For one moment she contemplates running back to answer it but she is late already, and it's probably just her mum or sister to find out how the interview went. At the end of the hall she can hear the lift door opening. She runs to catch it, and the doors of the lift close just as the answering machine picks up.

'. . . leave your message after the beep and I'll get back to you.'

'Hi there, Emma, it's Dexter here. What was I going to say? Well I was going to say I'm at this train station near home and I've just come from Mum's and . . . and I wondered what you were doing tonight. I have tickets for the *Jurassic Park* premiere! Actually we've missed that I think, but maybe the party afterwards? Me and you? Princess Di will be there. Sorry, I'm waffling, in case you're there. Pick up the phone, Emma. Pick up pick up pick up pick up. No? Okay, well I've just remembered, you have your date tonight, don't you? Your hot date. Well – have fun, call me when you get in, *if* you get in. Let me know what happens. Seriously, call me, soon as you can.'

He stumbles, catches his breath, then says:

'Just an unbelievably shitty day, Em,' and falters again. 'I've just done something so, so bad.' He should hang up, but he doesn't want to. He wants to see Emma Morley so that he might confess his sins, but she's on a date. He pulls his mouth into a grin and says 'I'll call you tomorrow. I want to know everything! Heartbreaker you.' He hangs up. Heartbreaker you.

The rails are clicking now, and he can hear the hum of the train approaching, but he can't get on board, not in this state. He'll just have to wait for the next one. The London train arrives and seems to be waiting for him, ticking politely, but Dexter stands shielded by the plastic carapace of the payphone booth, feels his face crumple inwards and his breath become broken and jagged, and as he starts to cry he tells himself that it's just chemical, chemical, chemical.

CHAPTER SEVEN
G.S.O.H.

Covent Garden and King's Cross

Ian Whitehead sat alone at a table for two in the Covent Garden branch of Forelli's, and checked his watch: fifteen minutes late, but he imagined that this was part of the exquisite game of cat-and-mouse that is dating. Well, let the games commence. He dunked his ciabatta in the little dish of olive oil as if loading a paintbrush, opened the menu and worked out what he could afford to eat.

Life as a stand-up comedian had yet to bring the wealth and TV exposure that it had once promised. The Sunday papers weekly proclaimed that comedy was the new rock and roll, so why was he still hustling for open-mike spots at Sir Laffalots on Tuesday nights? He had adapted his material to fit with current fashions, pulling back on the political and observational material and trying out character-comedy, surrealism, comic songs and sketches. Nothing seemed to raise a laugh. A detour into a more confrontational style had led to him being punched and kicked, and his residency with a Sunday night improv comedy team had proved only that he could be unfunny in an entirely unplanned, spontaneous way. Yet still he soldiered on, up and down the Northern Line, round and round the Circle, in search of the big laughs.

Perhaps there was something about the name 'Ian Whitehead' that made it resistant to being spelt out in lightbulbs. He had even considered changing it to something punchy, boysy and monosyllabic – Ben or Jack or Matt – but until he found his comic persona he had taken a job in Sonicotronics, an electronics shop on Tottenham Court Road where unhealthy young men in t-shirts sold ROM and graphics cards to unhealthy young men in t-shirts. The money wasn't great, but his evenings were free for gigs, and he frequently cracked up his co-workers with new material.

But the best, the very best thing about Sonicotronics was that during his lunch break he had bumped into Emma Morley. He had been standing outside the offices of the Church of Scientology, debating whether or not to take the personality test, when he saw her, almost obscured by a huge wicker laundry basket, and as he threw his arms around her Tottenham Court Road was lit by glory and transformed into a street of dreams.

Date number two, and here he was in a sleek modern Italian near Covent Garden. Ian's personal tastes tended towards the hot and spicy, salty and crispy, and he would have preferred a curry. But he was wise enough in the vagaries of womankind to know that she would be expecting fresh vegetables. He checked his watch again – twenty minutes late – and felt a pang of longing in his stomach that was partly hunger, partly love. For years now his heart and stomach had been heavy with love for Emma Morley, and not just sentimental platonic love, but a carnal desire too. All these years later he still carried with him, would carry for life, the image of her standing in mismatched underwear in the staffroom of Loco Caliente, illuminated by a shaft of afternoon sun like the light in a cathedral, as she yelled at him to get out and shut the bloody door.

Unaware that he was thinking of her underwear, Emma Morley stood watching Ian from the maître d's station and noted that he was definitely better looking these days. The crown of tight fair curls had gone, trimmed short now and slicked slightly with a little wax, he had lost that new-boy-in-the-city look. In fact, if it weren't for the terrible clothes and the way his mouth hung open, he would actually be attractive.

Although the situation was unusual for her, she recognised this as a classic date restaurant – just expensive enough, not too bright, not pretentious but not cheap either, the kind of place where they put rocket on the pizzas. The place was corny but not ridiculous and at least it was not a curry or, God forbid, a fish burrito. There were palm trees and candles and in the next room an elderly man played Gershwin favourites on a grand piano: '*I hope that he/turns out to be/someone to watch over me.*'

'Are you with someone?' asked the maître d'.

'That man over there.'

On their first date he had taken her to see *Evil Dead III, The Medieval Dead* at the Odeon on the Holloway Road. Neither squeamish nor a snob, Emma enjoyed a horror film more than most women, but even so she had thought this a strange, curiously confident choice. *Three Colours Blue* was playing at the Everyman, but here she was, watching a man with a chainsaw for an arm, and finding it strangely refreshing. Conventionally, she had expected to be taken to a restaurant afterwards but for Ian it seemed a trip to the cinema wasn't complete without a three-course meal thrown in. He contemplated the concession stand as if were an à la carte menu, choosing nachos to begin with, a hot-dog for the entrée, Revels for dessert, his palette cleansed with a pail of iced Lilt the size of a human torso, so that the *Evil Dead III*'s few meditative scenes were accompanied by the warm tropical hiss of Ian belching into his fist.

And yet despite all this – the love of ultra-violence and salty foods, the mustard on his chin – Emma had enjoyed herself more than she had expected. On the way to the pub he had changed sides on the pavement so that she wouldn't get hit by a runaway bus – a weirdly old-fashioned gesture that she'd never been subject to before – and they discussed the special effects, the beheadings and eviscerations, Ian declaring, after some analysis, that it was the best of the 'Dead' trilogy. Trilogies and box-sets, comedy and horror loomed large in Ian's cultural life, and in the pub they'd had an interesting debate about whether a graphic novel could ever have as much depth and meaning as, say, *Middlemarch*. Protective, attentive, he was like an older brother who knew about lots of really cool stuff, the difference being that he clearly wanted to sleep with her. So intent, so doting was his gaze that she frequently found herself feeling for something on her face.

That was how he grinned at her now, in the restaurant, standing with such enthusiasm that he knocked the table with his thighs, spilling tap water onto the complimentary olives.

'Shall I get a cloth?' she said.

'No, it's alright, I'll use my jacket.'

'Don't use your jacket, here – here's my napkin.'

'Well I've fucked the olives. Not literally I might hasten to add!'

'Oh. Right. Okay.'

'Joke!' he bellowed, as if shouting 'Fire!' He hadn't been this nervous since the last disastrous night at the improv, and he firmly told himself to calm down as he blotted at the tablecloth, glancing upwards to see Emma wriggling out of her summer jacket, pushing her shoulders back and her chest forward in that way that women do without realising the ache they cause. There it was, the evening's second great bubble of love and desire for Emma Morley. 'You look so lovely,' he blurted, unable to contain himself.

'Thank you! You too,' she said reflexively. He wore the stand-up comic's uniform of a crumpled linen jacket over a plain black t-shirt. In honour of Emma, there were no band names or ironic remarks: dressy then. 'I like this,' she said, indicating the jacket. 'Pretty sharp!' and Ian rubbed his lapel between finger and thumb as if saying 'what, *this* old thing?'

'Can I take your jacket?' said the waiter, sleek and handsome.

'Yes, thank you.' Emma handed it over, and Ian imagined he'd have to tip for it later. Never mind. She was worth it.

'Any drinks?' asked the waiter.

'You know, I think I'd like a vodka and tonic.'

'A double?' said the waiter, tempting her into further expense.

She looked to Ian and saw a flicker of panic cross his face. 'Is that reckless?'

'No, you go on.'

'Okay, a double!'

'You, sir?'

'I'll wait for the wine, thank you.'

'Mineral water?'

'TAP WATER!' he yelled, then, calmer, 'Tap water's fine, unless you . . .'

'Tap water's fine,' Emma smiled reassuringly. The waiter left. 'And by the way, this goes without saying, but we are going dutch tonight, okay? No arguments. It's 1993 for crying out loud,' and Ian found himself loving her even more. For form's sake, he thought he had better put on a show.

'But you're a student, Em!'

'Not anymore. I am now a fully qualified teacher! I had my first job interview today.'

'And how did it go?'

'Really, really well!'

'Congratulations, Em, that's fantastic,' and he threw himself across the table to kiss her on the cheek, no, both cheeks, no, hang on, just the one cheek, no, okay both cheeks.

The menu had been prepped in advance for humour, and while Emma tried to concentrate, Ian went into his act and ran through some of the choicer puns: penne for your thoughts, etc. The presence of grilled sea bass allowed him to do the one about how you wait ages for one bass, then three come along at the same time, and was this a minute steak or a mine-ute, like a really, really small steak? and what was it with 'ragu' these days, when did good old spag bol become 'ragu'? What, he speculated, would they, like, call 'alphabetti spaghetti?' Moist alphabetical forms in a sauce rouge? Or what?

As line followed line, Emma felt her hopes for the evening fade.

He is trying to laugh me into bed, she thought, when in fact what he is really doing is laughing me onto the tube home. In the cinema there had at least been the Revels and the violence to distract him, but here, face to face, there was nothing but a compulsion to riff. Emma got this a lot. The boys on her PGCE course were all pro-am gagsters, especially in the pub after a few pints, and while it drove her crazy she knew that she encouraged it too, the girls sitting and grinning while the boys did tricks with matchsticks and jammed on Children's TV or Forgotten Confectionery of the Seventies. Spangles Disease, the maddening non-stop cabaret of boys in pubs.

She gulped down her vodka. Ian had the wine list now, and was doing his schtick about how snooty wine is: *a voluptuous mouthful of forest fire with a back note of exploding toffee apple* etc. The C-major scale of the amateur stand-up, this routine had the potential to be infinite, and Emma found herself trying to imagine a notional man, a fantastical figure who didn't make a big deal about it, just looked at the wine list and ordered, unpretentiously but with authority.

'. . . flavours of smoky bacon Wotsits with a succulent back note of giraffe . . .'

He's laughing me into a stupor, she thought. I could heckle, I suppose, I could throw a bread roll at him, but he's eaten them all. She glanced at the other diners, all of them going into their act, and thought is this what it all boils down to? Romantic love, is this all it is, a talent show? Eat a meal, go to bed, fall in love with me and I promise you years and years of top notch material like this?

'. . . imagine if they sold lager this way?' A Glaswegian accent. 'Our Special Brew sits heavy on the palate, with a strong hint of council estate, old shopping trolley and urban decay. Goes particularly well with domestic violence! . . .'

She wondered where the fallacy had come from, that there was something irresistible about funny men; Cathy doesn't long for Heathcliff because he's a really great laugh, and what was all the more galling about this barrage was that she actually quite liked Ian, had set out with high hopes and even some excitement about seeing him again, but instead he was saying . . .

'. . . our orange juice is orange with a heavy bass note of oranges . . .'

Right, that's enough now.

'. . . squeezed, no, *seduced* from the teets of cows, the 1989 vintage milk has a distinctive milkiness . . .'

'Ian?'

'What?'

'Shut up, will you?'

A silence followed, with Ian looking hurt and Emma feeling embarrassed. It must have been that double vodka. To cover it up, she said loudly, 'How about we just get Valpolicella?'

He consulted the menu. 'Blackberries and vanilla, it says here.'

'Perhaps they write that because the wine tastes a bit of blackberries and vanilla?'

'Do you like blackberries and vanilla?'

'I love them.'

His eyes flicked to the price. 'Then let's get it then!'

And after that, thank God, things began to get a little better.

Hi, Em. Me again. I know you're out on the town with Laughing Boy, but I just wanted to say that when you get in, assuming you're alone, I've decided not to go the premiere after all. I'm home all night, if you want to come round. I mean, I'd like that. I'll pay for your taxi, you could stay over. So. Anytime you come in, just give me a call, then get in a cab. That's all. Hope to see you later. Love and all that. Bye, Em. Bye.

They reminisced about the old times, all of three years ago. While Emma had the soup then fish, Ian had gone for a medley of carbohydrates, starting with an immense bowl of meaty pasta which he buried between snow banks of parmesan. This and the red wine had sedated him a little, and Emma had relaxed too, was in fact well on her way to drunkenness. And why not? Didn't she deserve it? The last ten months had been spent working hard at something she believed in, and though some of the teaching placements had been frankly terrifying, she was clear-sighted enough to realise she was good at it. At her interview this afternoon they had obviously felt the same way, the headmaster nodding and smiling in approval, and though she didn't dare say it out loud, she knew that she had the job.

So why not celebrate with Ian? As he talked, she scrutinised his face and decided that he was definitely more attractive than he used to be; looking at him, she no longer thought of tractors. There was nothing refined or delicate about him; if you were casting a war film, he'd be the plucky Tommy maybe, writing letters to his mum, while Dexter would be – what? An effete Nazi. Even so, she liked the way he looked at her. Fond, that was the word. Fond and drunk, and she too felt heavy-limbed and sultry and fond of him in return.

He poured the last of the wine into her glass. 'So do you see any of the old gang?'

'Not really. I bumped into Scott once, in Hail Caesar's, that awful Italian. He was fine, still angry. Apart from that, I try to avoid it. It's a bit like prison – best not to associate with the old lags. Except you of course.'

'It wasn't that bad, was it? Working there?'

'Well it's two years of my life I'll never get back.' Spoken aloud, the observation shocked her but she shrugged it away. 'I don't know, I suppose it wasn't a very happy time, that's all.'

He smiled ruefully and nudged her knuckles with his. 'That why you didn't answer my phone-calls?'

'Didn't I? I don't know, maybe.' She raised the glass to her lips. 'We're here now. Let's change the subject. How's the stand-up career going?'

'Oh, alright. I've got this improv gig which is real seat-of-the-pants stuff, really unpredictable. Sometimes I'm just not funny at all! But I suppose that's the joy of improv, isn't it?' Emma wasn't sure that this was true, but nodded just the same. 'And I do this Tuesday night gig at Mr Chuckles in Kennington. It's a bit more hard-edged, more topical. Like I do this kind of Bill Hicks thing about advertising? Like the stupid adverts on TV? . . .'

He slipped into his routine and Emma freeze-framed her smile. It would kill him to say it but in all the time she had known Ian he had caused her to laugh perhaps twice, and one of those was when he fell down the cellar stairs. He was a man with a great sense of humour while at the same time being in no way funny. Unlike Dexter: Dexter had no interest at all in jokes, probably thought that a sense of humour, like a political conscience, was a little embarrassing and un-cool, and yet with Dexter she laughed all the time, hysterically, sometimes, frankly, until she peed a little. On holiday in Greece, they had laughed for ten days straight, once they'd settled that little misunderstanding. Where was Dexter right now? she wondered.

'Have you been watching him on telly then?' said Ian.

Emma flinched, as if she'd been caught out. 'Who?'

'Your friend Dexter, on that stupid programme.'

'Sometimes. You know, if it's on.'

'And how is he?'

'Oh fine, the usual. Well, a bit nutty to be honest, a bit off the rails. His mother's sick and, well, he's not taking it very well.'

'I'm sorry to hear that.' Ian frowned with concern and tried to work out a way of changing the subject. Not callously; he just didn't want a stranger's illness to get in the way of his evening. 'Do you speak a lot?'

'Me and Dex? Most days. I don't see him much though, with his TV commitments, and his *girlfriends*.'

'Who's he seeing now then?'

'No idea. They're like funfair goldfish; no point giving them names, they never last that long.' She had used the line before and hoped that Ian might like it, but he was still frowning. 'What's that face?'

'Just never liked him, I suppose.'

'No, I remember.'

'I tried.'

'Well you mustn't take it personally. He's not that good with other men, he doesn't see the point of them.'

'As a matter of fact, I always thought—'

'What?'

'That he took you a bit for granted. That's all.'

Me again! Just checking in. Bit drunk now actually. Bit senti-mental. You're a great thing, Emma Morley. Be nice to see you. Call when you get in. What else did I want to say? Nothing, except that you are a great, great thing. So. When you get in. Call me. Give me a call.

By the time the second brandies arrived there was no doubting that they were drunk. The whole restaurant seemed drunk, even the silver-haired pianist, clattering sloppily through 'I Get a Kick Out of You', his foot pumping the sustain pedal as if someone had cut his brake cable. Forced to raise her voice, Emma could hear it echoing in her head as she spoke with great passion and force about her new career.

'It's a big comprehensive in north London, teaching English and a bit of Drama. Nice school, really mixed, not one of those cushy suburban numbers where it's all yes-miss no-miss. So the kids are a bit of a challenge, but that's alright isn't it? That's what kids are meant to be. I say that now. They'll probably eat me alive, little sods.' She rolled the brandy round the glass in a way that she'd seen in films. 'I've got this vision of me sitting on the edge of the desk, talking about how Shakespeare was the first rapper or something, and all these kids are just gazing at me with their mouths open just – hypnotised. I sort of imagine being carried aloft on inspired young shoulders. That's how I'm going to get around the school, the car park, the canteen, everywhere I go I'm going to be on the shoulders of adoring kids. One of those carpe diem teachers.'

'Sorry, what-teachers?'

'Carpe diem.'

'Carpe—?'

'You know, seize the day!'

'Is that what it means? I thought it meant seize the carpet!'

Emma gave a polite hiccough of mirth, which for Ian was like a starting pistol. 'That's where I went wrong! Wow, my school days would have been so different if I'd known! All those years, scrambling around on the floor . . .'

Enough of this. 'Ian, don't do that,' she said sharply.

'What?'

'Slip into your act. You don't have to, you know.' He looked hurt, and she regretted her tone, leaning across the table to take his hand. 'I just don't think you have to be *observing* all the time, or riffing or quipping or punning. It's not improv, Ian, it's just, you know, talking and listening.'

'Sorry, I—'

'Oh, it's not just you, it's men in general, all of you doing your number all the time. God, what I'd give for someone who just talked and listened!' She was aware of saying too much, but momentum carried her on. 'I just can't work out why it's necessary. It's not an audition.'

'Except it sort of is, isn't it?'

'Not with me. It doesn't have to be.'

'Sorry.'

'And don't keep apologising either.'

'Oh. Okay.'

Ian was silent for a moment, and now it was Emma who felt like apologising. She shouldn't speak her thoughts; nothing good ever came of speaking your thoughts. She was about to apologise, when Ian sighed and rested his cheek against his fist.

'I think what it is is, if you're at school and you're not that bright or good-looking or popular or whatever, and one day you say something and someone laughs, well, you sort of grab onto it, don't you? You think, well I run funny and I've got this stupid big face and big thighs and no-one fancies me, but at least I can make people laugh. And it's such a nice feeling, making someone laugh, that maybe you get a bit reliant on it. Like, if you're not funny then you're not . . . anything.' He was looking at the table-cloth now, pinching the crumbs into a little pyramid with his fingertips as he said, 'Actually I thought you might know what that's like yourself.'

Emma's hand went to her chest. 'Me?'

'Putting on an act.'

'I don't put on an act.'

'That bit about the funfair goldfish, you've said that before.'

'No, I . . . so?'

'So I just think we're quite similar, you and me. Sometimes.'

Her first thought was to be offended. No I'm not, she wanted to say, what an absurd idea, but he was smiling at her so — what was the word — fondly, and perhaps she had been a little harsh on him. Instead, she shrugged. 'I don't believe it anyway.'

'What?'

'That no-one fancied you.'

He spoke in a jokey, nasal voice. 'Well, documentary evidence would seem to suggest otherwise.'

'I'm here, aren't I?' There was a silence; she really had drunk too much, and now it was her turn to play with the crumbs on the table. 'S'matter of fact, I was thinking how much better looking you were these days.'

He grasped his belly with both hands. 'Well, I've been working out.'

She laughed, quite naturally, looked at him and decided that it really wasn't such a bad face after all; not some silly pretty boy's face, just a decent, proper man's face. She knew that after the bill was paid that he would try and kiss her, and this time she would let him.

149

'We should go,' she said.

'I'll get the bill.' He made the little bill-writing sign at the waiter. 'It's weird, isn't it, that little mime that everyone does? Whose idea was that, I wonder?'

'Ian?'

'What? Sorry. Sorry.'

They split the bill two ways as promised and on the way out Ian pulled the door open, sharply kicking the bottom so that it gave the illusion of having hit him in the face. 'Little bit of physical comedy there . . .'

Outside a heavy curtain of black and purple clouds had formed across the sky. The warm wind had that ferric tang that precedes a storm, and Emma felt pleasantly woozy and brandy-flavoured as they walked north across the piazza. She had always hated Covent Garden, with its Peruvian pipe bands, jugglers and forced fun, but tonight it seemed fine, just as it seemed fine and natural to hang on the arm of this man who was always so nice and interested in her, even if he did carry his jacket slung over his shoulder by that little loop in the collar. Looking up, she saw that he was frowning.

'What's up?' she asked, squeezing his arm with hers.

'Just, you know, feel like I've blown it a bit, that's all. Getting nervous, trying too hard, making daft remarks. Do you know the worst thing about being a stand-up comedian?'

'Is it the clothes?'

'It's that people always expect you to be "on". You're always chasing the laugh—'

And partly to change the subject, she put her hands on his shoulders, using his body to brace herself as she stepped up on tip-toe to kiss him. His mouth was damp but warm. 'Blackberries and vanilla,' she murmured with their lips pressed together, though in truth he tasted of parmesan and booze. She didn't mind. He laughed into the kiss and she stepped down, held his face and looked up at him. He seemed as if he might cry with gratitude and she felt pleased that she'd done it.

'Emma Morley, can I just say—' He gazed down at her with great solemnity. 'I think you are absolutely The Bollocks.'

'You, with your honeyed words,' she said. 'Let's get back to your place, shall we? Before it starts to rain.'

Guess who? Half-eleven now. Where are you, dirty stop-out? Oh well. Call me anytime, I'm here, I'm not going anywhere. Bye. Bye.

At street level on the Cally Road, Ian's studio flat was lit only by the sodium of the street lamps and the occasional searchlight of the passing double-decker buses. Several times a minute the whole room vibrated, shaken by one or more of the Piccadilly, Victoria or Northern lines and buses 30, 10, 46, 214 and 390. In terms of public transport it was possibly the greatest flat in London, but only in those terms. Emma could feel the tremors in her back as she lay on the bed that folded into a sofa, her tights some way down her thighs.

'What was that one?'

Ian listened to the tremor. 'Eastbound Piccadilly.'

'How do you stand it, Ian?'

'You get used to it. Also I've got these—' and he pointed towards two fat maggots of grey wax on the window ledge. 'Mouldable wax ear-plugs.'

'Oh that's nice.'

''Cept I forgot to take them out the other day. Thought I had a brain tumour. All got a bit Children-of-a-Lesser-God, if you know what I mean.'

Emma laughed, then groaned as another bubble of nausea was released. He took her hand.

'Feeling any better?'

'I'm fine as long as I keep my eyes open.' She turned to look at him, pushing down the folds of the duvet to see his face and noting a little queasily that the duvet had no cover and was the colour of mushroom soup. The room smelt like a charity shop, the odour of men who live alone. 'I think it was the second brandy that did it.' He smiled, but the white light from a passing bus swept the room, and she could see that he looked troubled. 'Are you angry with me?'

'Course not. It's just, you know, you're kissing a girl and she breaks off because she's nauseous . . .'

'I told you, only because of the booze. I'm having a lovely time, really I am. I just need to catch my breath. Come here—' She sat to kiss him, but her best bra had rucked up so that the underwiring was digging into her armpit. 'Ow, ow, ow!' She hauled it back into place, then slumped forwards with her head between her knees. His hand was rubbing her back now, like a nurse and she felt embarrassed for spoiling everything. 'I'd better head off, I think.'

'Oh. Okay. If that's what you want.'

They listened to the sound of tyres on the wet street, white light scanning the room.

'That one?'

'Number 30.'

She hauled at her tights, then stood unsteadily and twisted her skirt round. 'I've had a lovely time!'

'Me too—'

'Just too much booze—'

'Me too—'

'I'll go home and sober up—'

'I understand. Still. It's a shame.'

She looked at her watch. 11.52 p.m. Beneath her feet a tube train rumbled by, reminding her that she stood in the dead centre of a remarkable transport hub. Five minutes walk to King's Cross, Piccadilly Westbound, home by 12.30 easy. There was rain on the windowpane, but not much.

But she imagined the walk at the other end, the silence of the empty flat as she fumbled with the keys, her wet clothes sticking to her back. She imagined herself alone in bed, the ceiling spinning, the Tahiti bucking beneath her, nauseous, regretful. Would it really be the worst thing to stay here, to have some warmth, affection, intimacy for a change? Or did she really want to be one of those girls she saw sometimes on the tube: hungover, pale and fretful in last night's party dress? Rain blew against the windows, a little harder this time.

'Want me to walk you to the station?' said Ian, tucking in his t-shirt. 'Or maybe—'

'What?'

'You could stay over, sleep it off here? Just, you know, cuddles.'

'"Cuddles".'

'Cuddles, hugs. Or not even that. We could just lie rigid with embarrassment all night if you like.'

She smiled, and he smiled back, hopefully.

'Contact lens solution,' she said. 'I don't have any.'

'I do.'

'I didn't know you wore contact lenses.'

'There you go then – something else we've got in common.' He smiled and she smiled back. 'Might even have a spare pair of wax ear-plugs if you're lucky.'

'Ian Whitehead. You old smoothie, you.'

'. . . *pick up, pick up, pick up. Nearly midnight now. At the stroke of midnight I will turn into a, what, I don't know, an idiot probably. So anyway, if you get this . . .*'

'*Hello? Hello?*'

'*You're there!*'

'*Hello, Dexter.*'

'*I didn't wake you, did I?*'

'*Just got in. Are you alright, Dexter?*'

'*Oh, I'm fine.*'

'*Because you sound pretty wasted.*'

'*Oh I'm just having a party. Just me. A little private party.*'

'*Turn the music down, will you?*'

'*Actually I just wondered . . . hold on, I'll turn the music down . . . if you wanted to come round. There's champagne,*' *there's music, there might even be some drugs. Hello? Hello, are you there?'*

'I thought we decided this wasn't a good idea.'

'Did we? Because I think it's a great idea.'

'You can't just phone up out of the blue and expect me to—'

'Oh come on, Naomi, please? I need you.'

'No!'

'You could be here in half an hour.'

'No! It's pouring with rain.'

'I didn't mean walk. Get a cab, I'll pay.'

'I said no!'

'I really need to see someone, Naomi.'

'So call Emma!'

'Emma's out. And not that kind of company. You know what I mean. The fact is, if I don't touch another human being tonight I think I actually might die.'

'—'

'I know you're there. I can hear you breathing.'

'Okay.'

'Okay?'

'I'll be there in half an hour. Stop drinking. Wait for me.'

'Naomi? Naomi, do you realise?'

'What?'

'Do you realise that you are saving my life?'

CHAPTER EIGHT
Showbusiness

FRIDAY 15 JULY 1994

Leytonstone and the Isle of Dogs

Emma Morley eats well and drinks only in moderation. She gets eight good hours sleep, then wakes promptly and of her own accord at just before six-thirty and drinks a large glass of water – the first 250ml of a daily 1.5 litres, which she pours from the matching glass and carafe set that stands in a shaft of morning sunlight by her double bed.

The clock radio clicks on and she allows herself to lie in bed and listen to the news headlines. The Labour leader John Smith has died, and there's a report on his memorial service at Westminster Abbey; respectful cross-party tributes, 'the greatest Prime Minister we never had', discreet speculation on who will replace him. Once again she reminds herself to look into the possibility of joining the Labour Party, now that her CND membership has long since lapsed.

More of the endless World Cup news forces her out of bed, throwing off the summer duvet, putting on her old thick-rimmed spectacles and sliding into the tiny corridor of space between the bed and the walls. She heads towards the tiny bathroom and opens the door.

'One minute!!' She pulls the door closed again, but not fast enough to prevent herself from seeing Ian Whitehead doubled over on the toilet.

'Why don't you lock it, Ian?' she shouts at the door.
'Sorry!'

Emma turns, pads back to bed and lies there listening grumpily to the farming forecast and, in the background, the flush of a toilet, then another flush, then a honking sound as Ian blows his nose, then another flush. Eventually he appears in the doorway, red-faced and martyred. He is wearing no underwear and a black t-shirt that stops a little above his hips. There isn't a man in the world that can carry off this look, but even so Emma makes a conscious effort to keep her eyes focussed on his face, as he slowly blows air out through his mouth.

'Well. That was quite an experience.'

'Not feeling any better then?' She removes her spectacles, just to be on the safe side.

'Not really,' he pouts, his hands rubbing his stomach. 'I've got an upset tummy now.' He talks in a low, pained voice and even though Emma thinks Ian is terrific there's something about the word 'tummy' that makes her want to close the door sharply on his face.

'I told you that bacon was off, but you wouldn't listen to me—'

'It's not that—'

'Oh no, bacon doesn't go off you say. Bacon's cured.'

'I think it's a virus—'

'Well maybe it's that bug that's going round. They've all got it at school, maybe I gave it to you.'

He doesn't contradict her. 'Been up all night. Feel rotten.'

'I know you do, sweetheart.'

'Diarrhoea on top of catarrh—'

'It's a winning combination. Like moonlight and music.'

'And I hate having summer colds.'

'It's not your fault,' says Emma, sitting up.

'I reckon it's gastric flu,' he says, relishing the pairing of words.

'Sounds like gastric flu.'

'I feel so . . .' Fists clenched, he searches for the word that sums up the injustice of it all. 'So – bunged up! I can't go to work like this.'

'So don't.'

'But I've got to go.'

'So go.'

'I can't, can I? It feels like I've got two pints of mucus right here.' He spreads his hand across the width of his forehead. 'Two pints of thick phlegm.'

'Well there's an image to carry me through the day.'

'Sorry, but that's how I feel.' He squeezes round the edge of the bed to his side, and with another martyred sigh, climbs beneath the duvet.

She gathers herself before standing. Today is a big day for Emma Morley, a monumental day, and she can do without this. Tonight is the premiere of Cromwell Road Comprehensive School's production of *Oliver!* and the potential for disaster is almost infinite.

It's a big day for Dexter Mayhew too. He lies in a tangle of damp sheets, eyes wide, and imagines all of the things that might go wrong. Tonight he is appearing on live national television in his very own TV show. A vehicle. It's a vehicle for his talents, and he is suddenly not sure that he possesses any.

The previous evening he went to bed early like a small boy, alone and sober while it was still light outside in the hope of being fresh-faced and quick-witted this morning. But he has been awake for seven of the nine hours now, and is exhausted and nauseous with anxiety. The phone rings and he sits up sharply and listens to his own voice on the answering machine. 'So – talk to me!' the voice says, urbane and confident, and he thinks *Idiot. Must change message*.

The machine beeps. 'Oh. Okay then. Hi there. It's me.' He feels the familiar relief at the sound of Emma's voice, and is about to pick it up when he remembers that they've argued and he is meant to be sulking. 'Sorry to call so early and all that, but some of us have proper jobs to go to. Just wanted to say, big night tonight so really, really good luck. Seriously, good luck.

You'll be fine, more than fine, you'll be great. Just wear something nice and don't talk in that weird voice. And I know you're annoyed with me for not coming but I'll be watching and cheering at the TV like some idiot—'

He is out of bed now, naked, staring at the machine. He contemplates picking up.

'I don't know what time I'll get back, you know how wild these school plays can get. This crazy business we call show. I'll call later. Good luck, Dex. Loads of love. And by the way, you've *got* to change that answering machine message.'

And she's gone. He contemplates calling straight back, but feels that tactically he ought to sulk a little longer. They have argued again. She thinks that he doesn't like her boyfriend, and despite his passionate denials there's no getting over the fact that he doesn't like her boyfriend.

He has tried, really he has. The three of them have sat together in cinemas and cheap restaurants and dingy old boozers, Dexter meeting Emma's eyes and smiling his approval as Ian snuffles at her neck; love's young dream with a pair of pints. He has sat at the tiny kitchen table of her tiny Earls Court flat and played a game of Trivial Pursuit so savagely competitive that it was like bare-knuckle boxing. He has even joined the blokes from Sonicotronics at The Laughter Lab in Mortlake to watch Ian's observational stand-up, Emma grinning nervously at his side and nudging him so that he knows when to laugh.

But even on his best behaviour the hostility is tangible, and mutual too. Ian takes every opportunity to imply that Dexter is a fake because he happens to be in the public eye, a snob, a fop just because he prefers taxis to night buses, members' clubs to saloon bars, good restaurants to take-away. And the worst of it is that Emma joins in with the constant belittling, the reminders of his failings. Don't they appreciate how hard it is, staying decent, keeping your head on straight when so much is happening to you and your life is so full and eventful? If Dexter picks up the bill at dinner, or offers to pay for a taxi instead of the bus, the two of them mumble and mope as if he has insulted them in some way. Why can't people be pleased that he's doing so well, grateful for his generosity? That last excruciating evening – a 'vid night' on a decrepit sofa, watching *Star Trek: Wrath of Khan* and drinking 'tinnies' while a curry leaked fluorescent ghee onto his Dries van Noten trousers – that was the last straw. From now on if he's going to see Emma, then he's going to see her alone.

Irrationally, unreasonably, he has become – what? Jealous? No, not jealous, but resentful perhaps. He has always expected Emma to be there, a resource he can call upon at any time like the emergency services. Since the cataclysm of his mother's death last Christmas he has found himself more and more reliant on her at exactly the point that she has become less available to him. She used to return phone-calls immediately, now days go by without a word. She's been 'away with Ian' she says, but where do they go? What do they do? Buy furniture together? Watch 'vids'? Go to pub quizzes? Ian has even met Emma's parents, Jim and Sue. They love him, she says. Why has Dexter never met Jim and Sue? Wouldn't they love him more?

Most annoyingly of all, Emma seems to be relishing this new-found independence from Dexter. He feels as if he's being taught a lesson, as if he's being slapped round the face with her new-found contentment. 'You can't expect people to build their lives around you, Dexter,' she has told him, gloatingly, and now they've argued once again, and all because she won't be there in the studio for the live broadcast of his show.

'What do you want me to do, cancel *Oliver!* because you're on telly?'

'Can't you come along afterwards?'

'No! It's miles!'

'I'll send a car!'

'I need to talk to the kids afterwards, the parents—'

'Why do you?'

'Dexter, be reasonable, it's my job!'

And he knows he's being churlish, but it would help to see Emma in the audience. He's a better person when she's around, and isn't that what friends are for, to raise you up and keep you at your best? Emma is his talisman, his lucky charm, and now she won't be there and his mother won't be there and he will wonder why he's doing it at all.

After a long shower he feels a little better and pulls on a light v-neck cashmere sweater worn with no shirt, some pale linen drawstring trousers worn with no underpants, steps into a pair of Birkenstocks and bounds down to the paper-shop to read the TV previews and check that Press and Publicity have been doing their job. The newsagent smiles at his celebrity customer with a due sense of occasion, and Dexter trots home with his arms full of newspapers. He feels better now, full of trepidation but exhilarated too, and while the espresso machine is warming up, the phone rings once again.

Even before the machine picks up something tells him that it will be his father and that he will screen the call. Since his mother's death the calls have become more frequent and more excruciating: stuttering, circular and distracted. His father, the self-made man, now seems defeated by the simplest of tasks. Bereavement has unmanned him and on Dexter's rare visits home he has seen him staring helplessly at the kettle as if it were some alien technology.

'So – talk to me!' says the idiot on the machine.

'Hello, Dexter, it's your father here.' He uses his ponderous phone voice. 'I am just phoning to say good luck for your television show tonight. I will be watching. It's all very exciting. Alison would have been very proud.' There's a momentary pause as they both realise that this probably isn't true. 'That's all I wanted to say. Except. Also, don't pay any attention to the news-papers. Just have fun. Goodbye. Goodbye—'

Don't pay any attention to the *what*? Dexter grabs at the phone.

'—Goodbye!'

His father has gone. He has set the timer on the explosives then hung up, and Dexter looks across at the pile of newspapers, now full of menace. He tightens the drawstring on his linen trousers and turns to the TV pages.

When Emma steps from the bathroom, Ian is on the phone and she can tell from the flirty, larky tone of his voice that he is talking to her mother. Her boyfriend and Sue have been conducting a borderline affair ever since they met in Leeds at Christmas: 'Lovely sprouts, Mrs M' and 'Isn't this turkey moist?' It's electric, the mutual longing between them and all Emma and her dad can do is tut and roll their eyes.

She waits patiently for Ian to tear himself away. 'Bye, Mrs M. Yeah I hope so too. It's just a summer cold, I'll pull through. Bye, Mrs M. Bye.' Emma takes the receiver as Ian, mortally ill once more, shuffles back to bed.

Her mother is flushed and giddy. 'Such a lovely lad. Isn't he a lovely lad?'

'He is, Mum.'

'I hope you're looking after him.'

'I've got to go to work now, Mum.'

'Now, why was I calling? I've completely forgotten why I was calling.'

She was calling to talk to Ian. 'Was it to wish me good luck?'

'Good luck for what?'

'The school production.'

'Oh yes, good luck for that. Sorry we can't come down to see it. It's just London's so expensive . . .'

Emma ends the phone-call by pretending that the toaster is on fire then goes to see the patient, sweltering beneath the duvet in an attempt to 'sweat it out'. Part of her is vaguely aware of failing as a girlfriend. It's a new role for her, and she sometimes finds herself plagiarising 'girlfriend behaviour': holding hands, cuddling up in front of the television, that kind of thing. Ian loves her, he tells her so, if anything a little too often, and she thinks she may be able to love him back, but it will take some practice. Certainly she intends to try and now, in a self-conscious gesture of sympathy, she curls herself around him on the bed.

'If you don't think you can come to the show tonight—'

He sits up, alarmed. 'No! No, no, no, I'm definitely coming—'

'I'll understand—'

'—if I have to come by ambulance.'

'It's only a silly school play, it's going to be so embarrassing.'

'Emma!' She lifts her head to look at him. 'It's your big night! I wouldn't miss it for the world.'

She smiles. 'Good. I'm pleased.' She leans and kisses him anti-septically with closed lips, then picks up her bag and pads out of the flat, ready for her big day.

The headline reads:

IS THIS THE MOST ODIOUS MAN ON TELEVISION?

– and for a while Dexter thinks there must be a mistake, because beneath the headline they have accidentally printed his picture, and beneath that the single word 'Smug' as if Smug were his surname. Dexter Smug.

With the tiny espresso cup pinched tight between finger and thumb, he reads on.

Tonight's TV

Is there a more smug, self-satisfied smart-arse than Dexter Mayhew on TV today? A subliminal burst of his cocky, pretty-boy face makes us want to kick the screen in. At school we had a phrase for it: here's a man who clearly thinks he's IT. Weirdly, someone out there in MediaLand must love him as much as he loves himself because after three years of *largin' it* (dontcha hate that lower case? So 1990) he's now presenting his own late-night music show, the *Late-Night Lock-In*. So

He should stop reading here, just close the paper and move on, but his peripheral vision has already glimpsed a word or two. 'Inept' was one. He reads on –

So if you really want to see a public schoolboy trying to be a new lad, dropping his aitches and flirting with the ladeez, trying to stay hip with the kidz unaware that the kidz are laughing at him, then this one is for you. It's live, so there might be some pleasure in watching his famously inept interviewing technique, or alternatively you could brand your face with a steam iron set to 'linen'. Co-presenter is 'bubbly' Suki Meadows, music from Shed Seven, Echobelly and the Lemonheads. Don't say you weren't warned.

Dexter has a clippings file, a Patrick Cox shoebox in the bottom of a wardrobe, but he decides to let this one go. With a great deal of clatter and mess he makes himself another espresso.

Tall poppy syndrome that's what it is, the British Disease, he thinks. *A little bit of success and they want to knock you down well I don't care I like my job and I'm bloody good at it and it's much much harder than people think balls of steel that's what you need to be a TV presenter and a mind like a like a well quick-thinking anyway and besides you mustn't take it personally critics who needs critics no-one ever woke up and decided they wanted to be a critic well I'd rather be out there doing it putting myself on the line rather than be some some eunuch being spiteful for twelve grand a year well no-one ever built a statue to a critic and I'll show them I'll show them all.*

Variations of this monologue run through Dexter's head throughout his big day; on his trip to the production office, during his chauffeured drive in the saloon car to the studio on the Isle of Dogs, throughout the afternoon's dress rehearsal, the production meeting, the hair and make-up sessions, right up until the moment when he is alone in his dressing room and is finally able to open his bag, take out the bottle he placed there that morning, pour himself a large glass of vodka, top it up with warm orange juice and proceed to drink.

'Fight, fight, fight, fight, fight—'

Forty-five minutes to go before curtain up, and the chanting can be heard the whole length of the English block.

'Fight, fight, fight—'

Hurrying up the corridor, Emma sees Mrs Grainger stumble from the dressing room as if fleeing a fire. 'I've tried to stop them, they won't listen to me.'

'Thank you, Mrs Grainger, I'm sure I can handle it.'

'Should I get Mr Godalming?'

'I'm sure it'll be fine. You go and rehearse the band.'

'I said this was a mistake.' She hurries away, hand to her chest. 'I said it would never work.'

Emma takes a deep breath, enters and sees the mob, thirty teenagers in top hats and hooped skirts and stick-on beards shouting and jeering as the Artful Dodger kneels on Oliver Twist's arms and presses his face hard into the dusty floor.

'WHAT is going on here, people?'

The Victorian mob turns. 'Get her off me, Miss,' mumbles Oliver into the lino.

'They're fighting, Miss,' says Samir Chaudhari, twelve years old with mutton chop sideburns.

'I can see that thank you, Samir,' and she pushes through the crowd to pull them apart. Sonya Richards, the skinny black girl who plays The Dodger, still has her fingers tangled in the flicked blond bangs of Oliver's hair, and Emma holds onto her shoulders and stares into her eyes. 'Let go, Sonya. Let go now, okay? Okay?' Eventually Sonya lets go and steps back, her eyes moistening now that the rage is leeching away, replaced by wounded pride.

Martin Dawson, the orphan Oliver, looks dazed. Five feet eleven and stocky, he is bigger even than Mr Bumble, but nevertheless the meaty waif looks close to tears. 'She started it!' he quavers between bass and treble, wiping his smudgy face with the heel of his hand.

'That's enough now, Martin.'

'Yeah, shut your face, Dawson . . .'

'I mean it, Sonya. Enough!' Emma stands in the centre of the circle now, holding the adversaries by the elbows like a boxing referee, and she realises that if she is to save the show she is going to have to improvise a rousing speech, one of the many Henry V moments that make up her working life.

'Look at you! Look at how great you all look in your costumes! Look at little Samir there with his massive sideburns!' The crowd laugh, and Samir plays along, scratching at the stuck-on hair. 'You've got friends and parents outside and they're all going to see a great show, a real performance. Or at least I thought they were.' She folds her arms, and sighs, 'Because I think we're going to have to cancel the show . . .'

She's bluffing of course, but the effect is perfect, a great communal groan of protest.

'But we didn't do anything, Miss!' protests Fagin.

'So who was shouting fight, fight, fight, Rodney?'

'But she just went completely ape-shit, Miss!' warbles Martin Dawson, and now Sonya is straining to get at him.

'Oi, Oliver, do you want some *more*?'

There's laughter, and Emma pulls out the old triumph against the odds speech. 'Enough! You lot are meant to be a company, not a mob! You know I don't mind telling you there are people out there tonight who don't think you can do this! They don't think you're capable, they think it's too complicated for you.

It's Charles Dickens, Emma! they say, they're not bright enough, they haven't got the discipline to work together, they're not up to *Oliver!*, give them something nice and easy.'

'Who said that, Miss?' says Samir, ready to key their car.

'It doesn't matter who said it, it's what they think. And maybe they're right! Maybe we should call the whole thing off!' For a moment, she wonders if she's over-egging it, but it's hard to overestimate the teenage appetite for high drama, and there's a great moan of protest from all of them in their bonnets and top hats. Even if they know she's faking, they are relishing the jeopardy. She pauses for effect. 'Now. Sonya and Martin and I are going to go and have a little talk, and I want you to continue to get ready, then sit quietly and think about your part, and then we'll decide what to do next. Okay? I said okay?'

'Yes, Miss!'

The dressing room is silent as she follows the adversaries out, bursting into noise again the moment she closes the door. She escorts Oliver and The Dodger down the corridor, past the sports hall where Mrs Grainger leads the band through a fiercely dissonant 'Consider Yourself' and she wonders once again what she is letting herself in for.

She talks to Sonya first. 'So. What happened?'

Evening light slants in through the large reinforced windows of 4D, and Sonya stares out at the science block, affecting boredom. 'We just had words, that's all.' She sits on the edge of a desk, her long legs swinging in old school trousers slashed into tatters, tin-foil buckles stuck onto black trainers. One hand picks at her BCG scar, her small, hard, pretty face bunched up tight as a fist as if to warn Emma off trying any of that seize-the-day crap. The other kids are frightened of Sonya Richards, and even Emma sometimes fears for her dinner money. It's the level stare, the rage. 'I'm not saying sorry,' she snaps.

'Why not? And please don't say "he started it".'

Her face opens with indignation. 'But he did!'

'Sonya!'

'He said—' She stops herself.

'What did he say? Sonya?'

Sonya makes a calculation, weighing up the dishonour of telling tales against her sense of injustice. 'He said the reason I could play the part was 'cause it wasn't really acting because I was a peasant in real life too.'

'A peasant.'

'Yeah.'

'That's what Martin said?'

'S'what he said, so I hit him.'

'Well.' Emma sighs and looks at the floor. 'The first thing to say is that it doesn't matter what anyone says, ever, you can't just hit people.' Sonya Richards is her project. She knows she shouldn't really have projects, but Sonya is so clearly smart, the smartest in her class by some way but aggressive too, a whip-thin figure of resentment and wounded pride.

'But he's such a little prick, Miss!'

'Sonya, please, don't!' she says, though a little part of her thinks that Sonya has a valid point about Martin Dawson. He treats the kids, the teachers, the whole comprehensive system as if he were a missionary who has deigned to walk among them. Last night at the dress rehearsal he had cried real tears during 'Where is Love?', squeezing the high notes out like kidney stones, and Emma had found herself idly wondering what it would feel like to walk on stage, place one hand over his face and push him firmly backwards. The peasant remark is entirely in character, but even so –

'If that is what he said—'

'It is, Miss—'

'I'll talk to him and find out, but if it is what he said it just reveals how ignorant he is, and how daft you are too, for rising to it.' She stumbles on 'daft', an Ilkley Moor word. Street, be more street, she tells herself. 'But, hey, if we can't settle this . . . *beef*, then we really can't do the show.'

167

Sonya's face tightens again, and Emma is startled to notice that she seems as if she might cry. 'You wouldn't do that.'

'I might have to.'

'Miss!'

'We can't do the show, Sonya.'

'We can!'

'What, with you bitch-slapping Martin during "Who Will Buy"?' Sonya smiles despite herself. 'You are smart, Sonya, so so smart, but people set these traps for you and you walk right into them.' Sonya sighs, sets her face and looks out at the small rectangle of parched grass outside the science block. 'You could do so well, not just in the play but in class too. Your work this term's been really intelligent and sensitive and thoughtful.' Unsure how to deal with praise, Sonya sniffs and scowls. 'Next term you could do even better, but you've got to control your temper, Sonya, you've got to show people you're better than that.' It's another speech, and Emma sometimes thinks she expends too much energy making speeches like this. She had hoped that it might have some kind of inspirational effect, but Sonya's gaze has drifted over Emma's shoulder now, towards the classroom door. 'Sonya, are you listening to me?'

'Beard's here.'

Emma glances round and sees a dark-haired face at the door's glass panel, two eyes peering through like a curious bear. 'Don't call him Beard. He's the headmaster,' she tells Sonya, then beckons him in. But it's true, the first, and second words that enter her head whenever she sees Mr Godalming are 'beard'. It's one of those startling full-face affairs: not straggly, cut very close and neat but very, very black, a Conquistador, his blue eyes peeping out like holes cut in carpet. So he is The Beard. As he enters Sonya starts to scratch at her chin and Emma widens her eyes in warning.

'Evening all,' he calls, in his jaunty out-of-hours voice. 'How's it going? Everything alright, Sonya?'

'Bit hairy, sir,' says Sonya, 'but I think we'll be okay.'

Emma snuffles, and Mr Godalming turns to her. 'Everything alright, Emma?'

'Sonya and I were just having a little pre-show pep-talk. Do you want to go and carry on getting ready, Sonya?' With a smile of relief, she pushes herself off the desk and saunters to the door. 'Tell Martin I'll be two minutes.'

Emma and Mr Godalming are alone.

'Well!' he smiles.

'Well.'

In a fit of informality Mr Godalming goes to sit astride a chair, showbiz-style, appearing to change his mind halfway through the action before deciding that there's no going back. 'Bit of a handful, that Sonya.'

'Oh, just bravado.'

'I heard reports of a fight.'

'That was nothing. Pre-show nerves.' Straddling his chair, he really does look fantastically uncomfortable.

'I heard your protégé has been laying into our future head-boy.'

'Youthful high spirits. And I don't think Martin was completely innocent.'

'Bitch-slapped was the phrase I heard.'

'You seem very well informed.'

'Well I am the headmaster.' Mr Godalming smiles through his balaclava, and Emma wonders if you looked long enough, would you actually be able to see the hair grow? What's going on under all that stuff? Might Mr Godalming actually be quite good-looking? He nods towards the door. 'I saw Martin in the corridor. He's very . . . emotional.'

'Well he's been in character for the last six weeks. He's taking a Method approach. I think if he could he'd have given himself rickets.'

'Is he any good?'

'God no, he's awful. An orphanage's the best place for him. You're welcome to jam bits of the programme in your ears during

169

"Where is Love?".' Mr Godalming laughs. 'Sonya's great though.'
The headmaster looks unconvinced. 'You'll see.'

He shifts uneasily on the chair. 'What can I expect tonight, Emma?'

'No idea. Could go either way.'

'Personally I'm more of a *Sweet Charity* man. Remind me, why couldn't we do *Sweet Charity*?'

'Well it's a musical about prostitution, so . . .'

Once more Mr Godalming laughs. He does this a lot with Emma, and others have noticed it too. There is gossip in the staffroom, dark murmurs about favouritism, and certainly he's looking at her very intently tonight. A moment passes, and she glances back towards the door where Martin Dawson peeks tearfully through the glass panel. 'I'd better have a word with Edith Piaf out there, before he goes off the rails.'

'Of course, of course.' Mr Godalming seems pleased to dismount the chair. 'Good luck tonight. My wife and I have been looking forward to it all week.'

'I don't believe that for a second.'

'It's true! You must meet her afterwards. Perhaps Fiona and I can have a drink with your . . . fiancé?'

'God, no, just boyfriend. Ian—'

'At the after-show drinks—'

'Beaker of dilute squash—'

'Cook's been to the cash-and-carry—'

'I hear rumours of mini kievs—'

'Teaching, eh?—'

'And people say it's not glamorous—'

'You look beautiful, Emma, by the way.'

Emma holds her arms out to the side. She is wearing makeup, just a little lipstick to go with a vintage floral dress which is dark pink and a little on the tight side perhaps. She looks down at her dress as if it has taken her by surprise, but really it's the remark that has thrown her. 'Ta very much!' she says, but he has noticed her hesitation.

A moment passes, and he looks towards the door. 'I'll send Martin in, shall I?'

'Please do.'

He heads to the door, then stops and turns. 'I'm sorry, have I broken some sort of professional code? Can I say that to a member of my staff? That they look nice?'

'Course you can,' she says, but both know that 'nice' was not the word he had used. The word was 'beautiful.'

'Excuse me, but I'm looking for the most odious man on television?' says Toby Moray from the doorway, in that whiny, pinched little voice of his. He's wearing a tartan suit and his on-screen make-up, his hair slick and oiled into a jokey quiff and Dexter wants to throw a bottle at him.

'I think you'll find that that's you who you're looking for, not me,' says Dexter, concise speech suddenly beyond him.

'Nice come-back, superstar,' says his co-presenter. 'So you saw the previews then?'

'Nope.'

'Because I can run off some photocopies for you—'

'Just one bad write-up, Toby.'

'You didn't read the *Mirror* then. Or the *Express*, *The Times* . . .'

Dexter pretends to be studying his running order. 'No-one ever built a statue of a critic.'

'True, but no-one built a statue of a TV presenter either.'

'Fuck off, Toby.'

'Ah, *le mot juste*!'

'Why are you here anyway?'

'To wish you luck.' He crosses, places his hands on Dexter's shoulders and squeezes. Round and waspish, Toby's role on the show is a kind of irreverent, say-anything jester figure and Dexter despises him, this jumped-up little warm-up man, and envies him too. In the pilot and in rehearsals he has run rings around Dexter, slyly mocking and deriding him, making him feel fat-tongued, slow-witted, doltish, the pretty boy who can't think on his feet. He shrugs Toby's hands away. This antagonism is meant to be the stuff of great TV they say, but Dexter feels paranoid, persecuted. He needs another vodka to recover some of his good spirits, but he can't, not while Toby's smirking at him in the mirror with his little owlish face. 'If you don't mind I'd like to gather my thoughts.'

'I understand. Focus that mind of yours.'

'See you out there, yeah?'

'See you, handsome. Good luck.' He pulls the door closed then opens it again. 'No, really. I mean it. Good luck.'

When Dexter's sure he's alone he pours himself that drink and checks himself in the mirror. Bright red t-shirt worn under black dinner jacket over washed out jeans over pointed black shoes, his hair cut short and sharp, he is meant to be the picture of metropolitan male youth but suddenly he feels old and tired and impossibly sad. He presses two fingers against each eye and attempts to account for this crippling melancholy, but is having trouble with rational thought. It feels as if someone has taken his head and shaken it. Words are turning to mush and he can see no plausible way of getting through this. Don't fall apart, he tells himself, not here, not now. Hold it together.

But an hour is an impossibly long time on live TV, and he decides that he might need a little help. There's a small water bottle on his dressing table, and he empties it into the sink then, glancing at the door, takes the bottle of vodka from the drawer once again and pours three, no, four inches of the viscous liquid into the bottle and replaces the lid. He holds it up to the light. No-one would ever tell the difference and of course he's not going to drink it all, but it's there, in his hand, to help him out and get him through. The deceit makes him feel excited and confident again, ready to show the viewing public, and Emma, and his father at home just what he can do. He is not just some presenter. He is a *broadcaster*.

The door opens. 'WAHEY!' says Suki Meadows, his co-presenter. Suki is the nation's ideal girlfriend, a woman for whom bubbliness is a way of life, verging on a disorder. Suki would probably start a letter of condolence with the word 'Wahey!' and Dexter might find this relentless perkiness a bit wearing if she weren't so attractive and popular and crazy about him.

'HOW ARE YOU, SWEETHEART? SHITTING BRICKS, I EXPECT!' and this is Suki's other great talent as a TV presenter, to hold every conversation as if she's addressing the Bank Holiday crowd on the sea-front at Weston-super-Mare.

'I am a little nervous, yes.'

'AWWWW! COME HERE YOU!' She wraps her arm around his head and holds it like a football. Suki Meadows is pretty and what used to be called petite, and fizzes and bubbles like a fan-heater dropped into a bath. There has been some flirtation between them recently, if you can call this flirtation, Suki pushing his face into her breast like this. Like a head-boy and head-girl, there has been some pressure for the two stars to get together, and it does sort of make sense from a professional, if not emotional point of view. She squeezes his head beneath her arm – 'YOU'RE GOING TO BE GREAT' – then suddenly holds onto his ears and jerks his face towards her. 'LISTEN TO ME. YOU'RE GORGEOUS, YOU KNOW THAT, AND WE ARE GOING TO BE SUCH A GREAT TEAM, YOU AND ME. MY MUM'S HERE TONIGHT AND SHE WANTS TO MEET YOU AFTERWARDS. BETWEEN ME AND YOU I THINK SHE FANCIES YOU. I FANCY YOU, SO SHE MUST FANCY YOU TOO. SHE WANTS YOUR AUTOGRAPH BUT YOU HAVE TO PROMISE NOT TO GET OFF WITH HER!'

'I'll do my best, Suki.'

'YOU GOT FAMILY IN?'

'No—'

'FRIENDS?'

'No—'

'WHAT DO YOU THINK OF THIS OUTFIT?' She's wearing

a clubby top and a tiny skirt, and carries the obligatory bottle of water. 'CAN YOU SEE MY NIPPLES?'

Is she flirting? 'Only if you look for them,' he flirts back mechanically, smiling weakly, and Suki senses something. She holds out his hands to the side and intimately bellows, 'WHAT'S UP WITH YOU, SWEETHEART?'

He shrugs. 'Toby's been in here, winding me up . . .' and before he can finish she has pulled him to his feet and her arms are round his waist, her hands twanging the waistband of his underpants in sympathy. 'YOU IGNORE HIM, HE'S JUST JEALOUS 'CAUSE YOU'RE BETTER AT THIS THAN HE IS.' She looks up at him, her chin poking his chest. 'YOU'RE A NATURAL, YOU KNOW YOU ARE.'

The floor manager is at the door. 'Ready for you now, guys.'

'WE'RE GREAT TOGETHER, AREN'T WE, ME AND YOU. SUKI AND DEX, DEX AND SUKI? WE'RE GOING TO KNOCK EM DEAD.' Suddenly she kisses him once, very hard, as if rubber-stamping a document. 'MORE OF THAT LATER, GOLDEN BOY,' she says in his ear, then picks up her bottle of water and bounds out onto the studio floor.

Dexter takes a moment to look at his reflection in the mirror. *Golden Boy*. He sighs and presses all ten fingers hard into his skull and tries not to think about his mother. Hold it together, don't foul this up. Be good. Do something good. He smiles the smile that he keeps especially for use on television, picks up his spiked water bottle, and heads out onto the studio floor.

Suki waits for him at the edge of the immense set, taking his hand and squeezing it. The crew are running round, patting his shoulder and punching his arm matily as they pass, and high above their heads ironic go-go dancers in bikinis and cowboy boots stretch out their calves in their ironic cages. Toby Moray is doing the warm-up, and getting big laughs too, until suddenly he's introducing them, a big hand please for your hosts tonight, Suki Meadows and Dexter Mayhew!

He doesn't want to go. Music thumps from the speakers: 'Start the Dance' by The Prodigy, and he wants to stay here in the wings, but Suki is tugging on his hand, and suddenly she is bounding out into the bright studio lights, bawling:

'ALLLLLLLLLLLRIGGGGGGGHHHHHT!'

Dexter follows on, the suave and urbane half of the presenting duo. As always the set involves a lot of scaffolding, and they climb the ramps until they're looking down at the audience below them, Suki chattering all the way: 'LOOK AT YOU, YOU'RE ALL GORGEOUS, ARE YOU READY TO HAVE A GREAT TIME? MAKE SOME NOISE!' Dexter stands mute on the gantry next to her, the microphone dead in his hand as he realises that he is drunk. His big break on live national television and he is sodden with vodka, dizzy with it. The gantry seems impossibly high, far higher than in rehearsals, and he wants to lie down but if he does this there's a chance that two million people will notice, so he assumes the manner and offers:

'Elloyoulothowareyouallfeelingalright?'

A single clear male voice sails up to the gantry. '*Wanker!*'

Dexter seeks out the heckler, a skinny, grinning twerp with Wonder Stuff hair, but it gets a laugh, a big laugh. Even the cameramen are laughing. 'My agent, ladies and gentlemen,' replies Dexter, and there's a ripple of amusement, but that's all. They must have read the papers. Is this the most odious man on television? Good God, it's true, he thinks. They hate me.

'One minute everyone,' shouts the floor manager, and Dexter suddenly feels like he's standing on a scaffold. He searches the crowd for a friendly face, but there are none and once again he wishes Emma were here. He could show-off for Emma, be at his best if Emma or his mother were here, but they're not, just this leering, jeering crowd of people much, much younger than himself. He has got to find a bit of spirit from somewhere, a bit of attitude and with the laser logic of the drunk he decides that alcohol might help, because why not? The damage is already done. The go-go dancers stand poised in their cages, the cameras glide into place, and he unscrews the lid of his illicit bottle, raises it, swallows and winces. Water. The water bottle contains water. Someone has replaced the vodka in his water bottle with—

Suki has his bottle.

Thirty seconds to air. She has picked up the wrong bottle. She is holding it in her hand now, a clubby little accessory.

Twenty seconds to air. She is unscrewing the lid.

'Are you keeping hold of that?' he squeaks.

'THAT'S ALRIGHT, ISN'T IT?' She bounces on her toes like a prizefighter.

'I've got your bottle by mistake.'

'SO? WIPE THE TOP!'

Ten seconds to air and the audience starts to cheer and roar, the dancers hold onto the bars of their cages and start to gyrate as Suki raises the bottle to her lips.

Seven, six, five . . .

He reaches for the bottle, but she knocks his hand away laughing.

'GET OFF, DEXTER, YOU'VE GOT YOUR OWN!'

Four, three, two . . .

'But it isn't water,' he says.

She gulps it down.

Roll titles.

And now Suki is coughing, red-faced and spluttering as guitars crash over the speakers, drums pound, go-go dancers writhe and a camera on wires swoops down from the high ceiling like a bird of prey, soaring over the audience's heads towards the presenters, so that it seems to the viewers at home as if three hundred young people are cheering an attractive woman as she stands on scaffolding and retches.

The music fades, and all you can hear is Suki coughing. Dexter has frozen, dried, dead on air and drunkenly crashing his own vehicle. The plane is going down, the ground looming up to meet him. 'Say something Dexter,' says a voice in his earpiece. 'Hello? Dexter? Say something?' but his brain won't work and his mouth won't work, and he stands there, dumb in every way. The seconds stretch.

But thank God for Suki, a true professional, wiping her mouth with the back of her hand. 'WELL PROOF THERE THAT WE'RE GOING OUT LIVE!' and there's a relieved little flurry of laughter from the audience. 'IT'S ALL GOING VERY WELL SO FAR, ISN'T IT, DEX?' She jabs him in the ribs with a finger, and he springs to life.

'Sorry about Suki there—' he says. 'The bottle's got vodka in it!' and he does the little comic wriggle of the wrist that suggests a secret drinker, and there's another laugh, and he feels better. Suki laughs too, nudges him and raises a fist, says, 'Why I oughta . . .' Three Stooges-style, and only he can see the glint of contempt behind the bubbliness. He latches onto the safety of the autocue.

'Welcome to the *Late-Night Lock-In*, I'm Dexter Mayhew—'

'—AND I'M SUKI MEADOWS!'

And they're back on course, introducing the Friday night feast of great comedy and music, appealing and attractive like the two coolest kids at school. 'So without further ado, let's make some noise please—' He flings his arm out behind him, like a ring-master '—and give a big *Late-Night Lock-In* welcome to Shed! Seven!'

The camera swoops away from them as if it has lost interest, and now the voices from the gallery are chattering in his head over the sound of the band. 'Everything alright there, Suki?' says the producer. Dexter looks at Suki pleadingly. She looks back, eyes narrowed. She could tell them: Dexter's on the booze, he's drunk, the man's a mess, an amateur, not to be trusted.

'All fine,' she says. 'Just went down the wrong way, that's all.'

'We'll send someone to fix your make-up. Two minutes, people. And Dexter, keep it together, will you?'

Yes, keep it together, he tells himself, but the monitors tell him there are fifty-six minutes and twenty-two seconds to go, and he's really not sure if he can.

* * *

Applause! Applause like she has never heard, rebounding off the walls of the sports hall. And yes, the band were flat and the singers sharp, and yes there were a few technical problems with missing props and collapsing sets, and of course it's hard to imagine a more forgiving audience, but still it is a triumph. The death of Nancy leaves even Mr Routledge, Chemistry, weeping and the chase over the London rooftops, with the cast in silhouette, is a spectacular coup de théâtre met by the kind of cooing and gasping that usually greets fireworks displays. As predicted Sonya Richards has shone, leaving Martin Dawson grinding his teeth as she soaks up the largest round of applause. There have been ovations and encores and now people are stamping on the benches and hanging off the climbing apparatus and Emma is being dragged on stage by Sonya who is crying, God, actually crying, clutching Emma's hand and saying well done, Miss, amazing, amazing. A school production, it is the smallest imaginable triumph but Emma's heart is beating in her chest and she can't stop grinning as the band play a cacophonous 'Consider Yourself' and she holds the hands of fourteen-year-olds and bows and bows again. She feels the elation of doing something well, and for the first time in ten weeks she no longer wants to kick Lionel Bart.

At the drinks afterwards, own-brand cola flows like wine, and there are also five bottles of sparkling perry to share among the adults. Ian sits in a corner of the sports hall with a plate of mini kievs and a plastic cup of Beecham's Powders that he has brought to the party specially, and he massages his sinuses, smiles and waits patiently as Emma soaks up the praise. 'Good enough for the West End!' someone says, somewhat unrealistically, and she doesn't even mind when Rodney Chance, her Fagin, boozy on spiked Panda Pops, tells her that she's 'pretty fit for a teacher'. Mr Godalming ('please, call me Phil') congratulates her while Fiona, ruddy-cheeked like a farmer's wife, looks on, bored and bad tempered. 'We should talk, in September, about your future here,' says Phil, leaning in and kissing her goodbye, causing some of the kids, and some of the staff, to make a 'whoooo' noise.

Unlike most showbusiness parties it's all over by nine forty-five, and instead of a stretch limo, Emma and Ian take the 55, the 19 and the Piccadilly Line home. 'I'm so proud of you—' says Ian, his head resting against hers '—but I think it's settled on my lungs.'

As soon as she enters the flat she can smell the flowers. The vast bouquet of red roses lolls in a casserole on the kitchen table.

'Oh my God, Ian, they're beautiful.'

'Not from me,' he mumbles.

'Oh. Who then?'

'Golden Boy, I expect. They came this morning. Completely over the top if you ask me. I'm going to have a hot bath. See if I can shift it.'

She removes her coat and opens the small card. 'Apologies for sulking. Hope it goes well tonight. Much love Dx'. That's all. She reads it twice, looks at her watch, and quickly turns on the TV to watch Dexter's big break.

Forty-five minutes later, as the final credits roll, she frowns and tries to make sense of what she has just seen. She doesn't know much about television, but she is pretty sure that Dexter hasn't shone. He has looked shaky, actually frightened some-times. Fluffing lines, looking at the wrong camera, he has seemed amateurish and inept and as if sensing his unease the people he has interviewed – the rapper on tour, the four cocky young Mancunians – have responded with disdain or sarcasm. The studio audience glares too, like surly teenagers at a pantomime, arms crossed high on their chests. For the first time since she met him he appears to be making an effort. Might he be, well, drunk? She doesn't know much about the media, but she can recognise a car crashing. By the time the last band plays out her hand has come to cover her face, and she knows enough about TV to know this is not ideal. There's a lot of irony about these days, but surely not to the extent that booing is good.

She turns the TV off. From the bathroom comes the sound of Ian honking into a flannel. She closes the door and picks up the phone, moulding her mouth into a congratulatory smile and in an empty flat in Belsize Park the answering machine picks up. 'So – talk to me!' says Dexter, and Emma goes into her act. 'Hey you! Hiya! I know you're at the party so just wanted to say, well first of all, thank you for the flowers. So beautiful, Dex, you shouldn't have. But mainly – Well! Done! You! You were fantastic, just really relaxed and funny, I thought it was fantastic, just a really, really, great, great show, really.' She hesitates: don't say 'really'. If you say 'really' too often it sounds like 'not-really'. She continues. 'I'm still not sure about that t-shirt-under-suit-jacket-thing, and it's always refreshing to see women dancing in cages, but Dexter, apart from that, it was just excellent. Really. I'm really so *proud* of you, Dex. In case you're interested, *Oliver!* went alright too.'

She senses her own performance is losing conviction now, and decides to bring it to a close.

'So. There you go. We've both got something to celebrate! Thanks again for the roses. Have a good night. Let's talk tomorrow. I'm seeing you Tuesday, is that right? And well done, you. Seriously. Well done you. Bye.'

At the party afterwards Dexter stands alone at the bar, arms crossed, shoulders hunched. People cross to congratulate him but no-one lingers long and the pats on the shoulder have come to feel like consolation or, at best, well done on missing that penalty. He has continued to drink steadily but the champagne seems stale in his mouth and nothing seems to lift the sense of disappointment, anti-climax, creeping shame.

'Wahey,' says Suki Meadows in a contemplative mood. Once the co-star, now clearly the star, she sits next to him. 'Look at you, all mean and moody.'

'Hey, Suki.'

'So! That went well, I thought!'

Dexter is unconvinced but they chink glasses just the same. 'Sorry about that . . . booze thing. I owe you an apology.'

'Yes you do.'

'It was just something to loosen me up, you know.'

'Still, we should talk about it. Some other time.'

'Okay.'

'Because I'm not going out there again with you off your tits, Dex.'

'I know. You won't. And I'll make it up to you.'

She leans her shoulder against his, and puts her chin on his shoulder. 'Next week?'

'Next week?'

'Buy me dinner. Somewhere expensive, mind. Next Tuesday.'

Her forehead is touching his now, her hand on his thigh. He was meant to be having dinner with Emma on Tuesday, but knows that he can always cancel Emma, she won't mind. 'Okay. Next Tuesday.'

'Can't wait.' She pinches his thigh. 'So. You gonna cheer up now?'

'I'll try.'

Suki Meadows leans over and kisses his cheek, then puts her mouth very, very close to his ear.

'NOW COME AND SAY HELLO TO MY MUUUUUUM!'

CHAPTER NINE
Cigarettes and Alcohol

SATURDAY, 15 JULY 1995

Walthamstow and Soho

Portrait In Crimson
A novel
by Emma T. Wilde

Chapter 1

  DCI Penny Something had seen some murder scenes in her
time, but never one as   as this.
    'Has the body been moved?' she snapped

The words glowed in bilious green on the word-processor's
screen: the product of a whole morning's work. She sat at the
tiny school desk in the tiny back room of the tiny new flat, read
the words, then read them again while behind her the immer-
sion heater gurgled in derision.

At weekends, or in the evenings if she could find the energy,
Emma wrote. She had made a start on two novels (one set in a
gulag, the other in a post-apocalyptic future), a children's picture
book, with her own illustrations, about a giraffe with a short
neck, a gritty, angry TV drama about social workers called
'Tough Shit', a fringe play about the complex emotional lives
of twenty-somethings, a fantasy novel for teenagers featuring
evil robot teachers, a stream-of-consciousness radio play about

a dying Suffragette, a comic strip and a sonnet. None had been completed, not even the fourteen lines of sonnet.

These words on the screen represented her latest project, an attempt at a series of commercial, discreetly feminist crime novels. She had read all of Agatha Christie at eleven years old, and later lots of Chandler and James M. Cain too. There seemed no reason why she shouldn't try writing something in between, but she was discovering once again that reading and writing were not the same – you couldn't just soak it up then squeeze it out again. She found herself unable to think of a name for her detective, let alone a cohesive original plot, and even her pseudonym was poor: Emma T. Wilde? She wondered if she was doomed to be one of those people who spend their lives *trying* things. She had tried being in a band, writing plays and children's books, she had tried acting and getting a job in publishing. Perhaps crime fiction was just another failed project to place alongside trapeze, Buddhism and Spanish. She used the computer's word-count feature. Thirty-five words, including the title page and her rotten pseudonym. Emma groaned, released the hydraulic lever on the side of her office chair and sank a little closer to the carpet.

There was a knock on the plywood door. 'How are things in the Anne Frank wing?'

That line again. For Ian, a joke was not a single-use item but something you brought out again and again until it fell apart in your hands like a cheap umbrella. When they had first started seeing each other, approximately ninety per cent of what Ian said came under the heading of 'humour' in that it involved a pun, a funny voice, some comic intent. Over time she had hoped to get this down to forty per cent, forty being a workable allowance, but nearly two years later the figure stood at seventy-five, and domestic life continued against this tinnitus of mirth. Was it really possible for someone to be 'on' for the best part of two years? She had got rid of his black bedsheets, the beer mats, secretly culled his underpants and there were fewer of his famous 'Summer Roasts', but even so she was reaching the limits of how much it's possible to change a man.

'Nice cup of tea for the lady?' he said, in the voice of a cockney char.

'No thanks, love.'

'Eggy bread?' Scottish now. 'Can ae do you some eggy bread, ma wee snootch?'

Snootch was a recent development. When pressed to justify himself, Ian had explained that it was because she was just so snootchy, so very, very snootch. There'd been a suggestion that she might reciprocate by calling him skootch; skootch and snootch, snootchy and skootchy, but it hadn't stuck.

'. . . wee slice of eggy bread? Line your stomach for tonight?'

Tonight. There it was. Often when Ian was working through his dialects it was because he had something on his mind that couldn't be said in a natural voice.

'Big night, tonight. Out on the town with Mike TV.'

She decided to ignore the remark, but he wasn't making it easy. His chin resting on her head, he read the words on the screen.

'*Portrait in Crimson . . .*'

She covered the screen with her hand. 'Don't read over my shoulder, please.'

'Emma T. Wilde. Who's Emma T. Wilde?'

'My pseudonym. Ian—'

'You know what the T stands for?'

'Terrible.'

'Terrific. Tremendous.'

'Tired, as in sick and—'

'If you ever want me to read it—'

'Why would you want to read it? It's crap.'

'Nothing you do is crap.'

'Well this is.' Twisting her head away, she clicked the monitor off and without turning round she knew he'd be doing his hangdog look. All too often this was how she found herself with

Ian, switching back and forth between irritation and remorse. 'Sorry!' she said, taking his hand by the fingers and shaking it.

He kissed the top of her head, then spoke into her hair. 'You know what I think it stands for? "The" as in "The Bollocks". Emma T. B. Wilde.'

With that, he left; a classic technique, compliment and run. Keen not to cave in straightaway, Emma pushed the door to, turned the monitor back on, read the words there, shuddered visibly, closed the file and dragged it to the icon of the waste-basket. An electronic crumpling noise, the sound of writing.

The squeal of the smoke alarm indicated that Ian was cooking. She stood and followed the smell of burning butter down the hall into the kitchen/diner; not a separate room, just the greasi-est quarter of the living room of the flat that they had bought together. Emma had been unsure about buying; it felt like the kind of place that the police get called to, she said, but Ian had worn her down. It was crazy to rent, they saw each other most nights anyway, it was near her school, a foot on the ladder etc. and so they had scraped together the deposit and bought some books on interior decoration, including one that told you how to paint plywood so that it looked like fine Italian marble. There had been inspirational talk of putting the fireplace back in, of bookshelves and fitted cupboards and storage solutions. Exposed floorboards! Ian would hire a sander and expose the floorboards as law demanded. On a wet Saturday in February they had lifted the carpet, peered despondently underneath at the mess of moul-dering chipboard, disintegrating underlay and old newspapers, then guiltily nailed it all back in place as if disposing of a corpse. There was something unpersuasive and impermanent about these attempts at home-making, as if they were children building a den, and despite the fresh paint, the prints on the walls, the new furni-ture, the flat retained its shabby, temporary air.

Now Ian stood in the kitchenette in a shaft of smoky sunlight with his broad back towards her. Emma watched him from the doorway, taking in the familiar old grey t-shirt with the holes in, an inch of his underpants visible above his track-suit bottoms, his 'tracky botts'. She could see the words Calvin Klein against the brown hair on the small of his back and it occurred to her that this was probably not at all what Calvin Klein had in mind.

She spoke to break the silence. 'Isn't that getting a bit burnt?'

'Not burnt, *crispy*.'

'I say burnt, you say crispy.'

'*Let's call the whole thing off!*'

Silence.

'I can see the top of your underpants,' she said.

'Yes, that's deliberate.' Lisping, effeminate voice. 'It's called fashion, sweetheart.'

'Well it's certainly very provocative.'

Nothing, just the sound of food burning.

But it was Ian's turn to cave this time. 'So. Where's Alpha Boy taking you then?' he said, without turning round.

'Somewhere in Soho, I don't know.' In fact she did know, but the restaurant's name was a recent by-word for modish, metropolitan dining and she didn't want to make matters worse. 'Ian, if you don't want me to go tonight—'

'No, you go, enjoy yourself—'

'Or if you want to come with us?—'

'What, Harry and Sally and me? Oh, I don't think so, do you?'

'You'd be very welcome.'

'The two of you bantering and talking over me all night—'

'We don't do that—'

'You did last time!'

'No, we didn't!'

'You're sure you don't want some eggy bread?'

'No!'

'And anyway, I've got a gig tonight, haven't I? House of Ha Ha, Putney.'

'A *paid* gig?'

'Yes, a *paid* gig!' he snapped. 'So I'm fine, thank you very much.'

He started searching noisily in the cupboard for some brown sauce. 'Don't you worry about me.'

Emma sighed irritably. 'If you don't want me to go, just say so.'

'Em, we're not joined at the hip. You go if you want. Enjoy yourself.' The sauce bottle wheezed consumptively. 'Just don't get off with him, will you?'

'Well that's hardly going to happen, is it?'

'No, so you keep saying.'

'He's going out with Suki Meadows.'

'But if he wasn't?'

'If he wasn't it wouldn't make the slightest bit of difference, because I love you.'

Still this wasn't enough. Ian said nothing and Emma sighed, crossed the kitchen, her feet sucking on the lino, and looped her arms around his waist, feeling him pull it in as she did so. Pressing her face against his back, she inhaled the familiar warm body smell, kissed the fabric of his t-shirt, mumbled 'Stop being daft' and they stood like this for a while, until it became clear that Ian was keen to start eating. 'Right. Better mark these essays,' she said, and walked away. Twenty-eight numbing opinions on viewpoint in *To Kill a Mockingbird*.

'Em?' he said as she reached the door. 'What are you doing this afty? Round about seventeen-hundred hours?'

'Should be finished. Why?'

He hitched himself up onto the kitchen units with the plate on his lap. 'Thought we might go to bed, for, you know, a bit of afternoon delight.'

I love him, she thought, I'm just not *in* love with him and also I don't love him. I've tried, I've strained to love him but I can't. I am building a life with a man I don't love, and I don't know what to do about it.

'Maybe,' she said from the doorway. 'May-be,' and she pouted her lips into a kiss, smiled and closed the door.

* * *

There were no more mornings, only mornings after.

Heart thumping, soaked with sweat, Dexter was woken just after midday by a man bellowing outside, but it turned out to be M People. He had fallen asleep in front of the television again, and was now being urged to search for the hero inside himself.

The Saturdays after the *Late-Night Lock-In* were always spent like this, in the stale air, blinds drawn against the sun. Had she still been around, his mother would have been shouting up the stairs for him to get up and do something with the day, but instead he sat smoking on the black leather sofa in last night's underpants, playing *Ultimate Doom* on the PlayStation and trying not to move his head.

By mid-afternoon he could feel weekend melancholy creep up on him and so decided to practise his mixing. Something of an amateur DJ, Dexter had a wallful of CDs and rare vinyl in bespoke pine racks, two turntables and a microphone, all tax-deductible, and could often be spotted in record shops in Soho, wearing an immense pair of headphones like halved coconuts. Still in his underpants, he mixed idly back and forth between break-beats on his brand new CD mixing decks in preparation for the next big-night-in with mates. But something was missing, and he soon gave up. 'CD's not vinyl,' he announced, then realised that he had said this to an entirely empty room.

Melancholy again, he sighed and crossed to the kitchen, moving slowly like a man recovering from surgery. The massive fridge was full to overflowing with bottles of an exciting new brand of upmarket cider. As well as presenting the show ('Car-crash television' they called it, apparently a good thing), he had recently expanded into voiceovers. He was 'classless' they said, also apparently a good thing, the exemplar of a new breed of British man: metropolitan, moneyed, not embarrassed by his masculinity, his sex-drive, his liking for cars and big titanium watches and gadgets in brushed steel. So far he had done voiceovers for this premium bottled cider, designed to appeal to a young Ted Baker-wearing crowd, and a new breed of men's razor, an extraordinary sci-fi object with a multitude of blades and a lubricating strip that left a mucal trail, as if someone had sneezed on your chin.

He had even dipped his toe into the world of modelling, a long-standing ambition that he had never dared to voice, and which he was quick to dismiss as 'just a bit of a laugh'. Only this month he had featured in a fashion spread in a men's magazine, the theme 'gangster-chic', and over nine pages he had chewed cigars or lain riddled with bullets in a number of tailored double-breasted suits. Copies of the magazine were accidentally scattered round the flat, so that guests might casually stumble upon it. There was even a copy by the toilet, and he sometimes found himself sitting there and staring at his own photo, dead but beautifully tailored and splayed across the bonnet of a Jag.

Presenting car-crash television was fine for a while, but you could only crash the car so many times. At some point in the future he would have to do something good as opposed to so-bad-it's-good, and in an attempt to acquire some credibility he had set up his own production company, Mayhem TV plc. At the moment Mayhem only existed as a stylish logo on some heavy stationery, but that would surely change. It would have to; as his agent Aaron had said, 'You're a great Youth Presenter, Dexy. Trouble is, you're not a Youth.' What else might he be capable of, given the breaks? Acting? He knew a lot of actors, both professionally and socially, played poker with a few of them, and frankly if *they* could do it . . .

Yes, professionally and socially, the last couple of years had been a time of opportunity, of great new mates, canapés and premieres, helicopter rides and a lot of yammering about football. There had been low points of course: a sense of anxiety and crippling dread, one or two instances of public vomiting. There was something about his presence in a bar or club that made other men want to shout abuse or even hit him, and recently he had been bottled off-stage while introducing a Kula Shaker concert – that was no fun. In a recent what's hot and what's not column, he had been listed as not-hot. This not-hotness had weighed heavily on his mind, but he tried to dismiss it as envy. Envy was just the tax you paid on success.

There had been other sacrifices on his part. Regretfully he had been obliged to shuffle off some old friends from University, because after all it wasn't 1988 anymore. His old flatmate Callum, the one he was meant to start a business with, continued to leave increasingly sarcastic messages, but Dexter hoped he'd get the idea soon. What were you meant to do, all live in a big house together for the rest of your lives? No, friends were like clothes: fine while they lasted but eventually they wore thin or you grew out of them. With this in mind, he had adopted a three-in, one-out policy. In place of the old friends he had let go, he had taken on thirty, forty, fifty more successful, better-looking friends. It was impossible to argue with the sheer volume of friends, even if he wasn't sure he actually liked all of them. He was famous, no, notorious for his cocktails, his reckless generosity, his DJ-ing and his after-after-show parties back at his flat, and many were the mornings that he had woken in the smoky wreckage to find that his wallet had been stolen.

Never mind. There had never been a better time to be young, male, successful and British. London was buzzing and he felt as if this was somehow down to him. A VAT-registered man in possession of a modem and a mini-disk player, a famous girlfriend and many, many cufflinks, he owned a fridge full of premium cider and a bathroom full of multi-bladed razors, and though he disliked cider and the razors gave him a rash, life was pretty good here, with the blinds down in the middle of the afternoon, in the middle of the year, in the middle of the decade, close to the centre of the most exciting city on earth.

The afternoon stretched before him. Soon it would be time to call his dealer. There was a party tonight in a huge house off Ladbroke Grove. He had to see Emma for dinner first, but could probably get rid of her by eleven.

* * *

Emma lay in the avocado bathtub and heard the front door close as Ian set off on the long journey to the House of Ha Ha in Putney to perform his stand-up act: fifteen unhappy minutes on some differences between cats and dogs. She reached for her glass of wine on the bathroom floor, held it in both hands and frowned at the mixer taps. It was remarkable how quickly the glee of home ownership had faded, how insubstantial and tatty their combined possessions seemed in the small flat with its thin walls and someone else's carpets. It wasn't that the place was dirty – every single surface had been scrubbed with a wire-brush – but it retained an unnerving stickiness and a smell of old cardboard that seemed impossible to shift. On their first night, after the front door had closed and the champagne had been opened, she had felt like bursting into tears. It's bound to take time before it feels like our home, Ian had said as he held her in bed that night, and at least they had their foot on the ladder. But the idea of scaling that ladder together, rung by rung over the years, filled her with a terrible gloom. And what was at the top?

Enough of this. Tonight was meant to be a special occasion, a celebration, and she hauled herself from the bathtub, brushed and flossed her teeth until her gums were sore, sprayed herself liberally with an invigorating floral woodiness, then searched her sparse wardrobe for an outfit that didn't make her look like Miss Morley the English teacher on a night out with her famous friend. She decided on some painful shoes and a small black cocktail dress that she had bought while drunk in Karen Millen.

She looked at her watch and, with time to kill, flicked on the television. On a nationwide quest to find Britain's Most Talented Pet, Suki Meadows was standing on Scarborough sea-front, introducing the viewers to a dog who could play the drums, the dog waving his limbs in the direction of a tiny snare, drumsticks gaffer-taped to his paws. Instead of finding this image justly disturbing, Suki Meadows was laughing, bubbling and fizzing away, and for a moment Emma contemplated phoning Dexter, making up an excuse and going back to bed. Because, really, what was the point?

It wasn't just the effervescing girlfriend. The fact was Em and Dex didn't get on that well these days. More often than not he would cancel their meetings at the last minute, and when they did see each other he seemed distracted, uncomfortable. They spoke to each other in strange, strangulated voices, and had lost the knack of making each other laugh, jeering at each other instead in a spiteful, mocking tone. Their friendship was like a wilted bunch of flowers that she insisted on topping up with water. Why not let it die instead? It was unrealistic to expect a friendship to last forever, and she had lots of other friends: the old college crowd, her friends from school, and Ian of course. But to whom could she confide about Ian? Not Dexter, not anymore. The dog played the drums and Suki Meadows laughed and laughed and Emma snapped the TV off.

In the hallway she examined herself in the mirror. She had been hoping for understated sophistication, but she felt like a make-over, abandoned halfway through. Recently she had been eating more pepperoni than she had ever thought possible, and there was the result; a little pot belly. Had he been there, Ian would have said that she looked beautiful, but all she saw was the swell of her belly through black satin. She placed her hand on it, closed the front door, and began the long journey from an ex-council flat in E17 to WC2.

'WAHEY!'

A hot summer night on Frith Street, and he was on the phone to Suki.

'DID YOU SEE IT?'

'What?'

'THE DOG! PLAYING THE DRUMS! IT WAS AMAZING!'

Dexter stood outside Bar Italia, sleek and matt black in shirt and suit, a little trilby-style hat pushed back on his head, the mobile phone held four inches from his ear. He had the sensation that if he hung up he would still be able to hear her.

'. . . LITTLE DRUMSTICKS ON HIS LITTLE PAWS!'

'It was hysterical,' he said, though in truth he couldn't bring himself to watch. Envy was not a comfortable emotion for Dexter, but he knew the whispers – that Suki was the real talent, that she had been carrying him – and comforted himself with the notion that Suki's current high profile, large salary and popular appeal were a kind of artistic compromise. Britain's Most Talented Pet? He would never sell out like that. Even if someone asked him to.

'NINE MILLION VIEWERS THEY RECKON THIS WEEK. TEN, MAYBE . . .'

'Suki, can I just explain something about the telephone? You don't have to shout into it? The phone does that bit for you . . .'

She huffed and hung up on him, and from across the road, Emma took a moment to stand and watch as Dexter swore at the phone in his hand. He still looked great in a suit. It was a shame about the hat but at least he wasn't wearing those ridiculous headphones. She watched his face brighten as he saw her and she felt a swell of affection and hope for the evening.

'You really should get rid of that,' she said, nodding towards the phone.

He slipped it into his pocket and kissed her cheek. 'So you've got a choice, you can either phone me, actually me personally, or you can phone a building in which I might just happen to be at the time—'

'Phone the building.'

'And if I miss the call?'

'Well God forbid you should miss a call.'

'It's not 1988 anymore, Em—'

'Yes, I know that—'

'Six months, I give you six months before you cave—'

'Never—'

'A bet—'

'Okay a bet. If I ever, ever buy a mobile phone I'll buy you dinner.'

'Well, that'll make a change.'

'Besides, they give you brain damage—'

'They do *not* damage your brain—'

'How can you tell?'

And they stood for a moment in silence, both with a vague sense that the evening had not started well.

'Can't believe you're getting at me already,' he said sulkily.

'Well that's my job.' She smiled and embraced him, pressing her cheek against his. 'I'm not getting at you. Sorry, sorry.'

His hand was on her bare neck. 'It's been ages.'

'Far too long.'

He stepped back. 'You look beautiful by the way.'

'Thank you. So do you.'

'Well, not beautiful . . .'

'Handsome then.'

'Thank you.' He took her hands and held them out to the side. 'You should wear dresses more often, you look almost feminine.'

'I like your hat now take it off.'

'And the shoes!'

She twisted an ankle towards him. 'It's the world's first orthopaedic high-heel.'

They began to walk through the crowds towards Wardour Street, Emma taking his arm then holding the material of his suit between finger and thumb, rubbing at the strange nap of the fabric. 'What is this, by the way? Velvet? Velour?'

'Moleskin.'

'I had a track-suit in that material once.'

'We're quite a pair, aren't we? Dex and Em—'

'Em and Dex. Like Rogers and Astaire—'

'Burton and Taylor—'

'Mary and Joseph—'

Dexter laughed and took her hand and soon they were at the restaurant.

Poseidon was a huge bunker excavated from the remains of an underground car park. Entrance was by way of a vast, theatrical staircase that seemed miraculously suspended above the main room and formed a permanent distraction to the diners below, who spent much of the evening assessing the beauty or fame of the new arrivals. Feeling neither beautiful nor famous, Emma sloped down the stairs, one hand on the banister, the other cupping her belly until Dexter took this arm and stopped, surveying the room as proudly as if he were the architect.

'So. What do you think?'

'Club Tropicana,' she said.

The interior had been styled to suggest the romance of a luxury liner from the 20s: velvet booths, liveried waiters bearing cocktails, decorative portholes that opened onto a view of nothing, and this lack of natural light gave the place a submarine aspect, as if it had already hit the iceberg and was on its way down. The intended air of inter-war elegance was further undermined by the clamour and ostentation of the room, the pervading atmosphere of youth and sex, money and deep-fat-frying. All the burgundy velvet and pressed peach linen in the world couldn't stifle the tumultuous noise from the open-plan kitchen, a blur of stainless steel and white. So here it is at last, thought Emma: The Eighties.

'Are you sure this is okay? It looks quite expensive.'

'I told you. My treat.' He tucked the label into the back of her dress, having glanced at it first, then took her hand and led her down the rest of the stairs with a little Astaire trot, into the heart of all that money, sex and youth.

A sleek handsome man in absurd naval epaulettes told them their table would be ten minutes so they pushed their way to the cocktail lounge where another faux naval man was busy juggling bottles.

'What do you want, Em?'

'Gin and tonic?'

Dexter tutted. 'You're not in the Mandela Bar now. You've

got to have a proper drink. Two martinis, Bombay Sapphire, very dry, with a twist.' Emma made to speak, but Dexter held up an autocratic finger. 'Trust me. Best martinis in London.'

Obediently she ummed and awwed at the bartender's performance, Dexter commentating throughout. 'The trick is to get everything really, really cold before you start. Iced water in the glass, gin in the freezer.'

'How do you know all this?'

'My mum taught me when I was, what, nine?' They touched glasses, silently toasting Alison, and both felt hope again, for the evening and for their friendship. Emma raised the martini to her lips. 'I've never had one of these before.' The first taste was delicious, icy and immediately intoxicating, and she tried not to spill it as she shuddered. She was about to thank him when Dexter placed his glass in Emma's hand, a good half of it already gone.

'Off to the loo. They're incredible here. The best in London.'

'Can't wait!' she said, but he had already gone, and Emma stood alone with two drinks in her hand, attempting to exude an aura of confidence and glamour so as not to look like a waitress.

Suddenly a tall woman stood over her in a leopard-skin corset, stockings and suspenders, her appearance so sudden and startling that Emma gave a little yelp as her martini sloshed over her wrist.

'Cigarettes?' The woman was extraordinarily beautiful, voluptuous and barely dressed, like a figure from the fuselage of a B-52, her breasts seeming to recline on a cantilevered tray of cigars and cigarettes. 'Would you like anything?' she repeated, smiling through powdery foundation and adjusting with one finger the black velvet choker around her neck.

'Oh, no, I don't smoke,' said Emma, as if this were a personal failing she intended to address, but the woman had already redirected her smile over Emma's shoulder, fluttering the sticky black lace of her eyelashes.

'Cigarettes, sir?'

Dexter smiled, sliding his wallet from the inside of his jacket as he scanned the wares on display below her bosom. With a connoisseur's flourish, he settled on twenty Marlboro Lights, and the Cigarette Girl nodded as if sir had made an excellent choice.

Dexter handed her a five-pound note folded lengthwise. 'Keep the change,' he smiled. Was there ever a more empowering phrase than 'Keep the change'? He used to feel self-conscious saying it, but not anymore. She gave an extraordinary aphrodisiac smile, and for one callous moment Dexter wished it were the Cigarette Girl, not Emma, who would be joining him for dinner.

Look at him, the little dear, thought Emma, noticing this little flicker of self-satisfaction. There had been a time, not so long ago, when the boys all wanted to be Che Guevara. Now they all wanted to be Hugh Hefner. With a games console. As the Cigarette Girl wiggled into the crowd, Dexter really looked as if he might try and pat her bottom.

'You've got drool on your moleskin.'

'Pardon?'

'What was that all about?'

'Cigarette Girl,' he shrugged, sliding the unopened packet into his pocket. 'This place is famous for it. It's glamour, a bit of theatre.'

'So why's she dressed as a prostitute?'

'I don't know, Em, maybe her woolly black tights are in the wash.' He took his martini and drained it. 'Post-feminism, isn't it?'

Emma looked sceptical. 'Oh, is that what we're calling it now?'

Dexter nodded towards the Cigarette Girl's bottom. 'You could look like that if you wanted to.'

'No-one misses a point quite like you, Dex.'

'What I mean is, it's about choice. It's empowering.'

'Mind like a laser—'

'If she chooses to wear the outfit, she can wear the outfit!'

'But if she refused she would be sacked.'

'And so would the waiters! And anyway, maybe she likes wearing it, maybe it's fun, maybe she feels sexy in it. That is feminism, isn't it?'

'Well, it's not the *dictionary* definition . . .'

'Don't make me out to be some kind of chauvinist, I'm a feminist too!' Emma tutted and rolled her eyes and he was reminded just how annoying and preachy she could be. 'I am! I am a feminist!'

'. . . and I will fight to the death, to the *death*, mind, for the right of a woman to display her breasts for tips.'

And now it was his turn to roll his eyes, and give a patronising laugh. 'It's not 1988, Em.'

'What does that mean? You keep saying it and I still don't know what it means.'

'It means don't keep fighting battles that are already lost. The feminist movement should be about equal pay and equal opportunities and civil rights, not deciding what a woman can or can't wear of her own free will on a Saturday night!'

Her mouth fell open in indignation. 'That's not what I—'

'And anyway, I'm buying you dinner! Don't give me a hard time!'

And it was at moments like this that she had to remind herself that she was in love with him, or had once been in love with him, a long time ago. They stood on the edge of a long pointless argument that she felt she would win, but which would leave the evening in tatters. Instead, she hid her face in her drink, her teeth biting the glass, and counted slowly before saying: 'Let's change the subject.'

But he wasn't listening, gazing over her shoulder instead as the maître d' beckoned them over. 'Come on – I've managed to get us a banquette.'

They settled into the purple velvet booth and scrutinised the menus in silence. Emma had been expecting something fancy and French, but this was basically expensive canteen food:

fishcakes, shepherd's pie, burgers, and she recognised Poseidon as the kind of restaurant where the ketchup comes on a silver salver. 'It's Modern British,' explained Dexter patiently, as if paying all that money for sausage and mash was very Modern, very British.

'I'm going to have oysters,' said Dexter. 'The natives, I think.'

'Are they friendly?' said Emma weakly.

'*What?*'

'The natives – are they friendly?' she persevered and thought My God, I'm turning into Ian.

Uncomprehending, Dexter frowned and returned to the menu. 'No, they're just sweeter, pearly and sweet and finer than rock oysters, more delicate. I'll get twelve.'

'You're very knowledgeable all of a sudden.'

'I love food. I've always loved food and wine.'

'I remember that tuna stir-fry you cooked me that time. I can still taste it in the back of my throat. Ammonia—'

'Not *cooking*, restaurants. I eat out most days now. As a matter of fact I've been asked if I want to review for one of the Sundays.'

'Restaurants?'

'Cocktail bars. Weekly column called "Barfly", sort of man-about-town thing.'

'And you'd write it yourself?'

'Of course I'd write it myself!' he said, though he had been assured that the column would be heavily ghosted.

'What is there to say about cocktails?'

'You'd be surprised. Cocktails are very cool now. Sort of a retro glamour thing. In fact—' He put his mouth to the empty martini glass '—I'm something of a mixologist myself.'

'Misogynist?'

'Mix*o*logist.'

'I'm sorry, I thought you said "misogynist".'

'Ask me how to make a cocktail, any cocktail you like.'

She pressed her chin with her finger. 'Okay, um . . . lager top!'

'I'm serious, Em. It's a real skill.'

'What is?'

'Mixology. People go on special courses.'

'Maybe you should have done it for your degree.'

'It would certainly have been more fucking useful.'

The remark was so belligerent and sour that Emma visibly winced, and Dexter seemed a little taken aback too, hiding his face in the wine list. 'What do you want: red or white? I'm going to get another martini, then we'll start with a nice biscuity Muscadet for the oysters then go onto something like a Margaux. What d'you think?'

He ordered and then was off to the loo again, taking his second martini with him, which Emma found unusual and vaguely unsettling. The minutes stretched. She read the wine label then read it again then stared into space and wondered at what point he had become such a, such a . . . mixologist? And why was she sounding so spiky, mean and joyless? She didn't care what the Cigarette Girl wore, not really, not that much, so why did she sound so priggish and judgemental? She resolved to relax and enjoy herself. This was Dexter after all, her best friend whom she loved. Didn't she?

In London's most amazing toilets, Dexter hunched over the cistern and thought much the same thing. He loved Emma Morley, supposed he did, but more and more resented that air of self-righteousness, of the community centre, the theatre co-op, of 1988. She was so, so . . . subsidised. It wasn't appropriate, especially not in a setting like this, a place specifically designed to make a man feel like a secret agent. After the grim ideological gulag of a mid-Eighties education, its guilt and bolshy politics, he was finally being allowed to have some fun, and was it really such a bad thing to like a cocktail, a cigarette, a flirtation with a pretty girl?

And the jokes; why was she always getting at him, reminding him of his failings? He hadn't forgotten them. All that stuff about things being 'posh' and my-fat-bum and orthopaedic high-heels, the endless, endless self-deprecation. Well God save me from comedi*ennes*, he thought, with their put-downs and their smart asides, their insecurities and self-loathing. Why couldn't a woman have a bit of grace and elegance and self-confidence, instead of behaving all the time like some chippy stand-up?

And class! Don't even mention class. He takes her to a great restaurant at his own expense, and on goes the cloth cap! There was a kind of vanity and self-regard in that working-class-hero act that sent him crazy. Why is she still harping on about how she went to a comp, never went abroad on holiday, has never eaten an oyster? She's nearly thirty years old, all that was a long, long time ago, and it's time she took responsibility for her own life. He gave a pound to the Nigerian man who passed him his hand towel, stepped out into the restaurant, saw Emma across the room fiddling with her cutlery in her High Street funeral dress, and he felt a new wave of irritation. In the bar, to his right, he could see the Cigarette Girl, standing alone. She saw him, and smiled, and he decided to make a detour.

'Twenty Marlboro Lights, please.'

'What, again?' she laughed, her hand touching his wrist.

'What can I say? I'm like one of those beagles.'

She laughed again, and he pictured her in the banquette next to him, his hand under the table on her stockinged thigh. He reached for his wallet. 'Actually, I'm going to this party later with my old mate from college over there—' Old mate, he thought, was a nice touch. '—and I don't want to run out of cigarettes.' He handed her a five-pound note, folded crisply lengthwise in two, held between first and second finger. 'Keep the change.'

She smiled, and he noticed a tiny speck of ruby lipstick on her white front teeth. He wanted very much to hold her chin and wipe it off with his thumb.

'You have lipstick . . .'

'Where?'

He extended his arm until his finger was two inches from her mouth. 'Just. There.'

'Can't take me anywhere!' She ran the point of her pink tongue back and forth across her teeth. 'Better?' she grinned.

'Much.' He smiled and stepped away, then turned back to her.

'Just out of interest,' he said, 'what time do you finish here tonight?'

The oysters had arrived, lying glossy and alien on their bed of melting ice. Emma had been passing the time by drinking heavily, with the fixed smile of someone who's been left alone and really doesn't mind at all. Finally she saw him weaving across the restaurant a little unsteadily. He bundled into the booth.

'I thought you'd fallen in!' This was something that her granny used to say. She was using her grandmother's material.

'Sorry,' he said, but nothing more. They began on the oysters. 'So listen, there's a party later tonight. My mate Oliver, who I play poker with. I've told you about him.' He tipped the oyster into his mouth. 'He's a baronet.'

Emma felt sea-water dribble down her wrist. 'And what's that got to do with anything?'

'What do you mean?'

'Him being a baronet.'

'I'm just saying, he's a nice bloke. Lemon on that?'

'No thank you.' She swallowed the thing, still trying to work out if she had been invited to the party or just informed that a party was taking place. 'So where is this party then?' she said.

'Holland Park. Massive great house.'

'Oh. Okay.'

Still not sure. Was he inviting her, or excusing himself early? She ate another oyster.

'You're very welcome to come along,' he said finally, reaching for the Tabasco sauce.

'Am I?'

'Absolutely,' he said. She watched as he unblocked the sticky neck of the Tabasco bottle with the tine of his fork. 'It's just you won't know anyone there, that's all.'

Clearly she was not invited. 'I'll know you,' she said weakly.

'Yes, I suppose so. And Suki! Suki will be there.'

'Isn't she filming in Scarborough?'

'They're driving her back tonight.'

'She's doing very well, isn't she?'

'Well, we both are,' he said, quickly and a little too loud.

She decided to let it pass. 'Yes. That's that what I meant. You both are.' She picked up an oyster, then put it back. 'I really like Suki,' she said, though she had met her only once, at an intimidating Studio 54-themed party in a private club in Hoxton. And Emma had liked her, though she couldn't escape the feeling that Suki treated her as rather quaint, one of Dexter's homely, old-style friends, as if she were only at the party because she'd won the phone-in competition.

He necked another oyster. 'She's great, isn't she? Suki.'

'Yes, she is. How's it going with you two?'

'Oh alright. Bit tricky, you know, being in the public eye all the time . . .'

'Tell me about it!' said Emma, but he didn't seem to hear.

'And I sometimes feel like I'm going out with this public address system, but it's great. Really. You know the best thing about the relationship?'

'Go on.'

'She knows what it's like. Being on the telly. She understands.'

'Dexter – that is *the* most romantic thing I've ever heard.'

And there she goes again, he thought, the snippy little comments. 'Well it's true,' he shrugged and decided that as soon as he could pay the bill, their evening would be over. As if as an afterthought, he added, 'So, this party. I'm just worried about you getting home, that's all.'

'Walthamstow's not Mars, Dex, it's just North East London. It supports human life.'

'I know!'

'It's on the Victoria Line!'

'But it's just a long way on public transport, and the party won't get going 'til midnight. You'll arrive and then you'll have to go. Unless I give you money for the cab—'

'I do have money, they do pay me.'

'Holland Park to Walthamstow though?'

'If it's awkward for me to come—'

'It's not! It's not awkward. I want you to come. Let's decide later, shall we?' and without excusing himself he went to the toilet again, taking his glass with him as if he had another table in there. Emma sat and drank glass after glass of wine and continued to simmer, building to a steady rolling boil.

And so the pleasure wore on. He returned just as the main courses arrived. Emma examined her beer-battered haddock with minted pea puree. The thick pale chips had been machine-cut into perfect oblongs and were stacked up like building blocks with the battered fish teetering precariously on top, six inches off the plate, as if it might hurl itself into the pool of thick green gloop below. What was that game? The stacked wooden blocks? Carefully, she extracted a chip from the top of the pile. Hard and cold inside.

'How's the King of Comedy?' Since returning from the toilet, Dexter's tone had become even more belligerent and provoking.

Emma felt traitorous. This might have been her cue to confide in someone about the mess of her relationship and her confusion as to what to do next. But she couldn't talk to Dexter, not now. She swallowed raw potato.

'Ian's great,' she said emphatically.

'Co-habiting okay? Flat coming along, is it?'

'Fantastic. You haven't seen it yet, have you? You should come round!' The invite was half-hearted and the reply a non-committal 'Hm,' as if Dexter was doubtful of the existence of pleasure beyond Underground Zone 2. There was a silence, and they returned to their plates.

'How's your steak?' she asked, eventually. Dexter seemed to have lost his appetite, dissecting the bloody red meat without actually eating it.

'Sensational. How's the fish?'

'Cold.'

'Is it?' He peered at her plate then shook his head sagely. 'It's opaque, Em. That's how fish *should* be cooked, so it just turns opaque.'

'Dexter—' Her voice was hard and sharp. '—it's *opaque* because it's deep-frozen. It hasn't been defrosted.'

'Is it?' He prodded angrily inside the sleeve of batter with his finger. 'Well, we'll send it back!'

'It's fine. I'll just eat the chips.'

'No, fuck it! Send it back! I'm not paying for fucking frozen fish! What is this, Bejams? We'll get you something else.' He waved a waiter over and Emma watched Dexter assert himself, insisting that it wasn't good enough, it said fresh fish on the menu, he wanted it taken off the bill and a replacement main course provided free of charge. She tried to insist she wasn't hungry anymore while Dexter in turn insisted that she had to have a proper main course because it was free. There was no choice but to stare at the menu all over again, while the waiter and Dexter glared at her and all the time his own steak sat there, mauled but uneaten, until finally it was settled, she got her free green salad, and they were alone again.

They sat in silence in the wreckage of the evening in front of two plates of unwanted food and she thought that she might cry.

'Well. This is going well,' he said, and tossed down his napkin.

She wanted to go home. She would skip dessert, forget the party – he clearly didn't want her there anyway – and go home. Maybe Ian would be back, kind and considerate and in love with her, and they could sit and talk, or just cuddle up and watch TV.

'So.' His eyes were scanning the room as he spoke. 'How's the teaching?'

'It's fine, Dexter,' she scowled.

'What? What have I done?' he replied indignantly, eyes snapping back to her.

She spoke levelly. 'If you're not interested, don't ask.'

'I am interested! It's just . . .' He poured himself more wine. 'I thought you were meant to be writing some *book* or something?'

'I am writing some-book-or-something, but I also have to earn a living. And also more to the point I enjoy it, Dexter, *and* I'm a bloody good teacher!'

'I'm sure you are! It's just, well, you know the expression. "Those who can . . ."'

Emma's mouth fell open. *Stay calm—*

'No, I'm not familiar with it, Dexter. Tell me. What expression?'

'You know . . .'

'No, seriously, Dexter, tell me.'

'It's not important.' He was starting to look sheepish.

'I'd like to know. Finish the sentence. "Those who can . . ."'

He sighed, a glass of wine in his hand, then spoke flatly. 'Those who can, *do*, those who can't, *teach* . . .'

She spat the words. 'And those who teach say go fuck yourself.'

And now his glass of wine was in his lap as Emma shoved the table away and jumped to her feet, grabbing her bag, knocking over bottles, clattering plates as she clambered out of the booth, storming through that hateful, hateful place. All around her people were staring now but she didn't care, she just wanted to be out. *Do not cry, you will not cry*, she commanded herself and, glancing behind her, saw Dexter mopping furiously at his lap, placating the waiter then following on in pursuit. She turned, broke into a run, and now here was the Cigarette Girl striding down the stairs towards her on long legs and high heels, a grin splitting her scarlet mouth. Despite her vow, Emma felt hot tears of humiliation prick her eyes, and now she was falling onto the stairs, stumbling on those stupid, stupid high shoes, and there was an audible gasp from the audience of diners behind her as she fell to her knees. The Cigarette Girl was beside her, holding onto her elbow, with a look of maddening, genuine concern.

'Are you alright there?'

'Yes, thank you, I'm fine—'

But now Dexter had caught up with her, was helping her up. Firmly she shook herself free from his grip.

'Get off me, Dexter!'

'Don't shout, calm down—'

'I will *not* calm down—'

'Alright, I'm sorry, I'm sorry, I'm sorry. Whatever it is you're angry about, I'm sorry!'

She turned to him on the stairs, eyes blazing. 'What, you don't *know*?'

'No! Come back to the table, and you can tell me!' But she was tumbling on, through the swing doors now, pushing them closed behind her so that the metal edge cracked him sharply on the knee. He limped after her. 'This is stupid, we're both a bit drunk, that's all—'

'No, *you're* drunk! You're always drunk or off your face on something or other, every time I see you. D'you realise I literally haven't seen you sober for, what, three years? I've forgotten what you're like sober, you're too busy boring on about yourself or your new pals or running to the loo every ten minutes – I don't know if it's dysentery or too much coke, but either way it's fucking rude and most of all it's boring. Even when you talk to me you're always looking over my shoulder in case there's some better option . . .'

'That's not true!'

'It is true, Dexter! Well bollocks to it. You're a *TV presenter*, Dex. You've not invented penicillin, it's TV, and crap TV at that. Well sod it, I've had enough.'

They were out amongst the crowds on Wardour Street in the fading summer light.

'Let's go somewhere and talk about this.'

'I don't want to talk about it, I just want to go home . . .'

'Emma, please?'

'Dexter, just leave me alone, will you?'

'You're being hysterical. Come here.' He took her arm once again and, idiotically, tried to hug her. She pushed him away, but he held onto her. People were staring at them now, another couple fighting in Soho on a Saturday night, and she relented finally, allowing herself to be pulled into a side street.

They were silent now, Dexter stepping away from her so that he could take her in. She was standing with her back to him, wiping her eyes with the heel of her hand, and he suddenly felt a hot pang of shame.

Finally, she spoke, in a quiet voice, her face to the wall.

'Why are you being like this, Dexter?'

'Like what?'

'You know what.'

'I'm just being myself!'

She spun to face him. 'No, you're not. I know what you're like and this isn't you. You're horrible like this. You're obnoxious, Dexter. I mean you always *were* a bit obnoxious, every now and then, a bit full of yourself, but you were funny too, and kind sometimes, and interested in people other than yourself. But now you're just out of control, with the booze, the drugs—'

'I'm just having fun!'

She sniffed, once, and looked up at him, through smudged black eyes.

'And sometimes I get carried away, that's all. If you weren't so . . . judgemental all the time—'

'Am I? I don't think I am. I try not to be. I just don't . . .' She stopped herself speaking, shook her head. 'I know you've been through a lot, in the last few years, and I've tried to understand that, really I have, with your mum and all, but . . .'

'Go on,' he said.

'I just don't think you're the person I used to know. You're not my friend anymore. That's all.'

He could think of nothing to say to this, so they stood in

silence, until Emma put her hand out, took two fingers of his hand, squeezed them in her palm.

'Maybe . . . maybe this is it, then,' she said. 'Maybe it's just over.'

'Over? What's over?'

'Us. You and me. Friendship. There are things I needed to talk to you about, Dex. About Ian and me. If you're my friend I should be able to talk to you but I can't, and if I can't talk to you, well, what is the point of you? Of us?'

'"What's the point?"'

'You said yourself, people change, no use getting sentimental about it. Move on, find someone else.'

'Yeah, but I didn't mean *us* . . .'

'Why not?'

'Because we're . . . us. We're Dex and Em. Aren't we?'

Emma shrugged. 'Maybe we've grown out of each other.'

He said nothing for a moment, then spoke. 'So, do you think I've grown out of you, or you've grown out of me?'

She wiped her nose with the back of her hand. 'I think you think I'm . . . dreary. I think you think I *cramp your style*. I think you've lost interest in me.'

'Em, I do *not* think you're dreary.'

'And neither do I! Neither do I! I think I'm fucking *marvellous* if you only knew it, and I think you used to think so too! But if you don't or if you're going to just take it for granted, then that's fine. I'm just not prepared to be treated like this anymore.'

'Treated like *what*?'

She sighed, and it was a moment before she spoke.

'Like you always want to be somewhere else, with someone else.'

He would have denied this, but the Cigarette Girl was waiting in the restaurant at that very moment, the number of his mobile phone tucked into her garter. Later he would wonder if there was something else he might have said to save the situation, a

209

joke perhaps. But nothing occurred to him and Emma let go of his hand.

'Well off you go,' she said. 'Go to your party. You're rid of me now. You're free.'

With failing bravado, Dexter tried to laugh. 'You sound like you're dumping me!'

She smiled sadly. 'I suppose I am in a way. You're not who you used to be, Dex. I really, really liked the old one. I'd like him back, but in the meantime, I'm sorry, but I don't think you should phone me anymore.' She turned and, a little unsteadily, began to walk off down the side alley in the direction of Leicester Square.

For a moment, Dexter had a fleeting but perfectly clear memory of himself at his mother's funeral, curled up on the bathroom floor while Emma held onto him and stroked his hair. Yet somehow he had managed to treat this as nothing, to throw it all away for dross. He followed a little way behind her. 'Come on, Em, we're still friends, aren't we? I know I've been a little weird, it's just . . .' She stopped for a moment, but didn't turn round, and he knew that she was crying. 'Emma?'

Then very quickly she turned, walked up to him and pulled his face to hers, her cheek warm and wet against his, speaking quickly and quietly in his ear, and for one bright moment he thought he was to be forgiven.

'Dexter, I love you so much. So, *so* much, and I probably always will.' Her lips touched his cheek. 'I just don't like you anymore. I'm sorry.'

And then she was gone, and he found himself on the street, standing alone in this back alley trying to imagine what he would possibly do next.

Ian returns at just before midnight to find Emma curled up on the sofa, watching some old movie. 'You're back early. How was Golden Boy?'

'Awful,' she murmurs.

If Ian feels any glee at this, he doesn't let it into his voice. 'Why, what happened?'

'I don't want to talk about it. Not tonight.'

'Why not? Emma, tell me! What did he say? Did you argue? . . .'

'Ian, please? Not tonight. Just come here, will you?'

She shuffles up so that he can join her on the sofa, and he notices the dress that she is wearing, the kind of thing she never wears for him. 'Is that what you wore?'

She holds the hem of the dress between finger and thumb. 'It was a mistake.'

'I think you look beautiful.'

She curls up against him, her head on his shoulder. 'How was the gig?'

'Not great.'

'Did you do the cats and dogs stuff?'

'Uh-huh.'

'Was there heckling?'

'Little bit of heckling.'

'Maybe it's not your best material.'

'Bit of booing.'

'That's part of it, though, isn't it? Everyone gets heckled sometimes.'

'I suppose so. I suppose sometimes I just worry . . .'

'What?'

'That I might just be . . . not very funny.'

She speaks into his chest. 'Ian?'

'What?

'You are a very, very funny man.'

'Thanks, Em.'

He rests his head against her and thinks about the small crimson box lined with crumpled silk that contains the engagement ring. For the last two weeks it has been tucked inside a balled-up pair of walking socks, waiting for its moment. Not right now though. In three weeks' time they'll be on the beach in Corfu. He imagines a restaurant overlooking the sea, a full moon, Emma in her summer dress, freshly tanned and smiling, perhaps a bowl of calamari between them. He imagines presenting the ring to her in an amusing way. For some weeks he has been devising different romantic-comedy scenarios in his head – perhaps dropping it into her wine glass while she's in the loo, or finding it in the mouth of his grilled fish, and complaining to the waiter. Getting it muddled up with the calamari rings, that might work. He might even just give it to her. He tries out the words in his head. *Marry Me, Emma Morley. Marry Me.*

'Love you lots, Em,' he says.

'Love you too,' says Emma. 'Love you too.'

The Cigarette Girl sits at the bar on her twenty-minute break, her costume on beneath her jacket, sipping whisky and listening to this man as he talks on and on about his friend, that poor pretty girl who fell down the staircase. They've had some kind of row apparently. The Cigarette Girl tunes in and out of the man's monologue, nodding every now and then and glancing surreptitiously at her watch. It is five minutes to midnight, and she should really get back to work. The hour between twelve and one is the best for tips, the high-water mark of lust and stupidity on the part of the male customers. Five more minutes and she'll go. Poor guy can barely stand up anyway.

She recognises him from that stupid TV programme – and doesn't he go out with Suki Meadows? – but can't recall his name. Does anyone watch that show anyway? The man's suit is stained, the pockets bulging with packets of unsmoked cigarettes, there's a sheen of oil on his nose, his breath is bad. What's more, he still hasn't even bothered to ask her real name.

The Cigarette Girl is called Cheryl Thomson. She works most days as a nurse, which is exhausting, but does an occasional shift here too because she went to school with the manager and the tips are incredible if you're prepared to flirt a little. At home in her flat in Kilburn her fiancé is waiting for her. Milo, Italian, 6' 2", once a footballer, now also a nurse. Very good-looking, they're getting married in September.

She would tell all this to the man if he asked, but he doesn't, so at two minutes to midnight on St Swithin's Day, she excuses herself – got to get back to work, no I can't go to the party, yes I've got your number, hope you and your friend work things out – and leaves the man alone at the bar, ordering another drink.

Part Three

1996–2001

Early Thirties

'Sometimes you are aware when your great moments are happening, and sometimes they rise from the past. Perhaps it's the same with people.'

James Salter, *Burning the Days*

CHAPTER TEN
Carpe Diem

Leytonstone and Walthamstow

Emma Morley lies on her back on the floor of the headmaster's office, with her dress rucked up around her waist and exhales slowly through her mouth.

'Oh, and by the way. Year Nine need new copies of *Cider With Rosie.*'

'I'll see what I can do,' says the headmaster, buttoning up his shirt.

'So while you've got me here on your carpet, is there anything else you'd like to discuss? Budget issues, Ofsted inspection? Anything you want to go over again?'

'I'd like to go over *you* again,' he says, laying down again and nuzzling her neck. It's the kind of meaningless innuendo that Mr Godalming – Phil – specialises in.

'What does that mean? That doesn't mean anything.' She tuts and shrugs him away and wonders why sex, even when enjoyable, leaves her so ill-tempered. They lie still for a moment. It's six-thirty in the evening at the end of term and Cromwell Road Comprehensive has the eerie quiet of a school after hours. The cleaners have been round, the office door is closed and locked from the inside, but still she feels uneasy and anxious. Isn't there meant to be some sort of afterglow, some sense of communion or well-being? For the last nine months she has been making love on institutional carpet, plastic chairs and laminated tables. Ever considerate of his staff, Phil has taken the foam cushion from the office armchair and it now rests beneath her hips, but even so she would one day like to have sex on furniture that doesn't stack.

'You know what?' says the headmaster.

'What?'

'I think you're sensational,' and he squeezes her breast for emphasis. 'I don't know what I'm going to do without you for six weeks.'

'At least it'll give your carpet burn a chance to heal.'

'Six whole weeks without you.' His beard is scratching at her neck. 'I'll go crazy with desire—'

'Well you've always got Mrs Godalming to fall back on,' she says, hearing her own voice, sour and mean. She sits and pulls her dress down over her knees. 'And anyway, I thought the long holidays were one of the perks of teaching. That's what you told me. When I first applied . . .'

Hurt, he looks up at her from the carpet. 'Don't be like this, Em.'

'What?'

'The woman-scorned act.'

'Sorry.'

'I don't like it anymore than you do.'

'Except I think you do.'

'No I don't. Let's not spoil it, eh?' He places one hand on her back, as if consoling her. 'This is our last time 'til September.'

'Alright, I said sorry, okay?' To mark a change in subject, she twists at the waist and kisses him, and is about to pull away when he places one hand on the nape of her neck and kisses her again with a gentle scouring action.

'Christ, I'm going to miss you.'

'You know what I think you should do?' she says, her mouth on his. 'It's quite radical.'

He looks at her anxiously. 'Go on . . .'

'This summer, soon as term's over . . .'

'Tell me.'

She places one finger on his chin. 'I think you should shave this off.'

He goes to sit. 'No way!'

'All this time and I don't know what you actually look like!'

'This IS what I look like!'

'But your *face*, your actual face. You might even be quite handsome.' She puts her hand on his forearm, and pulls him back down. 'Who's behind the mask? Let me in, Phil. Let me know the real you.'

They laugh for a while, comfortable again. 'You'd be disappointed,' he says, rubbing it like a favoured pet. 'Anyway, it's either this or shave three times a day. I used to shave in the morning but I looked like a burglar by lunch time. So I thought I'd let it grow, let it be my trademark.'

'Oh, a *trademark*.'

'It's informal. The kids like it. Makes me look anti-authority.'

Emma laughs again. 'It's not 1973, Phil. A beard means something different these days.'

He shrugs defensively. 'Fiona likes it. Says I have a weak chin otherwise.' A silence follows, as it always does when his wife is mentioned. To lighten things he says, self-deprecatingly: 'Of course you know the kids all call me The Beard.'

'I wasn't aware of that, no.' Phil laughs and Emma smiles. 'And anyway it's not The Beard, it's just Beard. No definite article, Monkey Boy.'

He sits suddenly, frowning sternly. '*Monkey Boy?*'

'That's what they call you.'

'Who?'

'The kids.'

'*Monkey Boy?*'

'Didn't you know?'

'No!'

'Oops. Sorry.'

He flops back down on the floor, sulky and hurt. 'Can't believe they call me Monkey Boy!'

'Only in fun,' she says, soothingly. 'It's affectionate.'

'Doesn't sound very affectionate.' He rubs his chin, as if comforting a pet. 'It's because I've got too much testosterone, that's all.' The use of the word 'testosterone' is enough to perk him up, and he pulls Emma back towards the floor and kisses her once more. He tastes of staffroom coffee and the bottle of white wine he keeps in his filing cabinet.

'I'll get a rash,' she says.

'So?'

'So people'll know.'

'Everyone's gone home.' His hand is on her thigh when the phone rings on the desk and he recoils as if bitten. He staggers to his feet.

'Leave it!' groans Emma.

'I can't leave it!' He's dragging on his trousers, as if talking to Fiona whilst naked from the waist down would be a betrayal too far, as if he's terrified of sounding in some way bare-legged.

'Hi, there! Hello, love! Yes, I know! Just walking out the door . . .' Domestic issues are debated – pasta or stir-fry, TV or a video – and Emma distracts herself from her lover's home life by retrieving her rolled-up underwear from beneath the desk where it lies with the paper-clips and pen tops. Dressing, she crosses to the window. There's dust on the blades of the venetian blinds, outside a pink light hits the science block, and suddenly Emma wishes that she were in a park or on a beach or a European city square somewhere, just anywhere but here in this airless institutional room with a married man. How does it happen that you wake up one day, find yourself in your thirties and someone's mistress? The word is repulsive, servile and she would rather not have it present in her mind, but can come up with no other. She is the boss's mistress and the best that can be said of the circumstances is that at least there are no children involved.

The affair – another awful word – began the previous September, after the disastrous holiday in Corfu, the engagement ring in the calamari. 'I think we want different things' was the best that she could come up with, and the rest of the long, long fortnight passed in a haze of sunburn and sulking, self-pity and anxiety about whether the jewellers would take the ring back. Nothing in the world could be more melancholy than that unwanted engagement ring. It sat in the suitcase in their hotel room, emanating sadness like radiation.

She returned from the holiday looking brown and unhappy. Her mother, who knew about the proposal, who had practically bought her own dress for the wedding, raged and moaned at Emma for weeks until she began to question her rejection of the offer. But saying yes would feel like caving in, and Emma knew from novels that you should never cave in to marriage.

The affair had settled it. During a routine meeting she had burst into tears in Phil's office, and he had crossed from behind the desk, put his arm round her, and pressed his mouth to the top of her head, almost as if to say 'at last'. After work, he took her to this place he'd heard of, a gastropub, where you could get a pint but the food was great too. They had rib-eye steaks and goat's cheese salad, and as their knees made contact beneath the big wooden table she had let it all flood out. After the second bottle of wine, it was all just a formality; the hug that became a kiss in the taxi home, the brown internal envelope in her pigeon hole (*about last night, can't stop thinking about you, felt this way for years, we need to talk, when can we talk?*).

Everything Emma knew about adultery had come from TV dramas of the Seventies. She associated it with Cinzano and Triumph TR7s and cheese and wine parties, thought of it as something the middle-aged did, the middle classes mainly; golf, yachts, adultery. Now that she was actually involved in an affair – its paraphernalia of secret looks, hands held under tables, fondles in the stationery cupboard – she was surprised at how familiar it all was, and what a potent emotion lust could be, when combined with guilt and self-loathing.

One night, after sex on the set of her Christmas production of *Grease*, he had solemnly handed her a gift-wrapped box.

'It's a mobile phone!'

'In case I need to hear your voice.'

Sitting on the bonnet of the Greased Lightning, she stared at the box and sighed. 'Well I suppose it was bound to happen eventually.'

'What's up? Don't you like it?'

'No, it's great.' She smiled, remembering. 'I just lost a bet with someone, that's all.'

Sometimes, walking and talking on a clear autumn evening in a secret part of Hackney Marshes, or giggling at the school carol service, drunk on mulled wine with their hips touching – sometimes she thought she was in love with Phillip Godalming. He was a good, principled, passionate teacher, if a little pompous sometimes. He had nice eyes, he could be funny. For the first time in her life she was the subject of an almost obsessive sexual infatuation. Of course, at forty-four he was far too old and his body, beneath the pelt, had that slipped doughy quality, but he was an earnest and intense lover, sometimes a little too intense for her liking; a face-puller, a talker. She found it hard to believe that the same man who stood in assembly to talk about the charity fun run would use that kind of language. Sometimes she wanted to break off during sex and say 'Mr Godalming – you *swore*!'

But nine months have passed now, the excitement has faded and she finds it harder to understand why she's here, loitering in a school corridor on a beautiful summer's evening. She should be with friends, or with a lover whom she's proud of and can mention in front of other people. Sulky with guilt and embarrassment, she waits outside the boys' loos while Phil washes himself with institutional soap. His Deputy Head of English and Theatre Studies and his mistress. Oh good God.

'All done!' he says, stepping out. He takes her hand in his, still damp from the washbasin, dropping it discreetly as they step out into the open air. He locks the main door, sets the alarm, and they walk to his car in the evening light, a professional distance apart, his leather briefcase occasionally banging the back of her shin.

'I'd drive you to the tube, but—'

'—best be on the safe side.'

They walk a little further.

'Four more days to go!' he says jauntily, to fill the silence.

'Where are you off to again?' she asks, even though she knows.

'Corsica. Walking. Fiona loves to walk. Walking, walking, walking, always walking. She's like Gandhi. Then in the evening, off come the walking boots, out like a light . . .'

'Phil, please – don't.'

'Sorry. Sorry.' To change the subject, he asks, 'How about you?'

'Might see family in Yorkshire. Staying here, working mostly.'

'Working?'

'You know. Writing.'

'Ah, the *writing*.' Like everyone, he says it as if he doesn't believe her. 'It's not about you and me, is it? This famous book?'

'No it's not.' They're at his car now, and she is keen to be gone. 'And anyway, I don't know if you and me are all that interesting.'

He's leaning against his blue Ford Sierra, gearing up for the big farewell, and now she has spoilt it. He frowns, bottom lip showing pink through his beard. 'What's that supposed to mean?'

'I don't know, just . . .'

'Go on.'

'Phil, this, us. It doesn't make me happy.'

'You're unhappy?'

'Well, it's not ideal is it? Once a week on an institutional carpet.'

'You seemed pretty happy to me.'

'I don't mean *satisfied*. Good God, it's not about sex, it's the . . . circumstances.'

'Well it makes me happy—'

'Does it? Does it really though?'

'As I recall it used to make you happy too.'

'Excited I suppose, for a while.'

'For Christ's sake, Emma!' He glares down at her as if she has been caught smoking in the girls' loos. 'I've got to go now! Why bring this up just as I've got to go?'

'I'm sorry, I—'

'I mean for fuck's sake, Emma!'

'Hey! Don't talk to me like that!'

'I'm not, I just, I'm just . . . Let's just get through the summer holiday, shall we? And then we'll work out what to do.'

'I don't think there's anything we can do, is there? We either stop or we carry on, and I don't think we should carry on . . .'

He lowers his voice. 'There is something else we can do . . . I can do.' He looks around, then when he's sure it's safe he takes her hand. 'I could tell her this summer.'

'I don't want you to tell her, Phil . . .'

'While we're away, or before even, next week . . .'

'I don't want you to tell her. There's no point . . .'

'Isn't there?'

'No!'

'Because I think there is, I think there might be.'

'Fine! Let's talk next term, let's, I don't know – pencil-in a meeting.'

Heartened, he licks his lips, and checks once more for onlookers. 'I love you, Emma Morley.'

'No you don't,' she sighs. 'Not really.'

He tilts his chin down, as if peering at her over imaginary glasses. 'I think that's for me to decide, don't you?' She hates that headmasterly look and tone of voice. She wants to kick him in the shins.

'You had better go,' she says.

'I'll miss you, Em—'

'Have a nice holiday, if we don't talk—'

'You've no idea how much I'll miss you—'

'Corsica, lovely—'

'Every day—'

'See you then, bye—'

'Here . . .' Raising his briefcase, using it a shield, he kisses her. Very discreet, she thinks, standing impassively. He opens the car door and steps in. A navy blue Sierra, a proper head-master's car, its glove compartment packed with Ordnance Survey maps. 'Still can't believe they call me Monkey Boy . . .' he mumbles, shaking his head.

She stands for a moment in the empty car park and watches him drive off. Thirty years old, barely in love with a married man, but at least there are no kids involved.

Twenty minutes later, she stands beneath the window of the long, low red-brick building that contains her flat, and notices a light on in the living room. Ian is back.

She contemplates walking off and hiding in the pub, or perhaps going round to see friends for the evening, but she knows that Ian will just sit in that armchair with the light off and wait, like an assassin. She takes a deep breath, and looks for her keys.

The flat seems much bigger since Ian moved out. Stripped of the video box-sets, the chargers and adapters and cables, the vinyl in gatefold sleeves, it feels as if it has been recently burgled, and once again Emma is reminded of how little she has to show for the last eight years. She can hear a rustling from the bedroom. She puts down her bag and walks quietly towards the door.

The contents of the chest of drawers are scattered on the floor: letters, bank statements, torn paper wallets of photographs and negatives. She stands silent and unobserved in the doorway and watches Ian for a moment, snorting with the effort of reaching deep into the back of the drawer. He wears unlaced trainers, track-suit bottoms, an un-ironed shirt. It's an outfit that has been carefully put together to suggest maximum emotional disarray. He is dressed to upset.

'What are you doing, Ian?'

He is startled, but only for a moment, after which he glares back indignantly, a self-righteous burglar. 'You're home late,' he says, accusingly.

'What's that got to do with you?'

'Just curious as to your *whereabouts*, that's all.'

'I had rehearsals. Ian, I thought we agreed you can't just drop in like this.'

'Why, got someone *with* you, have you?'

'Ian, I am so not in the mood for this . . .' She puts down her bag, takes off her coat. 'If you're looking for a diary or something, you're wasting your time. I haven't kept a diary for years . . .'

'As a matter of fact I'm just getting my *stuff*. It is *my* stuff, you know, I do *own* it.'

'You've got all your stuff.'

'My passport. I don't have my passport!'

'Well I can tell you right now, it's not in my underwear drawer.' He is improvising of course. She knows that he has his passport, he just wanted to poke through her belongings and show her that he's not okay. 'Why do you need your passport? Are you going somewhere? Emigrating maybe?'

'Oh you'd love that, wouldn't you?' he sneers.

'Well I wouldn't *mind,*' she says, stepping over the mess and sitting on the bed.

He adopts a gumshoe voice. 'Well, tough *shit*, sweetheart, 'cause I ain't going *nowhere*.' As a jilted lover, Ian has found a commitment and aggression that he never possessed as a stand-up comedian, and he is certainly putting on quite a show tonight. 'Couldn't afford to anyway.'

She feels like heckling him. 'I take it you're not doing a lot of stand-up comedy at the moment, then, Ian?'

'What do *you* think, sweetheart?' he says, putting his arms out to the side, indicating the stubble, the unwashed hair, the sallow skin; his look-what-you've-done-to-me look. Ian is making a spectacle of his self-pity, a one-man-show of loneliness and rejection that he's been working up for the last six months and, tonight at least, Emma has no time for it.

'Where's this "sweetheart" thing come from, Ian? I'm not sure if I like it.'

He returns to his search and mumbles something into the drawer, 'fuck off, Em' perhaps. Is he drunk, she wonders? On the dressing table, there's an open can of strong cheap lager. Drunk – now *there's* a good idea. At that moment, Emma decides to set out to get drunk as soon as possible. Why not? It seems to work for everyone else. Excited by the project, she walks to the kitchen to make a start.

He follows her through. 'So, where were you then?'

'I told you. At school, rehearsing.'

'What were you rehearsing?'

'*Bugsy Malone*. It's a lot of laughs. Why, you want tickets?'

'No thanks.'

'There's splurge guns.'

'I reckon you've been with someone.'

'Oh, please – here we go again.' She opens the fridge. There's half a bottle of wine, but this is one of those times when only spirits will do. 'Ian, what is this obsession with me being *with* someone? Why can't it just be that you and me weren't right for each other?' With a hard yank, she cracks the seal of the frosted-up freezer compartment. Ice scatters on the floor.

'But we *are* right for each other!'

'Well fine then, if you say so, let's get back together!' Behind some ancient minced beef crispy pancakes, there is a bottle of vodka. 'Yes!' She slides the crispy pancakes to Ian. 'Here – these are yours. I'm granting you custody.' Slamming the fridge, she reaches for a glass. 'And anyway, what if I *was* with someone, Ian? So what? We broke up, remember?'

'Rings a bell, rings a bell. So who is he then?'

She's pouring the vodka, two inches. 'Who's who?'

'Your new *boyfriend*? Go on, just tell me, I won't mind,' he sneers. 'We're still *friends* after all.'

Emma gulps from her glass then stoops for a moment, elbows on the counter top, the heels of her hands pressed against her eyes as she feels the icy liquid slide down her throat. A moment passes.

'It's Mr Godalming. The headmaster. We've been having this affair on and off for the past nine months, but I think it's mainly been about the sex. To be honest, the whole thing's a bit degrading for both of us. Makes me a bit ashamed. Bit sad. Still, like I keep saying, at least there are no kids involved! There you go—' She speaks into her glass. 'Now you know.'

The room is silent. Eventually . . .

'You're kidding me.'

'Look out the window, have a look, see for yourself. He's waiting in the car. Navy blue Sierra . . .'

He sniffs, incredulous. 'It's not fucking funny, Emma.'

Emma places her empty glass on the counter and exhales slowly. 'No, I know it's not. In no way could the situation be described as funny.' She turns and faces him. 'I've told you, Ian, I'm not seeing anyone. I'm not in love with anyone and I don't want to be. I just want to be left alone . . .'

'I've got a theory!' he says, proudly.

'What theory?'

'I know who it is.'

She sighs. 'Who is it then, Sherlock?'

'*Dexter!*' he says, triumphantly.

'Oh for Christ's sake—' She drains the glass.

'I'm right, aren't I?'

She laughs bitterly. 'God, I wish—'

'What does that mean?'

'Nothing. Ian, as you well know, I haven't spoken to Dexter for months—'

'Or so you say!'

'You're being ridiculous, Ian. What, you think we've been having this secret love affair behind everyone's back?'

'That's what the evidence seems to suggest.'

'Evidence? What *evidence*?'

And for the first time, Ian looks a little sheepish. 'Your notebooks.'

A moment, then she puts her glass out of reach so that she won't be tempted to throw it. 'You've been reading my notebooks?'

'I've glanced. Once or twice. Over the years.'

'You *bastard*—'

'The little bits of poetry, those magical ten days in Greece, all that yearning, all that desire—'

'How *dare* you! How dare you go behind my back like that!'

'You left them lying round! What do you expect!'

'I expected some *trust* and I expected you to have some dignity—'

'And anyway I didn't need to read them, it was so bloody obvious, the two of you—'

'—but I have limited reserves of sympathy, Ian! Months of you moaning and moping and whining and hanging round like a kicked dog. Well if you ever turn up out of the blue like this and start going through my drawers, I swear I will call the fucking police—'

'Go on then! Go on, call them!' and he steps towards her, his arms out to the side filling the little room. 'It's my flat too, remember?'

'Is it? How come? You never paid the mortgage! I did that! You never did anything, just lay around feeling sorry for yourself—'

'That's not true!'

'And whatever money you did earn went on stupid videos and take-away—'

'I chipped in! When I could—'

'Well it wasn't enough! Oh, God I hate this flat, and I hate my life here. I have got to get out of here or I will go crazy—'

'This was our home!' he protests, desperately.

'I was never happy here, Ian. Why couldn't you see that? I just got . . . stuck here, we both did. Surely you must know that.'

He has never seen her like this, or heard her say these things. Shocked, his eyes wide like a panicked child, he stumbles towards her. 'Calm down!' He's gripping her arm now. 'Don't say things like that—'

'Get away from me, Ian! I mean it, Ian! Just get away!' They're shouting at each other now and she thinks, Oh God, we've become one of those crazy couples you hear through the walls at night. Somewhere, someone's thinking, should I call the police? How did it come to this? 'Get out!' she shouts as he desperately tries to put his arms around her. 'Just give me your keys and get out, I don't want to see you anymore—'

And then just as suddenly, they're both crying, slumped on the floor in the narrow hallway of the flat they had bought together with such hope. Ian's hand is covering his face, and he's struggling to speak between great sobs and gulps of air. 'I can't stand this. Why is this happening to me? This is hell. I'm in hell, Em!'

'I know. I'm sorry.' She wraps her arms around his shoulder.

'Why can't you just love me? Why can't you just be in love with me? You were once, weren't you? In the beginning.'

'Course I was.'

'Well why can't you be in love with me again?'

'Oh Ian, I can't. I've tried, but I can't. I'm sorry. I am so, so sorry.'

Some time later they lie together on the floor in the same spot, as if they've been washed up there. Her head is on his shoulder, her arm across his chest, taking in the smell of him, the warm, comfortable smell that she had become so used to. Eventually, he speaks.

'I should go.'

'I think you should.'

Keeping his red, swollen face averted, he sits and nods towards the mess of paper, notebooks and photographs on the bedroom floor. 'You know what makes me sad?'

'Go on.'

'That there aren't more photographs of us. Together I mean. There's thousands of you and Dex, hardly any of just you and me. Not recent anyway. It's like we just stopped taking them.'

'No decent camera,' she says weakly, but he chooses to accept it.

'Sorry for . . . you know, flipping out like that, going through your stuff. Completely unacceptable behaviour.'

'S'alright. Just don't do it again.'

'Some of the stories are quite good, by the way.'

'Thank you. Though they were meant to be private.'

'What's the point of that? You'll have to show them to someone someday. Put yourself out there.'

'Okay, maybe I will. One day.'

'Not the poems. Don't show them the poems, but the stories. They're good. You're a good writer. You're clever.'

'Thank you, Ian.'

His face starts to crumple. 'It wasn't so bad, was it? Living here with me?'

'It was great. I'm just taking it all out on you, that's all.'

'Do you want to tell me about it?'

'Nothing to tell.'

'So.'

'So.' They smile at each other. He is standing by the door now, one hand on the handle, not quite able to leave.

'One last thing.'

'Go on.'

'You're not seeing him, are you? I mean Dexter. I'm just being paranoid.'

She sighs and shakes her head. 'Ian, I swear to you on my life. I am not seeing Dexter.'

''Cos I saw in the papers that he'd split up with his girlfriend and I thought, you and me breaking up, and him being single again—'

'I haven't seen Dexter for, God, ages.'

'But did anything happen? While you and I were together? Between you and Dexter, behind my back? Because I can't bear the idea—'

'Ian – nothing happened between me and Dexter,' she says, hoping he'll leave without asking the next question.

'But did you want it to?'

Did she? Yes, sometimes. Often.

'No. No, I didn't. We were just friends, that's all.'

'Okay. Good.' He looks at her, and tries to smile. 'I miss you so much, Em.'

'I know you do.'

He puts his hand to his stomach. 'I feel sick with it.'

'It'll pass.'

'Will it? Because I think I might be going a bit mad.'

'I know. But I can't help you, Ian.'

'You could always . . . change your mind.'

'I can't. I won't. I'm sorry.'

'Righto.' He shrugs and smiles with his lips tucked in, his Stan Laurel smile. 'Still. No harm in asking is there?'

'I suppose not.'

'I still think you're The Bollocks, mind.'

She smiles because he wants her to smile. 'No, *you're* The Bollocks, Ian.'

'Well I'm not going to stand here and argue about it!' He sighs, unable to keep it up, and reaches for the door. 'Okay then. Love to Mrs M. See you around.'

'See you around.'

'Bye.'

'Bye.'

He turns and pulls the door open sharply, kicking the bottom so that it gave the illusion of having hit him in the face. Emma laughs dutifully, then Ian takes a deep breath and is gone. She sits on the floor for one minute more then stands suddenly, and with a renewed sense of purpose grabs her keys and strides out of the flat.

The sound of a summer evening in E17, shouts and screams echoing off the buildings, a few St George's flags still hanging limply. She strides across the forecourt. Isn't she meant to have a close circle of kooky friends to help her get through all this? Shouldn't she be sitting on a low baggy sofa with six or seven attractive zany metropolitans, isn't that what city life is meant to be like? But either they live two hours away or they're with families or boyfriends, and thankfully in the absence of kooky pals, there is the off-licence called, confusingly, depressingly, Booze'R'Us.

Intimidating kids are cycling in lazy circles near the entrance, but she's fearless now, and marches through their centre, eyes fixed forward. In the shop she picks out the least dubious bottle of wine and joins the queue. The man in front of her has a cobweb tattooed on his face, and while she waits for him to count out enough small change for two litres of strong cider, she notices the bottle of champagne locked in a glass cabinet. It's dusty, like a relic of some unimaginably luxurious past.

'I'll have that champagne too, please,' she says. The shop-keeper looks suspicious, but sure enough the money is there, bunched tightly in her hand.

'Celebration, is it?'

'Exactly. Big, big celebration.' Then, on a whim. 'Twenty Marlboro too.'

With the bottles swinging in a flimsy plastic bag against her hip, she steps out of the shop, cramming the cigarette into her mouth as if it were the antidote to something. Immediately she hears a voice.

'Miss Morley?'

She looks around, guiltily.

'Miss Morley? Over here!'

And striding towards her on long legs is Sonya Richards, her protégé, her project. The skinny, bunched-up little girl who played the Artful Dodger has transformed, and Sonya is startling now: tall, hair scraped back, self-assured. Emma has a perfect vision of herself as Sonya must see her; hunched and red-eyed, fag in mouth on the threshold of Booze'R'Us. A role model, an inspiration. Absurdly, she hides the lit cigarette behind her back.

'How are you, Miss?' Sonya is looking a little ill at ease now, eyes flicking from side to side as if regretting coming over.

'I'm great! Great? How are you, Sonya?'

'Okay, Miss.'

'How's college? Everything going alright?'

'Yeah, really good.'

'A-levels next year, right?'

'That's right.' Sonya is glancing furtively at the plastic bag of booze chinking at Emma's side, the plume of smoke curling from behind her back.

'University next year?'

'Nottingham, I hope. If I get the grades.'

'You will. You will.'

'Thanks to you,' says Sonya, but without much conviction.

There's a silence. In desperation Emma holds up the bottles in one hand, the fags in the other and waggles them. 'WEEKLY SHOP!' she says.

Sonya seems confused. 'Well. I'd better get going.'

'Okay, Sonya, really great to see you. Sonya? Good luck, yeah? Really good luck,' but Sonya is already striding off without looking back and Emma, one of those carpe diem-type teachers, watches her go.

Later that night, a strange thing happens. Half asleep, lying on the sofa with the TV on and the empty bottle at her feet, she is woken by Dexter Mayhew's voice. She doesn't understand quite what he's saying – something about first-person-shooters and multiplayer options and non-stop shoot-em-up action.

Confused and concerned she forces her eyes open, and he is standing right in front of her.

Emma hauls herself upright and smiles. She has seen this show before. *Game On* is a late-night TV programme, with all the hot news and views from the computer games scene. The set is a red-lit dungeon composed of polystyrene boulders, as if playing computer games were a sort of purgatory, and in this dungeon whey-faced gamers sit hunched in front of a giant screen as Dexter Mayhew urges them to press their buttons faster, faster, shoot, shoot.

The games, the *tournaments,* are inter-cut with earnest reviews in which Dexter and a token woman with orange hair discuss the week's hot new releases. Maybe it's just Emma's tiny television, but he looks a little puffy these days, a little grey. Perhaps it's just that small screen, but something has gone missing. The swagger she remembers has gone. He is talking about *Duke Nukem 3D* and he seems uncertain, a little embarrassed even. Nevertheless she feels a great wave of affection for Dexter Mayhew. In eight years not a day has gone by when she hasn't thought of him. She misses him and she wants him back. I want my best friend back, she thinks, because without him nothing is good and nothing is right. I will call him, she thinks, as she falls asleep.

Tomorrow. First thing tomorrow, I will call him.

CHAPTER ELEVEN
Two Meetings

Soho and the South Bank

'So. The bad news is, they're cancelling *Game On*.'

'They are? Really?'

'Yes, they are.'

'Right. Okay. Right. Did they give a reason why?'

'No, Dexy, they just don't feel they've cracked a way of conveying the piquant romance of computer gaming to a late-night TV audience. The channel thinks that they haven't got the ingredients quite right, so they're cancelling the show.'

'I see.'

'. . . starting again with a different presenter.'

'And a different name?'

'No, they're still calling it *Game On*.'

'Right. So – so it's still the same show then.'

'They're making a lot of significant changes.'

'But it's still called *Game On*?'

'Yes.'

'Same set, same format and everything.'

'Broadly speaking.'

'But with a different presenter.'

'Yes. A different presenter.'

'Who?'

'Don't know. Not you though.'

'They didn't say who?'

'They said younger. Someone younger, they were going younger. That's all I know.'

'So . . . in other words, I have been sacked.'

'Well, I suppose another way of looking at it is that, yes, in this instance, they've decided to go in a different direction. A direction that's away from you.'

'Okay. Okay. So – what's the good news?'

'Sorry?'

'Well, you said "the bad news is they're cancelling the show". What's the good news?'

'That's it. That's all. That's all the news I have.'

At that precise same moment, barely two miles away across the Thames, Emma Morley stands in an ascending lift with her old friend Stephanie Shaw.

'The main thing is, and I can't say this enough – don't be intimidated.'

'Why would I be intimidated?'

'She's a legend, Em, in publishing. She's notorious.'

'Notorious? For what?'

'For being a . . . big personality,' and even though they are the only people in the lift, Stephanie Shaw drops her voice into a whisper. 'She's a wonderful editor, she's just a little . . . eccentric that's all.'

They ride the next twenty storeys in silence. Beside her Stephanie Shaw stands smart, petite in a crisp white shirt – no, not a shirt, a *blouse* – tight black pencil skirt, a neat little bob, years away from the sullen Goth who sat next to her in tutorials all that time ago, and Emma is surprised to find herself intimidated by her old acquaintance; her professional demeanour, her no-nonsense manner. Stephanie Shaw has probably *sacked* people. She probably says things like 'photocopy this for me!' If Emma did the same at school they'd laugh in her face. In the lift, hands clasped in front of her, Emma has a sudden urge to giggle. It's like they're playing at a game called 'Offices'.

The lift door slides open onto the thirtieth floor, a vast open-plan area, its high smoked-glass windows looking out across the Thames and Lambeth. When Emma had first come to London she had written hopeful, ill-informed letters to publishers and imagined the envelopes being sliced open with ivory paper knives in cluttered, shabby Georgian houses by ageing secretaries in half-moon glasses. But this is sleek and light and youthful, the very model of the modern media workplace. The only thing that reassures her are the stacks of books that litter the floor and tables, teetering piles of the things dumped seemingly at random. Stephanie strides and Emma follows and around the office faces pop up from behind walls of books and peer at the new arrival as she struggles to remove her jacket and walk at the same time.

'Now, I can't guarantee that she'll have read it all, or read it *at* all in fact, but she's asked to see you, which is great, Em, really great.'

'I appreciate this so much, Stephanie.'

'Trust me, Em, the writing's really good. If it wasn't I wouldn't have given it to her. It's not in my interest to give her rubbish to read.'

It was a school story, a romance really, for older kids, set in a comp in Leeds. A sort of real-life, gritty Mallory Towers, based around a school production of *Oliver!* and told from the point of view of Julie Criscoll, the mouthy, irresponsible girl playing the Artful Dodger. There were illustrations too, scratchy doodles and caricatures and sarcastic speech bubbles like you might find in a teenage girl's diary, all jumbled in with the text.

She had sent out the first twenty thousand words and waited patiently until she had received a rejection letter from every single publisher; a complete set. *Not for us, sorry not to be more helpful, hope you have better luck elsewhere* they said, and the only encouraging thing about all those rejections was their vagueness; clearly the manuscript wasn't getting read much, just declined with a standard letter. Of all the things she had written and abandoned, this was the first which, after reading, she hadn't wanted to hurl across the room. She knew it was good. Clearly she would have to resort to nepotism.

Despite various influential contacts from college, she had taken a private vow never to resort to asking favours; tugging at the elbow of her more successful contemporaries was too much like asking a friend for money. But she had filled a loose-leaf binder with rejection letters now, and as her mother was fond of reminding her, she wasn't getting any younger. One lunch break, she had found a quiet classroom, taken a deep breath and made a phone-call to Stephanie Shaw. It was the first time they had spoken in three years, but at least they actually liked each other and after some pleasant catching up, she came out with it: Would she read something? This thing I've written. Some chapters and an outline for a silly book for teenagers. It's about a school musical.

And now here she is, actually meeting a publisher, a real-life publisher. She feels shaky from too much coffee, sick with anxiety, her febrile state not helped by the fact that she has been forced to bunk off school herself. Today is a vital staff meeting, the last before the holidays, and like an errant pupil she had woken that morning, held her nose and phoned the secretary, croaking something about gastric flu. The secretary's disbelief was audible down the phone-line. She will be in trouble with Mr Godalming too. Phil will be furious.

No time to worry about that now because they are at the corner office, a glass cube of prime commercial space in which she can see a reedy female figure with her back to Emma, and beyond that a startling panorama from St Paul's down to Parliament.

Stephanie indicates a low chair by the door.

'So. Wait there. Come and see me afterwards. Tell me how it went. And remember – don't be scared . . .'

'Did they give a reason? For dumping me?'

'Not really.'

'Come on, Aaron, just tell me.'

'Well, the exact phrase was that, well, the exact phrase was that you were just a little bit 1989.'

'Wow. Wow. Right, okay. Okay, well – fuck 'em, right?'

'Exactly, that's what I said.'

'Did you?'

'I told them I wasn't best pleased.'

'Okay, well what else is coming up?'

'Nothing.'

'Nothing?'

'There's this thing where they have robots fighting and you have to sort of introduce the robots . . .'

'Why do the robots fight?'

'Who can say? It's in their nature, I suppose. They're aggressive robots.'

'I don't think so.'

'Okay. Car show on *Men and Motors*?'

'What, *satellite*?'

'Satellite and cable's the future, Dex.'

'But what about terrestrial?'

'It's just a little quiet out there.'

'It's not quiet for Suki Meadows, it's not quiet for Toby Moray. I can't walk past a television without seeing Toby-bloody-Moray.'

'That's TV, Dex, it's faddy. He's just a fad. You were the fad, now he's the fad.'

'I was a *fad*?'

'You're not a *fad*. I just mean you're bound to have ups and downs, that's all. I think you need to think about a change of

240

direction. We need to change people's perception of you. Your reputation.'

'Hang on – I have a *reputation*?'

Emma sits in the low leather chair and waits and waits, watching the office at work, feeling a slightly shameful envy of this corporate world and the smart-ish, young-ish professionals who occupy it. Water Cooler envy, that's what it is. There's nothing special or distinctive about this office, but compared to Cromwell Road Comp, it's positively futuristic; a sharp contrast to her staffroom with its tannin-stained mugs, torn furniture and surly rotas, its general air of grouchiness and complaint and dissatisfaction. And of course the kids are great, some of them, some of the time, but the confrontations these days seem more frequent and more alarming. For the first time she has been told to 'talk to the hand', a new attitude that she finds hard to reason with. Or perhaps she's just losing her knack, her motivation, her energy. The situation with her headmaster certainly isn't helping.

What if life had taken a different route? What if she had persevered with those letters to publishers when she was twenty-two? Might it have been Emma, instead of Stephanie Shaw, eating Pret A Manger sandwiches in a pencil skirt? For some time now she has had a conviction that life is about to change if only because it must, and perhaps this is it, perhaps this meeting is the new start. Her stomach churns once more in anticipation as the PA puts down her phone and approaches. Marsha will see her now. Emma stands, smoothes down her skirt because she has seen people do it on television, and enters the glass box.

Marsha – Miss Francomb? – is tall and imposing, with aqua-line features that give her an intimidating Woolfish quality. In her early forties, her grey hair cropped and brushed forward Soviet-style, her voice husky and commanding, she stands and offers her hand.

'Ah you must be my twelve-thirty.'

Emma squeaks a reply, yes, that's right twelve-thirty, though technically it was meant to be twelve-fifteen.

'*Setzen Sie, bitte hin,*' says Marsha, unaccountably. German? Why German? Oh well, best play along.

'*Danke,*' Emma squeaks again, looks around, settles on the sofa, and takes in the room: trophies on shelves, framed book covers, souvenirs of an illustrious career. Emma has the overwhelming feeling that she shouldn't be here, doesn't belong, is wasting this redoubtable woman's time; she publishes books, real books that people buy and read. Certainly Marsha isn't making it easy for her. A silence hangs in the air as she lowers the venetian blinds then adjusts them so that the exterior office is obscured. They sit in the half-light, and Emma has the sudden feeling that she is about to be interrogated.

'So sorry to have kept you waiting, it's unbelievably busy, I'm afraid. I'm only just able to fit you in. I don't want to rush this. With something like this it's so important to make the right decision, don't you think?'

'It's vital. Absolutely.'

'Tell me how long have you been working with children?'

'Um, let me see, '93 – about five years.'

Marsha leans forward, impassioned. 'And do you *love* it?'

'I do. Most of the time, anyway.' Emma feels as if she's being a little stiff, a little formal. 'When they're not giving me a hard time.'

'The children give you a hard time?'

'They can be little bastards sometimes, if I'm honest.'

'Really?'

'You know. Cheeky, disruptive.'

Marsha bridles, and sits back in her chair. 'So what do you do, for discipline?'

'Oh, the usual, throw chairs at them! Not really! Just the usual stuff, send them out the room, that kind of thing.'

'I see. I see.' Marsha says no more, but emanates deep disapproval. Her eyes return to the papers on the desk, and Emma wonders when they're going to actually start talking about the work.

'Well,' says Marsha, 'I have to say, your English is much better than I expected.'

'I'm sorry?'

'I mean, you're fluent. It's like you've been in England all your life.'

'Well . . . I have.'

Marsha looks irritated. 'Not according to your CV.'

'I'm sorry?'

'Your CV says that you're German!'

What can Emma do to make amends? Perhaps she should pretend to be German? No good. She can't speak German. 'No, I'm definitely English.' And what CV? She didn't send a CV.

Marsha is shaking her head. 'I'm sorry, we seem to be talking at cross-purposes. You are my twelve-thirty, aren't you?'

'Yes! I think so. Am I?'

'The nanny? You are here for the job of nanny?'

'I have a *reputation*?'

'A little bit. In the industry.'

'As what?'

'Just a bit . . . unreliable, that's all.'

'Unreliable?'

'Unprofessional.'

'In what way?'

'In a drunk way. In an off-your-face-on-camera kind of way.'

'Hey, I have never been—'

'—and arrogant. People think you're arrogant.'

'Arrogant? I'm confident, not arrogant.'

'Hey I'm just telling you what people say, Dex.'

'"People"! Who are these "people"?'

'People you've worked with—'

'Really? Good God—'

'I'm just saying, if you feel you've got a problem—'

'Which I haven't.'

'—now might be the time to address it.'

'I haven't though.'

'Well then we're fine. In the meantime, I think you might also want to watch what you're spending. For a couple of months at least.'

'Emma, I am so sorry . . .'

She walks towards the lifts, hot-eyed and embarrassed, Marsha walking close behind, Stephanie following behind her. Heads pop up from cubicles as they pass in procession. That'll teach her, they must think, for getting big ideas.

'I'm so sorry about wasting your time,' says Marsha, ingratiatingly. 'Someone was meant to call and cancel—'

'S'alright, not your fault—' Emma mumbles.

'Needless to say my assistant and I will be having words. Are you *sure* you didn't get the message? I hate to cancel meetings, but I simply hadn't got round to reading the material. I'd give it a quick read now, but poor old Helga is waiting in the boardroom apparently—'

'I quite understand.'

'Stephanie here assures me that you're extremely talented. I'm so looking forward to reading your work . . .'

Arriving at the lifts, Emma jabs the call button. 'Yes, well . . .'

'At least, if anything you'll have an amusing story.'

An amusing story? She jabs the call button as if poking an eye. She doesn't want an amusing story, she wants change, a break, not anecdotes. Her life has been stuffed with anecdotes, an endless string of the bastards, now she wants something to go right for once. She wants success, or at least the hope of it.

'I'm afraid next week is no good, then I'm on holiday, so it may be some time. But before the summer's out, I promise.'

Before the summer's out? Month after month slipping by with nothing changing. She jabs once more at the lift button and says nothing, a surly teenager, making them suffer. They wait.

Marsha, seemingly unflustered, examines her with sharp blue eyes. 'Tell me, Emma, what are you doing at the moment?'

'I teach English. A secondary school in Leytonstone.'

'That must be very demanding. When do you find the time to actually write?'

'At night. Weekends. Early mornings sometimes.'

Marsha narrows her eyes. 'You must be very passionate about it.'

'It's the only thing I really want to do now.' Emma surprises herself, not just at how earnest she must sound but also with the realisation that the remark is true. The lift opens behind her, and she glances over her shoulder, almost wishing now that she could stay.

Marsha is holding out her hand. 'Well, goodbye, Miss Morley. I look forward to talking to you further.'

Emma takes hold of her long fingers. 'And I hope you find your nanny.'

'I hope so too. The last one was a complete psychopath. I don't suppose you want the job anyway, do you? I imagine you'd be rather good.' Marsha smiles, and Emma smiles back, and behind Marsha, Stephanie bites her bottom lip, mouths sorry-sorry-sorry and mimes a little phone. 'Call me!'

The lift doors close and Emma slumps against the wall as the lift plummets thirty floors and she feels the excitement in her stomach curdle into sour disappointment. At three a.m. that morning, unable to sleep, she had fantasised an impromptu lunch with her new editor. She had pictured herself drinking crisp white wine in the Oxo Tower, beguiling her companion with engaging stories of school life, and now here she is, spat out onto the South Bank in less than twenty-five minutes.

In May she had celebrated the election result here, but there's none of that euphoria now. Having declared herself suffering from gastric flu, she can't even go to the staff meeting. She feels another argument brewing there too, recriminations, sly remarks.

To clear her head she decides to go for a walk, and heads off in the direction of Tower Bridge.

But even the Thames fails to lift her spirits. This stretch of the South Bank is in the process of renovation, a mess of scaffolding and tarpaulin, Bankside Power Station looming derelict and oppressive on this midsummer day. She is hungry, but there's nowhere to eat, no-one to eat with. Her phone rings, and she scrabbles for it in her bag, keen to vent some of her frustration and realising only too late who will be calling.

'So – gastric flu is it?' says the headmaster.

She sighs. 'That's right.'

'In bed with it, are you? Because it doesn't sound like you're in bed. It sounds to me like you're out enjoying the sun.'

'Phil, please – don't give me a hard time.'

'Oh, no, *Miss Morley*, you can't have it both ways. You can't end our relationship and then expect some kind of special dispensation—' It's the voice he has used for months now, officious, sing-song and spiteful and she feels a fresh burst of anger at the traps she lays for herself. 'If you want it to be purely professional, then we have to keep it purely professional! So! If you don't mind, could you tell me why you're not at this very important meeting today?'

'Don't do this, please, Phil? I'm not in the mood.'

'Because I'd hate to have to make this a *disciplinary* issue, Emma . . .'

She takes the phone away from her ear while the headmaster drones on. Chunky and old-fashioned now, it's the phone he bought her as a lover's gift so that he could 'hear her voice whenever he needed to'. My God, they had even had phone-sex on the thing. Or he had anyway—

'You were expressly informed that the meeting was obligatory. Term's not over yet, you know.'

—and for one moment she contemplates how pleasant it would feel to hurl the wretched thing into the Thames, watch the phone hit the water like half a brick. But she would have to remove the SIM card first, which would deaden the symbolism somewhat, and such dramatic gestures are for films and TV. Besides, she can't afford to buy another phone.

Not now that she has decided to resign.

'Phil?'

'Let's stick to Mr Godalming, shall we?'

'Okay – Mr Godalming?'

'Yes, Miss Morley?'

'I resign.'

He laughs, that maddening fake laugh of his. She can see him now, shaking his head slowly. 'Emma, you can't resign.'

'I can and I have and here's something else. Mr Godalming?'

'Emma?'

The obscenity forms on her lips, but she can't quite bring herself to say it. Instead she mouths the words with relish, hangs up, drops the phone into her bag and, dizzy with elation and fear of the future, she keeps on walking east along the River Thames.

'So, sorry I can't take you for lunch, I'm meeting another client . . .'

'Okay. Thanks, Aaron.'

'Maybe next time, Dexy. What's up? You seem downhearted, mate.'

'No, nothing. I'm just a little concerned, that's all.'

'What about?'

'About, you know. The future. My career. It's not what I expected.'

'It never is, is it? The future. That's what makes it so fucking EXCITING! Hey, come here you. I said come here! I've got a theory about you, mate. Do you want to hear it?'

'Go on then.'

'People love you, Dex, they really do. Problem is, they love you in an ironic, tongue-in-cheek, love-to-hate kind of way. What we need to do is get someone to love you *sincerely* . . .'

CHAPTER TWELVE
Saying 'I Love You'

WEDNESDAY 15 JULY 1998

Chichester, Sussex

Then, without quite knowing how it happened, Dexter finds that he has fallen in love, and suddenly life is one long mini-break.

Sylvie Cope. Her name is Sylvie Cope, a beautiful name, and if you asked him what she is like he would shake his head and blow air through his mouth and say that she is great, just great, just . . . amazing! She is beautiful of course, but in a different way from the others – not lads-mag-bubbly like Suki Meadows, or trendy-beautiful like Naomi or Ingrid or Yolande, but serenely, classically beautiful; in an earlier TV presenter incarnation, he might have called her 'classy', or even 'dead classy'. Long, straight fair hair, parted severely in the middle, small neat features set perfectly in a pale heart-shaped face, she reminds him of a woman in a painting that he can't remember the name of, someone mediaeval with flowers in her hair. That is what Sylvie Cope is like; the kind of woman who would look perfectly at home with her arms draped around a unicorn. Tall and slim, a little austere, frequently quite stern, with a face that doesn't move much except to frown or sometimes to roll her eyes at some stupid thing he's said or done; Sylvie is perfect, and demands perfection.

Her ears stick out just a tiny, tiny bit so that they glow like coral with the light behind her, and in the same light you can see a fine downy hair on her cheeks and forehead. At other, more superficial times in his life Dexter might have found these qualities, the glowing ears, the hairy forehead, off-putting but as he looks at her now, seated at the table opposite him on an English lawn in high summer, her perfect little chin resting on her long-fingered hand, swallows overhead, candles lighting her face just like in those paintings by the candle-guy, he finds her completely hypnotic. She smiles at him across the table and he decides that tonight is the night that he will tell her that he loves her. He has never really said 'I love you' before, not sober and on purpose. He has said 'I fucking love you', but that's different, and he feels that now is the time to use the words in their purest form. He is so taken with this plan that he is momentarily unable to concentrate on what is being said.

'So what *do* you do exactly, Dexter?' asks Sylvie's mother, from the far end of the table; Helen Cope, birdlike and aloof in beige cashmere.

Unhearing, Dexter continues to gaze at Sylvie, who is raising her eyebrows now in warning. 'Dexter?'

'Hm?'

'Mummy asked you a question?'

'I'm sorry, miles away.'

'He's a *TV presenter*,' says Sam, one of Sylvie's twin brothers. Nineteen years old with a college rower's back, Sam is a hulking, self-satisfied little Nazi, just like his twin brother Murray.

'Is or was? Do you still do presenting these days?' smirks Murray and they flick their blond fringes at each other. Sporty, clear-skinned, blue-eyed, they look like they were raised in a lab.

'Mummy wasn't asking *you,* Murray,' snaps Sylvie.

'Well, I still am a presenter, of sorts,' says Dexter and thinks, I'll get you yet, you little bastards. They've had run-ins before, Dexter and The Twins, in London. Through little smirks and twinkles they've revealed that they don't think much of sis's new boyfriend, think she can do better. The Cope family are Winners and will only tolerate Winners. Dexter's just a charm-boy, a has-been, a poser on the way down. There is silence at the table. Was he meant to keep talking? 'I'm sorry, what was the question?'

asks Dexter, momentarily lost but determined to get back on top of the game.

'I wondered what you were up to these days, work-wise?' she repeats patiently, making clear that this is a job interview for the post of Sylvie's boyfriend.

'Well, I've been working on a couple of new TV shows, actually. We're waiting to find out what's going to get commissioned.'

'What are they about, these TV shows?'

'Well one's about London nightlife, a sort of what's-on-in-the-capital thing, and the other's a sports show. Extreme Sports.'

'Extreme Sports? What are "Extreme Sports"?'

'Um, well mountain-biking, snow-boarding, skate-boarding—'

'And do you do any "Extreme Sports" yourself?' smirks Murray.

'I skate-board a little,' says Dexter, defensively, and he notices that at the other end of the table, Sam has stuffed his napkin into his mouth.

'Will we have seen you on anything on the BBC?' says Lionel, the father, handsome, plump, self-satisfied and still bizarrely blond in his late fifties.

'Unlikely. It's all rather late-night fare, I'm afraid.' '*Rather late-night fare, I'm afraid*', '*I skate-board a little*'. God, he thinks, what do you sound like? There's something about being with the Cope family that makes him behave as if he's in a costume drama. Perchance, 'tis rather late-night fare. Still, if that's what it takes . . .

Now Murray, the other twin – or is it actually Sam? – pipes up, his mouth full of salad, 'We used to watch that late night show you were on, *largin' it*. All swearing and dolly-birds dancing in cages. You didn't like us watching it, remember Mum?'

'God, that thing?' Mrs Cope, Helen, frowns. 'I *do* remember, vaguely.'

'You used to really, really *hate* it,' says Murray or Sam.

'Turn it off! you used to shout,' says the other one. 'Turn it off! You'll damage your brain!'

'Funny, that's exactly what my mother used to say too,' says

Dexter, but no-one picks up on the remark and he reaches for the wine bottle.

'So that was *you*, was it?' says Lionel, Sylvie's father, his eyebrows raised, as if the gentleman at his table has revealed himself to be rather the cad.

'Well, yes, but it wasn't all like that. I tended just to interview the bands and the movie stars.' He wonders if he sounds big-headed with this talk of bands and movie stars, but there's no chance of that because the twins are there, ready to shoot him down.

'So do you still hang out with a lot of *movie stars* then?' says one of them, in mock awe, the jumped-up little Aryan freakboy.

'Not really. Not anymore.' He decides to answer honestly, but without any regret or self-pity. 'That has all sort of . . . drifted away.'

'Dexter's being modest,' says Sylvie. 'He gets offers all the time. He's just very picky about his on-screen work. What he really wants to do is produce. Dexter has his own media production company!' she says proudly, and her parents nod approvingly. A businessman, an entrepreneur – that's more like it.

Dexter smiles too, but the fact is life has become a great deal quieter recently. Mayhem TV plc has yet to earn a commission, or a meeting with a commissioner, and at the moment still exists only in the form of expensively headed paper. Aaron, his agent, has dropped him. There are no voiceovers, no promotional work, not quite so many premieres. He is no longer the voice of premium cider, has been quietly expelled from poker school, and even the guy who plays the congas in Jamiroquai doesn't call him anymore. And yet despite all this, the downturn in professional fortunes, he's fine now, because now he has fallen in love with Sylvie, beautiful Sylvie, and now they have their mini-breaks.

Weekends frequently begin and end at Stansted airport, where they fly off to Genoa or Bucharest, Rome or Reykjavik, trips that Sylvie pre-plans with the precision of an invading army. A startlingly attractive, metropolitan European couple, they stay in exclusive little boutique hotels and walk and shop and shop and walk and drink tiny cups of black coffee in street cafés, then lock themselves into their chic minimal taupe-coloured bedroom with the wet-room and the single stick of bamboo in the tall thin vase.

If they're not exploring small independent shops in a major European city, then they're spending time in West London with Sylvie's friends: petite, pretty hard-faced girls and their pink-cheeked, large-bottomed boyfriends who, like Sylvie and her friends, work in marketing, or advertising or the City. In truth, they're not really his sort, these hyper-confident Über-boyfriends. They remind him of the prefects and head-boys he knew at school; not unpleasant, just not very cool. Never mind. You can't build your life around what's cool, and there are benefits to this less chaotic, more ordered lifestyle.

Serenity and drunkenness don't really go together and save for the occasional glass of champagne or wine with dinner, Sylvie doesn't drink alcohol. Neither does she smoke or take drugs or eat red meat or bread or refined sugar or potatoes. More significantly, she has no time for Dexter drunk. His abilities as a fabled mixologist mean nothing to her. She finds inebriation embarrassing and unmanly, and more than once he has found himself alone at the end of the evening because of that third martini. Though it has never been stated as such, he has been given a choice: clean up your act, sort out your life, or you will lose me. Consequently there are fewer hangovers these days, fewer nose-bleeds, fewer mornings spent writhing in shame and self-disgust. He no longer goes to bed with a bottle of red wine in case he gets thirsty in the night, and for this he is grateful. He feels like a new man.

But the single most striking thing about Sylvie is that he likes her so much more than she likes him. He likes her straightforwardness, her self-confidence and poise. He likes her ambition, which is ferocious and unapologetic, and her taste, which is expensive and immaculate. Of course he likes the way she looks, and the way they look together, but he also likes her lack of sentimentality; she is as hard, bright and desirable as a diamond and for the first time in his life, he has had to do the chasing. On their first date, a ruinously expensive French restaurant in Chelsea, he had wondered aloud if she was enjoying herself. She was having a wonderful time, she said, but she didn't like to laugh in company because she didn't like what laughter did to her face. And although a part of him felt a little chill at this, a part of him also had to admire her commitment.

This visit, his first to the parental home, is part of a long weekend, a stopover in Chichester before they continue down the M3 to a rented cottage in Cornwall, where Sylvie is going to teach him how to surf. Of course he shouldn't really be taking all this time off, he should be working, or looking for work. But the prospect of Sylvie, stern and rosy-cheeked in a wetsuit with her hair tied back, is almost more than he can bear. He looks across at her now to check on how he is performing, and she smiles reassuringly in the candlelight. He's doing fine so far, and he pours himself one last glass of wine. Mustn't have too much. Got to keep your wits about you, with these people.

After dessert – sorbet made from their very own strawberries, which he has praised excessively – Dexter helps Sylvie take the plates back into the house, a red-brick mansion like a high-end doll's house. They stand in the Victorian country kitchen, loading the dishwasher.

'I keep getting your brothers muddled up.'

'A good way to remember it is Sam's hateful and Murray's foul.'

'Don't think they like me very much.'

'They don't like anyone apart from themselves.'

'I think they think I'm a bit flash.'

She takes his hand across the cutlery basket. 'Does it matter what my family think of you?'

'Depends. Does it matter to you, what your family think of me?'

'A little, I suppose.'

'Well then it matters to me too,' he says, with great sincerity.

She stops loading the dishwasher, and looks at him intently. Like public laughter, Sylvie is not a big fan of ostentatious displays of affection, of cuddles and hugs. Sex with Sylvie is like a particularly demanding game of squash, leaving him aching and with a general sense that he has lost. Physical contact is rare and when it does come, tends to spring from nowhere, violently and swiftly. Now, suddenly, she puts her hand to the back of his head and kisses him hard, at the same time taking his other hand and jamming it between her legs. He looks into her eyes, wide and intent, and sets his own face to express desire, rather than discomfort at the dishwasher door chafing his shins. He can hear the family marching into the house, the twins' boorish voices in the hallway. He tries to pull away, but his lower lip is gripped neatly between Sylvie's teeth, stretching out comically like a Warner Brothers cartoon. He whimpers and she laughs then lets go of his lip so that it snaps back like a rollerblind.

'Can't wait for bed later,' she breathes, as he checks for blood with the back of his hand.

'What if your family hear?'

'I don't care. I'm a big girl now.' He wonders if he should do it now, tell her that he loves her.

'God, Dexter, you can't just put the saucepans in the dishwasher, you have to rinse them first.' She goes through to the living room, leaving him to rinse the pans.

Dexter is not easily intimidated by anyone, but there is something about this family, something self-sufficient and self-satisfied, that makes him feel defensive. It's certainly not a matter of class; his own background is just as privileged, if a lot more liberal and bohemian than the High Tory Copes. What makes him anxious is this obligation to prove himself a winner. The Copes are early risers, mountain-walkers, lake-swimmers; hale, hearty, superior and he resolves not to let them get to him.

As he enters the living room the Axis powers turn to face him, and there's a hasty hush as if they have just been discussing him. He smiles confidently, then flops into one of the low floral sofas. The living room has been done up to feel like a country house hotel, right down to the copies of *Country Life*, *Private Eye* and the *Economist*, fanned out on the coffee table. There's a momentary silence. A clock ticks, and he is contemplating reaching for a copy of *The Lady* when:

'I know, let's play "Are You There, Moriarty?",' says Murray, and there's general approval from the family, even Sylvie.

'What's "Are You There, Moriarty?"' asks Dexter, and the Copes all shake their heads in unison at this interloper's ignorance.

'It's a wonderful, wonderful parlour game!' says Helen, more animated than she has been all evening. 'We've been playing it for years!' Sam, meanwhile, is already rolling up a copy of the *Daily Telegraph* into a long stiff rod. 'Basically, one person is blindfolded, and they have this rolled-up newspaper and they sit kneeling opposite this other person . . .'

'. . . who's also blindfolded.' Murray takes over, at the same time digging in the drawers of the antique writing table for a roll of sellotape. 'The one with the rolled-up newspaper says, "Are you there, Moriarty?"' He tosses the tape to Sam.

'And the other person has to sort of contort and duck out of the way and then answer Yes! or Here!' Sam starts binding the newspaper into a tight baton. 'And judging from where the voice comes from, he has to try and hit them with the rolled-up newspaper.'

'You get three attempts, and if you miss all three you have to stay on and get hit by the next player,' says Sylvie, elated at the prospect of a Victorian parlour game, 'and if you hit the other person you get to choose your next contestant. That's how *we* play it anyway.'

'So—' says Murray, tapping the palm of his hand with the paper truncheon. 'Who's for some Extreme Sports?'

It is decided that Sam will take on Dexter the intruder and that, surprise surprise, Sam will get the baton. The field of battle is the large faded rug in the middle of the room, and Sylvie leads him into position then stands behind him, tying a large white napkin over his eyes, a princess favouring her loyal knight. He gets one last glimpse of Sam kneeling opposite him, smirking from behind his blindfold as he taps the palm of his hand with the baton, and Dexter is suddenly overwhelmed by the need to win this game and show the family what he's made of. 'Show them how it's done,' whispers Sylvie, her breath hot in his ear, and he remembers the moment in the kitchen, his hand between her legs. Now she takes his elbow and helps him kneel, and the adversaries face each other in silence like gladiators in the arena of the Persian rug.

'Let the games commence!' says Lionel, like an emperor.

'Are you there, Moriarty?' says Sam with a snigger.

'Here,' says Dexter, then like a limbo dancer deftly leans backwards.

The first blow hits him just below the eye, making a satisfying slapping sound that echoes round the room. 'Oooh!' and 'Ouch!' say the Copes, laughing at his pain. 'That's *gotta* hurt,' says Murray maddeningly, and Dexter feels a deep sting of humiliation while he laughs good-naturedly, a hearty, well-done-you laugh. 'You got me!' he concedes, rubbing his cheek, but Sam has smelt blood and is already asking—

'Are you there, Moriarty?'

'Ye . . .'

Before he can move, the second blow slaps against his buttock, causing him to flinch and stumble to the side, and again there is laughter from the family, and a low hissing 'yessssss' from Sam.

'Nice one, Sammy,' says the mother, proud of her boy, and Dexter suddenly has a deep hatred of this stupid fucking game, which seems to be some weird family ritual of humiliation . . .

'Two out of two,' guffaws Murray. 'Nice one, bro.'

. . . and don't say 'bro' either you little tit, thinks Dexter, fuming now because if there's one thing that he hates it's being laughed at, especially by this lot, who clearly think he's a loser, all washed-up and not up to the job of being their precious Sylvie's boyfriend. 'I think I've got the hang of it now,' he chortles, clinging to a sense of humour while at the same time wanting to pummel Sammy's face with his fists—

'Let's get ready to rumble . . .' says Murray, in that voice again.

—or a frying pan, a cast iron frying pan—

'So here goes – three out of three methinks . . .'

—a ball-peen hammer, or a mace—

'Are you there, Moriarty?' says Sam.

'Here!' says Dexter, and like a ninja he twists at his waist, ducking down and to the right.

The third blow is an insolent poke in the shoulder with the blunt end that sends Dexter sprawling backwards into the coffee table. The prod is so impertinent and precise that he's convinced that Sam must be cheating, and he tears his blindfold off to confront him, finding instead Sylvie leaning over him, laughing, actually laughing regardless of what it does to her face.

'A hit! A palpable hit!' shrieks that little shit Murray, and Dexter clambers to his feet, his face a grimace of delight. There's a little round of patronising applause.

'YESSSSSSSSSSSSSSSSSS!' crows Sam, teeth bared, his ruddy face screwed up, two fists pulled slowly towards his chest in victory.

'Better luck next time!' drawls Helen, the wicked Roman empress.

'You'll get the hang of it,' growls Lionel and, enraged, Dexter notices that the twins are holding finger and thumbs to their foreheads in an L shape. L for loser.

'Well I'm still proud of you,' pouts Sylvie, ruffling his hair and patting his knee, as he sinks into the sofa next to her. Shouldn't she be on his side? When it comes to loyalty, he thinks, she's still one of them.

The tournament continues. Murray beats Sam, then Lionel beats Murray, then Lionel gets beaten by Helen, and it's all very convivial and jolly, these neat little bops and taps with the rolled-up newspaper, all much jollier than when it was Dexter out there getting clubbed around the face with what felt like a length of scaffolding. From deep in the sofa he watches and scowls and, as part of his revenge, quietly sets about emptying a bottle of Lionel's very good claret. There was a time when he could do this kind of thing. If he was twenty-three again he would feel confident and charming and self-assured, but he has lost the knack somehow and his mood darkens as the bottle empties.

Then Helen beats Murray and Sam beats Helen and now it's Sam's turn to try and strike his sister, and there is at least some pleasure and pride in watching how good Sylvie is at the game, effortlessly avoiding her little brother's desperate swipes, twisting and ducking at the waist, supple and sporty, his golden girl. He watches, smiling, from deep in the sofa and just when he thinks they've all forgotten about him:

'Come on then. Your go!' Sylvie is holding out the baton towards him.

'But you just won!'

'I know, but you haven't had a chance to bat yet, poor thing,' she pouts. 'Come on. Have a go. Take me on!'

The Copes all love the idea of this – there's a low, pagan rumble of excitement, bizarrely vaguely sexual, and clearly he has no choice. His honour, the honour of the Mayhews is at stake here. Solemnly Dexter puts down his glass, stands and takes the baton.

'You're sure about this?' he says, kneeling on the carpet an arm's length away. 'Because I'm a pretty good tennis player.'

'Oh, I'm sure,' she says, grinning provocatively, shaking out her hands like a gymnast as the blindfold is tied.

'And I think I might be quite good at this.'

Behind him, Sam ties his blindfold tight as a tourniquet. 'We'll see, won't we?'

The arena falls silent.

'Okay, are you ready?' says Dexter.

'Oh yes.'

He grips the baton with both hands, arms level at his shoulder. 'Are you sure?'

'I'm ready when you . . .'

Momentarily an image flickers in his mind – a baseball player on his mound – as he slices diagonally with the bat, a tremendous uppercut that swishes audibly through the air and from behind the blindfold the impact feels fantastic as it sends tremors along both arms and into his chest. A moment of awed silence follows and for a moment Dexter is sure that he has done very, very well. And then he hears a crash, and an appalled cry goes up in unison from the whole family.

'SYLVIE!'

'Oh my God!'

'Sweetheart, darling, are you okay?'

Dexter tears off his blindfold to see that Sylvie has somehow been transported to the far side of the room, slumped over in the fireplace like a marionette with all her strings cut. Her eyes are blinking wide and her hand is cupped to her face, but it's already possible to see the dark rivulet of blood as it trickles down beneath her nose. She is moaning quietly to herself.

'Oh my God, I am so sorry!' he exclaims, horrified. Immediately he crosses towards her, but the family has already closed in.

'Good God, Dexter, what the hell were you thinking?' barks red-faced Lionel, drawing himself up to his full height.

'YOU DIDN'T EVEN ASK IF SHE WAS *THERE* MORIARTY!' shrieks her mother.

'Didn't I? Sorry—'

'No, you just lashed out crazily!'

'Like a madman—'

'Sorry. Sorry, I forgot. I was—'

'—*Drunk!*' says Sam. The accusation hangs in the air. 'You're drunk, man. You're completely pissed!'

They all turn and glare.

'It really was an accident. I just caught your face at an odd angle.'

Sylvie tugs on Helen's sleeve. 'How does it look?' she asks in a tearful voice as she discreetly removes her cupped hand from her nose. It's as if she's holding a fistful of strawberry sorbet.

'It's really not too bad,' gasps Helen, her hand clasped to her mouth in horror and Sylvie's face crumples further into tears. 'Let me see, let me see! The bathroom!' she whimpers, and the family haul her to her feet.

'It really was just some kind of flukey accident . . .' Holding her mother's arm, Sylvie hurries past him, eyes fixed straight ahead. 'Do you want me to come with you? Sylvie? Sylv?' There is no reply and he watches in misery, as her mother escorts her into the hall and up the stairs to the bathroom.

He listens to the footsteps fade.

And now it's just Dexter and the Cope menfolk. A primal scene, they glare and glare. Instinctively he feels his hand tighten around his weapon, the tightly rolled-up copy of today's *Daily Telegraph*, and says the only thing that he can think of to say.

'Ouch!'

'So – do you think I made a good impression?'

Dexter and Sylvie lie in the guest room's large soft double bed. Sylvie turns to look at him, her face unmoving, the small fine nose throbbing accusingly. She sniffs but says nothing.

'Do you want me to say I'm sorry again?'

'Dexter, it's *fine*.'

'You forgive me?'

'I forgive you,' she snaps.

'And you think they think I'm alright, they don't think I'm some sort of violent psychopath or something?'

'I think they think you're *fine*. Let's forget it shall we?' She turns onto her side, away from him, and turns out her light.

A moment passes. Like a shamed schoolboy, he feels as if he won't sleep, unless he gets some further reassurance. 'Sorry for . . . fucking up,' he pouts. '*Again!*' She turns once more, and lays one hand fondly on his cheek.

'Don't be ridiculous. You were doing fine until you hit me. They really, really liked you.'

'And what about you?' he says, still fishing.

She sighs and smiles. 'I think you're okay too.'

'Any chance of a kiss then?'

'I can't. I'll start bleeding. I'll make up for it tomorrow.' She turns away again. Satisfied now, he sinks lower and puts his hands behind his head. The bed is immense and soft and smells of freshly washed linen, and the windows open out onto a still summer night. Stripped of quilts and blankets, they lie beneath a single white cotton sheet, and he can see the wonderful line of her legs and narrow hips, the curve of her long smooth back. Tonight's sexual potential evaporated with the moment of impact and the possibility of concussion, but still he turns to her and places one hand beneath the sheet and onto her thigh. The skin is cool and smooth.

'Long drive tomorrow,' she mumbles. 'Let's go to sleep.'

He continues to look at the back of her head, where the long fine hair falls away from the nape of her neck, revealing the darker whorls beneath. You could take a photograph of that, he thinks, it is so beautiful. Call it 'Texture'. He wonders if he still might tell her that he loves her or, more tentatively, that he 'thinks he might be in love with her', which is both more touching and easier to back out of. But clearly this is not the time, not now with the plug of bloody tissue still on her bedside table.

He feels he ought to say something though. Inspired, he kisses her shoulder, and whispers. 'Well you know what they say—' He pauses for effect. 'You always hurt the one you love!'

This is pretty clever, pretty adorable he thinks, and there's a

261

silence while he waits, eyebrows raised expectantly, for the implication to sink in.

'Let's get some sleep, shall we?' she says.

Defeated, he lies back and listens to the gentle hum of the A259. Somewhere in the house right now her parents are tearing him to pieces and he realises, appallingly, that he has a sudden desire to laugh. He starts to giggle, then laugh outright, struggling to maintain the silence as his body starts to shake, making the mattress shudder.

'Are you *laughing*?' murmurs Sylvie into her pillow.

'No!' says Dexter, screwing his face tight to keep it in, but the laughter's coming in waves now and he feels another surge of hysterics starting to build in his stomach. There is a point in the future where even the worst disaster starts to settle into an anecdote, and he can see the potential for a story here. It's the kind of story that he would like to tell Emma Morley. But he doesn't know where Emma Morley is, or what she's doing, hasn't seen her for more than two years now.

He'll just have to remember the story. Tell her some other day.

He starts to laugh again.

CHAPTER THIRTEEN
The Third Wave

THURSDAY 15 JULY 1999

Somerset

They have started to arrive. An endless cascade of luxuriously quilted envelopes, thumping onto the doormat. The wedding invitations.

This wasn't the first wave of weddings. Some of their contemporaries had even got married at University, but in that self-consciously wacky, rag-week way, a let's-pretend parody of a wedding, like the jokey student 'dinner parties' where everyone wore evening dress to eat tuna pasta bake. Student wedding receptions were picnics in the local park, the guests in Oxfam suits and secondhand ballgowns, then onto the pub. In the wedding photos the bride and groom might be seen raising pint glasses to the camera, a fag dangling from the bride's rouged mouth, and wedding gifts were modest: a really cool compilation tape; a clip-framed photo-montage; a box of candles. Getting married at University was an amusing stunt, an act of benign rebellion, like a tiny tattoo that no-one ever sees or shaving your head for charity.

The second wave, the mid-twenties weddings, still retained a little of that tongue-in-cheek, home-made quality. The receptions took place in community centres and parents' gardens, vows were self-composed and rigorously secular, and someone always seemed to read that poem about the rain having such small hands. But a cold, hard edge of professionalism had started to creep in. The idea of the 'wedding list' had begun to rear its head.

At some point in the future a fourth wave is expected – the Second Marriages: bittersweet, faintly apologetic affairs that are over by 9.30 on account of all the kids. 'It's not a big deal,' they will say 'just an excuse for a party.' But for the moment this year is the year of the third wave, and it is the third wave that is proving the most powerful, the most spectacular, the most devastating. These are the weddings of people in their early-to-mid-thirties, and no-one is laughing anymore.

The third wave is unstoppable. Every week seems to bring another luxuriantly creamy envelope, the thickness of a letter-bomb, containing a complex invitation – a triumph of paper engineering – and a comprehensive dossier of phone numbers, email addresses, websites, how to get there, what to wear, where to buy the gifts. Country house hotels are being block-booked, great schools of salmon are being poached, vast marquees are appearing overnight like Bedouin tent cities. Silky grey morning suits and top hats are being hired and worn with an absolutely straight face, and the times are heady and golden for florists and caterers, string quartets and Ceilidh callers, ice sculptors and the makers of disposable cameras. Decent Motown cover-bands are limp with exhaustion. Churches are back in fashion, and these days the happy couple are travelling the short distance from the place of worship to the reception on open-topped London buses, in hot-air balloons, on the backs of matching white stallions, in micro-lite planes. A wedding requires immense reserves of love and commitment and time off work, not least from the guests. Confetti costs eight pounds a box. A bag of rice from the corner shop just won't cut it anymore.

Mr and Mrs Anthony Killick invite Emma Morley and partner to the wedding of their daughter Tilly Killick and Malcolm Tidewell.

In the motorway services Emma sat in her new car, her very first car, a fourth-hand Fiat Panda, and stared at the invite, knowing with absolute certainty that there would be men with cigars and someone English in a kilt.

'*Emma Morley and partner.*'

Her road atlas was an ancient edition, with several major conurbations missing. She turned it through one hundred and eighty degrees, then back ninety, but it was like trying to navigate with a copy of the Domesday Book and she slapped it onto the empty passenger seat where her imaginary partner should have been sitting.

Emma was a shocking driver, simultaneously sloppy and petrified, and for the first fifty miles had been absent-mindedly driving with her spectacles on top of her contact lenses so that other traffic loomed menacingly out of nowhere like alien space cruisers. Frequent rest stops were required to stabilise her blood pressure and dab the perspiration from her top lip, and she reached for her handbag and checked her make-up in the mirror, trying to sneak up on herself to gauge the effect. The lipstick was redder and more sultry than she felt she could carry off, and the small amount of powder she had applied to her cheeks now looked garish and absurd, like something from a Restoration comedy. Why, she wondered, do I always look like a kid trying on her mother's make-up? She had also made the elementary mistake of getting her hair cut, no, *styled*, just the day before, and it was still falling into an artful arrangement of layers and flicks; what her mum would have called a 'do'.

In frustration she tugged hard at the hem of her dress, a Chinese-style affair of rich blue silk, or some silk substitute, which made her look like the plump unhappy waitress in the Golden Dragon Take-away. Sitting down it bulged and stretched, and the combination of something in the 'silk' and motorway jitters was making her perspire. The car's air-conditioning had two settings, wind-tunnel and sauna, and all elegance had evaporated somewhere outside Maidenhead, to be replaced by two dark crescents of sweat beneath her arms. She raised her elbows to her head, and peered down at the patches and wondered if she should turn around, go home and change? Or just turn around. Go home, stay home, do some work on the book. After all, it's not as if she and Tilly Killick were still the best of pals. The dark days when Tilly had been her landlady in the tiny flat in Clapton had cast a long shadow, and they'd never quite settled the dispute over the non-return of the returnable deposit. It was hard to wish the newly-weds well when the bride still owed you five hundred quid.

On the other hand, old friends would be there. Sarah C, Carol, Sita, the Watson twins, Bob, Mari with the Big Hair, Stephanie Shaw from her publishers, Callum O'Neill the sandwich million-aire. Dexter would be there. Dexter and his girlfriend.

And it was at this exact moment, as she sat pointing her armpits at the air-conditioning vents and wondering what to do, that Dexter drove by unseen in his Mazda sports car, Sylvie Cope by his side.

'So who'll be there?' asked Sylvie, turning down the stereo. Travis – her choice for a change. Sylvie didn't much care for music, but made an exception for Travis.

'Just a whole lot of people from University. Paul and Sam and Steve O'D, Peter and Sarah, the Watsons. And Callum.'

'Callum. Good, I like Callum.'

'. . . Mari with the Big Hair, Bob. God, people I haven't seen for years. My old friend Emma.'

'Another ex?'

'No, not an ex . . .'

'A fling.'

'Not a fling, just an old, old friend.'

'English teacher?'

'Used to be an English teacher, writer now. You talked to her at Bob and Mari's wedding, remember? In Cheshire.'

'Vaguely. Quite attractive.'

'I suppose so.' Dexter shrugged hard. 'We fell out for a while. I told you about it. Remember?'

'They all melt into one.' She turned to the window. 'So did you have a thing with her?'

'No I did *not* have a thing with her.'

'What about the bride?'

'Tilly? What about her?'

'Did you ever have sex with the bride?'

December 1992, that horrible flat in Clapton that always smelt of fried onions. A foot massage that had spun wildly out of control while Emma was at Woolworths.

'Of course not. What do you think I am?'

'It seems like every week we go to some wedding with a coach-load of people you've slept with—'

'That's not true.'

'—a marquee-full. Like a conference.'

'Not true, not true—'

'It is true.'

'Hey, you're the only one for me now.' With one hand on the steering wheel, he reached across and placed the other on Sylvie's stomach, still flat beneath the peach shot-satin of her short dress, then rested it on the top of her bare thigh.

'Don't leave me talking to strangers, will you?' said Sylvie, and turned up the stereo.

It was mid-afternoon before Emma found herself, late and exhausted, at the security gates of the stately home, wondering if they would let her in. A vast estate in Somerset, shrewd investors had turned Morton Manor Park into a sort of all-in-one marriage compound, complete with its own chapel, banqueting hall, a privet maze, a spa, a selection of guest bedrooms with walk-through showers, all surrounded by a high wall topped with razor wire: a wedding camp. With follies and grottoes, ha-has and gazebos, a castle *and* a bouncy castle it was an upmarket marital Disneyland, available for whole week-ends at breathtaking expense. It seemed an unusual venue for the wedding of a former member of the Socialist Workers' Party, and Emma drove along the sweeping gravel drive, bemused and disconcerted by it all.

In sight of the chapel, a man dressed in the powdered wig and frock coat of a footman lunged in front of her, waving her down with frilly cuffs and leaning in at the window.

'Is there a problem?' she asked. She wanted to say 'officer'.

'I need the keys, ma'am.'

'The keys?'

'To park the car.'

'Oh God, really?' she said, embarrassed by the moss growing round the window seals, the mulch of disintegrated A to Zs and empty plastic bottles that littered the floor. 'Okay, well, the doors don't lock, you've got to use this screwdriver to hold it closed and there's no hand brake, so park it on the level or edged up against a tree or just leave it in gear, alright?' The footman took the keys between his finger and thumb as if he'd been handed a dead mouse.

She had been driving barefoot and now found that she had to stamp her swollen feet into her shoes, like an ugly stepsister. The ceremony had already started. From the chapel she could hear 'The Arrival of the Queen of Sheba' played by four, possibly five, gloved hands. She hobbled across the gravel towards the chapel, her arms raised to evaporate some of the perspiration, like a child pretending to be a plane, then with one last tug on the hem of her dress she slid discreetly through the large oak door and stood at the back of the packed congregation. An a capella group was performing now, clicking their fingers maniacally, singing 'I'm into Something Good' as the happy couple grinned toothily at each other, wet-eyed. This was Emma's first sighting of the groom: a rugby player type, handsome in pale grey morning suit and razor burn, he moved his big face at Tilly, working though different variations on 'my happiest moment'. Unusually, Emma noted, the bride had opted for a Marie-Antoinette theme – pink silk and lace, a hooped skirt, hair piled high, a beauty spot – causing Emma to wonder if Tilly's degree in History and French had perhaps fallen short of its mark. She looked very happy though, and he looked very happy, and the whole congregation looked very, very happy.

Song followed sketch followed song until the wedding began to resemble a Royal Variety Performance, and Dexter found his mind beginning to drift. Tilly's ruddy-cheeked niece was reading a sonnet now, something about the marriage of two minds not admitting impediment, whatever the hell *that* meant. He tried hard to concentrate on the poem's line of argument and to apply its romantic sentiment to his own feelings for Sylvie, then turned his attention back to how many of the congregation he had slept with. Not in a gloating way, not entirely, but with a sort of nostalgia. 'Love alters not with his brief hours and weeks . . .' read the bride's niece, as Dexter made it five. Five ex-lovers in one small chapel. Was this some kind of record? Should there be extra points for the bride? No sign of Emma Morley yet. With Emma, five-and-a-half.

From the back of the church Emma watched Dexter counting off on his fingers, and wondered what he was doing. He wore a black suit with a skinny black tie; like all the boys these days, trying to look like a gangster. In profile, there was the beginning of a slight sagging under his jaw, but he still looked handsome. Stupidly handsome actually, and far less pasty and bloated than before he had met Sylvie. Since their falling out Emma had seen him three times, always at weddings. Each time he had thrown his arms around her and kissed her as if nothing had changed, and said 'we must talk, we must talk', but it had never happened, not really. He had always been with Sylvie, the pair of them busy looking beautiful. There she was now, a proprietary hand on his knee, her head and neck like some long-stemmed flower, craning to take it all in.

The vows now. Emma glanced across in time to see Sylvie reach for Dexter's hand and squeeze the five fingers as if in soli-darity with the happy couple. She whispered in his ear, and Dexter looked up at Sylvie, smiling broadly and a little dopily, so Emma thought. He mouthed something back, and though not a practiced lip-reader Emma thought that there was a good chance it was 'I love you too.' Self-consciously, he glanced around and caught Emma's eye, grinning as if he'd been caught doing something he shouldn't.

The cabaret ended. There was just time for an uncertain rendition of 'All You Need is Love,' the congregation struggling to sing along in 7/4, before the guests followed the happy couple outside and the reunion began in earnest. Through the crowd of people, hugging, whooping and shaking hands, Dexter and Emma sought each other out and suddenly there they were.

'Well,' he said.

'Well.'

'Don't I know you?'

'Your face certainly rings a bell.'

'Yours too. You look different though.'

'Yes, I'm the only woman here who's drenched in sweat,' said Emma, plucking at the fabric beneath her arms.

'You mean "perspiration".'

'Actually, no, this is sweat. I look like I've been dragged from a lake. Natural silk my eye!'

'Sort of an oriental theme, isn't it?'

'I call it my Fall of Saigon look. Chinese technically. Of course the trouble with one of these dresses is forty minutes later you want another one!' she said, and had that feeling, halfway through the sentence that she would have been better off not starting it. Did she imagine it, or did he roll his eyes a little? 'Sorry.'

'That's okay. I really like the dress. In fact me love it long time.'

She rolled *her* eyes. 'There you go; now we're quits.'

'What I *meant* was that you look good.' He was peering at the top of her head now. 'Is that a . . . ?'

'What?'

'Is that what they call a *Rachel*?'

'Don't push your luck, Dex,' she said, immediately scrubbing at her hair with her fingertips. She glanced across to where Tilly and her brand new husband were posing for photographs,

Tilly fluttering a fan coquettishly in front of her face. 'Unfortunately I didn't realise there was a French Revolutionary theme.'

'The Marie-Antoinette thing?' said Dexter. 'Well at least we know there'll be cake.'

'Apparently she's travelling to the reception in a tumbril.'

'What's a tumbril?'

They looked at each other. 'You haven't changed, have you?' she said.

Dexter kicked at the gravel. 'Well I have. A bit.'

'That sounds intriguing.'

'I'll tell you later. Look—'

Tilly was standing on the running board of the Rolls-Royce Silver Ghost that would take them the hundred yards to the reception, the bouquet held low in both hands, ready to be tossed like a caber.

'Want to go and try your chances, Em?'

'Can't catch,' she said, placing her hands behind her back just as the bouquet was lobbed into the crowd and caught by a frail and elderly aunt, which seemed to anger the crowd somehow, as if someone's last chance for future happiness had been squandered. Emma nodded towards the embarrassed aunt, the bouquet dangling forlornly from her hand. 'There's me in forty years' time,' said Emma.

'Really? Forty?' said Dexter, and Emma pressed her heel down on his toe. Over her shoulder he could see Sylvie nearby, looking round for him. 'Better go. Sylvie doesn't really know anyone. I'm on strict orders never to leave her side. Come and say hi, will you?'

'Later. I'd better go and talk to the happy bride.'

'Ask her about that deposit she owes you.'

'D'you think? Today?'

'See you later. Maybe we'll be sitting next to each other at the reception.' He held up crossed fingers, and she crossed her fingers back.

The overcast morning had settled into a beautiful afternoon, high clouds rolling across the huge blue sky as the guests followed the Silver Ghost in procession to the Great Lawn for champagne and canapés. There, with a great whoop, Tilly finally saw Emma, and they hugged each other as best they could across the bride's vast hooped skirt.

'I'm so glad you could make it, Em!'

'Me too, Tilly. You look extraordinary.'

Tilly fluttered her fan. 'You don't think it's too much?'

'Not at all. You look stunning,' and her eye drifted once more to the beauty spot that made it look as if a fly had settled on her lip. 'The service was lovely too.'

'Awwww, was it?' This was an old trait of Tilly's to precede each sentence with a sympathetic 'aw', as if Emma were a kitten who had hurt her little paw. 'Did you cry?'

'Like an orphan . . .'

'Awww! I'm so, so glad you could make it.' Regally she tapped Emma's shoulder with her fan. 'And I can't wait to meet your boyfriend.'

'Well me too, but unfortunately I don't have one.'

'Awww, don't you?'

'Nope, not for some time now.'

'Really? Are you sure?'

'I think I'd notice, Tilly.'

'Awww! I'm sorry. Well get one! QUICK!!!! No seriously, boyfriends are great! Husbands are better! We must find you one!' she commanded. 'Tonight! We'll fix you up!' and Emma felt her head being verbally patted. 'Awwwww. So! Have you seen Dexter yet?'

'Briefly.'

'Have you met his girlfriend? With the hairy forehead? Isn't she beautiful? Just like Audrey Hepburn. Or is it Katharine? I can never remember the difference.'

'Audrey. She's definitely an Audrey.'

The champagne flowed on and a sense of nostalgia spread across the Great Lawn as old friends met and conversation turned into how much people earned now, how much weight they had gained.

'Sandwiches. That's the future,' said Callum O'Neill, who was both earning and weighing a great deal more these days. 'High-quality, ethically-minded convenience food, that's where it's at my friend. Food is the new rock and roll!'

'I thought that comedy was the new rock and roll.'

'It was, then it was rock and roll, now it's food. Keep up, Dex!' Dexter's old flatmate had transformed almost beyond recognition in the last few years. Prosperous, large and dynamic, he had moved on from refurbished computers, selling the business at a vast profit to start up the 'Natural Stuff' sandwich chain. Now, with his trim little goatee and close-cropped hair, he was the very model of the well-groomed, self-assured young entrepreneur. Callum tugged on the cuffs of an exquisite tailored suit and Dexter found himself wondering if this could really be the same skinny Irishman who wore the same trousers every day for three years.

'Everything's organic, everything's made fresh, we do juices and smoothies to order, we do fair-trade coffee. We've got four branches, and they're full all the time, seriously, constantly. We have to close at three o'clock, there's just no food left. I tell you, Dex, the food culture in this country, it's changing, people want things to be better. No-one wants a can of Tango and a packet of crisps anymore. They want hummus wraps, papaya juice, crayfish . . .'

'Crayfish?'

'In flatbread, with rocket. Seriously, crayfish is the egg sandwich of our time, rocket's the iceberg lettuce. Crayfish are cheap to produce, they breed like you wouldn't believe, they're delicious, the poor man's lobster! Hey, you should come and have a talk to me about it sometime.'

'About crayfish.'

'About the business. I think there could be a lot of opportunities for you.'

Dexter dug at the lawn with his heel. 'Callum, are you offering me a *job*?'

'No, I'm just saying, come in and—'

'I can't believe a friend of mine is offering me a *job*.'

'—come and have lunch! None of that crayfish crap either, a proper restaurant. My treat.' He draped a large arm over Dexter's shoulder, and in a lowered voice said, 'I haven't seen you much on TV these days.'

'That's because you don't watch cable and satellite. I do a lot of work on cable and satellite.'

'Like?'

'Well I'm doing this new show called *Sport Xtreme*. Xtreme with an X. Surfing footage, interviews with snow-boarders. You know. From all around the world.'

'So you're travelling a lot then?'

'I just present the footage. The studio's in Morden. So yes, I do travel a lot, but only to Morden.'

'Well, like I said, if you ever felt like a change in career. You know a bit about food and drink, you can get on with people if you put your mind to it. Business *is* people. I just think it might be for you. That's all.'

Dexter sighed through his nose, looked up at his old friend and tried to dislike him. 'Cal, you wore the same pair of trousers every day for three years.'

'Long time ago now.'

'For a whole term you ate nothing but tinned mince.'

'What can I say – people change! So what do you think?'

'Alright then. You can buy me lunch. But I warn you, I know nothing about business.'

'That's alright. It'll be nice to catch up anyway.' Half admonishingly, he tapped Dexter's elbow. 'You went very quiet on me for a while.'

'Did I? I was busy.'

'Not that busy.'

'Hey, you could have called me too!'

'I did, often. You never returned my calls.'

'Didn't I? Sorry. I had things on my mind.'

'I heard about your mum.' He looked into his glass. 'Sorry about that. Lovely lady, your mum.'

'S'alright. Long time ago now.'

There was a moment's silence, comfortable and affectionate, as they looked around the lawn at old friends talking and laughing in the late afternoon sun. Nearby, Callum's latest girl-friend, a tiny, striking Spanish girl, a dancer in hip-hop videos, was speaking to Sylvie who stooped down to hear her.

'It'll be nice to talk to Luiza again,' said Dexter.

'I shouldn't get too attached.' Callum shrugged. 'I think Luiza's on the way out.'

'Some things don't change then.' A pretty waitress, self-conscious in a mobcap, arrived to top up their glasses. They both grinned at her, caught each other grinning, and tapped their glasses together.

'Eleven years since we left.' Dexter shook his head, incredulous. 'Eleven years. How the fuck did that happen?'

'I see Emma Morley's here,' said Callum, out of nowhere.

'I know.' They glanced over and saw that she was talking to Miffy Buchanan, an old arch-enemy. Even at a distance, they could tell Emma's teeth were gritted.

'I'd heard you and Em fell out.'

'We did.'

'But you're alright now?'

'Not sure. We'll see.'

'Great girl, Emma.'

'She is.'

'Quite a beauty these days.'

'She is, she is.'

'Did you ever . . . ?'

'No. Nearly. Once or twice.'

'Nearly?' sniffs Callum. 'What does *that* mean?'

Dexter changed the subject. 'But you're alright, yeah?'

Callum took a sip of champagne. 'Dex, I'm thirty-four. I've got a beautiful girlfriend, my own house, my own business, I work hard at something I enjoy, I make enough money.' He placed his hand on Dexter's shoulder. 'And you, you've got a show on late-night TV! Life's been good for all of us.'

And partly from wounded pride, partly from a revived sense of competition, Dexter decided to tell him.

'So – do you want to hear something funny?'

Emma heard Callum O'Neill whoop from the other side of the Great Lawn and glanced across in time to see him holding Dexter in a head-lock, rubbing his knuckles on Dexter's scalp. She smiled then turned her full attention back to hating Miffy Buchanan.

'So I heard you were unemployed,' she was saying.

'Well I prefer to think of myself as self-employed.'

'As a writer?'

'Just for a year or two, a Sabbatical.'

'But you haven't actually had anything published?'

'Not as yet. Though I have actually been paid a small advance to—'

'Hm,' said Miffy, sceptically. 'Harriet Bowen has had three novels published now.'

'Yes, I've been made aware of that. Several times.'

'*And* she's got three kids.'

'Well. There you go.'

'Have you seen my two?' Nearby two immense toddlers in three-piece suits were rubbing canapés into each other's faces. 'IVAN. NO BITING.'

'They're lovely boys.'

'Aren't they? So have you had any *kids* yet?' said Miffy, as if it was an either/or situation, novels or kids.

'Nope—'

'Seeing anyone?'

'Nope—'

'No-one?'

276

'Nope—'

'Anyone on the horizon?'

'Nope—'

'Even so, you look much better than you did.' Miffy looked her up and down appraisingly, as if contemplating buying her at auction. 'You're actually one of the few people here who's actually *lost* some weight! I mean you were never massively *fat* or anything, just puppy-fat, but it's fallen off you!'

Emma felt her hand tighten around the champagne glass. 'Well it's good to know the last eleven years haven't been wasted.'

'And you used to have this really strong Northern accent, but now you just talk like everybody else.'

'Do I?' Emma said, taken aback. 'Well, that's a shame. I didn't lose it on purpose.'

'To be honest, I always thought you were putting it on. You know – an affectation—'

'*What?*'

'Your accent. You know – Ay oop! Miners-this, miners-that, Guat-e-mala Ra-ra-ra! I thought you were always rubbing it in everyone's face a bit. But now you're talking normally again!'

Emma had always envied those people who spoke their minds, who said what they felt without attention to social nicety. She had never been one of those people, but even so now felt an F-sound forming on her bottom lip.

'. . . and you were always so *angry* about everything all the time.'

'Oh, I still get angry, Miffy . . .'

'Oh my God, there's Dexter Mayhew.' Miffy was whispering in her ear now, one hand squeezing Emma's shoulder. 'Did you know we had a thing once?'

'Yes, you told me. Many, many times.'

'He still looks great? Doesn't he look great?' and she sighed swooningly. 'How come you two never got together?'

'I don't know: my accent, the puppy-fat? . . .'

'You weren't *that* bad. Hey, have you seen his girlfriend? Isn't she beautiful? Don't you think she's just exquisite?' and Miffy turned round for a reply, but was surprised to see that Emma had already gone.

The guests were gathering at the marquee now, huddling eagerly around the seating plan as if getting their exam results. Dexter and Emma found each other in the crowd.

'Table five,' said Dexter.

'I'm on table twenty-four,' said Emma. 'Table five's quite near the bride. Twenty-four's out near the chemical loos.'

'You mustn't take it personally.'

'What's the main course?'

'The rumour-mill says salmon.'

'Salmon. Salmon, salmon, salmon, salmon. I eat so much salmon at these weddings, twice a year I get this urge to swim upstream.'

'Come to table five. We'll swap the name cards around.'

'Tamper with the seating plan? They shoot people for less than that. There's a guillotine out back.'

Dexter laughed. 'We'll talk afterwards, yeah?'

'Come and find me.'

'Or you can come and find me.'

'Or you come find me.'

'Or you find me.'

As punishment for some past slight, Emma had been placed between the groom's elderly aunt and uncle from New Zealand, and the phrases 'beautiful landscape' and 'wonderful quality of life' were rotated for a good three hours. Occasionally she would be distracted by a great gale of laughter from the direction of table five, Dexter and Sylvie, Callum and his girlfriend Luiza; the glamorous table. Emma poured herself another glass of wine and asked once more about the landscape, the quality of life. Whales: had they ever seen real-life whales? she asked and glanced enviously at table five.

At table five, Dexter glanced enviously over at table twenty-four. Sylvie had devised a new game of quickly placing her hand over the top of Dexter's wine glass whenever he picked up the bottle, turning the long meal into a stern test of his reflexes. 'You will take it easy, won't you?' she whispered when he had scored a point, and he assured her that he would, but the result was mild boredom, and increasing envy at Callum's maddening self-assurance. At table twenty-four, he could see Emma talking politely and earnestly to a tanned elderly couple, noting the attentive way she listened, her hand placed now on the old man's arm, laughing at his joke, now taking their picture with the disposable camera, now leaning in to have her picture taken. Dexter noticed her blue dress, the kind of thing she never would have worn ten years ago, and noticed too that the zip had come undone by three inches or so at the back, that the hem had ridden up to halfway along her thigh, and there followed a fleeting but still vivid memory of Emma in an Edinburgh bedroom on Rankeillor Street. Dawn light through the curtains, a low single bed, her skirt around her waist, arms above her head. What had changed since then? Not that much. The same lines formed around her mouth when she laughed, they were etched just a little deeper now. She still had the same eyes, bright and shrewd, and she still laughed with her wide mouth tightly shut, as if holding in some secret. In many ways she was far more attractive than her twenty-two-year-old self. She was no longer cutting her own hair for one thing, and she had lost some of that library pallor, that shoe-gazing petulance and surliness. How would he feel, he wondered, if he were seeing that face for the first time now? If he had been allocated table twenty-four, had sat down and introduced himself. Of all the people here today, he thought, he would only want to talk to her. He picked up his drink and pushed back his chair.

But glasses were being tapped with knives. The speeches. As tradition demanded, the Father of the Bride was drunk and boorish, the Best Man was drunk and unfunny and also forgot to mention the Bride. With each glass of red wine Emma felt the energy leeching out of her, and she began to contemplate

'So how does it feel?' she asked. 'Losing an old flame to the arms of another man.'

'Tilly Killick's not an old flame.'

'Oh, Dexter . . .' Emma shook her head slowly. 'When will you learn?'

'I don't know what you're talking about.'

'Must have been, let me see . . . December 1992, that flat in Clapton. The one that smelt of fried onions.'

Dexter winced. 'How do you know about these things?'

'Well when I left to go to Woolworths you were massaging each other's feet with my best olive oil and when I got *back* from Woolworths she was crying and there were olive oil footprints all over my best rug and the sofa and on the kitchen table and half way up the wall too, I remember. So I carefully examined the forensic evidence and came to that conclusion. Oh, also, you left your birth control device at the top of the kitchen bin, so that was nice.'

'Did I? Sorry about that.'

'Plus the fact that she told me.'

'Did she?' He shook his head, betrayed. 'That was meant to be our secret!'

'Women talk about these things you know. It's no use swearing them to secrecy, it all comes out in the end.'

'I'll remember that in future.'

Now they had arrived at the entrance to the maze, a neatly trimmed privet hedge affair, a good ten feet high, its entrance marked by a heavy wooden door. Emma paused, her hand on the iron handle. 'Is this a good idea?'

'How hard can it be?'

'And if we got lost?'

'We'll use the stars or something.' The door creaked open. 'Right or left?'

'Right,' said Emma, and they stepped into the maze. The high hedges were lit at ground level with different coloured lights, and the air had that summer smell, thick and heady, almost oily from the warm leaves. 'Where's Sylvie?'

'Sylvie's okay, she's being Callumed. He's being the life and soul, the charming Oirish millionaire. I thought I'd leave them to it. I can't compete with him anymore. Too tiring.'

'He's doing very well, you know.'

'So everyone tells me.'

'Crayfish, apparently.'

'I know. He just offered me a job.'

'Crayfish wrangler?'

'Don't know yet. He wants to talk to me about "opportunities". Business is people he said, whatever that means.'

'But what about *Sport Xtreme*?

'Ah,' Dexter laughed and rubbed his hair with one hand. 'You've seen it then?'

'Never missed an episode. You know me, there's nothing I like more in the early hours of the morning than stuff about BMX. My favourite bit is when you say that things are "rad"—'

'They *make* me say that stuff.'

'"Rad" and "sweet". "Check out these sweet, old skool moves—"'

'I think I get away with it.'

'Not always, pal. Left or right?'

'Left, I think.' They walked a little way in silence, listening to the muffled thump of the band playing 'Superstition'. 'How's the writing going?'

'Oh, it's okay, when I do it. Most of the time I just sit around eating biscuits.'

'Stephanie Shaw says they gave you an advance.'

'Just a bit of money, enough to last 'til Christmas. Then we'll see. Back to teaching full-time probably.'

'And what's it about? This book.'

'Not sure yet.'

'It's about me, isn't it?'

'Yes, Dexter, it's a whole thick book entirely about *you*. It's called "Dexter Dexter Dexter Dexter Dexter". Right or left?'

'Let's try a left.'

'Actually it's just a book for kids. Teenagers. Boys, relationships, that kind of thing. It's about a school play, that production of *Oliver!* I did all those years ago. A comedy.'

'Well you look very well on it.'

'Do I?'

'Absolutely. Some people look better, some people look worse. You are definitely looking better.'

'Miffy Buchanan tells me I've finally lost my puppy-fat.'

'She's just jealous. You look great.'

'Thank you. Want me to say you look better too?'

'If you think you can pull it off.'

'Well you do. Left?'

'Left.'

'Better than during your rock and roll years anyway. When you were giving-it-large or whatever it was you were doing.' They walked a little way in silence, until Emma spoke again. 'I was worried about you.'

'Were you?'

'We all were.'

'Just a phase. Everybody's got to have a phase like that, haven't they? Go a bit wild.'

'Do they? I haven't. Hey, I hope you've stopped wearing that annoying flat cap too.'

'I haven't worn a hat for years.'

'Pleased to hear it. We were thinking about staging an intervention.'

'You know how it is, you start with the soft hats, just for kicks, then before you know it, you're into flat caps, trilbies, bowlers . . .'

Another junction. 'Right or left?' she said.

'No idea.'

They peered in either direction. 'Amazing, isn't it, how quickly this stopped being fun.'

'Let's sit down shall we? Over there.'

A small marble bench had been set into the hedge walls, lit

from beneath by a blue fluorescent light, and they sat on the cool stone, filled their glasses, tapped them together and bumped shoulders.

'God, I almost forgot . . .' Dexter reached into his trouser pocket, and very carefully removed a folded napkin, held it in his palm like a conjurer and unfolded it, a corner at a time. Nestling in the napkin like birds' eggs, were two crumpled cigarettes.

'From Cal,' he whispered, awed. 'Want one?'

'No thank you. Haven't touched one for years.'

'Well done you. I've stopped too, officially. But I feel safe here . . .' He lit the contraband, his hand shaking stagily. 'She can't find me here . . .' Emma laughed. The champagne and the solitude had lifted their mood, and both were now feeling sentimental, nostalgic, exactly as they should feel at a wedding, and they smiled at each other through the smoke. 'Callum says that we're the "Marlboro-Light-Generation".'

'God, that's depressing.' Emma sniffed. 'A whole generation defined by a brand of fag. I'd sort of hoped for more.' She smiled, and turned to Dexter. 'So. How are you these days?'

'I'm fine. Bit more sensible.'

'Sex in toilet cubicles lose its bittersweet charm?'

He laughed and examined the tip of the cigarette. 'I just had to get something out of my system, that's all.'

'And is it out now?'

'Think so, most of it.'

'Because of true love?'

'Partly. Also I'm thirty-four now. At thirty-four you start to run out of excuses.'

'Excuses?'

'Well, if you're twenty-two and you're fucking up, you can say, it's okay I'm only twenty-two. I'm only twenty-five, I'm only twenty-eight. But "I'm only thirty-four"?' He sipped from his glass, and leant back into the hedge. 'It's like everyone has a central dilemma in their life, and mine was can you be in a committed, mature, loving adult relationship and still get invited to threesomes?'

'And what's the answer, Dex?' she asked, solemnly.

'The answer is no, you can't. Once you've worked that out, it all gets a bit simpler.'

'It's true; an orgy won't keep you warm at night.'

'An orgy won't care for you when you're old.' He took another sip. 'Anyway, it's not even as if I was getting invited to any in the first place, just making a fool of myself, screwing things up. Screwed up my career, screwed up with Mum—'

'—well that's not true—'

'—screwed up all my friendships.' For emphasis, Dexter leant against her arm, and she leant back against his. 'I just thought it was time to do things properly for once. And now I've met Sylvie, and she's great, she really is, and she keeps me on the straight and narrow.'

'Well she's a lovely girl.'

'She is. She is.'

'Very beautiful. Serene.'

'A little bit scary sometimes.'

'She's got a lovely, warm sort of Leni Riefenstahl quality to her.'

'Lenny who?'

'Doesn't matter.'

'Of course she's got absolutely no sense of humour.'

'Well that's a relief. I think a sense of humour's over-rated,' said Emma. 'Goofing it up all the time, it's boring. Like Ian. 'Cept Ian wasn't funny. No, much better to have somebody you really fancy, someone who'll rub your feet.'

He tried and failed to imagine Sylvie touching his feet. 'She told me once that she never laughs because she doesn't like what it does to her face.'

Emma gave a low chuckle. 'Wow' was all she could say. 'Wow. But you love her, right?'

'I adore her.'

'Adore. Well "adore" is even better.'

'She's sensational.'

'She is.'

'And she's really turned things around for me too. I'm off the drugs and booze and not smoking.' She glanced at the bottle in his hand, the cigarette in his mouth. He smiled. 'Special occasion.'

'So true love found you in the end.'

'Something like that.' He filled her glass. 'How about you?'

'Oh, I'm fine. I'm fine.' As a distraction, she stood. 'Let's keep walking, shall we? Left or right?'

'Right.' With a sigh, he hauled himself to his feet. 'Do you still see Ian?'

'Not for years now.'

'Nobody else on the horizon?'

'Don't you start, Dexter.'

'What?'

'Sympathy for the spinster. I'm perfectly content, thank you. And I refuse to be defined by my boyfriend. Or lack of.' She was starting to speak with real zeal now. 'Once you decide not to worry about that stuff anymore, dating and relationships and love and all that, it's like you're free to get on with real life. And I've got my work, and I love that. I've got I reckon one more year to really make a go of it. The money's tiny, but I'm free. I go to the movies in the afternoon.' She paused momentarily. 'Swimming! I swim a lot. I swim and I swim and I swim, mile after mile. God, I fucking hate swimming. Turn left, I think.'

'You know, I feel the same. Not about swimming, I mean about not having to *date* anymore. Since I've been with Sylvie, it's like I've freed up this vast amount of time and energy and mental space.'

'And what do you do with it all, this mental space?'

'Play *Tomb Raider* mostly.'

Emma laughed, and walked a little further in silence, worrying that she was coming across as less self-contained and empowered than she had intended. 'And anyway, it's not like I'm completely, you know, boring and, and loveless. I have my moments. I had this thing with a guy called Chris. Called himself a dentist but he was really just a hygienist.'

'What happened to Chris?'

'Just fizzled out. Just as well. I was convinced that he was always staring at my teeth. Kept nagging me to floss, Emma, *floss*. Going on a date was like going for a check-up. Too much pressure. And before that there was Mr Godalming.' She shuddered. 'Mr Godalming. What a disaster.'

'Who was Mr Godalming?'

'Another time. Left, right?'

'Left.'

'Anyway, if I ever get really desperate, there's always your offer to fall back on.'

Dexter stopped walking. 'What offer?'

'Do you remember you used to say if I was still single when I got to forty you'd marry me?'

'Did I say that?' He winced. 'Bit patronising.'

'I thought so at the time. But don't worry, I don't think it's legally binding or anything, I'm not going to hold you to it. Besides, there's still seven years to go. Plenty of time . . .' She began walking again, but Dexter stood still behind her, rubbing his head like a boy who is about to reveal that he's broken the best vase.

'I'm afraid I'm sort of going to have to withdraw the offer anyway.'

She stopped and turned.

'Oh really? Why's that?' she said, but a part of her knew already.

'I'm engaged.'

Emma blinked once, very slowly.

'Engaged to what?'

'To be married. To Sylvie.'

A moment passed, perhaps half a second when their faces said

287

what they felt, and then Emma was smiling, laughing, her arms around his neck. 'Oh, Dexter. That's amazing! Congratulations!' and she went to kiss his cheek just as he turned his head, their mouths glancing for a moment so that they tasted the champagne on each other's lips.

'You're pleased?'

'Pleased? I'm destroyed! But really, seriously, that's fantastic news.'

'You think so?'

'More than fantastic, it's, it's . . . rad! It's rad and sweet. It's old skool!'

He stepped back from her and searched inside his jacket. 'In fact, that's why I dragged you in here. I wanted to give you this in person—'

A thick envelope of heavy lilac paper. Emma took it gingerly, and peered inside. The envelope was quilted with tissue paper and the invitation itself had hand-torn edges and seemed to be made of some sort of papyrus or parchment. 'Now that—' Emma balanced it like a table on her upturned fingertips '—*that* is what I call a wedding invitation.'

'Isn't it?'

'That is some elaborate stationery.'

'Eight quid each.'

'That's more than my car.'

'Smell it, go on . . .'

'Smell it?' Warily, she held it to her nose. 'It's *scented*! Your wedding invitations are *scented*?'

'It's meant to be lavender.'

'No, Dex – it's *money*. It smells of *money*.' Carefully, she opened the card, and he watched her as she read, remembering the way she used her fingertips to brush her fringe across her forehead. '"Mr and Mrs Lionel Cope invite you to the marriage of their daughter Sylvie to Mr Dexter Mayhew—" I can't believe I'm actually seeing this in print. Saturday, September 14th. Hang on, that's only . . .'

288

'Seven weeks away . . .' and he kept watching her face, that fantastic face to see how it might change when he told her.

'Seven weeks? I thought these things were years in the making?'

'Well they are usually, but I think this is what they call a shotgun wedding . . .'

Emma frowned, not quite there yet.

'For three hundred and fifty guests. With Ceilidh.'

'You mean? . . .'

'Sylvie's sort of pregnant. Well not sort of. She is. Pregnant. Actually pregnant. With a baby.'

'Oh, Dexter!' Once again, her face was against his. 'Do you know the father? I'm kidding! Congratulations, Dex. God, aren't you meant to space your bombshells out a bit, not just drop them all at once?' She held his face in both hands, looked at it. 'You're getting married?—'

'Yes!'

'—and you're going to be a *father*?'

'I know! Fuck me – a father!'

'Is that allowed? I mean will they let you?'

'Apparently.'

'Don't suppose you've still got that cigarette, have you?' He reached into his pocket for her. 'How's Sylvie about it?'

'She's delighted! I mean she's worried that it'll make her look fat.'

'Well I suppose that is a possibility . . .'

He lit her cigarette. '. . . but she wants to get on with it, get married, have kids, make a start. She doesn't want to end up mid-thirties and all alone—'

'Like ME!!!'

'Exactly, she doesn't want to end up like you!' He took her hand. 'That's not what I meant, of course.'

'I know. I'm kidding. Dexter, congratulations.'

'Thank you. Thank you.' A momentary pause. 'Let me have a go on that, will you?' he said as he took the last cigarette from her mouth, placing it between his own lips. 'Here, look at this . . .' From his wallet, he unfolded a square of smudgy paper, and held it down to the sodium light. 'It's the twelve-week scan. Isn't that incredible?'

Emma took the scrap of paper and peered at it dutifully. The beauty of the ultrasound scan is something that only parents can appreciate, but Emma had seen these things before and knew what was required of her. 'Beautiful,' she sighed, though in truth it could have been a Polaroid of the inside of his pocket.

'See – that's its spine.'

'Great spine.'

'You can even make out the tiny little fingers.'

'Awww. Boy or girl?'

'Girl, I hope. Or boy. Don't care. But you think it's a good thing?'

'Absolutely. I think it's wonderful. Fucking hell, Dexter, I turn my back for one minute . . . !'

She hugged him once again, her arms high round his neck. She felt drunk, full of affection and a certain sadness too, as if something was coming to an end. She wanted to say something along these lines, but thought it best to do this through a joke. 'Of course you've just destroyed any chance I had of future happiness, but I'm delighted for you, really.'

He twisted his head to look at her, and suddenly something was moving between them, something alive and vibrating in his chest.

Emma placed her hand there. 'Is that your heart?'

'It's my mobile.'

She stepped back and allowed him to retrieve his phone from his inside pocket. Glancing at the display, he gave his head a little sobering shake, and guiltily handed Emma the cigarette, as if it were a smoking gun. Quickly he recited, 'Don't sound drunk don't sound drunk,' assumed a tele-sales smile and answered.

'Hello, my love!'

Emma could hear Sylvie through the receiver. 'Where *are* you?'

'I've sort of got lost.'

'Lost? How can you get lost?'

'Well, I'm in a maze, so—'

'A *maze*? What are you doing in a *maze*?'

'Just . . . you know . . . hanging out. We thought it would be fun.'

'Well as long as *you're* having fun, Dex. I'm stuck here listening to some old dear bang on about New *Zealand* . . .'

'I know, and I've been trying to get out for ages, it's just, well you know – it's like a maze in here!' He giggled, but there was silence from the phone. 'Hello? Are you still there? Can you hear me?'

'Are you with anyone, Dexter?' said Sylvie, her voice low.

He glanced at Emma, still pretending to be captivated by the ultrasound scan. He thought for a moment, then turned his back to her and lied. 'Actually there's a whole gang of us in here. We're going to give it another fifteen minutes, then we're going to dig a tunnel, and if that doesn't work we're going to eat someone.'

'Thank God, here's Callum. I'm going to talk to Callum. Hurry up, will you?'

'Okay. I'm on my way. Bye, darling, bye!' He hung up. 'Did I sound drunk then?'

'Not in the least.'

'We've got to get out of here right now.'

'Fine by me.' She looked in both directions, hopeless. 'We should have left a trail of breadcrumbs.' As if in answer, there was a hum, a click, and each of the lights that illuminated the maze clicked off one by one, plunging them into darkness.

'That's handy,' said Dexter. They stood still for a moment as their eyes adjusted to the gloom. The band were playing 'It's Raining Men', and they listened hard to the muffled sound as if it held a clue to their whereabouts.

'We should get back,' said Emma. 'Before it starts raining men.'

'Good idea.'

'There's a trick, isn't there?' said Emma. 'As I remember it, you put your left hand on the wall, and as long as you don't let go, you get out eventually.'

'Then let's do it!' He poured the last two glasses from the champagne bottle and placed the empty bottle on the grass. Emma removed her heels, placed her fingertips on the hedge and, a little gingerly at first, they began to walk along the dim corridor of leaves.

'So you'll come? To my wedding.'

'Of course I will. I can't promise not to disrupt the service, mind.'

'It should have been me!' They both smiled in the darkness and walked a little further.

'As a matter of fact, I was going to ask you a favour.'

'Please, please, don't ask me to be the Best Man, Dex.'

'It's not that, it's just I've been trying to write a speech for ages now, and I was wondering if you might give me a hand?'

'No!' laughed Emma.

'Why not?'

'I just think it'll carry less emotional weight if it's written by me. Just write what you honestly feel.'

'Well I don't know if *that*'s such a good idea. "I'd like to thank the caterers, and by the way I'm scared shitless."' He squinted into the darkness. 'Are you sure this is working? It feels like we're going further in.'

'Trust me.'

'Anyway, I don't want you to write the whole thing, just give it a polish . . .'

'Sorry, you're on your own there.' They came to a halt at a three-way junction.

'We've definitely been here before.'

'Just trust me. We keep going.'

They walked on in silence. Nearby the band had segued into Prince's '1999', to cheers from the guests. 'When I first heard this song,' said Emma, 'I thought it was science-fiction. 1999. Hover cars and food in pill form and holidays on the moon. Now it's here and I'm still driving a Fiat bloody Panda. Nothing's changed.'

''Cept I'm a family man now.'

'A family man. Good God, aren't you scared?'

'Sometimes. But then you look at some of the idiots who manage to raise kids. I keep telling myself, if Miffy Buchanan can do it, how hard can it be?'

'You can't take babies to cocktail bars, you know. They get funny about that kind of thing.'

'S'okay. I'm going to learn to love staying in.'

'But you're happy?'

'Yeah? I think I am. Are you?'

'Happier. Happyish.'

'Happyish. Well, happyish isn't so bad.'

'It's the most we can hope for.' The fingertips of her left hand passed across the surface of a statute that seemed familiar, and now Emma knew exactly where they were. Turning right, and then left would bring them out into the rose garden again, back into the party, back to his fiancée and their friends, and there would be no more time to talk. She suddenly felt a startling sadness, so stopped for a moment, turned and took both of Dexter's hands in her own.

'Can I say something? Before we go back to the party?'

'Go on.'

'I'm a little drunk.'

'Me too. That's okay.'

'Just . . . I missed you, you know.'

'I missed you too.'

'But so, so much, Dexter. There were so many things I wanted to talk to you about, and you weren't there—'

'Same here.'

'And I feel a little guilty, sort of running away like that.'

'Did you? I didn't blame you. There were times when I was being a little . . . obnoxious.'

'More than a little, you were bloody awful—'

'I know—'

'Selfish, and stuck-up and boring actually—'

'Yes, you've made that point—'

'But even so. I should have stuck it out a bit, what with your mum and everything—'

'That's no excuse though.'

'Well, no, but it was bound to give you a knock.'

'I've still got that letter you wrote. It's a very beautiful letter, I appreciated it.'

'But still, I should have tried harder to get in touch. You're meant to stick by your friends aren't you? Take the blow.'

'I don't blame you—'

'But even so.' To her embarrassment, she found that there were tears in her eyes.

'Hey, hey, what's up, Em?'

'I'm sorry, drunk too much is all . . .'

'Come here.' He put his arms around her, his face against the bare skin of her neck, smelling shampoo and damp silk, and she breathed into his neck, his aftershave and sweat and alcohol, the smell of his suit, and they stood like this for a while until she caught her breath and spoke.

'I tell you what it is. It's . . . when I didn't see you, I thought about you every day, I mean *every day* in some way or another—'

'Same here—'

'—even if it was just "I wish Dexter could see this" or "where's Dexter now?" or "Christ, that Dexter, what an idiot", you know what I mean, and seeing you today, well, I thought I'd got you back – my *best* friend. And now all this, the wedding, the baby – I'm so, so happy for you, Dex. But it feels like I've lost you again.'

'Lost – how?'

'You know what happens, you have a family, your responsi-bilities change, you lose touch with people—'

'Not necessarily—'

'No really, it happens all the time, I know it. You'll have different priorities, and all these new friends, nice young couples that you met at ante-natal classes who'll have babies too and understand, or you'll be too tired because you've been up all night—'

'Actually, we're going to have one of those babies that aren't too much trouble. Just leave them in a room apparently. With a tin opener, a little gas stove.' He could feel her laughter against his chest, and at that moment he thought that there was no better feeling than making Emma Morley laugh. 'It won't be like that, I promise.'

'Do you?'

'Absolutely.'

She pulled away to look at him. 'You swear? No more disappearing?'

'I won't if you won't.'

Their lips touched now, mouths pursed tight, their eyes open, both of them stock still. The moment held, a kind of glorious confusion.

'What's the time?' said Emma, twisting her face away in panic.

Dexter tugged his sleeve and looked at his watch. 'Just coming up to midnight.'

'Well! We should go.'

They walked on in silence, unsure about what had happened and what would happen next. Two more turnings brought them once again to the exit of the maze, and back to the party. Emma was about to open the heavy oak door when he took her hand.

'Em?'

'Dex?'

He wanted to take hold of her hand and walk back into the maze. He would turn his phone off, and they would just stay in there until the party was over, get lost and talk about all that had happened.

'Friends again?' he said eventually.

'Friends again.' She let go of his hand. 'Now, let's go and find your fiancée. I want to *congratulate* her.'

CHAPTER FOURTEEN
Fathering

Richmond, Surrey

Jasmine Alison Viola Mayhew.

She was born in the late evening of the third day of the new Millennium, and so would always be as old as the century. A neat but healthy 6lbs 6ozs, and to Dexter's mind, inexpressibly beautiful, he knew that he would sacrifice his life for her, while at the same time feeling fairly confident that the situation was unlikely to arise.

That night, sitting in the low-slung vinyl hospital chair, clutching the tiny, crimson-faced bundle, Dexter Mayhew made a solemn resolution. He resolved to do the right thing from now on. A few biological and sexual imperatives aside, all his words and actions would now be fit for his daughter's ears and eyes. Life would be lived as if under Jasmine's constant scrutiny. He would never do anything that might cause her pain or anxiety or embarrassment and there would be nothing, absolutely nothing in his life to be ashamed of anymore.

This solemn resolution held for approximately ninety-five minutes. As he sat in a toilet cubicle, attempting to exhale cigarette smoke into an empty Evian bottle, a little must have escaped and set off the detector, waking his exhausted wife and daughter from their much-needed sleep and as he was escorted from the cubicle, still clutching the screw-top bottle of yellow grey smoke, the look in his wife's tired, narrowed eyes said it all: Dexter Mayhew was simply not up to it.

The growing antagonism between them was exacerbated by the fact that, as the new century began, he found himself without a job, or even the prospect of a job. The broadcast slot for *Sport Xtreme* had crept inexorably towards dawn, until it became clear that no-one, not even BMX riders, could stay up that late on a weeknight, no matter how rad, sweet or old skool the moves. The series limped to an end and Paternity Leave shaded into the less fashionable state of unemployment.

A temporary distraction was provided by moving house. After much resistance the bachelor flat in Belsize Park was rented out for a huge monthly sum, and exchanged for a neat terraced house in Richmond with, they told him, bags of potential. Dexter protested that he was too young to move to Surrey, by about thirty-five years, but there was no arguing with the quality of life, the good schools, the transport links, the deer roaming in the Park. It was close to her parents, the Twins lived nearby, so Surrey won out and in May they had begun the endless, bottomlessly expensive task of sanding every available wooden surface and knocking through every non-supporting wall. The Mazda sports car went too, sacrificed for a secondhand people carrier that smelt indelibly of the previous family's communal vomit.

It was a momentous year for the Mayhew family, yet Dexter found himself enjoying nest-building far less than he had thought. He had imagined family life as a sort of extended Building Society commercial: an attractive young couple in blue overalls, paint-rollers in hand, pulling crockery from an old tea chest and flopping down onto a big old sofa. He imagined walking shaggy dogs in the park and exhausted but good-humoured night-feeds. At some point in the near future, there would be rock pools, fires on the beach, mackerel cooked over driftwood. He would invent ingenious games and put up shelves. Sylvie would wear his old shirts over bare legs. Knitwear. He would wear a lot of knitwear and provide for his dependents.

Instead there was bickering, meanness and sullen looks through a fine haze of plaster dust. Sylvie began to spend more and more time at her parents' house, ostensibly to avoid the builders but more often to stay clear of her listless, ineffectual husband. Occasionally she would phone up to suggest that he go and see their friend Callum, the crayfish baron, and take him up on his offer of work, but Dexter resisted. Perhaps his presenting career might pick up again, he might find work as a producer or re-train as a cameraman or an editor. In the meantime he could help the builders, cutting down on labour costs and to this end he made tea and went for biscuits, picked up a little basic Polish, played PlayStation against the sonic boom of the floor-sander.

Once upon a time he had wondered what happened to all the old people in the TV industry, and now he had his answer. Trainee editors and cameramen were twenty-four, twenty-five, and he had no experience as a producer. Mayhem TV plc, his very own independent company, had become less a business, more an alibi for his inactivity. At the end of the tax year it was formally wound down to avoid accounting costs, and twenty reams of optimistically headed paper were shamefully consigned to the attic. The only bright spot came from spending time with Emma again, sneaking off to the movies when he should have been learning to grout with Jerzy and Lech. But that melancholy feeling, stepping out of a cinema into sunlight on a Tuesday afternoon, had become unbearable. What about his vow of perfect fatherhood? He had responsibilities now. In early June he finally cracked, went to see Callum O'Neill and was initiated into the Natural Stuff family.

And so this St Swithin's Day finds Dexter Mayhew in an oatmeal-coloured short-sleeve shirt and mushroom-coloured tie, supervising delivery of the vast daily supply of rocket to the new Victoria Station branch. He counts the boxes of the green

299

stuff while the driver stands by with a clipboard, staring openly, and instinctively Dexter knows what's coming next.

'Didn't you used to be on telly?'

And there it is . . .

'Back in the mists of time,' he replies, light-heartedly.

'What was it called? *largin' it* or something.'

Don't look up.

'That was one of them. So do I sign this receipt or what?'

'And you used to go out with Suki Meadows.'

Smile, smile, smile.

'Like I said it was a long, long time ago. One box, two, three—'

'She's everywhere these days, isn't she?'

'Six, seven, eight—'

'She's gorgeous.'

'She's very nice. Nine, ten.'

'What was that like then, going out with her?'

'Loud.'

'So – whatever happened to you?'

'Life. Life happened.' He takes the clipboard from him. 'I sign here, yes?'

'That's right. You sign there.'

Dexter autographs the invoice and places his hand into the top box, taking a handful of rocket and tasting it for freshness. 'Rocket – the iceberg lettuce *de nos jours*' Callum is fond of saying, but Dexter finds it bitter.

The real head-offices of Natural Stuff are in a warehouse in Clerkenwell, fresh and clean and modern, with juicers and bean-bags, unisex toilets, high-speed internet and pinball machines; immense, Warholesque canvases of cows, chickens and crayfish hang on the walls. Part workplace, part teenager's bedroom, the architects had labelled it not an office, but a 'dreamspace' in Helvetica, lower case. But before Dexter is allowed into the dreamspace, he has to learn the ropes. Cal is very keen that all his executives get their hands dirty, so Dexter is on a month-long trainee placement, working as the shadow manager of the latest outpost of the empire. In the last three weeks he has cleaned out the juicers, worn a hairnet to make the sandwiches, ground the coffee, served the customers and, to his surprise, it has been okay. This, after all, is what it's all about; business is people, as Callum likes to say.

The worst thing about it is the recognition, that flickering look of pity that passes over the customer's face when they see an ex-TV presenter serving up soup. The ones in their mid-thirties, his contemporaries, they're the worst. To have had fame, even very minor fame, and to have lost it, got older and maybe put on a little weight is a kind of living death, and they stare at Dexter behind the cash register as one might stare at a prisoner on a chain-gang. 'You seem smaller in real life,' they sometimes say, and it's true, he does feel smaller now. 'But it's okay,' he wants to say, ladling out the Goan-style lentil soup. 'It's fine. I'm at peace. I like it here, and it's only temporary. I'm learning a new business, I'm providing for my family. Would you like some bread to go with that? Wholemeal or multigrain?'

The morning shift at Natural Stuff lasts from 6.30 a.m. to 4.30 p.m., and after cashing up, he joins the Saturday shoppers on the train to Richmond. Then there's a boring twenty-minute walk back to the terrace of Victorian houses that are all much, much bigger on the inside than they appear on the outside, until he is home at The House of Colic. As he walks up the garden path (he has a garden path – how did that happen?), he sees Jerzy and Lech closing the front door, and he assumes the matey tone and mild cockney accent that is mandatory when talking to builders, even Polish ones.

'Cześć! Jak się masz?'

'Good evening, Dexter,' says Lech, indulgently.

'Mrs Mayhew, she is home?' You have to change the words round like this; it's the law.

'Yes, she's home.'

He lowers his voice. 'Today, how are they?'

'A little . . . tired, I think.'

Dexter frowns and sucks in his breath jokily. 'So – should I worry?'

'A little, perhaps.'

'Here.' Dexter reaches into his inside pocket, and hands them two contraband Natural Stuff Honey-Date-Oat Bars. 'Stolen property. Do not tell anyone, yes?'

'Okay, Dexter.'

'*Do widzenia.*' He steps up to the front door and takes out his key, knowing there's a good chance that somewhere in the house someone will be crying. Sometimes it seems as if they have a rota.

Jasmine Alison Viola Mayhew is waiting in the hallway, sitting up unsteadily on the plastic dust-sheets that protect the newly stripped floorboards. Small neat, perfect features set in the centre of an oval face, she is her mother in miniature, and once more he has that feeling of intense love tempered with abject terror.

'Hello, Jas. Sorry I'm late,' he says, scooping her up, his hands circling her belly, holding her above his head. 'What kind of day have you had, Jas?'

A voice from the living room. 'I wish you wouldn't call her that. She's Jasmine, not *Jazz.*' Sylvie lies on the dust-sheet-covered sofa, reading a magazine. 'Jazz Mayhew is *awful*. Makes her sound like a saxophonist in some lesbian *funk* band. *Jazz.*'

He drapes his daughter over his shoulder and stands in the doorway. 'Well if you're going to name her Jasmine, she's going to get called Jas.'

'*I* didn't name her, *we* named her. And I know it's going to happen, I'm just saying I don't like it.'

'Fine, I'll completely change the way I talk to my daughter.'

'Good, I'd like that.'

He stands at the end of the sofa, glances at his watch showily, and thinks *A new world record! I've been home, what, forty-five seconds, and already I've done something wrong!* The remark has just the right mix of self-pity and hostility; he likes it, and is about to say it out loud, when Sylvie sits and frowns, her eyes wet, hugging her knees.

'I'm sorry, sweetheart, I've had an awful day.'

'What's up?'

'She doesn't want to sleep at all. She's been awake all day, every single minute since five this morning.'

Dexter puts one fist on his hip. 'Well sweetheart, if you gave her the decaff, like I told you . . .' But this kind of banter doesn't come naturally to Dexter, and Sylvie does not smile.

'She's been crying, and whimpering all day, it's so hot outside, and so boring inside, with Jerzy and Lech banging away and, I don't know, I'm just frustrated, that's all.' He sits, puts his arm around her and kisses her forehead. 'I swear, if I have to walk around that bloody park again I'll scream.'

'Not long now.'

'I walk round the lake and round the lake and over to the swings and round the lake again. You know the highlight of my day? I thought I'd run out of nappies. I thought I'm going to have to go to Waitrose and get some nappies, and then I found some nappies. I found four nappies and I was *so* excited.'

'Still, back to work next month.'

'Thank God!' She keels over, her head against his shoulder and sighs. 'Perhaps I shouldn't go tonight.'

'No, you've got to! You've been looking forward to it for weeks!'

'I'm not really in the mood for it – a *hen night*. I'm too old for hen nights.'

'Rubbish—'

'And I worry—'

'Worry about what, about me?'

'Leaving you on your own.'

'Well I'm thirty-five years old, Sylvie, I've been in a house by myself before. And anyway, I won't be alone, I've got Jas to look after me. We'll both be fine, won't we, Jas? Min. Jasmine.'

'You're sure?'

'Absolutely.' *She doesn't trust me*, he thinks. *She thinks I'll drink. But I won't. No I won't.*

The hen night is for Rachel, the thinnest and most mean-spirited of his wife's friends, and a hotel suite has been hired for the sleepover, complete with a handsome cocktail waiter to use as they see fit. A limo, a restaurant, a table at a night-club, brunch the next day, it has all been planned through a series of bossy emails to ensure no possibility of spontaneity or joy. Sylvie won't be back until the following afternoon, and for the first time Dexter is to be left in charge overnight. She stands in the bathroom, putting on make-up and watching over him as he kneels to give Jasmine her bath.

'So put her down around eight, okay? That's in forty minutes.'

'Fine.'

'There's plenty of formula, and I've pureed the veggies.' *Veggies* – that's annoying, the way she says *veggies*. 'They're in the fridge.'

'Veggies in the fridge, I know that.'

'If she doesn't like it, there's some ready-made jars in the cupboard, but they're *only* for emergencies.'

'And what about crisps? I can give her crisps, can't I? If I brush the salt off—'

Sylvie clicks her tongue, shakes her head, applies lipstick. 'Support her head.'

'—and salted nuts? She's old enough, isn't she? Little bowl of peanuts?' He turns to look at her over his shoulder on the off-chance that she might be smiling, and is startled, as he often is, by how beautiful she looks, dressed simply but elegantly in a short black dress and high heels, her hair still damp from the shower. He takes one hand from Jasmine's bath, and cups his wife's brown calf. 'You look amazing, by the way.'

'Your hands are wet.' She twists her leg away. They haven't made love for six weeks now. He had anticipated a certain

304

coldness and irritability after the birth, but it's been a while, and sometimes there's a look she gives him, a look of – no, not contempt, but—

'Wish you were coming back tonight,' he says.

– disappointment. That's it. Disappointment.

'Watch out for Jasmine – support her head!'

'I know what I'm doing!' he snaps back. 'For Christ's sake!'

And there it is again, the look. There's no doubt about it, if Sylvie had a receipt, she would have taken him back by now; this one's gone wrong. It's not what I wanted.

The doorbell rings.

'That's my taxi. If there's an emergency, call my mobile, *not* the hotel, okay?' and she bends and taps her lips on the top of Dexter's head, then leans into the bath, and gives a second more persuasive kiss to her daughter. 'Goodnight, my precious. Look after daddy for me . . .' Jasmine frowns and pouts and as her mother leaves the bathroom, there is panic in her eyes. Dexter sees this and laughs. 'Where are you going, Mum?' he whispers. 'Don't leave me with this *idiot*!' Downstairs the front door is finally closed. Sylvie has gone, he is on his own and finally free to perform a whole series of idiotic actions.

It all begins with the television in the kitchen. Jasmine is already screaming as Dexter struggles to fasten her into the high-chair. She will do this for Sylvie, but now she's twisting and screaming, a compact parcel of muscle and noise, writhing with surprising strength and for no discernible reason, and Dexter finds himself thinking *just learn to talk, will you*? Just learn some bloody language and tell me what I'm doing wrong. How much longer until she can speak? A year? Eighteen months? It's insane, an absurd design error, this refusal to master speech just when it's needed most. They should come out talking. Not conversation, not repartee, just basic practical information. *Father, I have wind. This activity centre leaves me jaded. I am colicky.*

Finally she's in, but is alternating screaming and whining now, and he spoons the food into her mouth when he can, pausing every now and then to remove the smeared puree with the edge of the spoon as if it were a wet shave. In the hope that it might calm her down he turns on the small portable television on the counter, the one that Sylvie disapproves of. Because it's Saturday peak-viewing time, he inevitably sees Suki Meadows' face beaming out at him, live from TV Centre where she is bellowing the lottery results at a waiting nation. He feels his stomach contract in a little spasm of envy, then tuts and shakes his head, and is about to change channel when he notices that Jasmine is silent and still, entranced by his ex-girlfriend hollering 'wahey'.

'Look, Jasmine, it's Daddy's ex-girlfriend! Isn't she loud? Isn't she a loud, loud girl?'

Suki is wealthy now and ever more bubbly and famous and loved by the public, and even though they never got on and had nothing in common, he feels nostalgia for his old girlfriend, and for the wild years of his late twenties when his photo was in the papers. What is Suki doing tonight? he wonders. 'Maybe Daddy should have stuck with her,' he says aloud, treacherously, thinking back to the nights in black cabs and cocktail lounges, hotel bars and railway arches, the years before Saturdays were spent in a hairnet filling Mediterranean wraps.

Now Jasmine is crying again because somehow she has sweet potato in her eye, and as he wipes it away he feels the *necessity* of a cigarette. Why shouldn't he, after the day he's had, why shouldn't he treat himself? His back aches, a blue plaster is unpeeling from his thumb, his fingers smell of crayfish and old coffee, and he decides he needs a treat. He needs the gift of nicotine.

Two minutes later he is pulling on the baby harness, getting that little macho can-do thrill from the straps and buckles, as if hauling on a jet pack. He crams the crying Jasmine into the front, then sets out with real purpose down the long dull tree-lined street to that boring little arcade of shops. How did he get here, he wonders, a shopping arcade in Surrey on a Saturday night? It's not even Richmond proper, just a suburb of a suburb, and he thinks once again of Suki, out on the town somewhere with her attractive girlfriends. Maybe he could phone her once Jasmine is asleep, just to say hello. Have a drink, phone an old girlfriend; why not?

At the off-licence there's a tingle of anticipation as he pushes open the door and is immediately confronted by a high sheer wall of booze. Since the pregnancy there has been a policy of not keeping alcohol in the house in order to deter casual, everyday drinking. 'I'm just bored with sitting on a sofa on a Tuesday night,' said Sylvie, 'while you get drunk alone,' and taking this as a challenge he has stopped, more or less. But now he finds himself in an off-licence, and there seems to be so much great stuff here and it all looks so nice that it seems silly not to take advantage. Spirits and beers, wines white and red, he takes it all in and buys two bottles of good Bordeaux, just to be on the safe side, and twenty cigarettes. Then, because why not, he goes to the Thai take-away.

Soon the sun is setting and Jasmine is falling asleep on his chest as he walks briskly home down the pleasant streets to the neat little house that will be lovely when it's finished. He goes to the kitchen and without removing the sleeping baby from his sling, opens the bottle and pours a glass, his arms curled awkwardly around the bundle like a ballet dancer. He looks at the glass, almost ritualistically, then drains it, and thinks: not drinking would be so much easier if it wasn't so delicious. He closes his eyes, leans against the counter top as the tension goes out of his shoulders. There was a time when he used alcohol as a stimulant, something to lift his spirits and give him energy, but now he drinks like all parents drink, as a kind of early evening sedative. Feeling calmer, he props up the sleeping baby in a little nest of cushions on the sofa and enters the small, suburban garden: a rotary clothes line surrounded by timber and bags of cement. He keeps the baby harness on, letting it hang loose like a shoulder holster so that he might almost be an off-duty cop, homicide division, a jaded romantic, moody but dangerous, moonlighting with a little bit of childcare in Surrey. All he needs to complete the impression is a cigarette. It is his first for two weeks, and he lights it reverently, savouring that delicious first taste, sucking so hard that he can hear the tobacco crackle. Burning leaves and petrol, it tastes of 1995.

His brain gradually empties of work, of falafel wraps and oaty squares, and he starts to feel hopeful for the evening; perhaps he'll acquire that state of peaceful inactivity that is the nirvana of the exhausted parent. He pushes the butt deep into a pile of sand, retrieves Jasmine, tip-toes quietly up the stairs to her room and pulls down the blackout blinds. Like a master safe-cracker, he is going to change her nappy without waking her up.

As soon as he lays her on the changing mat she wakes and starts to cry again, that awful rasping cry. Breathing through his mouth, he changes her as quickly and efficiently as he can. Part of the positive press about having a baby was how inoffensive baby poo was, how poo and wee lost their taint and became, if not fun, at least innocuous. His sister had even claimed that you could 'eat it on toast', so benign and fragrant was this 'poo'.

Even so, you wouldn't want it underneath your fingernails and with the arrival of formula and solids it has taken on a decidedly more adult quality. Little Jasmine has produced what looks like a half-pound of peanut butter, which she has somehow contrived to smear up her back. With his head a little fuzzy from the wine on an empty stomach, he scoops and scrapes it up as best he can with half a pack of baby wipes and, when these run out, the edge of his one-day travelcard. He crams the still warm bundle into a chemical-smelling nappy bag, which he drops into a pedal bin, noting queasily that there is condensation on the lid. Jasmine cries throughout. When she is finally fresh and clean he scoops her up and holds her against his shoulder, bouncing on his toes until his calves ache and miraculously she is quiet again.

He crosses to the cot and lays her down, and she starts to scream. He picks her up and she is silent. Lays her down, she screams. He is aware of a pattern but it seems so unreasonable, so plain wrong, for her to demand so much when his spring rolls are getting cold, the wine is standing open and this small room smells so richly of hot poo. The phrase 'unconditional love' has been thrown around a lot, but right now he feels like imposing some conditions. 'Come on, Jas, play fair, be nice. Daddy's been up since five, remember?' She is quiet once again, her breath warm and steady against his neck, and so he tries once more to lay her down, taking it slowly, an absurd limbo dance, shifting imperceptibly from the vertical to the horizontal. He still wears the macho baby harness, and now imagines himself a bomb disposal expert; gently, gently, gently.

She starts to cry again.

He closes the door regardless and trots downstairs. Got to be tough. Got to be ruthless, that's what the books say. If she had some language, he'd be able to explain: *Jasmine, it is necessary for both of us to have some private time.* He eats in front of the television, but is once again struck by how hard it is to ignore a baby screaming. Controlled crying they call it, but he has lost control and wants to cry and starts to feel a Victorian indignation towards his wife – what kind of irresponsible harlot leaves a baby with his father? How dare she? He turns up the television and goes to pour another glass of wine, but is surprised to find the bottle empty.

Never mind. There is no parenting problem in the world that can't be solved by throwing milk at it. He makes some more formula, then climbs upstairs, his head a little fuzzy, blood ringing in his ears. The fierce little face softens as he places the milk bottle into her hands, but then she is screaming again, a ferocious wail as he sees that he has forgotten to screw the lid on the bottle and now warm formula has flooded out and soaked the bedclothes, the mattress, is in her eyes and up her nose, and she's screaming now, really screaming, and why shouldn't she scream, given that daddy has snuck into her room and flung half a pint of warm milk in her face. Panicked, he grabs a muslin square, finding instead her best cashmere cardigan on a pile of clean washing, and wipes off the excess clots of formula from her hair and out of her eyes, kissing her all the time, cursing himself – 'idiot idiot idiot sorry sorry sorry' – and with the other arm beginning the process of changing her formula-sodden bedding, her clothes, her nappy, flinging it all in a pile on the floor. Now he's relieved she isn't able to talk. '*Look at you, you idiot,*' she would say, '*can't even look after a baby.*' Back downstairs he makes more formula with one hand then carries her upstairs, feeding her in the darkened room until once again her head is on his shoulder, she is calm, is sleeping.

He closes the door silently then tip-toes down the bare wooden stairs, a burglar in his own home. In the kitchen the second bottle of wine sits open. He pours another glass.

It's nearly ten now. He tries to watch the television, this thing called *Big Brother*, but he can't understand what he's meant to be looking at and feels a curmudgeonly, old-timer's disapproval for the state of the TV industry. 'I don't understand,' he says aloud. He puts on some music, a compilation designed to make your home feel like the lobby of a European boutique hotel, and tries to read Sylvie's discarded magazine, but even that's beyond him now. He puts the games console on, but neither *Metal Gear Solid*, nor *Quake* nor *Doom*, not even *Tomb Raider* at its highest level brings him any peace. He needs some adult human company, conversation from someone who doesn't just scream and whimper and sleep. He picks up his phone. He is frankly drunk now, and with drunkenness has come the old compulsion: to say something stupid to an attractive woman.

Stephanie Shaw has a new breast pump. Top of the range, Finnish, it whirrs and chugs under her t-shirt like a small outboard motor as they sit on the sofa and try and watch *Big Brother*.

Emma had been led to believe that tonight would be a dinner party, but having made it to Whitechapel she has found that

Stephanie and Adam are too exhausted to cook; hope she doesn't mind. Instead they sit and watch the television and chat, while the breast pump whirrs and chugs away, giving the living room the atmosphere of a milking shed. Another big night in the life of a Godmother.

There are conversations Emma no longer wants to have and they all concern babies. The first few were novel enough, and yes, there was something intriguing, funny and touching about seeing your friends' features blended and fused in miniature like that. And of course there is always joy in witnessing the joy of others.

But not *that* much joy, and this year it seems that every time she leaves the house some new infant is being jammed in her face. She feels the same dread as when someone produces a brick-sized pile of their holiday snaps: great that you had a nice time, but what's it got to do with me? To this end, Emma has a fascinated-face that she puts on when a friend tells her about the miseries of labour, what drugs were used, whether they caved and went for the epidural, the agony, the joy.

But there's nothing transferable about the miracle of childbirth, or parenthood in general. Emma doesn't want to talk about the strain of broken sleep; hadn't they heard rumours of this in advance? Neither does she want to have to remark on the baby's smile, or how it started off looking like the mother but now looks like the father or started off looking like the father but now has the mother's mouth. And what is this obsession with the size of the hands, the tiny little hands with the tiny, tiny fingernails, when in a way it's big hands that would be more remarkable. 'Look at baby's massive great flapping hands!' Now *that* would be worth talking about.

'I'm falling asleep,' says Adam, Stephanie's husband, from the armchair, his head supported by his fist.

'Maybe I should go,' says Emma.

'No! Stay!' says Stephanie, but doesn't provide a reason.

Emma eats another Kettle Chip. What has happened to her

friends? They used to be funny and fun-loving, gregarious and interesting, but far too many evenings have been spent like this with pasty, irritable hollow-eyed couples in smelly rooms, expressing wonder that baby is getting bigger with time, rather than smaller. She is tired of squealing in delight when she sees a baby crawl, as if this was a completely unexpected development, this 'crawling'. What were they expecting, flight? She is indifferent to the smell of a baby's head. She tried it once, and it smelt like the back of a watchstrap.

Her phone rings in her bag. She picks it up and glances at Dexter's name but doesn't bother answering. No, she doesn't want to go all the way from Whitechapel to Richmond to watch him blowing raspberries on little Jasmine's belly. She is particularly bored by this, her male friends performing their New Young Dad act: harassed but good-tempered, weary but modern in their regulation jacket with jeans, paunchy in their ribbed tops with that proud, self-regarding little look they give as they toss junior in the air. Bold pioneers, the first men in the history of the world to get a little wee on their corduroy, a little vomit in their hair.

Of course, she can't say any of this out loud. There's something unnatural about a woman finding babies or, more specifically, conversation about babies, boring. They'll think she's bitter, jealous, lonely. But she's also bored with everybody telling her how *lucky* she is, what with all that sleep and all that freedom and spare time, the ability to go on dates or head off to Paris at a moment's notice. It sounds like they're consoling her, and she resents this and feels patronised by it. It's not like she's even going to Paris! In particular, she is bored with jokes about the biological clock, from her friends, her family, in films and on TV. The most idiotic, witless word in the English language is 'singleton', followed closely by 'chocoholic', and she refuses to be part of any Sunday supplement lifestyle phenomenon. Yes, she understands the debate, the practical imperatives, but it's a situation entirely out of her control.

And yes, occasionally she tries to picture herself in a blue hospital gown, sweaty and in agony, but the face of the man holding her hand remains stubbornly blurred, and it's a fantasy she chooses not to dwell on.

When it happens, if it happens, she will adore the child, remark on its tiny hands and even the smell of its scrofulous little head. She will debate epidurals, lack of sleep, colic, whatever the hell that is. One day she might even bring herself to coo at a pair of booties. But in the meantime she's going to keep her distance, and stay calm and serene and above it all. Having said that, the first one to call her Aunty Emma gets a punch in the face.

Stephanie has finished expressing and is showing her breast milk to Adam, holding it up to the light like a fine wine. It's a great little breast pump, they all agree.

'My turn next!' says Emma, but no-one laughs and right on cue the baby wakes upstairs.

'What someone needs to invent,' says Adam, 'is a chloroformed baby wipe.'

Stephanie sighs and trudges out, and Emma decides she will definitely head home soon. She can stay up late, work on the manuscript. The phone buzzes again. A message from Dexter, asking her to schlep out to Surrey to keep him company.

She turns the phone off.

'. . . I know it's a long way, it's just I think I might be suffering from post-natal depression. Get in a cab, I'll pay. Sylvie's not here! Not that it makes any difference, I know, but . . . there's a spare bedroom, if you wanted to stay over. Anyway, call me if you get this. Bye.' He hesitates, says another 'Bye' and hangs up. A pointless message. He blinks and shakes his head, and pours more wine. Scrolling through the phone's address book, he comes to S for Suki Mobile.

Initially there is no reply, and he finds himself relieved, because after all what good can come of it, the phone-call to an old girlfriend? He's about to hang up, when suddenly he hears the distinctive bellow.

'HELLO!'

'Hey there!' He dusts off his presenter's smile.

'WHO IS THIS?' She's shouting over the sound of a party, a restaurant perhaps.

'Make some noise!'

'WHAT? WHO IS THIS?'

'You have to guess!'

'WHAT? I CAN'T HEAR YOU . . .'

'I said "guess who?" . . .'

'I CAN'T HEAR YOU, WHO IS THIS?'

'You have to guess!'

'WHO?'

'I SAID YOU HAVE TO . . .' The game has become exhausting, so he just says 'It's Dexter!'

There's a moment's pause.

'Dexter? *Dexter Mayhew?*'

'How many Dexters do you know, Suki?'

'No, I know which Dexter, I'm just, like . . . WAHEY, DEXTER! Hello, Dexter! Hold on . . .' He hears the scrape of a chair and imagines eyes following her, intrigued, as she leaves the restaurant table and walks into a corridor. 'So how are you, Dexter?'

'I'm fine, I'm fine, I'm just, you know, phoning to say I saw you tonight on the telly, and it got me thinking about old times, and I thought I'd phone and say Hi. You looked great by the way. On TV. And I like the show. Great format.' Great *format*? You clown. 'So. How are you, Suki?'

'Oh, I'm fine, I'm fine.'

'You're everywhere! You're doing really well! Really!'

'Thank you. Thanks.'

There's a silence. Dexter's thumb caresses the off button. Hang up. Pretend the line's gone down. Hang up, hang up, hang up . . .

'It's been, what, five years, Dex!'

'I know, I was thinking about you just now, because I saw you on TV. And you looked great by the way. And how are you?' *Don't say that, you've said that already. Concentrate!* 'I mean, where are you? It's very noisy . . .'

'A restaurant. I'm having dinner, with some mates.'

'Anyone I know?'

'Don't think so. They're kind of *new* friends.'

New friends. Could that be hostility? 'Right. Okay.'

'So. Where are you, Dexter?'

'Oh, I'm at home.'

'Home? On a Saturday night? That's not like you!'

'Well, you know . . .' and he's about to tell her that he's married, has a kid, lives in the suburbs, but feels that this might serve to underline the sheer futility of the phone-call, so instead stays silent. The pause goes on for some time. He notices that there's an epaulette of snot on the cotton sweater he once wore to Pacha, and he has become aware of the new scent on his fingertips, an unholy cocktail of nappy sacks and prawn crackers.

Suki speaks. 'So, main course has just arrived . . .'

'Okay, well, anyway, I was just thinking about old times, and thinking it would be nice to see you! You know for lunch or a drink or something . . .'

The background music fades as if Suki has stepped into some private corner. In a hardened voice she says, 'You know what, Dexter? I don't think that's such a good idea.'

'Oh, right.'

'I mean I haven't seen you for five years now, and I think when that happens there's usually a reason, don't you?'

'I just thought—'

'I mean it's not as if you were ever that *nice* to me, never that interested, you were off your face most of the time—'

'Oh, that's not true!'

'You weren't even *faithful* to me, for fuck's sake, you were usually off fucking some runner or waitress or whatever so I don't know where you get off now, phoning up like we're old pals and getting *nostalgic* about "old times", our golden six months that were, quite frankly, pretty shitty for me.'

'Alright, Suki, you've made your point.'

'And anyway I'm with another guy, a really, really *nice* guy, and I'm very happy. In fact he's waiting for me right now.'

'Fine! So go! GO!' Upstairs, Jasmine starts to cry, with embarrassment perhaps.

'You can't just get pissed-up and phone out of the blue and expect me—'

'I'm not, I only, Jesus, okay, fine, forget it!' Jasmine's howl is echoing down the bare wooden stairs.

'What's that noise?'

'It's a baby.'

'Whose baby?'

'My baby. I have a daughter. A baby daughter. Seven months old.'

There's a silence, just long enough for Dexter to visibly wither, then Suki says:

'Then why the hell are you asking me out?'

'Just. You know. A friendly drink.'

'I *have* friends,' says Suki, very quietly. 'I think you'd better go and see to your daughter, don't you Dex?' and she hangs up.

For a while he just sits and listens to the dead line. Eventually he lowers the phone, stares at it, then shakes his head vigorously as if he has just been slapped. He *has* been slapped.

'Well, that went well,' he murmurs.

Address Book, Edit Contact, Delete Contact. 'Are you sure you want to delete Suki Mobile?' asks the phone. Fuck me, yes, yes, delete her, yes! He jabs at the buttons. Contact Deleted says the phone, but it's not enough; Contact Eradicated, Contact Vaporised, that's what he needs. Jasmine's crying is reaching the peak of its first cycle, so he stands suddenly and hurls the phone against the wall where it leaves a black scratch mark on the Farrow and Ball. He throws it again to leave a second.

Cursing Suki, cursing himself for being so stupid, he makes up a small bottle of milk, screws the lid on tight, puts it in his pocket, grabs the wine then runs up the stairs towards Jasmine's cry, an awful hoarse rasping sound now that seems to tear at the back of her throat. He bursts into the room.

'For fuck's sake, Jasmine, just shut up, will you?!' he shouts, instantly clapping his hand to his mouth with shame as he sees her sitting up in the cot, eyes wide in distress. Scooping her up, he sits with his back against the wall, absorbing her cries into his chest, then lays her in his lap, strokes her forehead with great tenderness, and when this doesn't work he starts to gently stroke the back of her head. Isn't there meant to be some secret pressure spot that you rub with your thumb? He circles the palm of her hand as it clenches and unclenches angrily. Nothing helps, his big fat fingers trying this, fumbling with that, nothing working. Perhaps she's not well, he thinks, or perhaps he is just not her mother. Useless father, useless husband, useless boyfriend, useless son.

But what if she is unwell? Could be colic, he thinks. Or teething, is she teething? Anxiety is starting to grip. Should she go to hospital? Perhaps, except of course he's too drunk to drive now. Useless, useless, useless man. 'Come on, *concentrate*,' he says aloud. There's some medicine on the shelf, on it the words 'may cause drowsiness' – the most beautiful words in the English language. Once it was 'do you have a t-shirt I can borrow?' Now it's 'may cause drowsiness'.

He bounces Jasmine on his knee until she's a little quieter, then puts the loaded spoon to her lips until he judges that 5ml has been swallowed. The next twenty minutes are spent putting on a demented cabaret, manically waggling talking animals at her. He runs through his limited repertoire of funny voices, pleading in high and low pitches and various regional accents for her to shush now, there there, go to sleep. He holds picture books in front of her face, lifting flaps, pulling tabs, jabbing at pages saying 'Duck! Cow! Choo-choo train! See the funny tiger, see it!' He puts on deranged puppet shows. A plastic chimpanzee sings the first verse of 'Wheels on the Bus' over and over again, Tinky Winky performs 'Old MacDonald', a stuffed pig gives her 'Into the Groove' for no reason. Together they squeeze beneath the arches of the baby gym and work out together. He stuffs his mobile phone into her little hands, lets her press the buttons, dribble into the keypad, listen to the speaking clock until finally, mercifully, she's quieter, just whimpering now, still wide awake but content.

There's a CD player in the room, a chunky Fisher Price in the shape of a steam train, and he kicks through discarded books and toys and presses play. *Relaxing Classics for Tots*, part of Sylvie's total baby-mind-control project. The 'Dance of the Sugar Plum Fairy' sounds from tinny speakers. 'Tuuuuuune!' he shouts, turns up the volume by way of the steam train's funnel and starts to waltz woozily around the room, Jasmine close to his chest. She stretches now, her tapered fingers balling into fists then flexing, and for the first time looks at her father with something other than a scowl. He catches a momentary glimpse of his own face smiling back up at him. She smacks her lips, eyes wide. She is laughing. 'That's my girl!' he says, 'that's my beauty.' His spirits lift and he has an idea.

Draping Jasmine over his shoulder, banging against door jambs on the way, he runs down to the kitchen where three large cardboard boxes temporarily hold all his CDs until the shelves are up. There are thousands of them, freebies mainly, the legacy of when he was held to be influential and the sight of them sends him back in time to his DJ days when he used to wander round Soho wearing those ridiculous headphones. He kneels and fishes through the box with one hand. The trick is not to make Jasmine *sleep,* the trick is to try and keep her awake, and to this end they're going to have a party, just the two of them, better by far than any night-club Hoxton can offer. Screw Suki Meadows, he's going to DJ for his daughter.

Energised now, he quarries deeper through the geological

layers of the CDs that represent ten years of fashion, picking out the occasional disc, stacking them up in a pile on the floor, warming to his plan. Acid Jazz and break-beats, 70s funk and acid house, give way to deep and progressive house, electronica and big beat and Balearic and compilations with the word 'chill' in and even a small, unconvincing selection of drum and bass. Looking through old music should be a pleasure, but he's surprised to find that even the sight of the artwork makes him feel anxious and jittery, tied up as it is with memories of sleepless, paranoid nights with strangers in his flat, idiotic conversations with friends he no longer knows. Dance music makes him anxious now. This must be it then, he thinks, this is getting old.

Then he sees the spine of a CD; Emma's writing. It's a compilation CD she made on her flashy new computer for his 35th birthday last August, just before his wedding. The compilation is called 'Eleven Years' and on the homemade inlay slip is a photograph, smudgy from Emma's cheap home printer, but nevertheless it is still possible to make out the two of them sitting on a mountainside, the peak of Arthur's Seat, the extinct volcano that looms over Edinburgh. It must have been that morning after graduation, what, twelve years ago? In the photo, Dexter in a white shirt leans against a boulder with a cigarette dangling from his lip. Emma sits a little distance away with her knees brought up to her chest, her chin on her knees. She wears 501s cinched tight at the waist, is a little plumper then than now, gawky and awkward with a ragged fringe of hennaed hair shading her eyes. It's the expression that she has used in photos ever since, smiling one-sidedly with her mouth closed. Dexter peers at her face and laughs. He shows it to Jasmine.

'Look at that! It's your godmother, Emma! Look how thin your dad was. Look – cheekbones. Daddy once had cheekbones.' Jasmine laughs soundlessly.

Back in Jasmine's bedroom he sets her in the corner and takes the CD out of the case. Tucked inside is a tightly written postcard, his birthday card from last year.

> 1st August 1999. Here it is – a homemade present. Keep telling yourself – it's the thought that counts it's the thought that counts. This is a loving CD reproduction of a cassette compilation I made for you ages ago. None of your chill-out rubbish; proper songs. Hope you enjoy this. Happy Birthday, Dexter, and congratulations on all your great news – A husband! A father! You will be great at both.
>
> It's good to have you back. Remember, I love you very much. Your old friend
> Emma x

He smiles, and puts the disc in the player that is shaped like a steam train.

It starts with Massive Attack, 'Unfinished Sympathy' and he picks up Jasmine and bounces at the knees with his feet planted, mumbling the words into his daughter's ear. Old pop music, two bottles of wine and no sleep are combining to make him feel light-headed and sentimental now. He cranks up the Fisher Price train as loud as it will go.

And then it's The Smiths, 'There is a Light That Never Goes Out', and though he never particularly cared for The Smiths he continues to bob around, head down, twenty again, drunk at a student disco. He is singing quite loudly, it's embarrassing, but he doesn't care. In the small bedroom of a terraced house, dancing with his daughter to music from a toy train, he suddenly has an intense feeling of contentment. More than contentment – elation. He spins, and steps on a pull-along wooden dog, and stumbles like a street drunk, steadying himself with one hand against the wall. *Whoa there, steady boy*, he says aloud, then looks down at Jasmine to see she's okay and she's fine, she's laughing, his own beautiful, beautiful daughter. *There is a light that never goes out.*

And now it's 'Walk On By', a song his mother used to play when he was a kid. He remembers Alison dancing to it in the living room, a cigarette in one hand, a drink in the other. He settles Jasmine on his shoulder, feeling her breath on his neck, and takes her other hand in his, kicking through the debris in an old-fashioned slow-dance. Through the middle of exhaustion and red wine he has a sudden desire to talk to Emma, to tell her what he's listening to, and as if on cue his phone rings just as the song fades. He forages amongst the discarded toys and books; perhaps it's Emma, calling back. The display says 'Sylvie' and he swears; he must answer. Sober, sober, sober, he tells himself. He leans against the cot, settles Jasmine in his lap and takes the call.

'Hello, Sylvie!'

At that moment Public Enemy's 'Fight the Power' suddenly kicks out from the Fisher Price, and he scrambles to jab at the stumpy buttons.

'What was that?'

'Just some music. Jasmine and I are having a little party, aren't we, Jas? I mean Jasmine.'

'She's still *awake*?'

''fraid so.'

Sylvie sighs. 'What have you been up to?'

I have smoked cigarettes, got drunk, doped our baby, phoned old girlfriends, trashed the house, danced around mumbling to myself. I have fallen over like a drunk in the street.

'Oh, just hanging out, watching telly. How about you? Having fun?'

'It's okay. Everyone's off their face of course—'

'Except you.'

'I'm too exhausted to get drunk.'

'It's very quiet. Where are you?'

'In my hotel room. I'm just going to have a lie-down, then go back for the next wave.' As she speaks, Dexter takes in the wreck of Jasmine's room – the milk-sodden sheets, the scattered toys and books, the empty wine bottle and greasy glass.

'How's Jasmine?'

'She's smiling, aren't you, sweetheart? It's Mummy on the phone.' Dutifully he presses the phone to Jasmine's ear, but she remains silent. It's no fun for anyone, so he takes it away. 'Me again.'

'But you've managed.'

'Of course. Did you ever doubt me?' There was a moment's pause. 'You should get back to your party.'

'Perhaps I should. I'll see you tomorrow. About lunch time. I'll be back at, I don't know, eleven-ish.'

'Fine. Goodnight then.'

'Goodnight, Dexter.'

'Love you,' he says.

'You too.'

She is about to hang up, but he feels compelled to say one more thing. 'And Sylvie? Sylvie? Are you there?'

She brings the phone back to her ear. 'Hm?'

He swallows, and licks his lips. 'I just wanted to say . . . I wanted to say I know I'm not very good at this at the moment, this whole father, husband thing. But I'm working on it, and I'm trying. I will get better, Sylv. I promise you.'

She seems to take this in because there's a short silence before she speaks again, her voice a little tight. 'Dex, you're doing fine. We're just . . . feeling our way, that's all.'

He sighs. Somehow he had hoped for more. 'You'd better get back to your party.'

'I'll see you tomorrow.'

'I love you.'

'You too.'

And she is gone.

The house seems very quiet. He sits there for a full minute, his daughter sleeping now on his lap, and listens to the roar of blood and wine in his head. For a moment he feels a pulse of dread and loneliness, but he shakes this away, then stands and raises his sleeping daughter to his face, loose-limbed now like a kitten. He inhales her scent: milky, almost sweet, his own flesh and blood. Flesh and blood. The phrase is a cliché but there are fleeting moments when he catches sight of himself in her face, becomes aware of the fact and can't quite believe it. For better or for worse, she is a part of me. He lowers her gently into her cot.

He steps on a plastic pig, sharp as flint, which embeds itself painfully in his heel and, swearing to himself, he turns off the bedroom light.

In a hotel room in Westminster, ten miles further east along the Thames, his wife sits naked on the edge of a bed with the phone held loosely in her hand and quietly starts to cry. From the bathroom comes the sound of a shower running. Sylvie doesn't like what crying does to her face, so when the sound stops she quickly wipes at her eyes with the heel of her hand and drops the phone onto the pile of discarded clothes on the floor.

'Everything fine?'

'Oh, you know. Not really. He sounded pretty drunk.'

'I'm sure he's fine.'

'No, but *really* drunk. He sounded strange. Perhaps I should go home.'

Callum belts his dressing-gown, walks back into the bedroom and leans at the waist to kiss her bare shoulder.

'Like I said, I'm sure he's fine.' She says nothing, so he sits and kisses her again. 'Try and forget about it. Have some fun. Do you want another drink?'

'No.'

'Do you want to lie down?'

'No Callum!' She shakes his arm off her. 'For Christ's sake!'

He resists the temptation to say something, turns and walks back to the bathroom to brush his teeth, his hopes for the night evaporating. He has a horrible feeling that she is going to want to talk about things – '*this isn't fair, we can't go on, perhaps I should tell him*,' all that stuff. For crying out loud, he thinks indignantly, I've already given the guy a job. Isn't that enough?

CHAPTER FIFTEEN
Jean Seberg

SUNDAY 15 JULY 2001

Belleville, Paris

He was due to arrive on 15th July on the 15.55 from Waterloo.

Emma Morley got to the arrival gate at the Gare du Nord in good time and joined the crowd, the anxious lovers clutching flowers, the bored chauffeurs, sweaty in suits with their hand-written signs. Might it be funny to hold up a sign with Dexter's name on? she wondered. Perhaps with his name spelt incorrectly? It might make him laugh, she supposed, but was it worth the effort? Besides, the train was pulling in now, the waiting crowd edging towards the gate in anticipation. A long hiatus before the doors hissed open, then the passengers spilled out onto the platform and Emma pressed forward with the friends and families, lovers and chauffeurs, all craning to see the arriving faces.

She set her own face into the appropriate smile. The last time she saw him, things had been said. The last time she saw him, something had happened.

Dexter sat in his seat in the very last carriage of the stationary train and waited for the other passengers to leave. He had no suitcase, just a small overnight bag on the seat next to him. On the table in front of him lay a brightly coloured paperback, on the cover a scratchy cartoon of a girl's face beneath the title *Big Julie Criscoll Versus the Whole Wide World*.

He had finished the book just as the train entered the Paris suburbs. It was the first novel he had finished in some months, his sense of mental prowess mitigated by the fact that the book was aimed at eleven- to fourteen-year-olds and contained pictures. Waiting for the carriage to clear, he turned once more to the inside of the back cover and the black and white photograph of the author and looked at it intently, as if committing her face to memory. In an expensive-looking crisp white shirt she sat a little awkwardly on the edge of a bentwood chair, her hand covering her mouth at just the moment that she burst into laughter. He recognised the expression and the gesture too, smiled, and placed the book in his bag, picked it up and joined the last few passengers as they waited to step down onto the platform.

The last time he had seen her, things had been said. Something had happened. What would he tell her? What would she say? Yes or no?

While she waited she played with her hair, willing it to grow longer. Shortly after arriving in Paris, dictionary in hand, she had plucked up the courage to go to a hairdresser – *un coiffeur* – to have her hair cropped. Though embarrassed to say it out loud, she had wanted to look like Jean Seberg in *A Bout de Souffle*, because after all if you're going to be a novelist in Paris you might as well do it properly. Now three weeks later, she no longer wanted to cry when she saw her reflection, but even so her hands kept going to her head as if adjusting a wig. With a conscious effort she turned her attention to the buttons on her brand new dove grey shirt, bought that morning from a shop, no, a boutique, on Rue de Grenelle. Two buttons undone looked too prim, three undone showed cleavage. She unfastened the third button, clicked her tongue and turned her attention back to the passengers. The crowd was thinning out now and she was starting to wonder if he had missed the train when she finally saw him.

He looked broken. Gaunt and tired, his face was shaded with scrappy stubble that didn't suit him, a prison beard, and she was reminded of the potential for disaster that this visit carried with it. But when he saw her he started to smile and quicken his pace, and she smiled too, then started to feel self-conscious as she waited at the gate wondering what to do with her hands, her eyes. The distance between them seemed immense; smile and stare, smile and stare for fifty metres? Forty-five metres. She looked at the floor, up into the rafters. Forty metres, she looked back at Dexter, back at the floor. Thirty-five metres . . .

While covering this vast distance, he was surprised to notice how much she had changed in the eight weeks since he had last seen her, the two months since everything had happened. Her hair had been cut very short, a fringe brushed across her forehead, and she had more colour in her face; the summer face that he remembered. Better dressed too: high shoes, a smart dark skirt, a pale grey shirt unbuttoned a touch too far, showing brown skin and a triangle of dark freckles below her neck. She still didn't seem to know what to do with her hands or where to look, and he was starting to feel self-conscious too. Ten metres. What would he say, and how would he say it? Was it a yes or no?

He quickened his pace towards her, and then finally they were embracing.

'You didn't have to meet me.'

'Of course I had to meet you. Tourist.'

'I like this.' He brushed his thumb across her short fringe. 'There's a word for it, isn't there?'

'Butch?'

'Gamine. You look *gamine*.'

'Not butch?'

'Not in the least.'

'You should have seen it two weeks ago. I looked like a collaborator!' His face didn't move. 'I went to a Parisian hairdresser for the first time. Terrifying! I sat in the chair, thinking *Arrêtez-vous, Arrêtez-vous*! The funny thing is even in Paris they ask you about your holidays. You think they're going to talk about contemporary dance or can-man-ever-truly-be-free? but it's "*Que faites-vous de beau pour les vacances? Vous sortez ce soir?*"' Still his face was fixed. She was talking too much, trying too hard. Calm down. Don't riff. *Arrêtez-vous*.

His hand touched the short hair at the back of her neck. 'Well I think it suits you.'

'Not sure I've got the features for it.'

'Really, you've got the features for it.' He held her at the top of her arms, taking her all in. 'It's like there's a fancy-dress party and you've come as Sophisticated Parisienne.'

'Or a Call Girl.'

'But a High-Class Call Girl.'

'Well even better.' She touched his chin with her knuckle, the stubble there. 'So what have you come as then?'

'I've come as Fucked-up Suicidal Divorcee.' The remark was glib and he regretted it immediately. Barely off the platform, and he was spoiling things.

'Well at least you're not bitter,' she said, reaching for the nearest off-the-shelf remark.

'Do you want me to get back on the train?'

'Not just yet.' She took him by the hand. 'Come on, let's go, shall we?'

They stepped outside the Gare du Nord into the stifling fume-filled air; a typical Parisian summer day, muggy, with thick grey clouds threatening rain. 'I thought we'd go for a coffee first, near the canal. It's a fifteen-minute walk, is that alright? Then another fifteen minutes to my flat. I have to warn you though, it's nothing special. In case you're imagining parquet floors and big windows with fluttering curtains or something. It's just two rooms over a courtyard.'

'A garret.'

'Exactly. A garret.'

'A writer's garret.'

In anticipation of this journey, Emma had memorised a scenic walk, or as scenic as possible in the dust and traffic of the north-east. *I'm moving to Paris for the summer, to write.* Back in April, the idea had seemed almost embarrassingly precious and fey, but she was so bored with married couples telling her that she could go to Paris at any time that she had decided actually to do it. London had turned into one enormous crèche, so why not get away from other people's children for a while, have an adventure? The city of Sartre and De Beauvoir, Beckett and Proust, and here she was too, writing teenage fiction, albeit with considerable commercial success. The only way she could make the idea seem less hokey was to settle as far away as she could from tourist Paris, in the working-class 19th arrondissement on the border of Belleville and Ménilmontant. No tourist attractions, few landmarks . . .

'—but it's really lively, and cheap, and multi-cultural and . . . God, I was about to say it's very "real".'

'Meaning what, violent?'

'No, just, I don't know, *real* Paris. I sound like a student, don't I? Thirty-five years old, living in a little two-room flat like I'm on a gap year.'

'I think Paris suits you.'

'It does.'

'You look fantastic.'

'Do I?'

'You've changed.'

'I haven't. Not really.'

'No, really. You look beautiful.'

Emma frowned and kept her eyes ahead, and they walked a little further, trotting down stone steps to the Canal St Martin, and a little bar by the water's edge.

'Looks like Amsterdam,' he said blandly, pulling out a chair.

'Actually it's the old industrial link to the Seine.' *Good*

God, I sound like some tour guide. 'Flows under the Place de la République, under the Bastille, then out into the river.' *Just calm down. He's an old friend, remember? Just an old friend.* They sat for a moment and stared at the water and she immediately regretted the self-consciously scenic choice of venue. This was terrible, like a blind date. She fumbled for something to say.

'So, shall we have wine, or—?'

'Better not. I'm sort of off it.'

'Oh. Really? For how long?'

'Month or so. It's not an AA thing. Just trying to avoid it.' He shrugged. 'Nothing good ever came of it, that's all. Not a big deal.'

'Oh. O-kay. Coffee then?'

'Just a coffee.'

The waitress arrived, dark, pretty and long-legged, but Dexter didn't even look up. There must be something seriously wrong, Emma thought, if he's not even ogling the waitress. She ordered in ostentatiously colloquial French, then smiled awkwardly at Dexter's raised eyebrow. 'I've been taking lessons.'

'So I hear.'

'Course she didn't understand a word. She'll probably bring us out a roast chicken!'

Nothing. Instead he sat grinding grains of sugar against the metal table with his thumbnail. She tried again, something innocuous.

'When were you last in Paris?'

'About three years ago. My *wife* and I came here on one of our famous mini-breaks. Four nights in the George Cinq.' He flicked a sugar-cube into the canal. 'So *that* was a waste of fucking money.'

Emma opened her mouth and closed it again. There was nothing to say. She had already made her 'at least you're not bitter' remark.

But Dexter blinked hard, shook his head then nudged her hand with his. 'So what I thought we'd do for the next couple of days is, you can show me the sights, and I'll just mope about and make stupid remarks.'

She smiled and nudged his hand back. 'It's hardly surprising, what you've been through, are going through,' and she covered his hand with her own. After a moment he covered her hand with his, she followed, covering his with hers, faster and faster, a children's game. But it was a piece of actors' business too, strained and self-conscious, and in her embarrassment she decided to pretend to need the bathroom.

In the small, stale room she glowered in the mirror and tugged at her fringe as if trying to pull more from her head. She sighed and told herself to calm down. The thing that happened, the event, it was just a one-off, not a big deal, he's just an old, old friend. She flushed the toilet for veracity's sake and stepped back out into the warm grey afternoon. On the table in front of Dexter was a copy of her novel. Warily, she sat back down, and poked it with her finger.

'Where did this come from then?'

'I bought it at the train station. Great piles of it, there were. It's everywhere, Em.'

'Have you read it yet?'

'Can't get past page three.'

'Not funny, Dex.'

'Emma, I thought it was wonderful.'

'Well it's just a silly kid's book.'

'No, really, I'm so proud of you. I mean I'm not a teenage girl or anything, but it really made me laugh. I read it straight through in one go. And I speak as someone who's been reading *Howard's Way* for the last fifteen years.'

'You mean *Howards End. Howard's Way* is something different.'

'Whatever. I've never read *anything* straight through before.'

'Well, the type is pretty large.'

'And that was my favourite thing about it really, the big type.

And the pictures. The illustrations are really funny, Em. I had no idea.'

'Well thank you . . .'

'Plus the fact that it's exciting and funny, and I'm so proud of you, Em. In fact—' He pulled a pen from his pocket. 'I want you to sign it.'

'Don't be ridiculous.'

'No, you've got to. You're . . .' He read from the back of the book '. . . the "most exciting children's author since Roald Dahl".'

'Says the publisher's nine-year-old niece.' He poked her with the pen. 'I'm still not signing it, Dex.'

'Go on. I insist.' He stood, pretending to need the toilet. 'I'm going to leave it there, and you've got to write something. Something personal, with today's date, in case you get really famous and I need the cash.'

In the small rank cubicle, Dexter stood and wondered how long he could keep this up. At some point they would need to talk, insane to tip-toe round the subject like this. He flushed the toilet for effect, washed his hands and dried them on his hair, then stepped back out onto the pavement, where Emma was just closing the book. He went to read the dedication, but she placed her hand on the cover.

'When I'm not around, please.'

He sat down and placed it in his bag, and she leant across the table, as if returning to business. 'So. I've got to ask. How are things?'

'Oh, fantastic. The divorce goes through in September, just before our anniversary. Almost two whole years of wedded bliss.'

'Have you spoken to her much?'

'Not if I can help it. I mean we've stopped screaming abuse and throwing things, now it's just yes, no, hello, goodbye. Which is more or less all we said when we were married anyway. Did you hear, they've moved in with Callum now? Into his ridiculous mansion in Muswell Hill where we used to go to *dinner* parties—'

'Yes, I heard.'

He looked at her sharply. 'Who from? Callum?'

'Of course not! Just, you know – people.'

'People feeling sorry for me.'

'Not sorry, just . . . concerned.' He wrinkled his nose in distaste. 'It's not a bad thing, Dex, people caring about you. Have you spoken to Callum?'

'No. He's tried. Keeps leaving messages, like nothing's happened. "Alright mate! Give us a call." He thinks we should go out for a beer, and "talk things through". Maybe I should go. Technically he still owes me three weeks' wages.'

'Are you working yet?'

'Not as such. We're renting out that bloody house in Richmond, and the flat, so I'm living off that.' He drank the dregs of his coffee and stared into the canal. 'I don't know, Em. Eighteen months ago I had a family, a career – not much of a career, but I had opportunities, I still got offers. People carrier, nice little house in Surrey—'

'Which you hated.'

'I didn't *hate* it.'

'You hated the people carrier.'

'Well, yes, I did hate that, but it was mine. And now all of a sudden I'm living in a bedsit in Kilburn with my half of the wedding list and I have . . . nothing. Just me and a shitload of Le Creuset. My life is effectively over.'

'You know what I think you should do?'

'What?'

'Maybe . . .' She took a deep breath, and held the fingers of his hand. 'Maybe you should beg Callum for your job back.' He glared and jerked his hand away. 'Joking! I'm joking!' she said and started to laugh.

'Well I'm glad you find the carnage of my marriage funny, Em.'

'I don't find it *funny*, I just think self-pity's probably not the answer.'

'It's not self-pity, it's the facts.'

'"My life is effectively over"?'

'I just mean. I don't know. Just . . .' He looked into the canal and gave a theatrical sigh. 'When I was younger everything seemed possible. Now nothing does.'

Emma, for whom the opposite was now true, simply said. 'It's not as bad as all that.'

'So there's a bright side, is there? To your wife running off with your best mate—'

'And he wasn't your "best mate", you hadn't spoken in years, that's just, I'm just saying . . . Okay, well for a start it's not a bedsit in Kilburn, it's a perfectly good two-bedroom flat in West Hampstead. I'd have killed to have a flat like that. And you're only there until you get your old flat back.'

'But I'm thirty-seven in two weeks! I'm practically middle-aged!'

'Thirty-seven is still mid-thirties! Just about. And no, you don't have a job at this exact moment, but you're not exactly living on benefits. You've an income from rent, which is unbelievably lucky if you ask me. And lots of people change track late in life. It's fine to be miserable for a while, but you weren't that happy when you were married, Dex. I know, I had to listen to it all the time. "We never talk, we never have fun, we never go out . . ." I know it's tough, but at some point you might be able to think of this as a new start! A new beginning. There are loads of things you could do, you just have to make a decision . . .'

'Like what?'

'I don't know – the media? You could try for some presenting jobs again?' Dexter groaned. 'Okay, something behind the scenes? Producer or director or something.' Dexter winced. 'Or, or photography! You used to talk about photography all the time. Or food, you could, I don't know, do something with food. And if none of that works, you've always got that low two-two in Anthropology to fall back on.' She patted the back of his hand for emphasis: 'People will always need anthropologists.' He smiled, then remembered he shouldn't be smiling. 'You're a healthy, capable, financially stable moderately attractive father in your mid-to-late-thirties. You're . . . alright, Dex. You just need to get your confidence back, that's all.'

He sighed and looked out at the canal. 'So was that your pep-talk then?'

'That was it. What did you think?'

'I still want to jump in the canal.'

'Maybe we should move on then.' She laid money on the table. 'My flat's about twenty minutes away in that direction. We can walk, or get a taxi . . .' She went to stand, but Dexter didn't move.

'The worst of it is I really miss Jasmine.' Emma sat again. 'I mean it's sending me insane and it's not even like I was a good *dad* or anything.'

'Oh come on—'

'I wasn't, Em, I was useless, completely. I resented it, I didn't want to be there. All the time we were pretending we were this perfect family, I always thought this is a mistake, this isn't for me. I used to think wouldn't it be great to *sleep* again, to go away for the weekend, or just go out, stay up late, have fun. To be free, to have no responsibilities. And now I've got all of that back, and all I do is sit with my stuff still in cardboard boxes and miss my daughter.'

'But you still see her.'

'Once a fortnight, one lousy overnight stay.'

'But you could see her more, you could ask for more time—'

'And I would! But even now you can see the fear in her eyes when her mum drives off; don't leave me here with this weird sad freak! I buy her all these presents, it's pathetic, there's a great pile of them every time she arrives, it's like Christmas morning every time, because if we're not opening presents I don't know what to do with her. If we're not opening presents

335

she'll just start crying and asking for Mummy, by which she means Mummy and that bastard Callum, and I don't even know what to buy her, because every time I see her she's different. You turn your back for one week, ten days and everything's changed! I mean, she started *walking* for Christ's sake and I didn't see that happen! How can that be? How can I be missing that? I mean, isn't that *my* job? I haven't even done anything wrong, and all of a sudden . . .' His voice quavered for a moment, and quickly he changed tone, grabbing onto anger: '. . . and meanwhile of course that fucker *Callum*'s there with them, in his big mansion in *Muswell fucking Hill . . .*'

But the momentum of his rage wasn't enough to prevent his voice cracking. Abruptly he stopped speaking, pressed his hands either side of his nose and opened his eyes wide, as if trying to suppress a sneeze.

'You okay?' she said, her hand on his knee.

He nodded. 'I'm not going to be like this all weekend, I promise.'

'I don't mind.'

'Well I mind. It's . . . demeaning.' He stood abruptly, and picked up his bag. 'Please, Em. Let's talk about something else. Tell me something. Tell me about you.'

They walked the length of the canal, skirting the edge of the Place de la République then turning east along rue du Faubourg du Temple as she talked about her work. 'The second one's a sequel. That's how imaginative I am. I'm about three-quarters of the way through. Julie Criscoll goes on this school trip to Paris and falls for this French boy and has all sorts of adventures, surprise suprise. That's my excuse for being here. "Research purposes".'

'And the first one's doing well?'

'So I'm told. Well enough for them to pay for two more.'

'Really? Two more sequels?'

''fraid so. *Julie Criscoll*'s what they call a franchise. That's where the money's at apparently. Got to have a franchise! And we're talking to TV people. For a show. An animated kid's show, based on my illustrations.'

'You're kidding me!'

'I know. Stupid, isn't it? I'm working in "the media"! I'm the Associate Producer!'

'What does that mean?'

'Nothing at all. I mean I don't mind. I love it. But I'd like to write a grown-up book one day. That's what I always wanted to write, this great, angry state-of-the-nation novel, something wild and timeless that reveals the human soul, not a lot of silly stuff about snogging French boys at discos.'

'It's not just about that though, is it?'

'Maybe not. And maybe that's just what happens; you start out wanting to change the world through language, and end up thinking it's enough to tell a few good jokes. God, listen to me. My life in art!'

He nudged her.

'What?'

'I'm pleased for you, that's all.' His arm curled round her shoulders and squeezed. 'An author. A proper author. You're finally doing what you always wanted to do.' They walked like this, a little self-consciously and awkwardly, the bag in the other hand banging against his leg, until the discomfort became too much and he took his arm away.

They walked on, and gradually their mood lifted. The blanket of cloud had broken and Faubourg du Temple was taking on a new lease of life as the evening began. Scrappy, gaudy and full of noise and life, parts of it almost souk-like, Emma kept stealing glances at Dexter, an anxious tour guide. They crossed the wide bustling Boulevard de Belleville and continued east along the border of the 19th and 20th. Climbing the hill, Emma pointed out the bars she liked, talked about the local history, Piaf and the Paris Commune of 1871, the local Chinese and North African communities, and

Dexter half-listened, half-wondered what would happen when they finally arrived at her flat. *Listen, Emma, about what happened . . .*

'. . . it's sort of like the Hackney of Paris,' she was saying.

Dexter smiled that maddening smile.

She nudged him. 'What?!'

'Only you would go to Paris and find the bit that's most like Hackney.'

'It's interesting. I think so, anyway.'

Eventually they turned down a quiet side street and came to what looked like a garage door where Emma punched a code into a panel and pressed against the heavy gate with her shoulder. They entered into an enclosed courtyard, cluttered and rundown and overlooked by apartments on all sides. Washing hung from rusting balconies, shabby pot plants wilted in the evening sun. The courtyard echoed with the noise of competing TVs and children playing soccer with a tennis ball, and Dexter fought down a little shiver of irritation. Rehearsing this occasion, he had pictured a tree-shaded square, louvred windows, a view of Notre-Dame perhaps. This was all fine enough, chic even in an urban, industrial way, but something more romantic would have made this all a little easier.

'Like I said, it's nothing grand. Fifth floor, I'm afraid.'

She pressed the light switch, which was on a timer, and they began the steep ascent of the wrought-iron stairs, tightly curled and seemingly sheering away from the wall in places. Emma was suddenly conscious of the fact that Dexter's eyes were exactly level with her backside and she began nervously reaching back to her skirt to smooth down creases that weren't there. As they reached the landing of the third floor the timer of the light clicked off, and they found themselves in darkness for a moment, Emma fumbling behind her to find his hand, and leading him up the stairs until they stood outside a door. In the dim light from the transom, they smiled at each other.

'Here we go. Chez Moi!'

From her bag, she produced an immense bunch of keys, and began work on a complex sequence of locks. After some time the door opened onto a small but pleasant flat with scuffed grey-painted floorboards, a large baggy sofa and a small neat desk overlooking the courtyard, its walls lined with austere-looking books in French, the spines a uniform pale yellow. Fresh roses and fruit stood on the table in a small adjoining kitchen, and through another door Dexter could glimpse the bedroom. They had yet to discuss the sleeping arrangements, but he could see the apartment's only bed, a large cast-iron affair, quaint and cumbersome like something from a farmhouse. One bedroom, one bed. Evening sunlight shone through the windows, drawing attention to the fact of it. He glanced at the sofa to check that it didn't fold out into anything. Nope. One bed. He could feel the blood pumping in his chest, though perhaps this was just from the long climb.

She closed the door and there was a silence.

'So. Here we are!'

'It's great.'

'It's okay. Kitchen's through here.' The climb and nerves had made Emma thirsty and she crossed to the fridge, opened it and took out a bottle of sparkling water. She had begun to drink, taking great gulps, when suddenly Dexter's hand was on her shoulder, then he was in front of her somehow, and kissing her. Her mouth still full of the effervescing water, she pursed her lips tight to prevent it squirting in his face like a soda siphon. Leaning away, she pointed at her cheeks, absurdly ballooned like a puffer fish, flapped her hands and made a noise that approximated to 'hold on a moment'.

Chivalrously, Dexter stepped back to allow her to swallow. 'Sorry about that.'

'S'okay. You took me by surprise, that's all.' She wiped her mouth with the back of her hand.

'Okay now?'

'Fine, but Dexter, I have to tell you . . .'

And he was kissing her again, clumsily pressing too hard as she leant backwards over the kitchen table, which suddenly juddered noisily across the floor, so that she had to twist away at the waist to stop the vase of roses falling.

'Oops.'

'The thing is, Dex—'

'Sorry about that, I just—'

'But the thing is—'

'Bit self-conscious—'

'I've sort of met someone.'

He actually took a step backwards.

'You've *met* someone.'

'A man. A guy. I'm seeing this guy.'

'A *guy*. Right. Okay. So. Who?'

'He's called Jean-Pierre. Jean-Pierre Dusollier.'

'He's *French*?'

'No, Dex, he's *Welsh*.'

'No, I'm just surprised, that's all.'

'Surprised he's French, or surprised that I should actually have a boyfriend?'

'No, just that – well it's pretty quick, isn't it? I mean you've only been here a couple of weeks. Did you unpack first, or . . .'

'Two months! I've been here two months, and I met Jean-Pierre a month ago.'

'And where did you meet him?'

'In a little bistro near here.'

'A little *bistro*. Right. How?'

'How?'

'—did you meet him?'

'Well, um, I was having dinner by myself, reading a book, and this guy was with some friends and he asked me what I was reading . . .' Dexter groaned and shook his head, a craftsman deriding another's handiwork. Emma ignored him and walked through to the living room. 'And anyway, we got talking—'

Dexter followed. 'What, in French?'

'Yes, in French, and we hit it off, and now we're . . . seeing each other!' She flopped onto the sofa. 'So. Now you know!'

'Right. I see.' His eyebrows rose then lowered again, his features contorting as he explored ways to sulk and smile at the same time. 'Well. Good for you, Em, that's really great.'

'Don't patronise me, Dexter. Like I'm some lonely old lady—'

'I'm not!' With feigned nonchalance, he turned to look out the window into the courtyard below. 'So what's he like then, this *Jean* . . .'

'Jean-Pierre. He's nice. Very handsome, very charming. An amazing cook, he knows all about food, and wine, and art, and architecture. You know, just very, very . . . French.'

'What, you mean rude?'

'No—'

'Dirty?'

'Dexter!'

'Wears a string of onions, rides a bike—'

'God, you can be unbearable sometimes—'

'Well what the hell is that supposed to mean, "very French"?'

'I don't know, just very cool and laidback and—'

'*Sexy?*—'

'I didn't say "sexy".'

'No but you've gone all sexy, playing with your hair, your shirt unbuttoned—'

'Such a stupid word, "sexy"—'

'But you're having a lot of sex, right?'

'Dexter, why are you being so—?'

'Look at you, you're glowing, you've got a little sweaty glow—'

'There's no reason for you to be – why are you anyway?'

'What?'

'Being so . . . mean, like I've done something wrong!'

'I'm not being mean, I just thought . . .' He stopped, and turned

341

to look out of the window, his forehead on the glass. 'I wish you'd told me before I came. I'd have booked a hotel.'

'You can still stay here! I'll just sleep with Jean-Pierre tonight.' Even with his back to her she could tell that he had flinched. 'Sleep *at* Jean-Pierre's tonight.' She leant forward on the sofa, her face cupped in both hands. 'What did you think was going to happen, Dexter?'

'I don't know,' he mumbled at the windowpane. 'Not this.'

'Well, I'm sorry.'

'Why do you think I came to see you, Em?'

'For a break. To get away from things. See the sights!'

'I came to talk about what happened. You and me, finally getting together.' He picked at the putty on the windows with his fingernail. 'I just thought it would have been a bigger deal for you. That's all.'

'We've slept together *once*, Dexter.'

'Three times!'

'I don't mean how many acts of *intercourse*, Dex, I mean the occasion, the night, we spent one night together.'

'And I just thought it might have been something worth remarking on! Next thing I know you've run off to Paris and thrown yourself under the nearest Frenchman—'

'I didn't "run off", the ticket was already booked! Why do you think that everything that happens happens because of you?'

'And you couldn't phone me up maybe, before you . . . ?'

'What, to ask your permission?'

'No, to see how I felt about it!'

'Hang on a minute – you're annoyed because we haven't examined our *feelings*? You're annoyed because you think I should have *waited* for you?'

'I don't know,' he mumbled. 'Maybe!'

'My God, Dexter, are you . . . are you actually *jealous*?'

'Of course I'm not!'

'So why are you sulking?'

'I'm not sulking.'

'Look at me then!'

He did so, petulant, his arms crossed high on his chest, and Emma couldn't help but laugh.

'What? *What?*' he asked, indignant.

'Well you do realise there's a certain amount of irony in this, Dex.'

'How is this ironic?'

'You getting all conventional and . . . monogamous all of a sudden.'

He said nothing for a moment, then turned back to the window.

More conciliatory, she said, 'Look – we were both a little drunk.'

'I wasn't *that* drunk . . .'

'You took your trousers off over your shoes, Dex!' Still he wouldn't turn around. 'Don't stand over by the window. Come and sit here, will you?' She lifted her bare feet up onto the sofa and curled her legs beneath her. He bumped the pane of glass with his forehead once, twice, then without meeting her eye, crossed the room and slumped next to her, a child sent home from school. She rested her feet against his thighs.

'Alright, you want to talk about that night? Let's talk about it.'

He said nothing. She poked him with her toes, and when he finally looked at her, she spoke. 'Okay. I'll go first.' She took a deep breath. 'I think that you were very upset and a little bit drunk and you came to see me that night and it just . . . happened. I think with all the misery of breaking up with Sylvie, and moving out and not seeing Jasmine, you were feeling a little lonely and you just needed a shoulder to cry on. Or to sleep with. And that's what I was. A shoulder to sleep with.'

'So that's what you think?'

'That's what I think.'

'. . . and you only slept with me to make me feel better?'

'Did you feel better?'

'Yes, much better.'

'Well so did I, so there you go. It worked.'

'. . . but that's not the point.'

'Well there are worse reasons to sleep with someone. You should know.'

'But pity sex?'

'Not pity, *compassion*.'

'Don't tease me, Em.'

'I'm not, I just . . . it was nothing to do with pity, and you know it. But it's . . . complicated. Us. Come here, will you?' She nudged him once more with her foot and after a moment he tipped over like a felled tree, his head coming to rest against her shoulder.

She sighed. 'We've known each other a long time, Dex.'

'I know. I just thought it might be a good idea. Dex and Em, Em and Dex, the two of us. Just try it for a while, see how it worked. I had thought that's what you wanted too.'

'It is. It was. Back in the late Eighties.'

'So why not now?'

'Because. It's too late. We're too late. I'm too tired.'

'You're thirty-five!'

'I just feel our time has passed, that's all,' she said.

'How do you know, unless we give it a try?'

'Dexter – I have met someone else!'

They sat in silence for a moment, listening to the children shouting in the courtyard below, the sound of distant televisions.

'And you like him? This guy.'

'I do. I really, really like him.'

He reached down, and took her left foot in his hand, still dusty from the street. 'My timing isn't great, is it?'

'No, not really.'

He examined the foot he held in his hand. The toenails were painted red, but chipped, the smallest nail gnarled and barely there. 'Your feet are disgusting.'

'I know they are.'

344

'Your little toe's like this little nub of sweetcorn.'

'Stop playing with it then.'

'So that night—' He pressed his thumb against the hard skin of her sole. 'So was it really so terrible?'

She poked him sharply in the hip with her other foot. 'Don't *fish*, Dexter.'

'No really, tell me.'

'*No*, Dexter, it was *not* such a terrible night, in fact it was one of the more memorable nights of my life. But I still think we should leave it at that.' She swung her legs off the sofa and sidled up until their hips were touching, taking his hand, her head on his shoulder now. Both stared forwards at the book-shelves, until Emma finally sighed. 'Why didn't you say all this, I don't know – eight years ago?'

'Don't know, too busy trying to have . . . fun, I suppose.'

She lifted her head to look at him sideways. 'And now you've stopped having fun, you think "good old Em, give her a go—"'

'That's not what I meant—'

'I'm not the consolation prize, Dex. I'm not something you *resort* to. I happen to think I'm worth more than that.'

'And I think you're worth more than that too. That's why I came here. You're a wonder, Em.'

After a moment she stood abruptly, picked up a cushion, threw it sharply at his head and walked towards the bedroom. 'Shut up, Dex.'

He reached for her hand as she passed, but she shook it free. 'Where are you going?'

'To have a shower, get changed. Can't sit around here all night!' she shouted from the other room, angrily pulling clothes from the wardrobe and dropping them onto the bed. 'After all, he'll be here in twenty minutes!'

'Who'll be here?'

'Who do you think? My NEW BOYFRIEND!'

'Jean-Pierre's coming here?'

'Uh-huh. Eight o'clock.' She started unbuttoning the tiny

buttons on her shirt, then gave up, pulled it impatiently over her head and whipped it at the floor. 'We're all going out for dinner! The three of us!'

He let his head fall backwards and let out a long low groan. 'Oh God. Do we have to?'

'I'm afraid so. It's all been arranged.' She was naked now, and furious, at herself, at the situation. 'We're taking you to the very restaurant where we first met! The famous *bistro*! We're going to sit there at the same table and hold hands and tell you all about it! It's all going to be very, *very* romantic.' She slammed the bathroom door, shouting through it. 'And in no way awkward!'

Dexter heard the sound of the shower running, and lay back on the sofa, looking at the ceiling, embarrassed now at this ridiculous expedition. He had thought that he had the answer, that they could rescue each other, when in truth Emma had been fine for years. If anyone needed rescuing, it was him.

And maybe Emma was right, maybe he was just feeling a little lonely. He heard the ancient plumbing gurgle as the shower ceased, and there it was again, that terrible, shameful word. Lonely. And the worst of it was that he knew it was true. Never in his life had he imagined that he would be lonely. For his thirtieth birthday he had filled a whole night-club off Regent Street; people had been queuing on the pavement to get in. The SIM card of his mobile phone in his pocket was over-flowing with telephone numbers of all the hundreds of people he had met in the last ten years, and yet the only person he had ever wanted to talk to in all that time was standing now in the very next room.

Could this be true? He scrutinised the notion once again and finding it to be accurate he stood suddenly with the inten-tion of telling her straightaway. He walked towards the bedroom then stopped.

He could see her through the gap in the door. She was sitting at a small 1950s dressing table, her short hair still wet from the shower, wearing a knee-length old-fashioned black silk dress, unzipped at the back to the base of her spine, opened wide enough to see the shade beneath her shoulder blades. She sat motionless and erect and rather elegant, as if waiting for someone to come and zip the dress up, and there was something so appealing about the idea, something so intimate and satisfying about that simple gesture, both familiar and new, that he almost stepped straight into the room. He would fasten the dress, then kiss the curve between her neck and her shoulder and tell her.

Instead he watched silently as she reached for a book on the dressing table, a large well-thumbed French/English dictionary. She began to leaf through the pages then stopped suddenly, her head slumping forwards, both hands spanning her brow and pushing her fringe back as she groaned angrily. Dexter laughed at her exasperation, silently he thought, but she glanced towards the door and he quickly stepped backwards. The floorboards popped beneath his feet as he pranced absurdly towards the kitchen area, running both taps and moving cups around uselessly under running water as an alibi. After a while he heard the ting of the old-fashioned phone being picked up in the bedroom, and he turned off the taps so that he might overhear the conversation with this Jean-Pierre. A low, lover's murmur, in French. He strained to listen, failing to understand a single word.

The bell sounded once again as she hung up. Some time passed, then she was standing in the doorway behind him. 'Who was that on the phone?' he asked over his shoulder, matter-of-factly.

'Jean-Pierre.'

'And how was Jean-Pierre?'

'He's fine. Just fine.'

'Good. So. I should get changed. What time is he coming round again?'

'He isn't coming round.'

Dexter turned.

'What?'

'I told him not to come round.'

'Really? You did?'

He wanted to laugh—

'I told him I had tonsillitis.'

—wanted to laugh so much, but he mustn't, not yet. He dried his hands. 'What is that? Tonsillitis. In French?'

Her fingers went to her throat. '*Je suis très désolé, mais mes glandes sont gonflées,*' she croaked feebly. '*Je pense que je peux avoir l'amygdalite.*'

'L'amy . . . ?'

'*L'amygdalite.*'

'You have amazing vocab.'

'Well, you know.' She shrugged modestly. 'Had to look it up.'

They smiled at each other. Then, as if an idea had suddenly occurred to her, she quickly crossed the room in three long strides, took his face between her hands, and kissed him, and he placed his hands upon her back, finding the dress still unfastened, the skin bare and cool and still damp from the shower. They kissed like this for some time. Then, still holding his face in her hands, she looked at him intently. 'If you muck me about, Dexter.'

'I won't—'

'I mean it, if you lead me on or let me down or go behind my back, I will murder you. I swear to God, I will eat your heart.'

'I won't do that, Em.'

'You won't?'

'I swear, I won't.'

And then she frowned, and shook her head, then put her arms around him once more, pressing her face into his shoulder, making a noise that sounded almost like rage.

'What's up?' he asked.

'Nothing. Oh, nothing. Just . . .' She looked up at him. 'I thought I'd finally got rid of you.'

'I don't think you can,' he said.

Part Four

2002–2005

Late Thirties

'They spoke very little of their mutual feelings: pretty phrases and warm attentions being probably unnecessary between such tried friends.'

Thomas Hardy, *Far From the Madding Crowd*

CHAPTER SIXTEEN
Monday Morning

MONDAY 15 JULY 2002

Belsize Park

The radio alarm sounds as usual at 07.05. It is already bright and clear outside, but neither of them move just yet. Instead they lie with his arm around her waist, their legs tangled at the ankle, in Dexter's double bed in Belsize Park in what was once, many years ago now, a bachelor flat.

He has been awake for some time, rehearsing in his head a tone of voice and phrasing that is both casual and significant, and when he feels her stir he speaks. 'Can I say something?' he says into the back of her neck, his eyes still closed, mouth gummed with sleep.

'Go on,' she says, a little wary.

'I think it's crazy, you having your own flat.'

With her back to him, she smiles. 'O-kay.'

'I mean you're here most nights anyway.'

She opens her eyes. 'I needn't be.'

'No, I want you to be.'

She turns in the bed to face him, and sees his eyes are still closed. 'Dex, are you? . . .'

'What?'

'Are you asking me to be your flatmate?'

He smiles and without opening his eyes, he takes her hand beneath the sheet and squeezes it. 'Emma, will you be my flatmate?'

'Finally!' she mumbles. 'Dex, it's all that I've lived for.'

'So, what, yes?'

'Let me think about it.'

'Well let me know, won't you? Because if you're not interested, I might get someone else in.'

'I said, I'll think about it.'

He opens his eyes. He had expected a yes. 'What's there to think about?'

'Just, I don't know. *Living together*.'

'We lived together in Paris.'

'I know, but that was Paris.'

'We more or less live together now.'

'I know, I just—'

'And it's insane for you to rent, renting is money down the drain, in the current property market.'

'You sound like my independent financial adviser. It's very romantic.' She pouts her lips and kisses him, a cautious morning kiss. 'This isn't just about sound financial planning, is it?'

'Mainly, but I also think it'd be . . . nice.'

'Nice.'

'You living here.'

'And what about Jasmine?'

'She'll get used to it. Besides, she's only two and a half, it's not up to her, is it? Or her mother.'

'And might it not get a bit . . . ?'

'What?'

'Cramped. The three of us at weekends.'

'We'll manage.'

'Where will I work?'

'You can work here while I'm out.'

'And where will you take your lovers?'

He sighs, a little bored with the joke after a year of almost maniacal fidelity. 'We'll go to hotels in the afternoon.'

They lapse into silence again as the radio burbles on and Emma closes her eyes once more and tries to imagine herself unpacking cardboard boxes, finding space for her clothes, her books. In truth, she prefers the atmosphere of her current flat, a pleasant, vaguely Bohemian attic off the Hornsey Road. Belsize Park is just too neat and chi-chi, and despite her best efforts and the gradual colonisation of her books and clothes, Dexter's flat still retains an atmosphere of the bachelor years: the games console, the immense television, the ostentatious bed. 'I keep expecting to open a cupboard and be buried under, I don't know . . . a cascade of *panties* or something.' But he has made the offer, and she feels as if she should offer something in return.

'Maybe we should think of buying somewhere together,' she says. 'Somewhere bigger.' Once again, they have grazed against the great unspoken subject. A long silence follows, and she wonders if he has fallen asleep again, until he says:

'Okay. Let's talk about it tonight.'

And so another weekday begins, like the one before and the ones to come. They get up and get dressed, Emma drawing on the limited store of clothes she keeps jammed into her allocated cupboard. He has the first shower, she has the second, during which time he walks to the shop and buys the newspaper and milk if necessary. He reads the sports pages, she the news and then after breakfast, eaten for the most part in comfortable silence, she takes her bike from the hallway and pushes it with him towards the tube. Each day they kiss each other goodbye at approximately eight twenty-five.

'Sylvie's dropping Jasmine off at four o'clock,' he says. 'I'll be back at six. You're sure you don't mind being there?'

'Course not.'

'And you'll be okay with Jasmine?'

'Fine. We'll go to the zoo or something.'

Then they kiss again, and she goes to work, and he goes to work, and so the days go by, faster than ever.

Work. He is working again in his own business, though 'business' feels a little too high-powered a word at present for this little delicatessen-café on a residential street between Highgate and Archway.

The idea was hatched in Paris, during that long strange summer in which they had dismantled his life, then put it back together again. It had been Emma's idea, sitting outside a café near the Parc des Buttes Chaumont in the north-east. 'You like food,' she had said, 'you know about wine. You could sell really good coffee by the pound, imported cheeses, all that swanky stuff that people want these days. Not pretentious or chi-chi, just this really nice little shop, with tables outside in the summer.' Initially he had bridled at the word 'shop', not quite able to see himself as a 'shopkeeper' or, even worse, a grocer. But an 'imported food specialist' had a ring to it. Better to think of it as a café/restaurant that also sold food. He would be an entrepreneur.

So in late September, when Paris had finally, finally started to lose some of its gleam, they had travelled back on the train together. With light tans and new clothes they walked arm-in-arm along the platform and it felt like they were arriving in London for the very first time, with plans and projects, resolutions and ambitions.

Their friends nodded sagely, sentimentally, as if they had known it all along. Emma was introduced once again to Dexter's father – 'Of course I remember. You called me a fascist' – and they put forward the idea of the new business in the hope that he might want to help with the financing. When Alison had died there had been a private understanding that some money might go to Dexter at an appropriate time, and this seemed like the moment. Privately, Stephen Mayhew still expected his son to lose every penny, but that was a small price to pay to know that he would never, ever appear on television ever again. And Emma's presence helped. Dexter's father liked Emma, and for the first time in some years found himself liking his son because of her.

They had found the property together. A video rental shop, already an anomaly with its shelves of dusty VHS, had finally given up the ghost, and, with one last push from Emma, Dexter had made his move and taken the property on a twelve-month lease. Through a long wet January they ripped out the metal shelving and distributed the remaining Steven Seagal videos around local charity shops. They stripped and painted the walls a buttery white, installed dark wooden panelling, scoured other bankrupt restaurants and cafés for a decent industrial coffee machine, chill cabinets, glass-fronted refrigerators; all those failed businesses reminding him of what was at stake, how likely he was to fail.

But all the time Emma was there, pushing him on, keeping him convinced that he was doing the right thing. The area was up-and-coming the estate agents said, slowly filling with young professionals who knew the value of the word 'artisan' and wanted jars of duck confit, customers who didn't mind paying two pounds for an irregular loaf of bread or a lump of goat's cheese the size of a squash ball. The café would be the kind of place where people came to ostentatiously write their novels.

On the first day of spring they sat in the sun on the pavement outside the partly refurbished shop and wrote down a list of possible names: corny combinations of words like magasin, vin, pain, Paris pronounced 'Paree', until they settled on Belleville Café, bringing a flavour of the 19th arrondissement to just south of the A1. He formed a limited company, his second after Mayhem TV plc, with Emma as his company secretary and, in a small but significant way, his co-investor. Money was starting to come in from the first two 'Julie Criscoll' books, the animated TV series had been commissioned for its second series, there was talk of merchandising: pencil cases, birthday cards, even a monthly magazine. There was no denying it, she was now what her mother would term 'well off'. After a certain amount of throat-clearing, Emma found herself in the strange, slightly unnerving position of being able to offer Dexter financial help. After a certain amount of foot shuffling, he accepted.

They opened in April, and for the first six weeks he stood by the dark wood counter, watched people walk in, look round, sniff and walk out again. But then word began to spread, things began to pick up and he found himself able to take on some staff. He began to acquire regulars, even to enjoy himself.

And now the place has become fashionable, albeit in a more sedate, domesticated way than he is used to. If he is famous now it is only locally, and only for his selection of herbal teas, but he's still a mild heartthrob to the flushed young mums who come in to eat pastries after their pram-ercise class, and in a small way he is almost, almost a success again. He unlocks the heavy padlock that holds down the metal shutters, already hot to the touch on this radiant summer's morning. He pulls them up, unlocks the door and feels, what? Content? Happyish? No, happy. Secretly, and for the first time in many years, he is proud of himself.

Of course there are long boring wet Tuesdays, when he wants to pull down the shutters and methodically drink all the red wine, but not today. It's a warm day, he is seeing his daughter tonight and will be with her for much of the next eight days while Sylvie and that bastard Callum go on another of their constant holidays. By some strange mystery Jasmine is now two and a half years old, self-possessed and beautiful like her mother, and she can come in and play shops and be fussed over by the other staff, and when he gets home tonight Emma will be there. For the first time in many years he is more or less where he wants to be. He has a partner whom he loves and desires and who is also his best friend. He has a beautiful, intelligent daughter. He does alright. Everything will be fine, just as long as nothing ever changes.

Two miles away, just off the Hornsey Road, Emma climbs the flights of stairs, unlocks the front door and feels the cool, stale air of a flat that has been unoccupied for four days. She makes tea, sits at her desk, turns on her computer, and stares at it for the best part of an hour. There's a lot to do – scripts for the second series of 'Julie Criscoll' to read and approve, five hundred words of the third volume to write, illustrations to work on. There are letters and emails from young readers, earnest and often disconcertingly personal notes that she must give some attention to, about loneliness and being bullied and this boy I really, really like.

But her mind keeps slipping back to Dexter's proposal. During the long, strange summer in Paris last year they had made certain resolutions about their future together – if in fact they did have a future together – and central to the scheme was that they would not live together: separate lives, separate flats, separate friends. They would endeavour to be together, and faithful of course, but not in any conventional way. No traipsing around estate agents at the weekend, no joint dinner parties, no Valentine's Day flowers, none of the paraphernalia of coupledom or domesticity. Both of them had tried it, neither had succeeded.

She had imagined this arrangement to be sophisticated, modern, a new design for living. But so much effort is required to pretend that they don't want to be together that it has recently seemed inevitable that one of them will crack. She just hadn't expected it to be Dexter. One subject has remained largely unspoken, and now there seems to be no way to avoid it. She will have to take a deep breath and just say the word. Children. No, not 'children', best not scare him, better use the singular. She wants a child.

They have spoken about it before, in a roundabout facetious way, and he has made noises about maybe, in the future, when things are a little bit more settled. But how much more settled can things be? The subject sits there in the middle of the room and they keep walking into it. It's there every time her parents telephone, it's there every time she and Dexter make love (less frequently now than in the debauch of the flat in Paris, but still often enough). It keeps her awake at night. Sometimes it seems that she can chart her life by what she worries about at three a.m. Once it was boys, then for too long it was money, then career, then her relationship with Ian, then her infidelity. Now it is this. She is thirty-six years old, a child is what she wants, and if he doesn't want it too, then perhaps they had better . . .

What? Call it a day? It seems melodramatic and degrading to issue that kind of ultimatum, and the thought of carrying out the threat seems inconceivable, for the moment at least. But she resolves that she will raise the subject tonight. No, not tonight, not with Jasmine staying, but soon. Soon.

After a distracted morning of time-wasting, Emma goes for a lunch-time swim, ploughing up and down the lanes yet still unable to clear her head. Then with her hair still wet she cycles back to Dexter's flat and arrives to find an immense, vaguely sinister black 4x4 waiting outside the house. It's a gangsters' car, two silhouettes visible against the windscreen, one broad and short, the other tall and slim; Sylvie and Callum, both gesticulating wildly in the middle of another argument. Even from across the road Emma can hear them, and as she wheels her bike closer she can see Callum's snarled face, and Jasmine in the back seat, eyes fixed on a picture book in an attempt to filter out the noise. Emma taps the window nearest Jasmine and sees her look up and grin, tiny white teeth in a wide mouth, straining forwards against her seatbelt to get out.

Through the car window, Emma and Callum nod. There's something of the playground about the etiquette of infidelity, separation and divorce, but allegiances have been declared, enmities sworn, and despite having known him for nearly twenty years Emma must no longer talk directly to Callum. As for the ex-wife, Sylvie and Emma have settled on a tone, self-consciously bright and grudge-free, but even so dislike shimmers between them like a heat haze.

'Sorry about that!' says Sylvie, unfolding her long legs from the car. 'Just a little disagreement about how much luggage we're taking!'

'Holidays can be stressful,' says Emma, meaninglessly. Jasmine is unbuckled from her car seat, and clambers up into Emma's arms, her face pressed into her neck, skinny legs wrapped around Emma's hips. Emma smiles, a little embarrassed, as if to say 'what can I do?' and Sylvie smiles back, a smile so stiff and unnatural that it's surprising she doesn't have to use her fingers.

'Where's Daddy?' says Jasmine into Emma's neck.

'He's at work, he'll be back very soon.'

Emma and Sylvie smile some more.

'How is that going then?' Sylvie manages. 'The café?'

'Really well, really well.'

'Well I'm sorry not to see him. Send him my love.'

More silence. Callum gives her a nudge by starting the engine.

'Do you want to come in?' asks Emma, knowing the answer.

'No, we should head off.'

'Where is it again?'

'Mexico.'

'Mexico. Lovely.'

'You've been?'

'No, though I worked in a Mexican restaurant once.'

Sylvie actually tuts, and Callum's voice booms from the front seat. 'Come on! I want to avoid the traffic!'

Jasmine is passed back into the car for goodbyes and be-goods and not-too-much-TV and Emma discreetly takes Jasmine's luggage inside, a candy-pink vinyl suitcase on wheels and a ruck-sack in the form of a panda. When she comes back Jasmine is waiting rather formally on the pavement, a pile of picture books held against her chest. She is pretty, chic, immaculate, a little mournful, every inch her mother's child, very much not Emma's.

'We must go. Check-in's a nightmare these days.' Sylvie tucks her long legs back into the car like some sort of folding knife. Callum stares forwards.

'So. Enjoy Mexico. Enjoy your snorkelling.'

'Not snorkelling, scuba-diving. Snorkelling is what children do,' says Sylvie, unintentionally harsh.

Emma bridles. 'I'm sorry. Scuba-diving! Don't drown!' Sylvie raises her eyebrows, her mouth forming a little 'o' and what can Emma say? *I meant it, Sylvie, please don't drown, I don't want you to drown?* Too late, the damage is done, the illusion of sorority shattered. Sylvie stamps a kiss on the top of Jasmine's head, slams the door and is gone.

Emma and Jasmine stand and wave.

'So, Min, your dad's not back until six. What do you want to do?'

'Don't know.'

'It's early. We could go to the zoo?'

Jasmine nods vigorously. Emma holds a family pass to the zoo, and she goes inside to get ready for another afternoon spent with someone else's daughter.

In the big black car the former Mrs Mayhew sits with her arms folded, her head resting against the smoky glass, her feet tucked up beneath her on the seat while Callum swears at the traffic on the Euston Road. They rarely speak these days, just shout and hiss, and this holiday, like the others, is an attempt to patch things up.

The last year of her life has not been a success. Callum has revealed himself to be boorish and mean. What she took to be drive and ambition have proved to be an unwillingness to come home at nights. She suspects him of affairs. He seems to resent Sylvie's presence in *his* home, and Jasmine's presence too; he shouts at her for merely behaving like a child, or avoids her company altogether. He barks absurd slogans at her: 'Quid pro quo, Jasmine, quid pro quo.' She's two and a half, for good-ness' sake. For all his ineptness and irresponsibility at least Dexter was keen, too keen sometimes. Callum on the other hand treats Jasmine like a member of staff who just isn't working out. And if her family were wary of Dexter, they actively despise Callum.

Now, whenever she sees her ex-husband he is smiling, smiling away advertising his happiness like the member of some cult.

He throws Jasmine in the air, gives her piggybacks, displays at every opportunity what a wonderful dad he has become. And this Emma person too, all Jasmine talks about is Emma-this and Emma-that and how Emma is her daughter's best, best friend. She brings home pieces of pasta glued to coloured card and when Sylvie asks what it is, she says it's Emma, then chatters on and on about how they went to the zoo together. They have a family pass, apparently. God, the insufferable smugness of the pair of them, Dex and Em, Em and Dex, him with his chintzy little corner shop – Callum has forty-eight branches of Natural Stuff now, by the way – and her with her push-bike and thickening waist, her studenty demeanour and wry bloody outlook. To Sylvie's mind there's also something sinister and calculating in the fact that Emma has been promoted from godmother to stepmother, as if she was always lurking there, circling, waiting to make her move. *Don't drown!* Cheeky cow.

Beside her, Callum swears at the traffic on the Marylebone Road and Sylvie feels intense resentment at the happiness of others, combined with misery at finding herself on the wrong team for once. Sadness too, at how ugly and ungracious and spiteful all of these thoughts are. After all, it was she who left Dexter and who broke his heart.

Now Callum is swearing at the traffic on the Westway. She wants to have another child sometime soon, but how? Ahead of her lies a week's scuba-diving at a luxury hotel in Mexico, and she knows already that this is not going to be enough.

CHAPTER SEVENTEEN
bigdayspeech.doc

North Yorkshire

The holiday cottage was not at all like in the photographs. Small and dark, it had that holiday cottage smell, air-freshener and stale cupboards, and seemed to have retained the winter's chill in its thick stone walls, so that even on a blazing July day it felt chilly and damp.

Still, it didn't seem to matter. It was functional, isolated and the view of the North Yorkshire Moors was startling, even through the tiny windows. Most days they were out walking or driving along the coast, visiting antiquated seaside resorts that Emma remembered from childhood excursions, dusty little towns that seemed stuck in 1976. Today, the fourth day of the trip, they were in Filey, walking along the broad promenade that overlooks the great expanse of beach, still fairly empty on a Tuesday during term-time.

'See over there? That's where my sister got bitten by a dog.'

'That's interesting. What kind of dog?'

'Oh I'm sorry, am I boring you?'

'Only a little.'

'Well tough, I'm afraid. Four more days to go.'

In the afternoon, they were meant to go on some ambitious hike to a waterfall that Emma had planned the night before, but after an hour they found themselves on the moors staring uncomprehendingly at the Ordnance Survey map before giving up, lying down on the parched heather and dozing in the sun. Emma had brought along a bird guide and an immense pair of ex-army binoculars, the size and weight of a diesel engine, which she now raised with some effort to her eyes.

'Look, up there. I think it's a hen harrier.'

'Hmmm.'

'Have a look. Go on – up there.'

'I'm not interested. I'm sleeping.'

'How can you not be interested? It's beautiful.'

'I'm too young to birdwatch.'

Emma laughed. 'You're being ridiculous, you know that.'

'It's bad enough that we're rambling. It'll be classical music next.'

'Too *cool* to birdwatch—'

'Then it'll be gardening, then you'll be buying jeans in Marks and Spencer's, you'll want to move to the country. We'll call each other "darling". I've seen it happen, Em. It's a slippery slope.'

She raised herself on one arm, leant across and kissed him. 'Remind me again, why am I marrying you?'

'It's not too late to cancel.'

'Would we still get our deposit back?'

'Don't think so.'

'Okay.' She kissed him again. 'Let me think about it.'

They were getting married in November, a small, discreet winter wedding at a registry office, followed by a small, restrained reception for close friends and family at a favoured local restaurant. It was, they insisted, not really a wedding, more an excuse for a party. The vows would be secular and not too sentimental and had yet to be written; almost too embarrassing, they imagined, actually to sit face-to-face and compose those promises to each other.

'Can't we just use the vows you made to your ex-wife?'

'But you are still going to promise to obey me, right?'

'Only if you vow that you'll never, ever get into golf.'

'And you're going to take my surname?'

'"Emma Mayhew". Could be worse, I suppose.'

'You could hyphenate.'

'Morley-Mayhew. Sounds like a village in the Cotswolds. "We've got a little place just outside Morley-Mayhew".'

And this was how they approached the big day: flippant, but privately, discreetly elated too.

This week in Yorkshire was their last chance of a holiday before their modest, discreet big day. Emma had a deadline and Dexter was anxious about leaving the business for a whole week, but at least the trip allowed them to stop off at Emma's parents, an event that her mother had treated like an overnight visit by royalty. Serviettes were on the table, rather than the usual kitchen roll, there was trifle and a bottle of Perrier in the fridge. After the end of Emma's relationship with Ian it had seemed that Sue Morley would never love again and yet, if anything, she was even more fixated on Dexter, flirting in a bizarre, over-enunciated voice, like a coquettish speaking clock. Dutifully, Dexter flirted back, while the rest of the Morley family could do nothing but stare silently at the floor tiles and try not to laugh. Sue didn't care; to her it seemed as if a long-held fantasy was finally coming true: her daughter was actually marrying Prince Andrew.

Watching him through her family's eyes, Emma had felt proud of Dexter; he twinkled at Sue, was boyish and funny with her cousins, seemed sincerely interested in her father's koi carp and United's chances in the league. Only Emma's younger sister seemed sceptical of his appeal and sincerity. Divorced with two boys now, resentful and perpetually exhausted, Marianne was not in the mood for another wedding. They spoke that night while washing up.

'Why's Mum talking in that daft voice, that's what I want to know.'

'She likes him.' Emma nudged her sister's arm. 'You like him too, don't you?'

'He's nice. I like him. Just I thought he was meant to be some famous shagger or summat.'

'A long time ago, maybe. Not now.'

And Marianne had sniffed and visibly resisted saying something about leopards and their spots.

They abandoned the search for the waterfall, and instead drove back to the local pub, eating crisps and playing closely matched games of pool through the late afternoon.

'I don't think your sister likes me very much,' said Dexter, racking up the balls for the deciding game.

'Course she does.'

'She barely spoke a word to me.'

'She's just shy and a bit grumpy. She's like that, our sis.'

Dexter smiled. 'Your accent.'

'What about it?'

'You've got dead Northern since we've been up here.'

'Have I?'

'Soon as we hit the M1.'

'Don't mind, do you?'

'Don't mind at all. Whose turn to break?'

Emma won the game, and they walked back to the cottage in the evening light, woozy and affectionate from beer on an empty stomach. A working holiday, the plan had been to spend the day together and for Emma to work at night, but the trip had coincided with the most fertile days of Emma's cycle, and they were obliged to take full advantage of these opportunities now. 'What, again?' mumbled Dexter as Emma closed the door and kissed him.

'Only if you want to.'

'No, I do. It's just I feel a bit like I'm on a . . . stud farm or something.'

'Oh, you are. You are.'

By nine o'clock, Emma was asleep in the large, uncomfortable bed. It was still light outside, and for a while Dexter lay listening to her breathing, looking out at the small patch of purple moor that could be seen through the bedroom window. Still restless, he slid from the bed, pulled on some clothes and stepped quietly downstairs to the kitchen, where he rewarded himself with a glass of wine and wondered what they were supposed to do now. Dexter, who was used to the wilds of Oxfordshire, found this kind of isolation unnerving. It was too much to hope for a broadband connection, but in the brochure the cottage had also proudly boasted its lack of a television, and the silence made him anxious. On his iPod he selected some Thelonious Monk – he found himself listening to more jazz these days – then flopped back onto the sofa, releasing a cloud of dust, and picked up his book. Half-jokingly, Emma had bought him a copy of *Wuthering Heights* to read on the trip, but he found the book almost entirely unreadable so instead he reached for his laptop, opened it and stared at the screen.

In a folder called 'Personal Documents' lay another folder called 'Random' within which lay a file of just 40KB called bigdayspeech.doc: the text of his groom's speech. The horror of his witless, incoherent, semi-improvised performance at his previous wedding still remained vivid, and he was determined to get this one right, and to start work on it early.

So far, the text in its entirety ran as follows.

My Groom's speech

After a whirlwind romance! etc.

How we met. At same Uni but never knew her. Seen her around. Always angry about something terrible hair. Show photographs? Thought I was toff. Dungarees, or did I imagine. Finally got to know her. Called Dad fascist.

Great friends on and off. Me being idiot. Sometimes don't see thing in front of face.(corny)

How to describe Em. Her many qualities. Funny. Intelligence. Good dancer when she does but terrible cook. Taste in music.

We argue. But can always talk laugh. Beautiful but doesn't always know it etc etc. Great with Jas, even gets on with my ex-wife! Ho ho ha. Everyone loves her.

We lost touch. Bit about Paris.

Finally together, whirlwind romance nearly 15 years, finally makes sense. All friends said told you so. Happier than ever been.

Pause wile guests vom in unison.

Acknowledge second wedding. Get right this time. Thank caterers. Thank Sue Jim making me welcome. Feel like honorary northerner gags here etc. Telegrams? Absent friends. Sorry Mum's not here. Would have approved. At last!

Toast to my beautiful wife blah-di-blah-di-blah-blah-blah-blah-blah.

It was a start, and the structure was there. He set to work in earnest, switching the font from Courier to Arial to Times New Roman and back again, changing it all to italics, counting the words, adjusting the paragraphs and margins so that it looked more substantial.

Finally, he started to speak it out loud, using the text as notes, trying to recall the fluency he had once had on TV.

'I'd just like to thank everyone for coming here today . . .'

But he could hear the creak of floorboards above his head and quickly he closed the lid of the laptop, slid it furtively beneath the sofa and reached for *Wuthering Heights*.

Naked and sleepy-eyed, Emma padded down the stairs, stopping halfway and sitting with her arms wrapped round her knees. She yawned. 'What time is it?'

'Quarter to ten. Wild times, Em.'

She yawned once more. 'You've tired me out.' She laughed. 'Stud.'

'Go and put some clothes on, will you?'

'What are you doing anyway?' He held up *Wuthering Heights* and Emma smiled. '"I cannot live without my life! I cannot live without my soul"! Or is it "love without my life". Or "live without my love"? Can't remember.'

'Haven't got to that bit yet. It's still some woman called Nelly banging on.'

'It gets better, I promise you.'

'Tell me again, why is there no television here?'

'We're meant to make our own entertainment. Come back to bed and talk to me.'

He stood and crossed the room, leaning over the banister and kissing her. 'Promise you won't force me to have sex again.'

'What shall we do instead then?'

'I know it sounds weird,' he said, looking a little sheepish. 'But I wouldn't mind a game of Scrabble.'

CHAPTER EIGHTEEN
The Middle

Belsize Park

Something strange was happening to Dexter's face.

Coarse, black hairs had begun to appear high up on his cheeks, joining the occasional long grey solitary hairs that crept from his eyebrows. As if that wasn't enough, a fine, pale fur was appearing around the opening of his ears and at the bottom of his earlobes; hair that seemed to sprout overnight like cress, and which served no purpose except to draw attention to the fact that he was approaching middle age. Was now middle-aged.

Then there was the widow's peak, particularly noticeable now after a shower; two parallel byways gradually widening and making their way to the crown of his head, where the two paths would one day meet and it would all be over. He dried his hair with the towel, then scrubbed it this way and that with his fingertips until the path was covered over.

Something strange was happening to Dexter's neck. He had developed this sag, this fleshy pouch under his chin, his bag of shame, like some flesh-toned roll-neck jumper. He stood naked in front of the bathroom mirror and put one hand on his neck as if trying to mould it all back into place. It was like living in a subsiding house – every morning he woke and inspected the site for fresh cracks, new slippage in the night. It was as if the flesh were somehow cleaving from the skeleton, the characteristic physique of someone whose gym membership had long since lapsed. He had the beginnings of a paunch and, most grotesquely, something strange was happening to his nipples. There were items of clothing that he could barely bring himself to wear now, fitted shirts and ribbed woollen tops, because you could see them there, like limpets, girlish and repulsive. He also looked absurd in any garment with a hood, and only last week he had caught himself standing in a trance, listening to *Gardeners' Question Time*. In two weeks' time he would be forty years old.

He shook his head, and told himself it wasn't that disastrous. If he turned and looked at himself suddenly, and held his head in a certain way, and inhaled, he could still pass for, say, thirty-seven? He retained enough vanity to know that he was still an unusually good-looking man, but no-one was calling him beautiful anymore, and he'd always thought he would age better than this. He had hoped to age like a movie star: wiry, aquiline, grey-templed, sophisticated. Instead he was ageing like a TV presenter. An ex-TV presenter. A twice-married ex-TV presenter who ate far too much cheese.

Emma came in, naked from the bedroom, and he began to brush his teeth, another obsession; he felt like he had an old mouth, like it would never be clean again.

'I'm getting fat,' he mumbled, mouth full of foam.

'No you're not,' she said without much conviction.

'I am – look.'

'So don't eat so much cheese then,' she said.

'I thought you said I wasn't getting fat.'

'If you feel you are, then you are.'

'And I don't eat too much cheese. My metabolism is slowing down, that's all.'

'So do some exercise. Go to the gym again. Come swimming with me.'

'No time, have I?' While the toothbrush was removed from his mouth she kissed him consolingly. 'Look, I'm a mess,' he mumbled.

'I've told you before, darling, you have beautiful breasts,' and she laughed, poked him in the buttock and stepped into the shower. He rinsed, sat on the bathroom chair and watched her.

'We should go and see that house this afternoon.'

Emma groaned over the sound of the water. 'Do we have to?'

'Well I don't know how else we're going to find—'

'Okay. Okay! We'll go and see the house.'

She continued to shower with her back to him and he stood and stalked into the bedroom to get dressed. They were scrappy and irritable once again, and he told himself that it was because of the strain of trying to find a place to live. The flat had already been sold and a large part of their possessions placed into storage just to make room for the two of them. Unless they found somewhere soon they would have to rent, and all this brought its tensions and anxieties.

But he knew that something else was going on and sure enough, as Emma waited for the kettle and read the paper, she suddenly said—

'I've just got my period.'

'When?' he asked.

'Just now,' she said, with studied calm. 'I could feel it coming on.'

'Oh well,' he said, and Emma continued to make coffee, her back to him.

He stood to wrap his arms around her waist and lightly kissed the nape of her neck, still damp from the shower. She didn't look up from the newspaper. 'Doesn't matter. We'll try again, yeah?' he said, standing there with his chin on her shoulder for a while. It was a winsome, uncomfortable stance, and when she turned the page of the paper, he took it as his cue to return to the table.

They sat and read, Emma the current affairs, Dexter the sport, both taut with irritation while Emma tutted and shook her head in that maddening way she sometimes had. The Butler Inquiry into the origins of the war dominated the headlines, and he could feel her building up to some kind of topical political comment. He focussed on the latest from Wimbledon, but—

'It's weird, isn't it? How there's this war going on, and virtually no protest? I mean you think there'd be marches or something, wouldn't you?'

That tone of voice riled him too. It was the one he remembered from all those years ago: her student voice, superior and self-righteous. Dexter made an uncontentious noise, neither challenging nor accepting, in the hope that this would be enough. Time passed, pages of the newspaper were turned.

'I mean you'd think there'd be something like the anti-Vietnam movement or something, but nothing. Just that one march, then everyone shrugged and went home. Even the students aren't protesting!'

'What's it got to do with the students?' he said, mildly enough, he thought.

'It's traditional, isn't it? That students are politically engaged. If we were still students, we'd be protesting.' She went back to the paper. '*I* would anyway.'

She was provoking him. Fine, if that's what she wanted. 'So why aren't you?'

She looked at him sharply. 'What?'

'Protesting. If you feel so strongly.'

'That's exactly my point. Maybe I should be! That was exactly my observation! If there was some kind of cohesive movement . . .'

He returned to the paper, resolving to keep quiet but unable to do so. 'Or maybe it's because people don't mind.'

'What?' She looked at him, eyes narrowed.

'The war. I mean if people were really affronted by it there'd be protests, but maybe people are glad that he's gone. I don't know if you noticed, Em, but he wasn't a very nice man . . .'

'You can be glad Saddam's gone and still be against the war.'

'That's my point. It's ambiguous, isn't it?'

'What, you think it's a *fairly* just war?'

374

'Not *me* necessarily. People.'

'But what about you?' She closed the newspaper, and he felt a genuine sense of unease. 'What do you think?'

'What do I think?'

'What do you think?'

He sighed. Too late now, no turning back. 'I just think it's pretty rich that a lot of people on the Left were against the war when the people that Saddam was murdering were exactly the people the Left should have been supporting.'

'Like who?'

'Trade unionists, feminists. Homosexuals.' Should he say the Kurds? Was that correct? He decided to chance it. 'The Kurds!'

Emma snuffled righteously. 'Oh, you think we're fighting this war to protect trade unionists?' You think Bush invaded because he was worried about the plight of Iraqi women? Or gays?'

'All I'm saying is that the anti-war march would have had a bit more moral credibility if the same people had protested against the Iraqi regime in the first place! They protested about apartheid, why not Iraq?'

'. . . and Iran? And China and Russia and North Korea and Saudi Arabia! You can't protest against everyone.'

'Why not? You used to!'

'That's beside the point!'

'Is it? When I first knew you, all you *did* was boycott things. You couldn't eat a bloody Mars Bar without a lecture on personal responsibility. It's not my fault you've become complacent . . .'

He returned to his ridiculous sports news with a little self-satisfied smirk, and Emma felt her face beginning to redden. 'I have not become . . . Don't change the subject! The point is, it's ridiculous to claim that this war is about human rights, or WMDs or anything like that. It's about one thing and one thing only . . .'

He groaned. It was inevitable now: she was going to say 'oil'. Please, please don't say 'oil' . . .

'. . . nothing to do with human rights. It's entirely to do with oil!'

'Well isn't that a pretty good reason?' he said, standing and deliberately scraping his chair. 'Or don't you use oil, Em?'

As last words go, he felt this was pretty effective, but it was hard to walk away from an argument in this bachelor flat that suddenly felt too small, cluttered and scuffed. Certainly Emma wasn't going to let a fatuous remark like that go unanswered. She followed him into the hall, but he was waiting for her, turning on her with a ferocity that unsettled them both.

'I tell you what this is *really* about. You've had your period and you're angry about it and you're taking it out on me! Well I don't like being harangued while I'm trying to eat my breakfast!'

'I'm not *haranguing* you—'

'Arguing then—'

'We're not arguing, we're discussing—'

'Are we? Because I'm arguing—'

'Calm down, Dex—'

'The war wasn't my idea, Em! I didn't order the invasion, and I'm sorry, but I don't feel as strongly about it as you do. Maybe I should, maybe I will, but I don't. I don't know why, maybe I'm too *stupid* or something—'

Emma looked startled. 'Where did that come from? I didn't say you were—?'

'But you treat me like I am. Or like I'm this right-wing nut because I don't spout platitudes about The War. I swear, if I sit at one more dinner party and hear someone say "It's all about the oil"! Maybe it is, so what? Either protest about that, or stop using oil or accept it and shut the fuck up!'

'Don't you dare tell me to—'

'I wasn't! I wasn't talking to . . . oh, forget it.'

He squeezed past that bloody bike of hers, cluttering up *his* hallway, and into the bedroom. The blinds were still drawn, the bed unmade, damp towels on the floor, the room smelling of their bodies from the night before. He began searching for his keys in the gloom. Emma watched him from the doorway, with that look of maddening concern, and he kept his eyes averted.

'Why are you so embarrassed about discussing politics?' she said calmly, as if he were a child having a tantrum.

'I'm not embarrassed, I'm just . . . bored.' He was searching through the laundry basket, pulling out discarded clothes, checking trouser pockets for keys. 'I find politics boring – there, I've said it now. It's out!'

'Really?'

'Yes, really.'

'Even at University?'

'Especially there! I just pretended I didn't because it was the thing to do. I used to sit there at two in the morning listening to Joni Mitchell while some clown banged on about apartheid, or nuclear disarmament or the objectification of women and I used to think, fuck, this is boring, can't we talk about, I don't know, family or music or sex or something, people or something—'

'But politics *is* people!'

'What does that *mean*, Em? It's meaningless, it's just something to say—'

'It means we talked about a lot of things!'

'Did we? All I remember about those golden days is a lot of people showing-off, men mostly, banging on about feminism so that they could get into some girl's knickers. Stating the bleeding obvious; isn't that Mr Mandela nice and isn't nuclear war nasty and isn't it rotten that some people don't have enough to eat—'

'And that's *not* what people said!'

'—it's exactly the same now, except the bleeding obvious has changed. Now it's global warming and hasn't Blair sold out!'

'You don't agree?'

'I *do* agree! I do! I just think it would be refreshing to hear someone we know, one single person, say Bush can't be all that stupid and thank God someone's standing up to this fascist dictator and by the way I love my big car. Because they'd be wrong, but at least there'd be something to talk about! At least they wouldn't be patting themselves on the back, at least it would make a change from WMDs and schools and fucking *house* prices.'

'Hey, you talk about house prices too!'

'I know! And I fucking bore myself too!' His shout echoed as he flung yesterday's clothes against the wall, and then they both stood there in the gloomy bedroom, the blinds still down, the stale bed unmade.

'Do I bore you then?' she said quietly.

'Don't be ridiculous! That's not what I said.' Suddenly exhausted, he sat on the bed.

'But do I?'

'No, you don't. Let's change the subject, can we?'

'So, what do you want to talk about?' she said.

He sat hunched on the edge of the mattress, pressed his hands to his face and exhaled through his fingers. 'We've only been trying for eighteen months, Em.'

'Two years.'

'Two years then. I don't know, I just hate that . . . look you give me.'

'What look?'

'When it doesn't work, like it's my fault.'

'I don't!'

'That's what it feels like.'

'I'm sorry. I apologise. I'm just . . . disappointed. I really want it, that's all.'

'So do I!'

'Do you?'

He looked hurt. 'Of course I do!'

'Because you didn't to begin with.'

'Well I do now. I love you. You know that.'

She crossed the room and joined him, and they sat for a moment holding hands, shoulders hunched.

'Come here,' she said, falling backwards onto the bed, and he followed, their legs dangling over the edge. A shaft of murky light leaked between the blinds.

'I'm sorry for taking it out on you,' she said.

'I'm sorry for . . . I don't know.'

She lifted his hand and pressed the back of it against her lips. 'You know. I think we should get checked out. Go to a fertility clinic or something. Both of us.'

'There's nothing wrong with us.'

'I know, and that's what we're going to confirm.'

'Two years isn't that long. Why not wait another six months?'

'I just don't feel like I've got another six months in me, that's all.'

'You're crazy.'

'I'll be thirty-nine next April, Dex.'

'I'm forty in two weeks!'

'Exactly.'

He exhaled slowly, visions of test tubes floating before his eyes. Depressing cubicles, nurses snapping on rubber gloves. Magazines. 'Alright then. We'll have some *tests*.' He turned to look at her. 'But what'll we do about the waiting list?'

She sighed. 'I suppose we might have to, I don't know. Go private.'

After a while, he spoke. 'My God. Now that's something I never thought you'd say.'

'No, me neither,' she said. 'Me neither.

With some sort of fragile peace in place, he got ready for work. The absurd row would make him late, but at least the Belleville Café was running fairly smoothly now. He had employed a sharp, reliable manager, Maddy, with whom he enjoyed good business relations and some mild flirtation, and he no longer had to open up in the mornings. Emma accompanied him downstairs and they walked out into the day, gloomy and nondescript.

'So where is this house then?'

'Kilburn. I'll send you the address. It looks nice. In the photos.'

'They all look nice in the photos,' she mumbled, hearing her own voice, sulky and dreary. Dexter chose not to speak, and a moment passed before she felt able to loop her arms around his waist and hold onto him. 'We're not being very good today, are we? Or I'm not. Sorry.'

'That's okay. We'll stay in tonight, you and me. I'll cook you dinner, or we'll go out somewhere. To the cinema or something.' He pressed his face to the top of the head. 'I love you and we'll sort this out, alright?'

Emma stood silent on the doorstep. The proper thing to do would be to tell him that she loved him too, but she still wanted to mope a little more. She resolved to sulk until lunch time, then make it up to him tonight. Perhaps if the weather cleared up, they could go and sit on Primrose Hill like they used to. *The important thing is that he will be there and it will be okay.*

'You should go,' she mumbled into his shoulder. 'You'll be late for *Maddy*.'

'Don't start.'

She grinned and looked up at him. 'I'll cheer up by tonight.'

'We'll do something fun.'

'Fun.'

'We still have fun, don't we?'

'Of course we do,' she said, and kissed him goodbye.

And they did have fun, though it was of a different kind now. All that yearning and anguish and passion had been replaced by a steady pulse of pleasure and satisfaction and occasional irritation, and this seemed to be a happy exchange; if there had been moments in her life when she had been more elated, there had never been a time when things had been more constant.

Sometimes, she thought, she missed the intensity, not just of their romance, but of the early days of their friendship. She remembered writing ten-page letters late into the night; insane, passionate things full of dopey sentiment and barely hidden meanings, exclamation marks and underlining. For a while she had written daily postcards too, on top of the hour-long phone-calls just before bed. That time in the flat in Dalston when they had stayed up talking and listening to records, only stopping when the sun began to rise, or at his parents' house, swimming in the river on New Year's Day, or that afternoon drinking absinthe in the secret bar in Chinatown; all of these moments and more were recorded and stored in notebooks and letters and wads of photographs, endless photographs. There was a time, it must have been in the early nineties, when they were barely able to pass a photo-booth without cramming inside it, because they had yet to take each other's permanent presence for granted.

But to just look at someone, to just sit and look and talk and then realise that it's morning? Who had the time or inclination or energy these days to stay up talking all night? What would you talk about? Property prices? She used to long for those midnight phone-calls; these days if a phone rang late at night it was because there had been an accident, and did they really need more photographs when they knew each other's faces so well, when they had shoeboxes full of that stuff, an archive of nearly twenty years? Who writes long letters in this day and age, and what is there to care so much about?

She sometimes wondered what her twenty-two-year-old self would think of today's Emma Mayhew. Would she consider her self-centred? Compromised? A bourgeois sell-out, with her appetite for home ownership and foreign travel, clothes from Paris and expensive haircuts? Would she find her conventional, with her new surname and hopes for a family life? Maybe, but then the twenty-two-year-old Emma Morley wasn't such a paragon either: pretentious, petulant, lazy, speechifying, judge-mental. Self-pitying, self-righteous, self-important, all the selfs except self-confident, the quality that she had always needed the most.

No, this, she felt, was real life and if she wasn't as curious

381

or passionate as she once had been, that was only to be expected. It would be inappropriate, undignified, at thirty-eight, to conduct friendships or love affairs with the ardour and intensity of a twenty-two-year-old. Falling in love like that? Writing poetry, crying at pop songs? Dragging people into photo-booths, taking a whole day to make a compilation tape, asking people if they wanted to share your bed, just for company? If you quoted Bob Dylan or T.S. Eliot or, God forbid, Brecht at someone these days they would smile politely and step quietly backwards, and who would blame them? Ridiculous, at thirty-eight, to expect a song or book or film to change your life. No, everything had evened out and settled down and life was lived against a general background hum of comfort, satisfaction and familiarity. There would be no more of those nerve-jangling highs and lows. The friends they had now would be the friends they had in five, ten, twenty years' time. They expected to get neither dramatically richer nor poorer; they expected to stay healthy for a little while yet. Caught in the middle; middle class, middle-aged; happy in that they were not over happy.

Finally, she loved someone and felt fairly confident that she was loved in return. If someone asked Emma, as they sometimes did at parties, how she and her husband had met, she told them:

'We grew up together.'

So they went to work as usual. Emma sat at her computer by the window overlooking the tree-lined street, writing the fifth and final 'Julie Criscoll' novel, in which her fictional heroine, ironically enough, became pregnant and had to decide between motherhood and university. It wasn't going very well; the tone was too sombre and introspective, the jokes wouldn't flow. She was keen to get it finished, and yet uncertain what to do next, or what she was capable of doing; a book for grown-ups perhaps, something serious and properly researched about the Spanish Civil War, or the near-future, something vaguely Margaret Atwoody, something her younger self might respect and admire.

That was the idea anyway. In the meantime, she tidied the flat, made tea, paid some bills, did a coloured wash, put CDs back in their cases, made more tea then finally turned on her computer and stared it into submission.

At the café, Dexter flirted a little with Maddy, then sat in the tiny stock room that smelt oppressively of cheese and attempted to complete the quarterly VAT return. But the gloom and guilt of this morning's outburst still clung to him, and when he could no longer concentrate he reached for his phone. It used to be Emma who made the conciliatory calls and smoothed things over, but in the eight months since their marriage they seemed to have changed places, and he now found himself incapable of doing anything while he knew she was unhappy. He dialled, imagining her at her desk, looking at her mobile phone, seeing his name appear and turning it off. He preferred it that way – much easier to be sentimental when no-one was going to answer back.

'So I'm here, doing my VAT, and I keep thinking about you and I just wanted to say don't worry. I've arranged for us to view this house at five o'clock. I'll text you the address, so, who knows. We'll see. Period property, good-sized rooms. It's got a breakfast bar apparently. I know you've always dreamt of one. That's all. Except to say I love you and don't worry. Whatever it is you're worrying about, don't. That's everything. See you there at five. Love you. Bye.'

As routine demanded, Emma worked until two, ate lunch, then went swimming. In July she sometimes liked to go to the ladies pool on Hampstead Heath, but the day had become precariously dark and overcast, and instead she braved the teenage kids at the indoor pool. For twenty minutes she weaved unhappily between them as they dive-bombed and ducked and flirted with each other, manic with the freedom of the end of term. Afterwards she sat in the changing rooms, listened to Dexter's message and smiled. She memorised the address of the property and called back.

'Hi there. It's me. Just to say, I'm setting out now and I can't wait to see the breakfast bar. I might be five minutes late. Also thank you for your message and I wanted to say . . . I'm sorry for being so snappy today, and for that stupid argument. Nothing to do with you. Just a bit nuts at the moment. The important thing is I love you very much. So. There you go. Lucky you! I think that's everything. Bye my love. Bye.'

Outside the sports centre the clouds had darkened and finally burst, letting loose fat grey drops of warm rain. She cursed the weather and the wet seat of her bicycle and set off across North London towards Kilburn, improvising a route through a maze of residential streets towards Lexington Road.

The rain became heavier, oily drops of brown city water, and Emma rode standing on the pedals with her head lowered so that she was only vaguely aware of a blur of movement in the side road to her left. The sensation is less of flying through the air, more of being picked up and hurled, and when she comes to rest on the roadside verge with her face against the wet pavement, her first instinct is to look for her bicycle, which has somehow disappeared from beneath her. She tries to move her head, but is unable to do so. She wants to take off her helmet, because people are looking at her now, faces craning over her and she looks ridiculous in a bicycle helmet, but the people crouching over her seem fearful and are asking her over and over again are you alright are you alright. One of them is crying and she realises for the first time that she is not alright. She blinks against the rain falling on her face. She is definitely going to be late now. Dexter will be waiting.

She thinks very distinctly of two things.

The first is a photograph of herself at nine years old in a red swimsuit on a beach, she can't remember where, Filey or Scarborough perhaps. She is with her mother and father who are swinging her towards the camera, their sunburnt faces buckled with laughter. Then she thinks of Dexter, sheltering from the rain on the steps of the new house, looking at his watch, impatient; he'll wonder where I am, she thinks. He'll worry.

Then Emma Mayhew dies, and everything that she thought or felt vanishes and is gone forever.

Part Five

Three Anniversaries

'She philosophically noted dates as they came past in the revolution of the year; . . . her own birthday; and every other day individualized by incidents in which she had taken some share. She suddenly thought one afternoon, when looking in the glass at her fairness, that there was yet another date, of greater importance to her than those; that of her own death, when all these charms would have disappeared; a day which lay sly and unseen among all the other days of the year, giving no sign or sound when she annually passed over it; but not the less surely there. When was it?'

Thomas Hardy, *Tess of the d'Urbervilles*

CHAPTER NINETEEN
The Morning After

Rankeillor Street, Edinburgh

When she opened her eyes again, the skinny boy was still there, his back to her now as he sat precariously on the edge of her old wooden chair, pulling on his trousers as quietly as possible. She glanced at her radio alarm clock: nine-twenty. They had slept for maybe three hours, and now he was sneaking off. She watched as he placed his hand in the trouser pocket to still the rattling of his loose change, then stood and started to pull on last night's white shirt. One last glimpse of his long brown back. Handsome. He really was stupidly handsome. She very much wanted him to stay, almost as much perhaps as he clearly wanted to leave. She decided that she would have to speak.

'Not going without saying goodbye, are you?'

He turned round, caught in the act. 'I didn't want to wake you.'

'Why not?'

'Just you looked so nice, sleeping there.'

Both knew this was a poor effort. 'Right. Right, I see.' She heard herself, needy and annoyed. Don't let him think you care, Em. Be cool. Be . . . blasé.

'I was going to leave you a note, but . . .' He pantomimed looking for a pen, oblivious to the jam jar full of them on the desk.

She lifted her head from the pillow and rested it on one hand. 'I don't mind. You can leave if you want to. Ships that pass in the night n'all that. Very, what d'you call it . . . bittersweet.'

He sat on the chair, and continued to button his shirt. 'Emma?'

'Yes, Dexter?'

'I've had a really nice time.'

'I can tell by the way you're searching for your shoes.'

'No, seriously.' Dexter leant forward on the chair. 'I'm really glad we finally got to talk. And the other stuff as well. After all this time.' He scrunched his face, looking for just the right words. 'You're really, *really* lovely, Em.'

'Yeah, yeah, yeah—'

'No, you are.'

'Well you're lovely too and now you can go.' She allowed him a small, tight smile. He responded by suddenly crossing the room, and she turned her face up towards him in anticipation, only to find that he was reaching beneath the bed for a discarded sock. He noticed her raised face.

'Sock under bed,' he said.

'Right.'

He perched uneasily on the bedframe, speaking in a strained, chipper tone as he pulled on his socks. 'Big day today! Driving back!'

'Where to, London?'

'Oxfordshire. That's where my parents live. Most of the time anyway.'

'Oxfordshire. Very nice,' she said, privately mortified at the speed with which intimacy evaporates, to be replaced by small talk. Last night they had said and done all those things, and now they were like strangers in a bus queue. The mistake she had made was to fall asleep and break the spell. If they had stayed awake, they might still have been kissing now, but instead it was all over and she found herself saying; 'How long will that take then? To Oxfordshire?'

''Bout seven, eight hours. My dad's an excellent driver.'

'Uh-huh.'

'You're not going back to . . . ?'

'Leeds. No I'm staying here for the summer. I told you, remember?'

'Sorry, I was really pretty drunk last night.'

'And that, m'lud, is the case for the defence . . .'

'It's not an excuse, it's . . .' He turned to look at her. 'Are you annoyed with me, Em?'

'Em? Who's Em?'

'Em*ma*, then.'

'I'm not annoyed, I just . . . wish you'd woken me up, instead of being all furtive and sneaking off . . .'

'I was going to write you a note!'

'And what was it going to say, this precious note?'

'It was going to say "I've taken your purse".'

She laughed, a low morning growl that caught the back of her throat, and there was something so gratifying about her smile, the two deep parentheses in the corners of her mouth, the way she kept her lips tightly closed as if holding something back, that he almost regretted telling his lie. He had no intention of leaving at lunch time. His parents were going to stay over and take him out to dinner that night, then leave tomorrow morning. The lie had been instinctive in order to facilitate a quick, clean escape, but now as he leant across to kiss her he wondered if there was a way to withdraw the deceit somehow. Her mouth was soft, and she allowed herself to fall back on the bed, which still smelt of wine, her warm body and fabric conditioner, and he decided that he really must try to be more honest in future.

She rolled away from the kiss. 'Just going to the loo,' she said, lifting his arm to pass beneath it. She stood, hooking two fingers in the elastic of her underpants and tugging the material down over her bottom.

'Is there a phone I can use?' he asked, watching her pad across the room.

'In the hallway. It's a novelty phone, I'm afraid. Very zany. Tilly finds it *hilarious*. Help yourself. Don't forget to leave ten p,' and she was out in the hall and heading towards the bathroom.

The bath was already running for one of her flatmate's epic all-day summer hot soaks. Tilly Killick waited for Emma in her dressing-gown, eyes goggling through the steam behind big red spectacle frames, mouth hanging open in a scandalised 'O'.

'Emma Morley, you dark horse!'

'What?'

'Have you got someone in your room?'

'Maybe!'

'It's not who I think it is . . .'

'Just Dexter Mayhew!' said Emma, nonchalantly, and the two girls laughed and laughed and laughed.

Dexter found the phone in the hallway, shaped like a startlingly realistic burger. He stood with the sesame seed bun flipped open in his hand, listening to the whispers from the bathroom and experiencing the satisfaction he always felt when he knew people were talking about him. Odd words and phrases were audible through the plasterboard: *So did you? No! So what happened? We just talked, and stuff. Stuff? What does that mean, stuff? Nothing! And is he staying for breakfast? I don't know. Well make sure he stays for breakfast.*

Dexter watched the door patiently, waiting until Emma reappeared. He dialled 123, the speaking clock, pressed the bap to his ear and spoke into the beef patty.

'. . . *the time sponsored by Accurist will be nine thirty-two and twenty seconds.*'

At the third stroke he went into his act. 'Hi, Mum, it's me . . . yeah, a bit worse for wear!' He ruffled his hair in a way that he believed to be endearing '. . . No, I stayed over at a friend's house . . .' and here he glanced over at Emma, who loitered nearby in t-shirt and underpants, pretending to go through the mail.

'. . . *the time sponsored by Accurist will be nine thirty-three precisely . . .*'

'So listen, something's come up and I wondered if we could postpone going home until first thing tomorrow, instead of today? . . . I just thought the drive might be easier for Dad . . . I don't mind if you don't . . . Is Dad with you? Ask Dad now then.'

Taking his cue from the speaking clock, he allowed himself thirty seconds and gave Emma his most amiable smile. She smiled back and thought: nice guy, altering his plans just for me. Perhaps she had misjudged him. Yes, he is an idiot, but he needn't be. Not always.

'Sorry!' he mouthed.

'I don't want you to change your plans for me—' she said, apologetically.

'No, I'd like to—'

'Really, if you've got to go home—'

'It's fine, it's better this way—'

'At the third stroke the time sponsored by Accurist will be nine thirty-four precisely.'

'I don't mind, I'm not offended or anything—'

He held up his hand for quiet. 'Hi, Mum? . . .' A pause; build anticipation, but don't overdo it. 'Really? Okay, that's great! Alright, I'll see you at the flat later! Okay, see you. Bye.' He snapped the bun closed like a castanet and they stood and grinned at each other.

'Great phone.'

'Depressing, isn't it? Every time I use it, makes me want to cry.'

'You still want that ten p?'

'Nah. You're alright. My treat.'

'So!' he said.

'So,' said Emma. 'What are we going to do with the day?'

CHAPTER TWENTY

The First Anniversary
A Celebration

FRIDAY 15 JULY 2005

London and Oxfordshire

Fun, fun, fun – fun is the answer. Keep moving and don't allow yourself a moment to stop or look around or think because the trick is to not get morbid, to have fun and see this day, this first anniversary as – what? A celebration! Of her life and all the good times, the memories. The laughs, all the laughs.

With this in mind he has ignored his manager Maddy's protests, taken two hundred pounds from the café's cash register and invited three of the staff – Maddy, Jack, and Pete who works on Saturdays – out on the town to welcome the special day in style. After all, it's what she would have wanted.

And so the first moments of this St Swithin's Day find him in a basement bar in Camden with his fifth martini in one hand and a cigarette in the other because why not? Why not have some fun and celebrate her *life*? He says this, slurs this to his friends who smile at him a little weakly and sip at their drinks so slowly that he begins to regret bringing them along. They're so stuffy and boring, accompanying him from bar to bar less like good mates, more like hospital orderlies, humouring him and making sure he doesn't bump into people or crack his head as he falls from the taxi. Well, he's had enough of it. He wants some release, wants to let his hair down, he deserves it after the year he has just had. With this in mind he suggests that they all go to a club he once went to on a stag night. A strip club.

'Don't think so, Dex,' says Maddy, quietly appalled.

'Oh, come on, Maddy! Why not?' he says, his arm draped around her shoulder. 'It's what she would have wanted!' and he laughs at this and raises his glass once more, reaching for it with his mouth and missing by some distance so that the gin spatters onto his shoes. 'It'll be a laugh!' Maddy reaches behind her for her coat.

'Maddy, you lightweight!' he shouts.

'I really think you ought to go home now, Dexter,' says Pete.

'But it's just gone midnight!'

'Goodnight, Dex. See you whenever.'

He follows Maddy to the door. He wants her to have fun, but she seems tearful and upset. 'Stay, have another drink!' he demands, tugging at her elbow.

'You will take it easy, won't you? Please?'

'Don't leave us boys alone!'

'Got to. I'm opening up in the morning, remember?' She turns and takes both his hands in hers in that maddening way she has, all caring and sympathetic. 'Just be . . . careful?'

But he doesn't want sympathy, he wants another drink, and so he drops her hands abruptly and heads back towards the bar. He has no trouble getting served. Just a week ago bombs have exploded on public transport. Strangers have set out to kill at random and despite all the pluck and bravado the city has an under-siege atmosphere tonight. People are scared to be out and so Dexter has no problem flagging down a taxi to take them towards Farringdon Road. His head is resting against the window as he hears Pete and Jack chickening out, offering up the usual excuses: it's late, they have work in the morning. 'I've got a wife and kids you know!' says Pete jokily; they're like hostages pleading for release. Dexter feels the party disintegrating around him but doesn't have the energy to fight it, so he stops the cab in King's Cross and sets them free.

'Come back with us, Dex mate? Yeah?' says Jack, peering in at the window with that stupid concerned look on his face.

'Nah, I'm alright.'

'You can always stay at mine?' says Pete. 'Sleep on the sofa?' but Dexter knows he doesn't really mean it. As Pete has pointed out, he's got a wife and kids, so why would he want this monster in his house? Sprawled stinking and unconscious on the sofa, weeping while Pete's kids try to get ready for school. Grief has made an idiot of Dexter Mayhew once again, and why should he impose this on his friends? Best just stick with strangers tonight. And so he waves goodbye and orders the taxi onto a bleak, shuttered side street off Farringdon Road, and Nero's night-club.

The outside is marked by black marble pillars, like a funeral directors. Falling from the cab, he worries that the bouncers won't let him in, but in fact he is their perfect customer: well dressed and stupid-drunk. Dexter grins ingratiatingly at the big man with the shaved head and the goatee, hands over his cash and is waved through the door and into the main room. He steps into the gloom.

There was a time, not so long ago, when a visit to a strip club would have seemed raffishly post-modern; ironic and titillating at the same time. But not tonight. Tonight Nero's night-club resembles a business-class departure lounge in the early Eighties. All silver chrome, low black leather sofas and plastic pot plants, it is a particularly suburban notion of decadence. An amateurish mural, copied from a children's textbook, of slave-girls bearing trays of grapes, covers the back wall. Polystyrene Roman pillars sprout here and there, and standing around the room in unflattering cones of orange light on what look like low coffee tables are the strippers, the dancers, the artistes, all performing in various styles to the blaring R & B; here a languid jig, there a sort of narcoleptic mime act, another girl performing startling aerobic high-kicks, all of them naked or nearly so. Beneath them sit the men, suited mainly, ties undone, slumped on the slippery booths with heads lolling backwards as if their necks had been crisply snapped: his people. Dexter takes the room in, his eyes slipping in and out of focus, grinning stupidly as he feels lust and shame combine in a narcotic rush. He stumbles on the stairs, steadies himself on the greasy chrome rail, then stands and shoots his cuffs and weaves between the podiums towards the bar where a hard-faced woman tells him single drinks can't be bought, just bottles, vodka or champagne, a hundred quid each. He laughs at the audacious banditry and hands over his credit card with a flourish, as if challenging them to do their worst.

He takes his bottle of champagne – a Polish brand that comes in a pail of tepid water – and two plastic glasses, carrying them to a black velvet booth where he lights a cigarette and starts to drink in earnest. The 'champagne' is as sugary as a boiled sweet, apple-flavoured and barely sparkling, but it doesn't matter. His friends have gone now and there is no-one to take the glass from his hand or distract him with conversation, and after the third glass the time itself begins to take on that strange elastic quality, speeding up and slowing down, moments disappearing altogether as his vision fades to black and back up again. He is about to slip into sleep, or unconsciousness, when he feels a hand on his arm and finds himself facing a skinny girl in a very short, sheer red dress with long blonde hair, shading into black an inch from her scalp. 'Mind if I have a glass of champagne?' she says, sliding into the booth. She has very bad skin beneath the thick foundation and speaks with a South African accent, which he compliments her on. 'You've got a lovely voice!' he shouts against the music. She sniffs and wrinkles her nose and introduces herself as Barbara in a way that suggests that 'Barbara' was the first name that came to hand. She is slight with bony arms and small breasts which he stares at baldly, though she doesn't seem to mind. A ballet dancer's physique. 'Are you a ballet dancer?' he says, and she sniffs and shrugs. He has decided that he really, really likes Barbara.

'What brings you here then?' she asks mechanically.

'It's my anniversary!' he says.

'Congratulations,' she says, absently, pouring herself some champagne and raising her plastic glass in the air.

'Aren't you going to ask me what it's the anniversary of?' he says, though he must be slurring his speech pretty badly because she asks him to repeat it three times. Best try something more straightforward. 'My wife had an accident exactly one year ago today,' he says. Barbara gives a nervous smile and starts to look around as if regretting sitting down. Dealing with drunks is part of the job but this one is plainly weird, out celebrating some accident, then whining on incoherently and at great length about some driver not looking where he was going, a court case that she can't understand and can't be bothered to understand.

'Do you want me to dance for you?' she says, if only to change the subject.

'What?' He falls towards her. 'What did you say?' His breath is rank and his spit flecks her skin.

'I said do you want me to dance for you, cheer you up a bit? You look like you might need cheering up.'

'Not now. Later maybe,' he says, slapping his hand on her knee now, which is as hard and unyielding as a banister. He is speaking again, not normal speech but a tangle of unconnected mawkish, sour remarks that he has made before – only thirty-eight years old we were trying for a baby the driver walked away scot-free wonder what that bastard's doing right this minute taking away my best friend hope he suffers only thirty-eight where's the justice what about me what am I meant to do now Barbara tell me what am I supposed to do now? He comes to a sudden halt.

Barbara's head is lowered and she's staring at her hands, which she holds devoutly in her lap as if in prayer and for a moment he thinks he has moved her with his story, this beautiful stranger, touched her deeply in some way. Perhaps she's praying for him, perhaps she's even crying – he has made this poor girl cry and he feels a deep affection for this Barbara. He puts his hand over hers in gratitude, and realises that she is texting. While he has been talking about Emma, she has had her mobile phone in her lap and is writing a text. He feels a sudden flush of rage and revulsion.

'What are you doing?' he asks, voice trembling.

'*What?*'

He is shouting now. 'I said what the fuck are you *doing*?' He swipes wildly at her hands, sending the phone skittering across the floor. 'I was talking to you!' he shouts, but she is shouting back now, calling him a nutter, a loony, then beckoning to the bouncer. It's the same immense goateed man who had been so friendly at the door, but now he just puts his massive arm around Dexter's shoulders, the other round his waist, scooping him up like a child and carrying him across the room. Heads turn, amused, as Dexter bawls over his shoulder, *you stupid, stupid cow, you don't understand*, and he catches one last glance of Barbara, both middle fingers raised and jabbing upwards, laughing at him. The fire exit is kicked open and he is out once again on the street.

'My credit card! You've got my fucking credit card!' he shouts, but like everyone else the bouncer just laughs at him, and pulls the fire exit closed.

Enraged now, Dexter steps straight off the pavement and waves his arms at the many black cabs that head westward, but none of them will stop for him, not while he's staggering in the road like this. He takes a deep breath, steps back onto the pavement, leans against a wall and checks his pockets. His wallet has gone, and so have his keys, to his flat and his car. Whoever's got the keys and wallet will have his address too, it's on his driving licence, he'll have to have the locks changed, and Sylvie's meant to be coming round at lunch time. She's bringing Jasmine. He kicks at the wall, rests his head against the bricks, checks his pockets again, finds a balled-up twenty-pound note in his trouser pocket, damp from his own urine. Twenty quid is enough to get him safely home. He can wake up the neighbours, get the spare key, sleep it off.

But twenty quid is also enough to get him into town, with change for another drink or two. Home or oblivion? Forcing himself to stand straight, he hails a cab and sends it into Soho.

Through a plain red door in an alley off Berwick Street he finds an illicit underground dive that he used to go to ten, fifteen years ago as a very last resort. It's a grubby windowless room, dark and dense with smoke and people drinking from cans of Red Stripe. He crosses to the formica table that doubles as a bar, using the crowd for support, but then discovers that he has no cash, has given the last of it to the taxi-driver, lost the change. He'll have to do what he always used to do when he had lost all his money, pick up the nearest drink and neck it. He walks back into the room, ignoring the abuse of the people he stumbles into, grabs what looks like a forgotten can and drains what's left, then boldly takes another and jams himself in a corner, sweating, his head against a loudspeaker, his eyes closed, the drink running down his chin and onto his shirt and suddenly there's a hand against his chest pushing him back into the corner and someone wants to know what the *fuck* he thinks he's playing at, nicking people's drinks. He opens his eyes: the man before him is old, red-eyed, squat like a toad.

'Actually, I think you'll find it's mine,' says Dexter, then sniggers at how unconvincing the lie is. The man snarls, bares his yellow teeth and shows his fist, and Dexter realises what he wants: he wants the man to hit him. 'Get your hands off me, you ugly old cunt,' he slurs, and then there's a blur and a noise like static, and he is lying on the floor with his hands to his face as the man kicks at his stomach and stamps on his back with his heel. Dexter tastes the foul carpet as the kicks come down, and then suddenly he is floating, face down, six men lifting him by the legs and arms, like at school when it was his birthday and all his mates threw him in the pool and he is whooping and laughing as they carry him along the corridor through a restaurant kitchen and out into the alley where he is bowled into a huddle of plastic bins. Still laughing he rolls off onto the hard, filthy ground and feels the blood in his mouth, the hot iron taste of it, and he thinks, well, it's what she would have wanted. This is what she would have wanted.

15th July 2005

Hello there, Dexter!

I hope you don't mind me writing. It's a weird thing to do, isn't it, writing a letter in these days of t'internet! but it felt more appropriate. I wanted to sit down and do something to mark the day, and this seemed like the best thing.

So how are you? And how are you keeping? We spoke briefly at the memorial service, but I did not want to intrude as it was clear how tough that day was for you. Brutal, wasn't it? Like you, I'm sure, I have been thinking of Emma all day. I'm always finding myself thinking of her, but today is especially tough and I know you must find it tough too, but I wanted to drop you a line with my thoughts for what they are worth (i.e. not very much!!!!). Here goes then.

When Emma left me all those years ago, I thought my life would go to bits, and it did too for a couple of years. To be honest, I think I went a bit nuts. But then I met this girl in a shop where I was working and for our first date I took her to see me do some stand-up comedy. Afterwards she said please not to take this the wrong way but that I was a very, very bad comedian and that the best thing I could do was give it up and be myself instead. That moment was the moment that I fell in love with her and now we have been married for four years and have three amazing kids (one of each! Ha ha). We live in the teeming metropolis that is Taunton to be near my parents (i.e. free baby-sitting!!!). I work in a big insurance office now, working in the customer enquiries department. No doubt this will sound a bit dullsville to you, but I am good at it and we have a really good laugh. All things considered I am really happy. Our kids are a boy and two girls. I know you have a kid too. Knackering, isn't it?!!!

But why am I telling you all this? We were never particularly good pals and you probably don't care very much what I am doing. I suppose if there is a reason for writing it is this.

After Emma left me I thought I was finished, but I wasn't,

because I met Jacqui my wife. Now you've lost Emma too, only you can never get her back, none of us can, but I just wanted to urge you not to give up. Emma always loved you, very, very much. For many years this caused me a great deal of pain and jealousy. I used to overhear your phone-calls and watch you together at parties, and she always lit up and sparkled with you in a way she never did with me. I'm ashamed to say I used to read her notebooks when she was out, and they were full of you and your friendship and I couldn't bear it. To be honest, mate, I didn't think you deserved her, but then I don't think any of us deserved her really. She was always going to be the smartest, kindest, funniest, loyalest person we would ever meet, and the fact of her not being here well it just isn't right.

So like I said, I didn't think you deserved her but I know from my brief contact with Emma that all that changed eventually. You were a shit and then you weren't a shit, and I know that in the years you finally got together that you made her very, very happy. She glowed, didn't she? She just glowed with it all shiny and I would like to thank you for this and say no hard feelings mate and wish you best of luck for the rest of your life.

I am sorry if this letter is getting a bit weepy. Anniversaries like this are hard for all of us, for her family and you especially, but I hate this date, and will always hate this day every year from now on whenever it comes round. My thoughts are with you today. I know you have a beautiful daughter and I hope you get some comfort and pleasure from her.

Well must close now! Be happy and be <u>good</u> and get on with life! Seize the day all that bollocks. I think that is what Emma would have wanted.

Best wishes (or at a push, love I suppose)
Ian Whitehead

'Dexter, can you hear me? Oh, God, what have you done? Can you hear me Dex? Open your eyes, will you?'

When he wakes, Sylvie is there. Somehow he is lying on the floor of his flat, jammed between the sofa and the table, and she is standing awkwardly above him, trying to pull him out of the narrow space and get him into a sitting position. His clothes are wet and sticky and he realises that he has been sick in his sleep. He is appalled and ashamed but powerless to move as Sylvie grunts and gasps, her hands beneath his armpits.

'Oh, Sylvie,' he says, struggling to help her. 'I'm sorry. I fucked up again.'

'Just sit up for me will you, honey?'

'I'm fucked up, Sylvie. I am so fucked up . . .'

'You'll be fine, you need to sleep it off that's all. Oh, don't cry, Dexter. Listen to me, will you?' She's kneeling with her hands on his face now, looking at him with a tenderness he rarely saw when they were married. 'We'll get you cleaned up and into bed, and you can sleep it off. Okay?'

Glancing past her he sees a figure loitering anxiously in the doorway: his daughter. He groans and thinks he might be sick again, so powerful is the sudden spasm of shame.

Sylvie follows his gaze. 'Jasmine sweetheart, please wait in the other room, will you?' she says, as levelly as possible. 'Daddy's not feeling very well.' Jasmine doesn't move. 'I told you, go next door!' says Sylvie, panic rising in her voice.

He wants very much to say something to reassure Jasmine, but his mouth is swollen and bruised and he can't seem to form the words, and instead he lies back down, defeated. 'Don't move,' says Sylvie, 'Just stay exactly where you are,' and she leaves the room, taking their daughter with her. He closes his eyes, waiting, praying for all of this to pass. There are voices in the hall. Phone-calls are made.

The next thing that he knows for sure is that he is in the back of a car, curled uncomfortably on the back seat beneath a tartan blanket. He pulls it tight around him – despite the warm day he can't seem to stop shivering – and realises that it's the old picnic blanket which, along with the smell of the car's scuffed burgundy upholstery, reminds him of family days out. With some difficulty he lifts his head to look out of the passenger window. They are on the motorway. Mozart plays on the radio. He sees the back of his father's head, fine silver-grey hair neatly trimmed apart from the tufts in his ears.

'Where are we going?'

'I'm taking you home. Go back to sleep.'

His father has abducted him. For a moment he considers arguing: Take me back to London, I'm fine, I'm not a child. But the leather is warm against his face, he doesn't have the energy to move, let alone argue. He shivers once more, pulls the blanket up to his chin and falls asleep.

He is woken by the sound of the wheels on the gravel of the large, sturdy family home. 'In you come then,' says his father, opening the car door like a chauffeur. 'Soup for tea!' and he walks towards the house, tossing the car keys jauntily into the air as he goes. Clearly he has decided to pretend that nothing out of the ordinary has happened, and Dexter is grateful for this. Hunched and unsteady, he clambers from the car, shrugs off the picnic blanket and follows him inside.

In the small downstairs bathroom he inspects his face in the mirror. His bottom lip is cut and swollen, and there's a large, yellow-brown bruise down one side of his face. He tries to roll his shoulders, but his back aches, the muscles stretched and torn. He winces, then examines his tongue, ulcerous, bitten at the sides and coated with a grey mould. He runs the tip of it over his teeth. They never feel clean these days, and he can smell his own breath reflecting back off the mirror. It has a faecal quality, as if something is decaying inside him. There are broken veins on his nose and cheek. He is drinking with a renewed sense of purpose, nightly and frequently during the day, and has gained a great deal of weight; his face is podgy and slack, his eyes permanently red and rheumy.

He rests his head against the mirror and exhales. In the years he was with Emma he sometimes wondered idly what life would

be like if she weren't around; not in a morbid way, just prag-
matically, speculatively, because don't all lovers do this? Wonder
what he would be without her? Now the answer is in the mirror.
Loss has not endowed him with any kind of tragic grandeur,
it has just made him stupid and banal. Without her he is
without merit or virtue or purpose, a shabby, lonely, middle-
aged drunk, poisoned with regret and shame. An unwanted
memory rises up of that morning, of his own father and his
ex-wife undressing him and helping him into the bath. In two
weeks time he will be forty-one, and his father is helping him
into the bath. Why couldn't they just have taken him to hospital
to have his stomach pumped? There would have been more
dignity in that.

In the hallway he can hear his father talking to his sister,
shouting into the telephone. He sits on the edge of the bath. It
requires no effort to eavesdrop. In fact it's impossible not to
hear.

'He woke the neighbours, trying to kick his own door down.
They let him in . . . Sylvie found him on the floor . . . It seems
he had a bit too much to drink that's all . . . just cuts and
bruises . . . Absolutely no idea. Anyway, we've cleaned him up.
He'll be fine in the morning. Do you want to come and say
hello?' In the bathroom, Dexter prays for a 'no', but his sister
clearly can see no pleasure in it either. 'Fair enough, Cassie.
Maybe give him a call in the morning will you?'

When he is sure his father has gone, Dexter steps out into
the hall and pads towards the kitchen. He drinks warm tap water
from a dusty pint glass and looks out at the garden in the evening
sun. The swimming pool is drained and covered with a sagging
blue tarpaulin, the tennis court scrappy and overgrown. The
kitchen, too, has a musty smell. The large family house has
gradually closed down room by room, so that now his father
occupies just the kitchen, living room and his bedroom, but even
so it is still too large for him. His sister says that sometimes he
sleeps on the sofa. Concerned, they have talked to him about

moving out, buying somewhere more manageable, a little flat in Oxford or London, but his father won't hear of it. 'I intend to die in my own house if you don't mind,' he says, a line of argument that's too emotive to counter.

'Feeling better then?' His father stands behind him.

'A little.'

'What's that?' He nods towards Dexter's pint glass. 'Gin, is it?'

'Just water.'

'Glad to hear it. I thought we'd have soup tonight, seeing as how it's a special occasion. Could you manage a tin of soup?'

'I think so.'

He holds two tins in the air. 'Mulligatawny or Cream of Chicken?'

So the two men shuffle around the large musty kitchen, a pair of widowers making more mess than is really necessary in warming two cans of soup. Since living alone, his father's diet has reverted to that of an ambitious boy-scout: baked beans, sausages, fish-fingers; he has even been known to make himself a saucepan of jelly.

The phone rings in the hall. 'Get that will you?' says his father, mashing butter onto sliced white bread. Dexter hesitates. 'It won't bite you, Dexter.'

He goes into the hall and picks up. It's Sylvie. Dexter settles on the stairs. His ex-wife lives alone now, the relationship with Callum having finally combusted just before Christmas time. Their mutual unhappiness, and a desire to protect Jasmine from this, has made them strangely close and for the first time since they got married they are almost friends.

'How are you feeling?'

'Oh, you know. Bit embarrassed. Sorry about that.'

'That's alright.'

'I seem to remember you and Dad putting me in the bath.'

Sylvie laughs. 'He was very unfazed by it all. "He's got nothing I've not seen before!"'

Dexter smiles and winces at the same time. 'Is Jasmine okay?'

'I think so. She's fine. She will be fine. I told her you had food poisoning.'

'I'll make it up to her. Like I said, I'm sorry.'

'These things happen. Just don't ever, ever do it again, will you?'

Dexter makes a noise that sounds like 'No, well, we'll see . . .' There is a silence. 'I should go, Sylvie. Soup's burning.'

'See you Saturday night, yes?'

'See you then. Love to Jasmine. And I'm sorry.'

He hears her adjust the receiver. 'We do all love you, Dexter.'

'No reason why you should,' he mumbles, embarrassed.

'No, maybe not. But we do.'

After a moment, he replaces the phone then joins his father in front of the television, drinking lemon barley water that has been diluted in homeopathic proportions. The soup is eaten off trays with specially padded undersides for comfortable laptop eating – a recent innovation that Dexter finds vaguely depressing, perhaps because it's the kind of thing his mother would have never let in the house. The soup itself is as hot as lava, stinging his cut lip as he sips it, and the sliced white bread his father buys is imperfectly buttered, torn and mashed into a putty-coloured pulp. But it is, bizarrely, delicious, the thick butter melting into the sticky soup, and they eat it while watching *EastEnders*, another recent compulsion of his father's. As the credits roll, he places the padded tray on the floor, presses the mute button on the remote control and turns to look at Dexter.

'So is this to become an annual festival, do you think?'

'I don't know yet.' Some time passes, and his father turns back to the muted TV. 'I'm sorry,' says Dexter.

'What for?'

'Well, you had to put me in the bath, so . . .'

'Yes I'd rather not do *that* again if you don't mind.' With the TV still muted, he starts to flick through the TV channels. 'Anyway, you'll be doing it for me soon enough.'

'God, I hope not,' says Dexter. 'Can't Cassie do it?'

His father smiles and glances back at him. 'I really don't want to have a heart-to-heart. Do you?'

'I'd rather not.'

'Well let's not then. Let's just say that I think the best thing you could do is try and live your life as if Emma were still here. Don't you think that would be best?'

'I don't know if I can.'

'Well you'll have to try.' He reaches for the remote control. 'What do you think I've been doing for the last ten years?' On the TV, his father finds what he has been looking for, and sinks further into his chair. 'Ah, *The Bill*.'

They sit and watch the TV in the light of the summer evening, in the room full of family photographs and to his embarrassment Dexter finds that he is crying once again, very quietly. Discreetly, he puts his hand to his eyes, but his father can hear the catching of his breath and glances over.

'Everything alright there?'

'Sorry,' says Dexter.

'Not my cooking, is it?'

Dexter laughs and sniffs. 'Still a bit drunk, I think.'

'It's alright,' says his father, turning back to the TV. '*Silent Witness* is on at nine.'

CHAPTER TWENTY-ONE
Arthur's Seat

FRIDAY 15 JULY 1988

Rankeillor Street, Edinburgh

Dexter showered in the shabby mildewed bathroom, then put on last night's shirt. It smelt of sweat and cigarettes so he put the suit jacket on too, to hold the odour in, then squeezed toothpaste onto his index finger and polished his teeth.

He joined Emma Morley and Tilly Killick in the kitchen, beneath a greasy wall-sized poster of Truffaut's *Jules et Jim*. Jeanne Moreau stood over them laughing as they ate an awkward, bowel-tweaking breakfast: brown toast with soya spread, some kind of aggregate muesli. Because this was a special occasion, Emma had washed out the continental-style espresso maker, the kind that always seemed to be mouldy inside, and after the first cup of oily black liquid Dexter began to feel a little bit better. He sat quietly, listening to the flatmates' self-consciously larky banter, their big spectacles worn as a badge of honour, and had the vague feeling that he had been taken hostage by a rogue fringe theatre company. Perhaps it had been a mistake to stay on after all. Certainly it had been a mistake to leave the bedroom. How was he supposed to kiss her with Tilly Killick sitting there, babbling on?

For her part, Emma found herself increasingly maddened by Tilly's presence. Did she have no discretion at all? Sat there with her chin cupped in her hand, playing with her hair and sucking her teaspoon. Emma had made the mistake of showering with an untested bottle of Body Shop strawberry gel and was painfully aware of smelling like a fruit yoghurt. She badly wanted to go and rinse it off, but didn't dare leave Dexter alone with Tilly, her dressing-gown gaping open on her best underwear, a red plaid all-in-one body from Knickerbox; she could be so *obvious* sometimes.

To go back to bed, that's what Emma really wanted, and to be partially dressed once again, but it was too late for that now, they were all too sober. Keen to get away, she wondered aloud what they should do today, the first day of their graduate lives.

'We could go to the pub?' suggested Dexter, weakly. Emma groaned with nausea.

'Go for lunch?' said Tilly.

'No money.'

'The movies then?' offered Dexter. 'I'll pay . . .'

'Not today. It's lovely out, we should be outside.'

'Okay, the beach, North Berwick.'

Emma shrank from the idea. It would mean wearing a swimming costume in front of him, and she wasn't strong enough for that kind of agony. 'I'm useless on the beach.'

'Okay then, what?'

'We could climb up Arthur's Seat?' said Tilly.

'Never done it,' said Dexter casually. Both girls looked at him, open-mouthed.

'You've never climbed Arthur's Seat?'

'Nope.'

'You've been in Edinburgh four years, and you've never? . . .'

'I've been busy!'

'Doing what?' said Tilly.

'Studying anthropology,' said Emma and the two girls cackled unkindly.

'Well we must go!' said Tilly, and a brief silence followed as Emma's eyes blazed a warning.

'I haven't got proper shoes,' said Dexter.

'It's not K2, it's just a big hill.'

'I can't climb it in brogues!'

'You'll be fine, it's not hard.'

'In my suit?'

'Yes! We could take a picnic!' But Emma could feel the enthusiasm starting to slip away, until Tilly finally spoke:

'Actually, you two should probably go without me. I've got . . . stuff to do.'

Emma's eyes flicked towards her, catching the end of a wink, and Emma thought she might very easily lean across and kiss her.

'Alright then. Let's do it!' said Dexter, brightening too, and fifteen minutes later they were stepping outside into the hazy July morning, the Salisbury Crags looming over them at the end of Rankeillor Street.

'We're really climbing up there?'

'A child could do it. Trust me.'

In the supermarket on Nicolson Street they shopped for a picnic, both a little uncomfortable in the strangely domestic rite of sharing a shopping basket, both self-conscious about their choices; were olives too fancy? Was it funny to take Irn Bru, ostentatious to buy champagne? They loaded Emma's army surplus rucksack with supplies – Emma's joky, Dexter's would-be sophisticated – then doubled back towards Holyrood Park and began the ascent along the base of the escarpment.

Dexter tagged along behind, sweaty in his suit and slippery shoes, a cigarette held between his lips, his head thumping with red wine and the morning's coffee. He was vaguely aware that he should be taking in the splendour of the view, but instead his eyes were fixed on Emma's bottom in faded blue 501s, cinched in tight at the waist, above black high-top Converse All-Stars.

'You're very nimble.'

'Like a mountain goat, me. I used to go hiking a lot at home, when I was in my Cathy phase. Out on the wild and windy moors. Dead soulful I was. "I cannot live without my life! I cannot live without my soul!"'

Half-listening, Dexter assumed that she was quoting something, but was distracted by a strip of dark sweat forming between her shoulder blades, a glimpse of a bra-strap at the slipped neck of her t-shirt. He had another momentary image of last night in bed, but she looked round at him as if warning him off the thought.

'How you doing there, Sherpa Tenzing?'

'I'm fine. I wish there was some grip on these shoes, that's all.' She was laughing now. 'What's funny?'

'Just I've never seen anyone smoke and hike at the same time.'

'What else am I meant to be doing?'

'Looking at the view!'

'A view's a view's a view.'

'Is that Shelley or Wordsworth?'

He sighed and stopped, his hands on his knees. 'Okay. Fine. I'll look at the view.' Turning, he saw the council estates, the spires and crenellations of the Old Town beneath the great grey hulk of the castle, then beyond that in the haze of the warm day, the Firth of Forth. Dexter had a general policy of not appearing impressed by anything, but it really was a magnificent view, the one he recognised from picture postcards. He wondered why he had never seen it before.

'Very nice,' he allowed himself and they kept climbing towards the summit, wondering what would happen when they got there.

CHAPTER TWENTY-TWO
The Second Anniversary
Unpacking

SATURDAY 15 JULY 2006

North London and Edinburgh

At six-fifteen that evening he pulls down the metal shutters of the Belleville Café and snaps the heavy padlock into place. Nearby Maddy waits for him, and he takes her hand as they walk together towards the tube station.

Finally, finally he has moved house, recently taking possession of a pleasant but unshowy three-bedroomed maisonette in Gospel Oak. Maddy lives in Stockwell, some distance away at the other end of the Northern Line, and sometimes it makes sense for her to stay over. But not tonight; there has been no melodrama or portentousness about it, but tonight he would like to have some time by himself. He has set himself a task tonight, and he can only do it alone.

They say goodbye outside Tufnell Park tube. Maddy is a little taller than him, with long straight black hair, and she has to stoop a little to kiss him goodbye. 'Call me later, if you want.'

'I might do.'

'And if you change your mind, and you want me to come up—'

'I'll be fine.'

'Alright then. See you tomorrow maybe?'

'I'll call you.'

They kiss goodnight again, briefly but fondly, and he carries on walking down the hill towards his new home.

He has been seeing Maddy, the café's manager, for two months now. They have yet to tell the other staff officially, but suspect they probably know already. It has not been a passionate affair, more a gradual acceptance over the last year of an inevitable situation. To Dexter, it has all been a little too practical and matter-of-fact, and he is privately a little uncomfortable about the transition that Maddy has made from confidante to lover; it casts a shadow over the relationship, that it should have originated in such gloom.

But it's true they get on very well, everyone says so, and Maddy is kind and sensible and attractive, long and slim, and a little awkward. She has ambitions to be a painter, and Dexter thinks she is good; small canvases hang in the café, and are sold occasionally. She is also ten years younger than he is – he imagines Emma rolling her eyes at this – but she is wise and smart and has been through her own share of unhappiness: an early divorce, various unhappy relationships. She is quiet, self-contained and thoughtful and has a melancholy air about her, which suits him at present. She is also compassionate and fiercely loyal; it was Maddy who saved the business during the time when he was drinking the profits and not turning up, and he is grateful to her for this. Jasmine likes her. They get on well enough, for the moment at least.

It's a pleasant Saturday evening and he walks on alone through residential back streets until he reaches the flat, the basement and ground floor of a red-brick mansion block not too far from Hampstead Heath. The flat retains the smell and the wallpaper of the elderly couple who lived there before, and he has only unpacked a few essentials: the TV and DVD, the stereo. It's a frumpy kind of place, at the moment anyway, with its dado rails and appalling bathroom and its many other small rooms, but Sylvie insists that it has great potential, once they've knocked the walls through and sanded the floors. There's a great room for when Jasmine comes to stay, and a garden too. A garden. For a while he joked about paving it over, but has now decided that he is going to learn to garden, and has bought a book on the subject. Somewhere deep in his consciousness he has become aware of the concept of the shed. Soon, it will be golf and pyjamas in bed.

Once inside and past the boxes that clutter the hall, he takes a shower then goes into the kitchen and orders Thai food to be delivered. In the living room he lies on the sofa and begins to compile a mental list of the things he must do before he can begin his task.

For a small, diverse circle of people, a previously innocuous date has taken on a melancholy weight, and there are certain calls that must now be made. He starts with Sue and Jim, Emma's parents in Leeds. The conversation is pleasant and straightforward enough and he tells them about the business, how Jasmine is getting on at school, repeating the conversation twice for both the mother and the father. 'Well, that's all the news really,' he tells Sue. 'Just to say, you know, thinking of you today, and hope you're alright.'

'You too, Dexter. Look after yourself, won't you?' she says, her voice unsteady, then hangs up. Dexter continues to work through the list, speaking to his sister, his father, his ex-wife, his daughter. The conversations are brief, ostentatiously light-hearted and don't mention the significance of the day, but the subtext is always the same: 'I'm fine.' He phones Tilly Killick, but she is mawkish and over-emotional: 'But how are you *really* sweetheart? I mean, *really*? Are you by yourself? Are you *okay* by yourself? Do you want us to come over?' Irritated, he re-assures her, then ends the call as quickly and politely as he can. He calls Ian Whitehead in Taunton, but he's putting the kids to bed, the little sods, and it's not a good time. Ian promises he'll call back in the week and maybe even come down and see him sometime, and Dexter says that it's a great idea in full knowledge that it will never happen. There's a general sense, as in all the calls, that the worst of the storm has passed. Dexter will probably never speak to Ian Whitehead again and this is fine too, for both of them.

He eats supper with the television on, hopping channels and restricting himself to the solitary beer that came free with the delivery. But there's something saddening about eating alone, hunched over on the sofa in this strange house and for the first time that day he feels a rush of despair and loneliness. These days grief seems like walking on a frozen river; most of the time he feels safe enough, but there is always that danger that he will plunge through. Now he hears the ice creak beneath him, and so intense and panicking is the sensation that he has to stand for a moment, press his hands to his face and catch his breath. He exhales slowly through his fingers, then rushes into the kitchen and throws dirty plates into the sink with a clatter. He has a sudden overwhelming need to drink, and to keep on drinking. He finds his phone.

'What's up?' says Maddy, concern in her voice.

'Just a little panic that's all.'

'Are you sure you don't want me to come up?'

'I'm fine now.'

'I can get a taxi? I can be with you in—'

'No, really. I'd rather be alone.' He finds that the sound of her voice is enough to calm him, and he reassures her once more then says goodnight. When he is sure that there is no conceivable reason for anyone to call him back, he turns the phone off, draws the blinds, goes upstairs and begins.

The spare bedroom contains nothing but a mattress, an open suitcase and seven or eight cardboard boxes, two of which are labelled 'Emma 1' and 'Emma 2' in her own handwriting in thick black marker pen. The last of Emma's possessions from his flat, the boxes contain notebooks, letters, wallets of photographs, and he carries them down to the living room and spends the rest of the evening unpacking them, sorting the meaningless ephemera – ancient bank statements, receipts, old take-away menus, all of which he stuffs into a black bin-liner – from the stuff he will send to her parents, and the items he would like to keep for himself.

The process takes some time, but is carried out in an entirely dry-eyed, pragmatic way, and he stops only occasionally. He avoids reading the journals and notebooks with their scraps of youthful poetry and plays. It seems unfair – he imagines Emma wincing over his shoulder or scrambling to knock them from his hand – and instead he concentrates on the letters and photographs.

The way the material has been packed means that he works through it in reverse chronological order, digging back through the strata, starting with their years together as a couple, back through the Nineties and eventually, at the bottom of box 2, into the Eighties. First there are dummy covers from the 'Julie Criscoll' novels, correspondence with her editor Marsha, press cuttings. The next layer reveals postcards and photos of Paris, including a snap of the famous Jean-Pierre Dusollier, dark-skinned and very handsome, the one that got away. In an envelope with Metro tickets, folded menus, a rental agreement in French, he stumbles on something that's so startling and affecting that he almost drops it on the floor.

It's a Polaroid, taken in Paris during that summer, of Emma lying naked on a bed, legs crossed at the ankle, her arms stretched languidly above her head. The photo was taken on a drunken, amorous evening after watching *Titanic* in French on a black and white TV, and even though he found the photograph beautiful, she had snatched it from him and insisted that she would destroy it. The fact that she kept the Polaroid and secreted it away should please him, suggesting as it does that Emma liked the photo more than she let on. But it also slams him up against her absence once more, and he has to take a moment to catch his breath. He places the Polaroid back in the envelope and sits in silence to gather himself. The ice creaks beneath him.

He continues. From the late Nineties he finds an assortment of birth announcements, wedding invitations and orders of service, an over-sized farewell card from the staff and pupils of Cromwell Road Comprehensive School and, stuffed in the same envelope, a series of letters from someone called Phil which are so sexually fixated and pleading that he quickly folds them up and stuffs them back into the envelope. There are flyers from Ian's comedy-improv nights and some tedious paperwork from solicitors concerning the purchase of the flat in E17. He finds a selection of witless picture postcards that he sent while travelling in the early Nineties – 'Amsterdam is MAD', 'Dublin ROCKS'. He is reminded of the letters he got in return, wonderful little packets of pale blue air-mail paper that he re-reads occasionally, and is embarrassed afresh by his callow twenty-four-year-old self: 'VENICE COMPLETELY FLOODED!!!!'. There's a copy of the photostat programme of 'Cruel Cargo – a play for young people by Emma Morley and Gary Cheadle' and then old essays, dissertations on 'Donne's Women' and 'Eliot and Fascism', a pile of postcard reproductions marked with the tiny holes from the pin-boards of student houses. He finds a cardboard tube and in it, rolled up tight, Emma's graduation certificate, untouched, he imagines, for nearly twenty years. He verifies this by looking at the date – 14 July 1988. Eighteen years ago yesterday.

In a torn paper wallet he finds the graduation photographs and flicks through them without any great nostalgia. Because the photos were taken by Emma herself she barely features in them, and he has forgotten many of the other students anyway; she was part of a different crowd in those days. Still, he is struck by the youth of the faces and also by the fact that Tilly Killick has the power to annoy him, even in a photo at a distance of nineteen years. A snap of Callum O'Neill, skinny and self-satisfied, is swiftly torn in two and plunged deep into the bin-bag.

But at some point she must have handed the camera to Tilly, because there is finally a sequence of Emma by herself, pulling mock-heroic faces in mortar board and gown, her spectacles perched bookishly on the end of her nose. He smiles, then gives a groan of amused shame as he finds a photo of his old self.

He is pulling an absurd male model's face, sucking in his

cheekbones and pouting while Emma wraps one arm around his neck, her face close to his, eyes wide, one hand pressed to her cheek as if star-struck. After this photo was taken they had gone to the graduation tea-party, the pub and then to the party at that house. He can't remember who lived there, only that the house was packed and virtually destroyed, the party spilling out onto the street and the back garden. Hiding from the chaos, they had found a spot on a sofa in the living room together and stayed rooted there all evening. This was where he had kissed her for the first time. He examines the graduation photo once again, Emma behind thick black frames, her hair a bottle red and badly cut, a little plumper in the face than he remembers her now, mouth split in a wide smile, her cheek pressed to his. He puts the photo to one side, and looks at the next.

It is the morning after. They are sitting together on a mountain-side, Emma in 501s cinched at the waist and black Converse All-Stars, Dexter a little way off in the white shirt and black suit that he had worn the day before.

The summit of Arthur's Seat was disappointingly crowded with tourists and other graduating students, all whey-faced and shaky from last night's celebrations. Dex and Em raised their hands sheepishly in greeting to a few acquaintances, but tried to keep their distance, keen to avoid gossip even now that it was too late.

They wandered idly around the scrappy rust-coloured plateau, taking in the view from all angles. Standing at the stone column that marked the summit, they made the remarks they were obliged to make in such situations: how far they had walked and how they could see their house from here. The column itself had been scratched with graffiti: private jokes, 'DG Was Here', 'Scotland Forever', 'Thatcher Out'.

'We should carve our initials,' suggested Dexter, weakly.

'What, "Dex 4 Em"?'

'4 Ever.'

Emma sniffed doubtfully and examined the most striking graf-fiti, a large penis drawn with indelible green ink. 'Imagine climbing all this way just to draw that. Did he bring the pen with him, d'you think? "It's a lovely view, natural beauty and all that, but what this spot really needs is a massive cock and balls."'

Dexter laughed mechanically, but once again, self-consciousness was starting to creep in; now they were here it felt like a mistake, and independently they wondered if they should skip the picnic and simply clamber back down and head home. But neither of them was quite prepared to suggest this, and instead they found a hollow a short way from the summit where the rocks seemed to provide some natural furniture, and they settled here and unpacked the rucksack.

Dexter popped the champagne, which was warm now and foamed forlornly over his hand and onto the heather. They took it in turns to swig but there was little sense of celebration and after a brief silence Emma resorted once more to remarking on the view. 'Very nice.'

'Hm.'

'No sign of rain!'

'Hm?'

'St Swithin's Day, you said it was. "If on Swithin's Day it do rain . . ."'

'Absolutely. No sign of rain.'

The weather; she was talking about the weather. Embarrassed by her own banality, she lapsed into silence before trying a more direct approach. 'So, how are you feeling, Dex?'

'Bit rough.'

'No, I mean about last night? Me and you.'

He glanced at her and wondered what he was expected to say. He was wary of a confrontation with no immediate means of escape, save hurling himself from the mountainside. 'I feel fine! How about you? How are you feeling about last night?'

'Fine. Bit embarrassed, I s'pose, harking on like that, you

know, 'bout the future. Changing the world, and all that. Bit corny in the harsh light of day. Must have sounded corny anyway, specially to someone with no principles or ideals—'

'Hey, I have ideals!'

'Sleeping with two women at the same time is not an ideal.'

'Well, you *say* that . . .'

She tutted. 'You can be really seedy sometimes, d'you know that?'

'I can't help it.'

'Well you should try.' She grabbed a handful of heather and tossed it limply towards him. 'You're much nicer when you do. Anyway. The point is, I didn't mean to sound such a drip.'

'You didn't. It was interesting. And like I said, I had a really nice time. It's just a shame the timing's not better.'

He was giving her an annoying little consolatory smile and she wrinkled her nose in irritation. 'What, you mean otherwise we'd be *boy*friend and *girl*friend?'

'I don't know. Who knows?'

He held out his hand, palm upwards, and she looked at it for a moment with distaste, then sighed and took it resignedly, and they sat there, their hands linked uselessly, feeling idiotic until their arms got tired and they both let go. The best solution, he decided, was to feign sleep until it was time to go, and with this in mind he removed his jacket, padded it into a pillow and closed his eyes against the sun. His body ached, the alcohol pulsed in his head, and he began to feel himself slipping into unconsciousness, when she spoke.

'Can I say something? Just to put your mind at rest?'

Groggily he opened his eyes. She was sitting with her legs raised to her chest, arms wrapped round them, chin resting on her knees. 'Go on.'

She inhaled, as if gathering her thoughts, then spoke.

'I don't want you thinking that I'm bothered or anything. I mean, what happened last night, I know it was only 'cause you were drunk . . .'

421

'Emma . . .'

'Let me finish, will you? But I had a really nice time anyway. I've not done a lot of . . . that kind of thing. I've not made a study of it, not like you, but it was nice. I think you're nice, Dex, when you want to be. And maybe it's just bad timing or whatever, but I think you should head off to China or India or wherever and find yourself, and I'll get on quite happily with things here. I don't want to come with you, I don't want weekly postcards, I don't even want your phone number. I don't want to get married and have your babies either, or even have another fling. We had one really, really nice night together, that's all. I'll always remember it. And if we bump into each other sometime in the future at a party or something, then that's fine too. We'll just have a friendly chat. We won't be embarrassed 'cause you've had your hand down my top and there'll be no awkwardness and we'll be, whatever, "cool" about it, alright? Me and you. We'll just be . . . friends. Agreed?'

'Alright. Agreed.'

'Right, that's that then. Now—' She reached for her rucksack and fumbled around inside, producing a battered Pentax SLR.

'What are you doing?'

'What does it look like? Taking a photo. Something to remember you by.'

'I look terrible,' he said, already adjusting his hair.

'Don't give me that, you love it . . .'

He lit a cigarette for a prop. 'What do you want a photo for?'

'For when you're famous.' She was balancing the camera on a boulder now, framing the shot through the viewfinder. 'I want to be able to say to my kids, see him there, he once stuck his hand up Mummy's skirt in a crowded room.'

'You started it!'

'No, you started it, pal!' She cocked the clockwork timer, scrubbed at her own hair with her fingertips, while Dexter set the cigarette in one side of his mouth and then the other. 'Right – thirty seconds.'

Dexter refined his pose. 'What do we say? "Cheese"?'

'Not "cheese". Let's say "one-night stand!"' She pressed the button and the camera began to whirr. 'Or "promiscuous!"' She clambered over the rocks.

'Or "thieves that pass in the night".'

'Thieves don't pass in the night. That's ships.'

'What do thieves do?'

'Thieves are thick.'

'What's wrong with just "cheese"?'

'Let's not say anything. Let's just smile, look natural. Look young and full of high ideals and hope or something. Ready?'

'Ready.'

'Okay then, smile and . . .'

CHAPTER TWENTY-THREE

The Third Anniversary
Last Summer

SUNDAY 15 JULY 2007

Edinburgh

'Ring-ring. Ring-ring.'

He is woken by his daughter's index finger pressing his nose as if it were a doorbell.

'Ring-ring. Ring-ring. Who's at the door? Jasmine's at the door!!'

'What are you doing, Jas?'

'I'm waking you up. Ring-ring.' Her thumb is in his eye now, pulling back the eyelid. 'Wake up, lazybones!'

'What time is it?'

'Daytime!'

Beside him in the hotel bed, Maddy reaches for her watch. 'Half past six,' she groans into the pillow and Jasmine laughs malevolently. Dexter opens both eyes, and sees her face on the pillow next to him, her nose inches away. 'Haven't you got books to read or dolls to play with or something?'

'Nope.'

'Go and colour something in, will you?'

'I'm hungry. Can we have room service? What time is the swimming pool open?'

The Edinburgh hotel is plush, traditional and grand, oak panels and porcelain baths. His parents stayed here once, for his graduation, and it's a little more old-fashioned and expensive.than he would like, but he thought that if they're going to do this, they should do it in some style. They are staying for two nights – Dexter, Maddy and Jasmine – before hiring a car and driving across to a holiday cottage near Loch Lomond. Glasgow is nearer of course, but Dexter hasn't been to Edinburgh for fifteen years, not since a debauched weekend when he presented a TV show from the Festival. All of that seems a long, long time ago now, another lifetime. Today he has a fatherly notion that he might show his daughter round the city. Maddy, aware of the date, has decided to leave them to it.

'You're sure you don't mind?' he asks her in the privacy of the bathroom.

'Of course not. I'll go to the gallery, see that exhibition.'

'I just want to show her some places. Memory Lane. No reason why you should suffer too.'

'Like I said, I really don't mind.'

He regards her carefully. 'And you don't think I'm nuts?'

She gives a faint smile. 'No, I don't think you're nuts.'

'You don't think it's ghoulish or weird?'

'Not at all.' If she does mind, she certainly isn't showing it. He kisses her lightly on the neck. 'You must do whatever you want,' she says.

The notion that it might rain for forty consecutive days had once seemed far-fetched, but not this year. All over the country it has poured daily for weeks now, high streets disappearing under flood water, and the summer has seemed so unique that it might almost be a new kind of season. A monsoon season, but as they step out onto the street, the day is still bright with high cloud, dry for the moment at least. They make plans for lunch with Maddy, and go their separate ways.

The hotel is in the Old Town, just off the Royal Mile, and Dexter takes Jasmine on the standard atmospheric tour, down alleyways and secret stairways until they find themselves on Nicolson Street, heading south out of the city centre. He remembers the street as hectic and hazy with bus fumes, but on a Sunday morning it is quiet and a little sad, and Jasmine is starting to get restless and bored now that they have left the tourist trail. Feeling her hand go heavy in his, Dexter keeps on walking. He has found the old address on one of Emma's letters and soon spots a sign. Rankeillor Street. They turn into the quiet residential road.

'Where are we going?'

'I'm looking for somewhere. Number seventeen.' They are outside now. Dexter peers up at the third-floor window, its curtains drawn, blank and nondescript.

'You see that flat there? That's where Emma used to live when we were at University together. In fact that's sort of where we met.' Jasmine looks up obediently, but there is nothing to distinguish the unremarkable terraced house from those on either side, and Dexter starts to question the wisdom of this expedition. It's indulgent, morbid and sentimental; what was he expecting to find? There is nothing here that he recalls, and the pleasure gained from nostalgia is slight and futile. For a moment he contemplates abandoning the tour, phoning Maddy and arranging to meet a little earlier, but Jasmine is pointing to the end of the street, the granite escarpment that looms incongruously over the estate below.

'What's that?'

'It's Salisbury Crags. Leads up to Arthur's Seat.'

'There's people up there!'

'You can climb it. It isn't hard. What do you think? Shall we try? Do you think you can do it?'

They head for Holyrood Park. Depressingly, his seven-and-a-half-year-old daughter clambers up the mountain path with far more energy than her father, pausing only intermittently to turn back and laugh at him, wheezing and sweating below.

'It's because I've got no grip on my shoes,' he protests, and they keep climbing, leaving the main path and clambering over rocks before finally stumbling onto the scrubby rust-coloured plateau at the top of Arthur's Seat. There they find the stone column that marks the highest point, and he inspects the scratchings and scribbles, half hoping to see his own initials there: 'Fight Faschism' 'Alex M 5/5/07' 'Fiona 4ever'.

To distract Jasmine from the lewder graffiti, he lifts her up and sits her on the column, one arm round her waist, her legs dangling as he points out the landmarks. 'That's the castle, near the hotel. There's the station. That's the Firth of Forth, leading out into the North Sea. Norway's over there somewhere. Leith, and that's the New Town, where I used to live. Twenty years ago now, Jas. Last century. And over there, with the tower, that's Calton Hill. We could climb that too, if you liked, this afternoon.'

'Aren't you too tired?' she asks, sardonically.

'Me? You're kidding. I'm a natural athlete.' Jasmine wheezes in imitation, one fist clutching at her chest. 'Comedian.' He lifts her off the pillar, hands tucked in her armpits, and makes to throw her off the mountainside before swinging her, screaming and laughing, under his arm.

They walk a little way from the summit and find a natural hollow nearby that overlooks the city. He lies with his hands behind his head, while Jasmine sits beside him eating salt and vinegar crisps and drinking her carton of juice with great concentration. The sun is warm on his face, but the early start to the day is starting to take its toll and within minutes he feels sleep creeping up on him.

'Did Emma come here too?' asks Jasmine.

Dexter opens his eyes and raises himself up onto his elbows.

'She did. We came here together. I've got a photo of us at home. I'll show you. Back when Dad was skinny.'

Jasmine puffs her cheeks out at him, then sets about licking the salt from her fingers. 'Do you miss her?'

'Who? Emma? Of course. Every day. She was my best friend.' He nudges her with his elbow. 'Why, do you?'

Jasmine frowns as she recalls. 'I think so. I was only four, I don't remember her that well, only when I look at pictures. I remember the wedding. She was nice though, wasn't she?'

'Very nice.'

'So who's your best friend now?'

He places a hand on the back of his daughter's neck, fitting his thumb into the hollow there. 'You, of course. Why, who's your best friend?'

Her forehead creases in serious thought. 'I think it's probably Phoebe,' she says, then sucks on the straw of her empty juice carton so that it gurgles rudely.

'You can go off people you know,' he says, and she laughs with the straw pinched between her lips. 'Come here,' he growls, making a grab and pulling her backwards so that she lies in the crook of his arm, her head on his shoulder. In a moment she is still and Dexter closes his eyes once again and feels the warmth of the mid-morning sun on his eyelids.

'Beautiful day,' he mumbles, 'No rain today. Not yet,' and once again sleep starts to creep up on him. He can smell the hotel shampoo on Jasmine's hair, feel her breath on his neck, salt and vinegar, slow and regular, as he drifts off into slumber.

He is unconscious for perhaps two minutes before her bony elbows are jabbing into his chest.

'Dad? I'm bored. Can we go now, please?'

Emma and Dexter spent the rest of that afternoon on the hillside laughing and talking, offering up information about themselves: what their parents did, how many siblings they had, telling favoured anecdotes. In the middle of the afternoon, as if by mutual agreement, they both fell asleep, lying chastely in parallel until at five Dexter woke with a start, and they gathered together the empty bottles and the remains of the picnic and started to head woozily down the hill towards the city and home.

As they approached the park exit, Emma became aware that they would soon be saying goodbye, and that there was every chance that they would never see each other again. There might be parties, she supposed, but they both knew a different crowd, and besides he would be off travelling soon. Even if they did see each other it would be fleeting and formal, and he would soon forget everything that had happened in that small rented room in the early hours of the morning. As they stumbled down the hill she began to feel regret creeping up on her, and realised she didn't want him to go yet. A second night. She wanted one more night at least, so that they could finish what they had started. How might she say that? She couldn't of course. Faint-hearted as usual, she had left it too late. In the future, I'll be braver, she told herself. In the future, I will always speak my mind, eloquently, passionately. They were at the park gates now, the place where she should probably say goodbye.

She kicked at the gravel footpath and scratched her head. 'Well, I suppose I'd better . . .'

Dexter took her by the hand. 'So, listen. Why don't you come for a drink?'

She instructed her features to show no delight. 'What, now?'

'Or at least walk back with me?'

'Aren't your mum and dad coming round?'

'Not 'til this evening. It's only half-five.'

He was rubbing the knuckle of her forefinger with his thumb. She made a pretence of making a decision. 'Go on then,' she shrugged, indifferent, and he let go of her hand and started walking.

As they crossed the railway at North Bridge and passed into the Georgian New Town, a plan was forming in his head. He would get home by six, immediately call his parents at their hotel and arrange to meet them at the restaurant at eight rather than at the flat at six-thirty. This would give him nearly two whole hours. Callum would be with his girlfriend, they'd have the flat to themselves for two whole hours, and he would be able to kiss her again. The high-ceilinged white-walled rooms were empty save for his suitcases and a few pieces of furniture, the mattress in his bedroom, the old chaise-longue. A couple of dust-sheets and it would look like the set of a Russian play. He knew enough about Emma to know that she would be a sucker for that, and he would almost certainly be able to kiss her, even sober. Whatever happened between them in the future, whatever rows and repercussions loomed, he knew that he very much wanted to kiss her now. The walk would take another fifteen minutes. He found himself slightly breathless. They should have got a cab.

Perhaps she had the same idea because they really were walking very fast as they headed down the steep incline of Dundas Street, their elbows occasionally brushing against each other, the Forth hazy in the distance. After all these years she was still elated by the sight of the iron-blue river in between the terraces of fine Georgian houses. 'I might have known you'd live round here,' she said, disapproving but envious, and as she spoke she found herself short of breath. She was going back to his well-appointed flat, they were going to do it, and she was embarrassed to find her neck flushing pink in anticipation. She ran her tongue over her teeth, attempting an ineffectual polish. Did she need to brush her teeth? Champagne always made her breath smell. Should they stop for chewing gum? Or condoms, would Dexter have condoms? Of course he would; it was like asking if he had shoes. But should she brush her teeth or should she just throw herself at him as the door closed? She tried to recall what underwear she was wearing, then remembered that it was her special mountain-climbing underwear. Too late to worry about that; they had turned into Fettes Row.

'Not far now,' he said and smiled, and she smiled too, and laughed, reaching for his hand, acknowledging what was about to happen. They were almost running now. He said he lived at number thirty-five, and she found herself counting down in her head. Seventy-five, seventy-three, seventy-one. Nearly there. Her chest was tightening, she felt sick. Forty-seven, forty-five, forty-three. There was a stitch in her side and an electric tingle in her fingertips and now he was pulling on her hand and they were both laughing as they ran down the street. A car horn blared. Ignore it, keep going, whatever happens do not stop.

But a woman's voice was calling 'Dexter! Dexter!' and all the hope fell out of her. It felt like running into a wall.

Dexter's father's Jaguar was parked opposite number thirty-five, and his mother was stepping from the car and waving at him from across the street. He had never imagined that he could be less pleased to see his parents.

'There you are! We've been waiting for you!'

Emma noticed how Dexter dropped her hand, almost throwing it away from him as he crossed the street and embraced his mother. With a further spasm of irritation she noticed that Mrs Mayhew was extremely beautiful and stylishly dressed, the father less so, a tall, sombre, dishevelled man, clearly unhappy to have been kept waiting. The mother met Emma's eyes over her son's shoulder and gave an indulgent, consolatory smile, almost as if she knew. It was the look a duchess might give, finding her errant son kissing the housemaid.

After that, things happened faster than Dexter would have liked. Remembering the faked phone-call, he realised that he was bound to be caught in a lie unless he got them into the flat as quickly as possible, but his father was asking about parking, his mother wondering where he had *been* all day, and why he hadn't called, while Emma stood a little way off to one side, still the housemaid, deferential and superfluous, wondering how soon she could accept defeat and head home.

'I thought we told you, we'd be coming here at six—'

'Six-thirty actually.'

'I left a message this morning on your machine—'

'Mum, Dad – this is my friend Emma!'

'Are you sure that I can park here?' said his father.

'Pleased to meet you, Emma. Alison. You've caught the sun. Where have you two been all day?'

'—because if I get a parking ticket, Dexter—'

Dexter turned to Emma, eyes blazing an apology. 'So, do you want to come in for a drink?'

'Or dinner?' said Alison. 'Why don't you join us for dinner?'

Emma glanced at Dexter, who seemed wild-eyed with what she took to be shock at the idea. Or was it encouragement? Either way, she would say no. These people seemed nice enough, but it wasn't what she wanted, gate-crashing someone else's family occasion. They would be going somewhere swanky and she looked like a lumberjack and besides, really, what was the point? Sitting there gazing at Dexter while they asked what her parents did for a living, where she went to school. Already she could feel herself shrinking from this family's brash self-confidence, their showy affection for each other, their money and style and grace. She would become shy or, worse, drunk and neither would help her chances. Best give up. She managed a smile. 'Actually, I better head back.'

'Are you sure?' said Dexter, frowning now.

'Yeah, stuff to do. You go on. I'll see you around, maybe.'

'Oh. Okay,' he said, disappointed. If she had wanted to come in she could have, but '*see you around, maybe*'? He wondered if perhaps she wasn't that bothered about him after all. There was a silence. His father wandered off to peer at the parking meter once more.

Emma raised her hand. 'Bye then.'

'See you.'

She turned to Alison. 'Nice to meet you.'

'And you, Emily.'

'Emma.'

'Of course. Emma. Goodbye, Emma.'

'And—' She shrugged towards Dexter while his mother spectated. 'Well, have a nice life, I suppose.'

'And you. Have a nice life.'

She turned and started to walk away. The Mayhew family watched her go.

'Dexter, I'm sorry – did we interrupt something?'

'No. Not at all. Emma's just a friend.'

Smiling to herself, Alison Mayhew regarded her handsome son intently, then reached out and took the lapels of his suit in both hands, tugging them gently to settle the jacket on his shoulders.

'Dexter – weren't you wearing this yesterday?'

* * *

And so Emma Morley walked home in the evening light, trailing her disappointment behind her. The day was cooling off now, and she shivered as she felt something in the air, an unexpected shudder of anxiety that ran the length of her spine, and was so intense as to make her stop walking for a moment. Fear of the future, she thought. She found herself at the imposing junction of George Street and Hanover Street as all around her people hurried home from work or out to meet friends or lovers, all with a sense of purpose and direction. And here she was, twenty-two and clueless and sloping back to a dingy flat, defeated once again.

'What are you going to do with your life?' In one way or another it seemed that people had been asking her this forever; teachers, her parents, friends at three in the morning, but the question had never seemed this pressing and still she was no nearer an answer. The future rose up ahead of her, a succession of empty days, each more daunting and unknowable than the one before her. How would she ever fill them all?

She began walking again, south towards The Mound. 'Live each day as if it's your last', that was the conventional advice, but really, who had the energy for that? What if it rained or you felt a bit glandy? It just wasn't practical. Better by far to simply try and be good and courageous and bold and to make a difference. Not change the world exactly, but the bit around you. Go out there with your passion and your electric typewriter and work hard at . . . something. Change lives through art maybe. Cherish your friends, stay true to your principles, live passionately and fully and well. Experience new things. Love and be loved, if you ever get the chance.

That was her general theory, even if she hadn't made a very good start of it. With little more than a shrug she had said goodbye to someone she really liked, the first boy she had ever really cared for, and now she would have to accept the fact that she would probably never see him again. She had no phone number, no address, and even if she did, what was the point?

He hadn't asked for her number either, and she was too proud to be just another moony girl leaving unwanted messages. *Have a nice life* had been her last line. Was that really the best she could come up with?

She walked on. The castle was just coming into view when she heard the footsteps, the soles of smart shoes slapping hard onto the pavement behind, and even before she heard her name and turned she was smiling, because she knew that it would be him.

'I thought I'd lost you!' he said, slowing to a walk, red-faced and breathless, attempting to regain some nonchalance.

'No, I'm here.'

'Sorry about that.'

'No, really, it's fine.'

He stood with his hands on his knees, catching his breath. 'I wasn't expecting my parents 'til later, and then they turned up out of the blue, and I got distracted, and I suddenly realised . . . bear with me . . . I realised I didn't have any way to get in touch with you.'

'Oh. Okay.'

'So – look. I don't have a pen. Do you have a pen? You must have.'

She crouched and rooted in her rucksack amongst the litter of their picnic. *Find a pen, please have a pen, you must have a pen . . .*

'Hurrah! A pen!'

'Hurrah'? You shouted 'hurrah!', you idiot. Stay calm. Don't blow it now.

She rooted in her wallet for a scrap of paper, found a supermarket receipt, and handed it over, then dictated her number, her parents' number in Leeds, their address and her own address in Edinburgh with special emphasis on the correct postcode, and in return he wrote down his.

'This is me.' He handed her the precious scrap of paper. 'Call me or I'll call you, but one of us will call, yes? What I mean is it's not a competition. You don't lose if you phone first.'

'I understand.'

'I'm away in France until August, but then I'm back and I thought you might want to come down and stay maybe?'

'Stay with *you*?'

'Not for ever. For a weekend. At mine. My parents', I mean. Only if you want to.'

'Oh. Okay. Yes. Okay. Yes. Yes. Okay. Yes.'

'So. I should get back. Are you sure you don't want to come for a drink or something? Or dinner?'

'I don't think I should,' she said.

'No, I don't think you should either.' He looked relieved and she felt slighted once again. Why not? she thought. Was he embarrassed by her?

'Oh. Right. Why's that?'

'Because I think if you did I'd go a bit mad. With frustration, I mean. You sitting there. Because I wouldn't be able to do what I want to do.'

'Why? What do you want to do?' she asked, though she knew the answer. He put one hand lightly on the back of her neck, and simultaneously she placed one hand lightly on his hip, and they kissed in the street as all around them people hurried home in the summer light, and it was the sweetest kiss that either of them would ever know.

This is where it all begins. Everything starts here, today.

And then it was over. 'So. I'll see you around,' he said, walking slowly backwards away from her.

'I hope so,' she smiled.

'And I hope so too. Bye, Em.'

'Bye, Dex.'

'Goodbye.'

'Goodbye. Goodbye.'

Acknowledgements

Continued thanks to Jonny Geller and Nick Sayers for their enthusiasm, insight and guidance. Also all at Hodder and Curtis Brown.

I'm grateful to those who submitted themselves to early drafts: Hannah MacDonald, Camilla Campbell, Matthew Warchus, Elizabeth Kilgarriff, Michael McCoy, Roanna Benn and Robert Bookman. Some points of detail were also provided by Ayse Tashkiran, Katie Goodwin, Eve Claxton, Anne Clarke and Christian Spurrier. I continue to be indebted to Mari Evans. Once again, Hannah Weaver is thanked for her support and inspiration, and for putting up with it all.

A debt is owed to Thomas Hardy, for unwittingly suggesting the premise and some clumsily paraphrased prose in the final chapter. Also to Billy Bragg, for his fine song 'St Swithin's Day'.

It is in the nature of this novel that certain smart remarks and observations may have been pilfered from friends and acquaintances over the years, and I hope that a collective thank you – or apology – will be enough.

'You're gorgeous, you old hag, and if I could
give you just one gift ever
for the rest of your life it would be this.
Confidence.
It would be the gift of confidence.
Either that or a scented candle.'

How is writing a screenplay different from writing a book?

There are so many differences, too many to go into detail here, but the most striking for me is that the screenplay isn't really literature at all. It can be beautifully written and read for entertainment, and a good screenplay can make you laugh or cry, but it's still basically an instruction manual, a set of preferred suggestions on how to make a film. The ways of making that film are infinitely variable, and dependent on the input of any number of people. The finished film might resemble the screenplay very precisely or hardly at all, and the screenwriter is only part of that process. This is the great pleasure and also the frustration of screenwriting. In fiction, the novel is the finished object – like a poem, that's all there is, and the success or failure of the novel is only down to the author. Writing for the screen is team-work.

What else? Film-making is practical and therefore expensive, and it's rarely the screenwriter who pays. Consequently there's a great deal more collaboration, or interference, depending on how well it's going. If the producers don't like it, they won't make it, and why should they? It's their money after all.

This may sound obvious, but film-making is expensive. If I write 'It rained that night' in prose, then it's just four words and the only expenditure is ink and paper. If I write it in a screenplay, then someone has to hire a rain-machine, and twenty people have to stand beneath it all night. Consequently, you'll always have someone looking at your script and asking 'Does it really have to rain? At night?' If you write the words 'Ext. Battlefield, the Somme – Night' in a screenplay, then a great many more questions will be asked. These parameters aren't always a bad thing – writing an entertaining movie with people talking for

2

ninety minutes, no explosions, no aliens, is a challenge in itself.

Genre plays a bigger role in screenwriting too. When people hear about a film, their first question is 'What is it?' Action? Rom-com? Film Noir? Of course screenplays don't have to fit into these boxes, and the best of them often defy categorisation, but even so, it's hard to ignore them entirely. When writing a novel, I don't think of genre at all. *One Day* has romantic-comedy elements, but there was no template, and I'd hate to think of it being marketed as a narrow type of book.

Novels can be discursive – it's fine to go off on a tangent occasionally, so long as you're still being entertaining. In films, scenes and dialogue tend to serve a purpose. Novel-writing is personal and immersive – even when a novel isn't autobiographical, something of the author's views and personality will come out. For me at least, screenwriting is a lot more objective, technical and structural. Often, in the case of adaptations, writing the screenplay is a form of editing rather than creation. A page of dialogue in a novel might often be a first draft, whereas I would expect a page of dialogue in a screenplay to be rewritten five, ten, fifteen times, with notes from five, ten, fifteen different people.

There's an obvious formal difference between writing a book and writing for the screen. Novels are read in anything between two and twenty sittings – they're episodic by their very nature. Films have to seem like a single journey – you have to fight quite hard to avoid that 'end-of-chapter' feeling.

Novelists have the luxury of the internal voice. 'He said X, but felt Y.' In films, the actor has to do this, or the screenwriter has to manipulate a situation where the internal thoughts are expressed, hence all those 'best friends' in films. Screenplays are about action, not in the sense of things exploding, but in the sense of characters doing and saying things. Thinking on screen is tricky.

Exposition in novels is much, much more straightforward.

The author is there to pass on information. It's not the most beautiful of sentences, but there's nothing wrong with – 'The two friends had known each other for twelve years, but had only been close for the last year or so.' On screen this gets mangled into 'How long have we known each other?' 'Oh, twelve years, but we've only really been friends for a year or so.' Why are they talking like this? Why are they telling each other information that they already know?

Finally, the main difference is that novelists are left alone. Screenwriters leave the house, go to meetings, argue. When I'm writing a script, I long to be writing a book, and vice-versa.

Were you nervous when One Day *was being made into a film (e.g. that they might change the ending!)?*

Of course. It's very nerve-wracking, especially on such a personal, heartfelt book. But there was never any question of changing the ending. We've tried hard to stay true to the spirit and story of the book, whilst always accepting the fact that 110 pages of screenplay can never be the same as 130,000 words of prose. An adaptation is never the same as a book read aloud. The demands of pacing, the running time and the lack of an inner voice all mean that things have to change. But the book was always there, on set and absorbed by the cast. But films have to live alongside their source material, rather than replacing them.

Did you have to fight hard to write the screenplay yourself?

Not fight exactly – I was a screenwriter before I became a novelist – but I would have had trouble letting it go completely. As I've said before, it's not an autobiographical book, but it is very personal and heartfelt, and it would have been hard to just hand it over to another writer.

4

You've written a lot for television & film. Do you prefer this kind of writing to writing novels?

I love both, though the experience of writing *One Day*, the novel, was the happiest, most satisfying writing experience I've had. I love screenwriting, but it is incredibly stressful sometimes. Writing fiction isn't care-free either, but the only debates I tend to have are with myself.

Does your training as an actor help writing screenplays?

As an actor, I was largely mute, and quite right too! I can't emphasise enough how terrible I was as an actor. But I do love writing dialogue. It reminds me of improvisation – that easy, funny, back-and-forth. I never write fiction with a film in mind, but I do like to imagine the lines spoken aloud, and I do keep an eye out for dialogue that sounds fake, verbose or stilted. As an ex-actor, I suppose I might have a lingering sense of what would be fun to perform, even if I rarely got the chance to perform anymore.

Did you draw on your own experiences while writing One Day *(and your earlier novels)?*

A few. I am, for instance, the same age as the characters, and have lived in all the same places, so it would be strange if a little personal experience didn't find its way into the book. But as I've written before, there's a difference between autobiography and a novel with a personal element. Certainly, my twenties were nothing like Dexter's. If anything, Emma and I have a lot more in common, in terms of background, ambition and anxieties, though Emma is a great deal smarter and more principled than I am. The terrible restaurant I worked in was French, not Mexican, and the flat was in Battersea, not Earl's Court. Ian, too, shares one or two of my less appealing qualities, though I won't go into that here!

5

Kingsley Amis once said that all books are autobiographical to the extent that it's impossible to write a thought that the author hasn't had, and there's a good deal of truth in that. But the reality is very heavily filtered and adapted to make fiction – real-life transcribed rarely makes satisfying literature, which is why I'm so wary of biopics. There's very little in the book that I could point to and say 'that's just how it was'. Certainly there's no individual real-life Emma or Dexter.

As for my previous novels, *Starter For Ten* is about being a student, and I was a student, and *The Understudy* is about being a failed actor, and I was a failed actor, so you might detect a pattern. But thankfully I was never quite as inept, foolish, unhappy or humiliated as those two characters. Having said that, if something embarrassing happens to Brian Jackson in *Starter For Ten*, then it probably happened in real-life.

What was the inspiration behind One Day?

There's no single inspirational moment. I'd read a passage in Hardy's *Tess of the D'Urbervilles* as a teenager, and that had always stayed with me. It seemed like an interesting starting point for a story – it's quoted in the novel, towards the end. Also, I had just turned forty, and my first novel was about what it felt like to be twenty, and I was curious to explore what happens to us in between. How are expectations of the future fulfilled or disappointed? How do we end up here? Do we change along the way, or stay the same?

I also wanted to write something that was a mixture of light and shade, of comedy and drama. My first two novels were quite straightforward comedies with male underdog protagonists, and I thought it was important to push myself a little further this time.

Did you know the ending of One Day *before you started writing?*

The ending was the beginning, if you see what I mean. It's a little hard to write about here, in case readers have skipped to this section first, but it's certainly fair to say that the ending certainly wasn't done on a whim. It was the central idea of the book.

Why did you choose Edinburgh as one of the central settings in the novel?

I've always loved Edinburgh; I think it's one of the most startling, atmospheric cites in the world. It's beautiful without being twee; elegant and tough at the same time. I first went there in the summer of 1988, just when the novel begins, performing at the Festival and staying at a tiny flat on Rankeillor Street, which became Emma and Tilly's student flat in the novel. It's another instance of how the book contains personal experience without being particularly autobiographical. In fact, I was in all the novel's locations at the same time as the characters (Paris in the summer of 2001, Greece in '92, Edinburgh in '88). Partly this is so that I can get the time and place right, partly it's probably laziness on my part. I really should learn to research! However, I've never been to India, and I'm ashamed to admit that this section of *One Day* is taken from travel guides.

Do you write every day?

I write something, though often only emails. The last two years have been spent working on scripts or publicising *One Day*. But when everything calms down then yes, I'll try and write every day.

Does anyone read your books while you're in the process of writing them?

I wrote half of *One Day* then gave it to three trusted friends, just to get some indication that I'd not gone completely mad, that it made sense. I then revised the first half according to their feedback, and completed the novel. When it was finished, a few other readers took a look. The idea of spending two or three years working on something only to have the first reader frown and shake their head is terrifying, but neither do I want to be constantly addressing notes before I've actually finished. One or two voices saying 'keep going' is all a writer really needs.

Who are your favourite writers?

I could quite literally write a book on this, but off the top of my head my favourites are Charles Dickens, particularly *Great Expectations*, *Bleak House* and *Our Mutual Friend*; George Orwell, especially the essays and *1984*; F. Scott Fitzgerald's *Tender is the Night*; J D Salinger (especially *Franny and Zooey*); Thomas Hardy's *Tess of the D'Urbervilles*, *Far From the Madding Crowd* and *The Mayor of Casterbridge*.

I also love Graham Greene, Muriel Spark, Evelyn Waugh and the great and under-rated Penelope Fitzgerald. Philip Roth, John Cheever, Richard Yates, John Updike, Kurt Vonnegut, James Salter, Jim Thompson, Tobias Wolff, Cormac McCarthy, Saul Bellow, William Maxwell, James Ellroy, Emile Zola, Vladimir Nabokov and Gustave Flaubert are also up there.

I admire the poets Philip Larkin, TS Eliot and John Donne. Anton Chekhov is my favourite playwright, along with Harold Pinter, Tom Stoppard and Alan Bennett. Billy Wilder, Preston Sturges, Woody Allen and François Truffaut are my favourite screenwriters.

Do you have any advice for aspiring writers?

Read. Read widely and constantly, and take in plays too, and movies and poetry and journalism. Don't watch too much TV (though I love some TV), read instead. And – I don't say this lightly – stay off the internet. You can't write anything really good and tweet at the same time.

What are you working on now?

As I write this, I'm doing the last few rewrites on a film that may or may not go into production in autumn 2011, a film version of *Great Expectations*, my favourite novel. But primarily, I'm trying to write a new novel. At present that's all I really want to do.

Have you read either of David Nicholls' previous bestselling novels?

Read on to find out more about

STARTER FOR TEN

and

THE UNDERSTUDY

STARTER FOR TEN

THINK YOU KNOW UNIVERSITY CHALLENGE?

COULD YOU COPE WITH JEREMY PAXMAN'S WITHERING GLARE?

ARE YOU READY FOR THE FUNNIEST NOVEL IN RECENT YEARS?

Q. What does a woman really look for in a man?

A. Advanced general knowledge, of course!

1985. Brian, a first-year student and ardent Kate Bush fan, falls for beautiful University Challenge queen, and would-be actress, Alice.

When Alice fails to respond to his charms, Brian comes up with a foolproof plan to capture her heart, once-and-for-all. He's going to win University Challenge. At any cost.

David Nicholls' first novel is a brilliant comedy about love, class, growing up, and the all-important difference between knowledge and wisdom.

THE UNDERSTUDY

HAVE YOU READ THE 'FUNNIEST BOOK OF THE YEAR' MARIE CLAIRE, THE 'ZIPPY COMEDY WITH LAUGH-OUT-LOUD LINES' DAILY MAIL WHICH 'COULD HOLD ITS OWN AGAINST A RICHARD CURTIS SCRIPT'? INDEPENDENT ON SUNDAY

For Josh Harper, being in show-business means money, fame, a beautiful wife, and a lead role on the London stage.

For Stephen C. McQueen, it means a disastrous career playing passers-by and dead people.

Stephen is stuck with an unfortunate name, a hopeless agent, a daughter he barely knows, and a job as understudy to *the* Josh Harper, the 12th Sexiest Man in the World.

When Stephen falls in love with Josh's clever, funny wife Nora, things get even more difficult.

But might there yet be a way for Stephen to get his Big Break?